BUFFALO RIDGE

Also by Forrest Peterson
Good Ice (2007)

BUFFALO RIDGE

A NOVEL

FORREST PETERSON

[signed] Forrest Peterson

NORTH STAR PRESS OF ST. CLOUD, INC.
St. Cloud, Minnesota

Copyright © 2012 Forrest Peterson

All rights reserved

This is a work of fiction. Any resemblance to any person, living or dead, is a coincidence.

ISBN: 978-0-87839-360-2

First edition, December 2012

Printed in the United States of America

Published by North Star Press of St. Cloud, Inc.
PO Box 451
St. Cloud, MN 56302
www.northstarpress.com

1

Tom Otto yawned. He shook his head, trying to dislodge the fatigue. Sometimes when the drive was long he would wrap his right arm over his head and try to keep his eyelids open by force. It seldom helped.

The worst time came right about sunrise. Except for early summer when the sun rose before 6:00 a.m., he would be on the road in early morning darkness. In summer, driving east on the two-lane highway, instead of stimulating his senses, the sunlight felt almost like a drug.

He drank thick, strong coffee. It was never enough, and too often it forced him to stop and pee. He had thought about taking something to keep him alert during those early morning hours. He knew other drivers took stuff. Methamphetamines, speed.

So far he had refused. It was a crutch, a weakness, some kind of failure. Then again, if it prevented him from falling asleep at the wheel, perhaps he could justify it. He wouldn't have to tell Jeri.

She still would be sleeping, her shoulder-length, bronze hair tied up in an unruly clump on top of her head, the way she always wore it at night. She wore it that way at work, too, enclosed in the white bonnet of line workers at the processing plant. Eight hours a day, minus a half-hour lunch and two fifteen-minute breaks, she eviscerated broiler chickens, moving unrelentingly down the line.

After three years, Jeri perpetually carried the odor of raw poultry from her clothes, hair, and skin, but he had become accustomed to it.

At first he opposed her going to work so soon, right after Jade was born. He had hoped that his business would gain traction right from the start, enough to allow her to stay home. All the articles he had been reading convinced him that consumers were eager for "natural" or "organic" meats and vegetables. Maybe that was true in the big cities and on the country's coasts. He believed the demand would grow in small towns on the Midwestern prairie, that some day there would be a fleet of "Tom's Fresh Meats and Produce, Naturally" trucks. Until then Jeri's job made up the difference.

He drove along heading west, away from the bright morning sun rising a few degrees above the horizon. It looked like the beginnings of a sweet, perfect June day.

Tom tried to map his route for greatest efficiency. In some cases, he asked customers further away from the route to pick up their orders from a drop point at a neighbor's closer to the route.

He made an exception for the Weavers and four other small farms in the area. They supplied him with fresh eggs, whole grains, vegetables in season, lamb, beef, butchered chickens, and goat cheese.

Today, as he turned into the Weavers' driveway, the refrigerated truck inventory included six cases of fresh romaine lettuce. Tom figured he'd depart the farm minus a couple heads of romaine after he picked up some fresh meats and produce.

He always looked forward to this stop, perhaps more for the setting and the enthusiastic welcome from the three Weaver kids. Stan and Tulie Weaver raised more than chickens, eggs, sheep, cattle, and fresh vegetables on their eighty-acre homestead. When his truck approached the old turn-of-the-century farmhouse, three children from the house usually came to greet him; the oldest often carrying the youngest still learning to walk.

A creek flowed through the farm site about seventy-five yards from the house. The bank nearest to the barn stretched out in a carpet of green prairie grasses opening up to the sun, displaying a bright green against the shaded opposite bank where trees grew thick, untrammeled by cattle or hogs. Several sheep grazed in the yard around the house, keeping the grass short and fertilized, and saving time that would have been wasted on mowing.

Tulie usually emerged from the farmhouse, following the kids. Stan most likely would be in the barn or tending one of the fields. Tulie, short for Tulip, had grown up in a commune in northern Idaho in the 1970s.

THIS MORNING ONLY THE DOGS surrounded the truck, barking and wagging their tails. Tom surveyed the farmyard expecting to see the kids.

"Okay, where is everyone?" he said aloud. He shut down the motor and stepped down. The dogs, a little rat terrier-schnauzer cross named Pee Wee, and Henry, a golden retriever-lab, enveloped him with their sniffing, licking snouts. Tom patted their heads and broke free. Looking around, his senses sharpened as he walked toward the farmhouse.

"Hello . . . anybody home?" he called. No kids laughing and talking, no Tulie's cheerful welcome.

Pee Wee and Henry followed Tom to the kitchen door, their barking became replaced by quiet, expectant looks.

Tom rapped on the door. Where is everyone?

He opened the door and entered the back hall, the mud room. "Hey, everybody! It's Tom. Hello!"

He stood straining to hear a response. A noise came from somewhere in the house, faintly as if from behind a door. A child crying.

If their pickup had not been parked under the lean-to attached to the barn, Tom might have assumed they weren't home. The coffee maker with its red "on" light glowing sat half-full on the kitchen counter. A National Public Radio news broadcast droned from a battery-powered radio on the far end of the seven-foot trestle table jutting out from a wall, the first of many similar tables built by Stan in the single stall garage he converted to a wood-working shop three years ago.

Tom stepped slowly into the kitchen, intently listening for another sound. The table held three bowls of oatmeal, cups, and pieces of toast—home-made whole grain bread—all looking like a meal in progress.

"Hello! Tulie? Stan? Anybody here?"

He heard the crying again. Not really crying, but more like a sobbing whimper. Dread began seeping into Tom, spreading out into a prickly chill. What's going on? What happened? Where is everyone?

Then he saw bare feet laying sideways on the floor in the doorway of the back hall connecting the kitchen to Stan and Tulie's bedroom.

"Tulie! Tulie!"

Tom sprang toward her, then froze.

Tulie lay motionless on her left side. A dark-red stain spread across the upper part of her nightgown from the ragged edges of a gaping wound. He knelt, reaching for her right wrist to find a pulse, already knowing it would not be there. He gently placed his hand on her forehead. It felt cool and clammy. Her open, unblinking eyes stared vacantly.

Filtering through the shock a deep sadness rose in his chest, then anger. Where's Stan? Where are the kids? Who did this? Why? Instinct added the questions: Where were the killers and was he in danger?

Slowly, quietly, Tom stood, tensing against the escape of any sound. He wondered if he should cover Tulie's body with a sheet or blanket for the childrens sake, or just leave her body untouched.

He crept through Stan and Tulie's bedroom, across the center hallway and into the living room. He peered into the dining room, then headed to the stairs to check the upper bedrooms. His teeth clenched at each creaky groan of the stair boards as he ascended.

He paused at the top of the stairs, reached for his cell phone and pressed 9-1-1.

"Nine-one-one. What is your emergency?" answered a terse female voice.

He spoke quietly, straining to suppress a quaver in his voice. "Hello. This is Tom Otto. I'm at the Stan and Tulie Weaver farm in the southwest part of the county. I just found Tulie's body in the house. It . . . it looks like a shotgun blast killed her."

"Is anyone else there? Are you in danger?" the dispatcher cut in.

"I'm looking for their kids and for Stan. I don't think anyone else is here."

"Stay there. Don't touch anything. Deputies are on the way. We can send an ambulance. Give me the address."

Tom knew the road but couldn't remember the house number. "It's the old Wegman place. Three quarters of a mile east of County Road 30, about seven miles south of Highway 45."

"I need the exact street address," ordered the dispatcher.

"I don't remember. I'll have to look. Everybody around here knows the old Wegman place."

"Well, I'm not everybody." She sounded young, probably a newcomer to the area. So many new people had been arriving in recent years. Tom believed that would help his business grow. Yet he could sympathize with old-timers who saw the familiarity of knowing all their neighbors beginning to fade.

He fumbled in his pocket for his customer list, found the street address and recited it to the dispatcher.

"What's your full name and address? What are you doing there?"

"I'm Tom Otto, 16843 225th Street Northeast. I was delivering produce on my route. You don't need to send an ambulance, at least for Tulie. Send the coroner. I'm going to hang up now and look for Stan and the kids."

"Stay where you are and stay on the line!" the dispatcher commanded.

"I have to find the kids. My phone's losing power."

"Do they have a land line, a regular phone? Call back on that."

"No, they don't. They just have a cell phone, but I don't know where it is."

"Well, you just stay put. It won't be long, and someone will be there. What's your cell number?"

"I'm going to find the kids," Tom replied, the quaver in his voice now from anger instead of fear. He punched the phone's disconnect button. He pushed aside the immediate regret that such an insolent act might haunt him later. He began searching for the kids. He heard it again, a small child's muffled cry.

"Hey, kids. It's me, Tom, Tom Otto," he announced loudly. He stood still to listen for a response, hearing only silence throughout the upstairs hallway and four bedrooms. He walked slowly down the hall, unable to hear anything. He looked in each room, cautiously opening each closet door.

In Stan and Tulie's room, something caught Tom's eye out of the bedroom window. A far off cloud of dust appeared to speed across a distant field. A vehicle was traveling fast along the gravel township road toward the turn leading to the long driveway into the Weaver farmstead. If it was a sheriff's deputy, it was an awfully quick response, Tom thought, but he felt relieved that they had arrived. He knew he would have to stay and help, especially with the kids. He still had a truck full of fresh meats and produce to deliver. And without the Weavers, where would Tom get a big part of his produce? Grief would have to wait.

THE SHERIFF'S DEPUTY PATROL CAR tore down the driveway, almost skidding to a stop next to Tom's truck. Tom went downstairs and waited just outside the kitchen door. The deputy approached, and Tom held out his hand. "I'm Tom Otto, the guy who called. You sure got here fast for this being down in this neck of the county."

"We patrol down here when we can, or as much as we need to. You said there's a body in there."

"It's Tulie Weaver. She took a shotgun blast at close range."

"I'd like to see some ID," said the deputy. Tom knew many of the officers, but not some of the younger recruits. This guy was only in his late twenties. Hearing the order, Tom suddenly felt apprehensive. He showed the deputy his driver's license, suddenly realizing that everyone—including him—would be a suspect.

"Where is she?" Tom motioned to the hallway behind him.

"You said something about kids. Is there anyone else? A father or husband? Did you see any other vehicles?"

"I thought I heard a child crying or something. I don't know where Stan is. He's the dad. I didn't see any other vehicles," Tom replied calmly. "You think I did this?" He could hardly believe what he had just heard. "The Weavers are good friends, business partners." He glared at the young officer.

The deputy stepped past him into the kitchen. He looked around warily, his right hand resting on the handle of his holstered pistol. He knelt and studied Tulie's body. He went into the bedroom and took the top sheet off the bed and draped it over the body. He went back into the kitchen where Tom stood and called in to dispatch on his radio.

"You said they have a cell phone?" the deputy asked. "What's the number? Do you know the number?" Tom nodded and the deputy asked him to dial it on his own cell phone. The deputy turned off the radio on the counter.

They stood still, Tom listening to the ring tones from his phone. They could barely hear the faint melody coming from somewhere—it sounded like from below. In seconds the faint sound ceased.

"Let's check the cellar," Tom said. He led the deputy outside around to the cellar door, the old kind with large double doors at an angle against the side of the house. The doors opened to a stairway leading down to a dark, clammy cave-like space surrounded by an ancient stone foundation.

Michael Weaver clamped his hand over the mouth of his baby brother. Anna Weaver clutched the cell phone. The first few bars of the ring tone had escaped before she could turn it off. Another muffled cry from Jonathan squeezed out between Michael's fingers.

The deputy handed Tom his flashlight and let him go down the stairway first.

"Michael? Hello. This is Tom Otto. Everything's going to be okay. Anna? Are all you kids down here?"

He panned the light around the cellar illuminating shelves of preserved fruits and vegetables in neat rows of Mason jars. A large wooden bin held potatoes. Dried herbs hung from several cords strung across between two shelves.

"C'mon kids. It's okay. We're going to help you. Come on out," Tom pleaded.

Slowly, cautiously, Michael Weaver stepped out from behind a 250-gallon fuel oil tank in one corner. The ten-year-old clutched his one-and-one-half-year-old brother, Jonathan. Anna, who just turned five, followed, grasping a cell phone in both hands. In the bright beam of the flashlight they looked stone-faced. Anna's eyes glistened in the light.

SMUDGED TRACKS OF TEARS trailed down her cheeks. They stood mute except for Jonathan who squirmed and whimpered in his brother's grasp.

Tom walked over and knelt down in front of them.

"Everybody okay? Can you tell us what happened? Is your dad around?"

"I don't know," Michael replied soberly. "I don't know where dad is."

"We're going to look for him," the deputy said. "Everything's going to be okay. Did you see anybody? Was anybody else here?"

"We were having breakfast. This car came down the driveway," Michael said. "Mom told us to go down here and be quiet."

What did you hear? Did you hear anything?"

"We heard mom talking to some guys. Then we heard some shots."

"How long ago was that?" the deputy asked.

"It was just before Tom came. We were going to go back outside. Then we heard Tom's truck. We didn't know it was him so we stayed here," Michael said, his composure weakening and voice beginning to tremble. Yet he withstood the pressure of tears damming up in his eyes.

"Okay, that's enough," Tom said to the deputy. "I'll take the kids out to the truck. They can wait there, and we can go check out the barn."

The deputy hesitated, then agreed because it was the logical thing to do. Truck or squad car made little difference.

Tom led the children out of the cellar and helped them climb into the cab of his truck. He tried to comfort little Anna, who cried for her mommy. She was about the same age as his own daughter, Jade. Anna clutched a rag doll with one hand and took Michael's hand with the other. Baby Jonathan fussed and squirmed out of Michael's grasp, insisting on walking over to the truck. He smiled up at Tom, pointing toward the barn saying, "Dada, Dada."

It would be at least another ten minutes before reinforcements arrived. That was too long to wait, so the deputy walked toward the barn. Tom hurried across the farmyard to catch up, looking back once to see the kids sitting in the truck. They were so trusting, so innocent, at least the two younger ones. Michael's grim expression hadn't changed.

"Why isn't the boy in school? Don't they ride the bus out here?" the deputy asked as they approached the barn.

"They're home-schooled," Tom replied. "Tulie taught them."

At the barn the deputy gave an "are you ready for this?" look over his shoulder at Tom, then opened the smaller door.

Back in the 1940s and 1950s that big barn stood out among others in the neighborhood for its size, its white-painted walls and red-shingled roof, a towering cap with broad, graceful arcs sweeping down from the peak to eaves on the sides, then flipping slightly outward.

When the Weavers bought the farm eight years ago, the barn needed a lot of repair, which Stan did even before they fixed up the house. As in the old days, the hay loft held small mountains of sweet-scented alfalfa and grass hay. Twelve milk cows stood in their tie stalls, munching hay and, this morning, bawling about their swollen udders needing to be milked. The goats wandered around in a pen waiting for their turn. They looked up curiously at the opening door.

The deputy held his left hand outstretched behind him, telling Tom to stay put. His right hand drew his nine millimeter Smith and Wesson from its holster. He walked slowly down the center aisle looking into each stall as he passed by.

He stopped, listening. Tom heard it too, the muffled whoosh of tires on a gravel road. The sheriff's squad car pulled to a skidding stop, leaving a dust cloud drifting across the farmyard. The deputy resumed his surveillance, this time announcing loudly, "Stan. Stan Weaver. Are you here, Stan?"

THEY COULD FIND NO SIGN of Stan Weaver other than his well-cared for livestock, neat rows of tools, and clean barn. Tom followed the deputy out of the barn to meet the sheriff approaching them.

"The coroner's on his way. So, what do we got?" the sheriff asked.

The deputy looked toward Tom's truck. The two older Weaver kids stared at the men through closed windows. Little Jonathan sitting on Michael's lap looked to be squirming and crying.

"There's a body in the house. Tom Otto here says it's Mrs. Weaver. What did you say her name was, Tulip?"

"Yes. Everyone calls her Tulie," Tom said.

"Anybody else here besides the kids?" the sheriff asked.

"We were looking in the barn for Stan, Tulie's husband," Tom said.

The sheriff shot him an "I wasn't talking to you" look. "You go wait by your truck. Stay with the kids," he ordered.

"I can help you look for Stan. The kids'll be okay."

"Other officers will be here soon. I want you to stay with the kids," the sheriff said in a firm but even voice.

Tom conceded. He offered some suggestions about where to look for Stan if he wasn't in the barn. The sheriff and deputy walked toward the machine shed.

Tom climbed into his truck. He lifted Jonathan from Michael's lap to his own. The toddler responded with a curious gaze. Tom smiled and his blue eyes captured Jonathan's attention, for a moment.

"I want mommy. Where's daddy?" Anna began to cry again, ending Michael's brief respite from wrestling with his younger brother.

"I don't know. Stop crying," Michael commanded.

"We'll find your folks." Tom tried to sound reassuring. "Everything's going to be okay."

By this time Michael understood that this clearly was not true.

"I have to go potty," Anna whined.

Failing to dissuade her, Tom lifted Jonathan back to Michael's lap. He took Anna's hand and they walked to the outhouse behind the farm house. Visiting the Weaver farm was like going back in time sixty, seventy, maybe a hundred years. No power line connected the farm to the rural electric co-op lines. No electric pump drew water from a deep well, no indoor plumbing except for the kitchen sink—a hand pump drew water from a cistern in the basement. Water drained to an old, leaky cesspool in the backyard.

An eighty-foot-tall wind generator provided up to twenty kilowatts of electricity, some stored in batteries to be available when the wind speed dropped. Stan had rigged up minimal electric and water service to the house, but for a toilet they still used an outhouse.

"I'm hungry. I want more breakfast," Anna whined when they walked past the kitchen door heading back to the truck. "Where's Mommy?"

A SMALL CARAVAN OF VEHICLES swept into the farmyard, a dark green, full-sized sedan in the lead, followed by another sheriff's patrol car, a big black Ford Expedition with dark-tinted windows, and an older, small foreign compact. Tom thought it looked like a late eighties vintage Subaru, and clearly out of place with the other vehicles.

The big sedan hadn't finished settling back to a stop and its transmission jammed into Park before the front passenger door flew open. A man wearing a dark suit leaped out and ran back toward the Subaru. He jerked open the driver's door and appeared to be yelling something and gesturing, his right arm pointing back toward the driveway.

A young man in the Subaru argued back, a defiant look on his face.

"You get the hell out of here!" the dark suit commanded loudly. "This is private property. We're investigating a possible crime scene. You want the story, you call me later."

"Can't I just get a couple photos?" the young man pleaded.

"Hell no! You try and I'll stick that camera up your ass!"

"This is public information! You can't keep me out of here," the reporter protested.

"You can kiss my ass! Now scram!"

The reporter turned the wheel and backed the Subaru around sideways across the driveway, and using his left hand turned the wheel out toward the road. His right hand reached for his camera. He twisted off the 35 mm lens and clicked on the telephoto lens. When he felt far enough from the BCI state agent he stopped, hung out the car window and pressed the shutter release with the motor drive turned on, slowly panning the camera after each click. The last frame caught the agent glaring and flipping him the bird. The reporter leaned back in and gunned the engine back out onto the road and headed towards town.

2

THE SEARCH TURNED UP NO CLUES to Stan Weaver's absence other than the bawling cows. A county social worker arrived to take the kids. With the officers' permission, Tom called one of the neighbors and asked him to come over and help with the chores. The cows had already been milked, but all the livestock needed to be fed and water replenished.

The officers completed the initial crime scene investigation and helped the funeral director load Tulie's body into the Expedition. Tom watched them wheel the gurney along the bumpy path. Now with the initial shock subsiding, a helpless sadness began to creep in. He felt anger. Why would anyone do this? He hurt for the kids. He prayed that Stan would be found okay.

Although well-acquainted with the Weavers, the Ottos were not close friends. They had visited the Weaver farm several times in the past couple of years, and despite their differences, they enjoyed each others' company. Their relationship consisted mostly of Tom's stops two or three times a week on his route.

With Jade and Trace now old enough to play with the Weaver kids, Tom and Jeri appreciated the occasional visits to an old-fashioned farm. In some ways it was like stepping back into the nineteenth century. It seemed almost perfect. The Weavers lived what appeared to be a peaceful, uncomplicated, pastoral life. If they needed modern medical care, power tools, or movie CDs they still could drive into town.

Jeri had already left for work by the time Tom returned home from his route in the afternoon. He had hoped she would still be home. Instead he saw her mom's 1992 cream-colored Buick in the driveway. It always irritated him when she left it blocking the driveway to the shop where he parked the delivery truck. Sometimes he felt that it was deliberate. Her occasional comments about his organic food venture sometimes seemed more critical than complimentary. She openly talked about her dislike of her daughter having to work the second shift at the plant. But she was good with the kids and Tom was glad to see her there.

He had called Jeri earlier to tell her the news.

Mrs. Meyers stayed for supper. Since her husband died she had been doing that more often. Tom appreciated the help as long as she didn't talk about his business venture or politics.

Chasing the remnants of his dinner around the plate, the crunch of wheels on the driveway pulled Tom's eyes away and out the window. The same dark, full-sized sedan that he saw earlier at the farm entered, rolling slowly toward the trailer house. That was another sore point with Jeri's mom. She wished they lived in a regular house in town, and not in a mobile home on five acres about four miles out of town.

The BCI agent stepped out, accompanied by the sheriff.

Tom walked over to the door. He hadn't yet said anything to Lynn and it was too late now. She asked who they were and what were they doing here. Tom couldn't say anything in front of the kids.

"I'll tell you later," he whispered, opening the door and inviting them in.

They asked Mrs. Meyers if she would kindly take the kids outside. They assured her it had nothing to do with Tom or his family, but they would like to ask him some questions.

Before leaving with the kids she offered the BCI agent a cup of coffee, which he accepted. He watched as she herded the kids outside with a bemused, patronizing smile on his face.

"Nice kids," he said. "Is that your mother?"

"Mother-in-law," Tom replied.

The agent nodded and settled in to a chair at the table. "How long have you known the Weavers?"

Tom sat down across the table, his hands fidgeting, struggling inside between defiance and fear. "I don't know. About five years maybe. Has Stan showed up yet?"

"No. We're still looking. Would you say you were close friends, or acquaintances? How would you describe your relationship?"

"I don't know. I guess we were good acquaintances. Not really close friends. They were a little different. We liked them. They were real nice. I still can't believe what happened."

"You were there with your truck. Were you delivering something, or what?"

"I already told you all that."

"Tell me again."

Tom looked at the sheriff, hoping to detect some guidance. "They're on my route. Mostly I get stuff from them. They raise organic produce, chickens and beef and stuff."

"Do you bring anything to them?"

"Sometimes they'll buy fresh vegetables. When they're out-of-season."

"Do you have any idea who might want to do them harm?"

"I have no idea. They're so nice. I don't know much about their past though. Who knows?"

"What did they do for a living? Did either one have a job?"

"Not as far as I know. I think the farm was it. They seemed to be pretty much self-sufficient. Going to their place was like going back a hundred years."

"Did they ever talk about anything, like any problems with somebody? Did you ever hear anybody talking about them?"

"No. Like I said, they were so nice, friendly. Where are the kids?" Tom asked.

"They're with a foster family for now."

"Is there anything we can do? Jeri and me would like to help. The kids know us. Maybe they could stay here."

"Right now we're looking for any relatives," the agent replied. "You know of any? If we can find some relatives we might send them there. With the investigation going on and what you know about the situation we think it'd be best if the kids were someplace else. You realize you still might be in danger? Whoever did this might know something about you and your family."

That thought never occurred to Tom. He remembered a few people in that part of the county who seemed like the anti-government, tax protester types. They pretty much kept to themselves. He'd heard stories about them, run-ins with law enforcement, printing their own money, weird stuff like that. They called it scrip. He kept trying to think of something, unconsciously biting his lip.

"What? What do you know?" the agent asked.

"I don't know. I was just thinking about these anti-government weirdos down there," Tom finally said.

"Why? Why would they want to hurt the Weavers?"

"I don't really know. In some ways they're kind of alike. I mean, the Weavers, they've got this organic farm. You know, like the old hippies, like a commune only it's just their family. But as far as I know they paid their taxes and stuff. I never heard Stan talk like that. He was, you know, real liberal, almost radical sometimes. But he wasn't crazy or anything. Some of these tax protester types, they're nuts."

"But you said they were kind of alike. What did you mean by that?"

"I just meant the way they lived. Out in the boondocks away from everybody. They try to be self-sufficient growing their own food. Stuff like that."

"Actually, we know quite a bit about those tax protesters," the agent said. "It's the Weaver's we don't know much about. I suppose because they've never caused any trouble. But what did they live on? Did either one have a job?"

"Not that I know of," Tom replied. "I already said that. They did all kinds of things. They didn't seem to really need a lot of stuff. I know Stan made furniture. Tulie made these rag rugs and they sold stuff at craft shows or right off the farm. Their produce was the main thing. Stan had some deal with a fancy grocery store in the city for organic meat. They made goat cheese. All kinds of stuff. They were pretty handy with a lot of things."

"I'm sure," the investigator said wryly. "Weaving rugs. I like that, the Weavers weaving rugs." He rose from the table and offered his hand to Tom.

"We'll be talking with you again," he said as they shook hands. "If you see or hear anything on your route be sure to let us know."

Tom said he would. The investigator asked if he could use the bathroom. He walked slowly down the narrow hall all the way to end, past the bathroom. He looked into other rooms and out the side windows as he passed by. He returned to the kitchen, sheepishly apologizing for not seeing the bathroom right away. Once outside he walked slowly toward his car scanning around the yard, noting the shed and grove in back. He stopped to chat with Lynn and the kids playing on the swing set.

He returned to the front door and asked Tom if he could take a quick look in the shed and around back. Tom shrugged and consented.

Lynn entered the kitchen looking more concerned than questioning. She kept an eye on the kids still outside while Tom told her everything he knew. He felt better, but he really wanted to talk with Jeri. They only had a few minutes on the phone earlier in the afternoon to give her a quick summary. He would have to wait until 11:30 when she came home.

Most weeknights he went to bed about nine, right after getting the kids tucked in. His workday began when the alarm went off at four a.m. Tonight he would have to sacrifice some sleep so he and Jeri could talk. Their schedule helped avoid daycare expenses. On her way to work Jeri dropped off the kids at her mom's. Tom picked them up on his way home from the route. Sometimes they stayed with Lynn for supper, or she brought them out. Twice a week when his route took him closer to town he would stop at home for lunch. They dreamed of the day when they could have a normal schedule.

Lynn said she would stay and help put the kids to bed. Tom appreciated the help and sought escape for about two hours working on the pickup.

The shop measured thirty feet by forty-eight feet, half as large as the mobile home. Sometimes, when they struggled trying to figure out how to pay their bills, he regretted building it. They were still paying on the mobile home and the lot. They had two years left on the loan for the pickup. Like a demanding patriarch, the old delivery truck required frequent repair.

But the kids came first. Tom and Jeri received much happiness and gratification in their care. It made the financial stress bearable and even challenging. At times minor disputes erupted over the pickup, but the indulgence survived as a part of their lives before marriage and children.

The 2000 Ford F-350 Lariat replaced Tom's previous pickup, in which he had gained the notice of Jeri and later courted her. They bought the new one just before Trace was born. Questions about the wisdom of doing so surfaced briefly, but insufficient to confront the struggle paying for it, still outweighed the pleasure it gave them.

Saturday they planned to take it off-roading in the river bottom. The last time out they broke the right rear shock absorber. Even though justifying the cost nagged him, Tom rationalized it because he did the work himself. Sometimes he had to choose between fixing the delivery truck, which always seemed to need fixing, or spending money on the pickup.

After Lynn had engaged the kids in bedtime stories and left, Tom returned to the shop and finished installing the shock. He sat on the workbench sipping a beer. His eyes roved over the shiny, red truck, the chassis a full two feet off the ground on high-rise springs and thirty-inch tires. He thought about starting it just to hear the 5.1-liter V-8 engine reverberating around the shop, the exhaust amplified to a throbbing rumble through the twin mufflers. Maybe the fumes would drive off the swarms of mosquitoes. But that might wake the kids. Instead he rubbed mosquito repellent on his face, neck, and arms.

He looked at his watch, almost 11:30. He avoided thinking about tomorrow and how tired he would be. His worries fled when he saw the headlights of Jeri's 1984 Crown Victoria turn into the driveway. He went out to meet her getting out of the car.

"Hey babe. How you doing? How was work?" He embraced her and buried his face in the side of her neck and shoulder, the scent of her skin intermingled with the odor of poultry flesh, which was strangely comforting.

"Hi. I'm really tired. I don't know. Some of those people at work, they seem like they're just getting going when it's time to quit. It's like they're really wired or something," Jeri replied. "So, what about you? What's going on? I still can't believe that."

"Believe it. I saw it with my own eyes. Then that BCI agent and the sheriff stopped over after supper and grilled me. It seemed like they were suspicious about me."

"Oh come on! That's crazy."

"It gave me the creeps. It made me feel guilty even though I'm not."

They went in and sat at the kitchen table. Tom twisted the caps off two MGDs and retold the day's events in greater detail.

"Those poor kids," Jeri said. "I wish we could do something. They're just not used to being away from their farm. I can't imagine them having to stay at some strange place. I wish we could have them stay here."

"I asked about that, but the sheriff said no way."

They sat quietly. Crickets chirped through the mild night air filtering through the window screen over the sink. Moths flailed their dusty wings at the outside light by the door until Tom turned it off.

"The BCI guy said we could be in danger," Tom said, sitting back down and looking seriously at Jeri.

"What? Why us?"

"He didn't really say. He just said right now everything's up in the air. He said we should be cautious. Your mom is all upset. She wants us to stay in town at her place for awhile."

"Don't be ridiculous," Jeri said. "That'd probably cause another crime scene," she laughed.

She rose from the table. "I got to take a shower. I'm glad you waited up. I know it makes you tired the next day. Maybe you should take something to help stay awake."

"I don't want to do that. I'll stick with coffee."

"Yeah, but it'd be better to take something a little stronger than to have something bad happen." Jeri didn't think about such things too much, but when she did she felt a pang in her gut if the possibility of life without him stole into her thoughts.

"When you're already in bed when I get home it's kind of lonesome," she said. "It's hard to go to bed right away. Sometimes I sit up watching TV or reading."

"I know," Tom said. "But if you worked the day shift then we'd have to pay for daycare. Right now we just can't afford it. Let's just forget about all that stuff for now." He stood behind her and wrapped his arms under her chin, nuzzling his face in her hair. She reached up and patted his arm. "Race you to the shower."

TOM LAY ON HIS BACK, Jeri's head and shoulders cradled in his arm. He looked at the clock showing fewer than three hours before his alarm buzzed. Thoughts about the day's events kept burrowing through the curtain of sleep trying to close, ending the long and stressful day. The dread of how tired he would be in the morning didn't help.

"I got the shock fixed on the truck," he said, trying to force his mind away from the worries.

"How much was that?"

"Not too much. It had to be done," Tom said, now sorry that he had mentioned it.

"How much is 'not too much'? We just can't afford that all the time. Here I have to drive that old beater Crown Vic and you get the truck," Jeri complained.

"I don't drive it anymore than you. During the week I'm always in the delivery truck," Tom countered. "It had to be fixed."

"If we didn't take it off-roading things like that wouldn't happen."

"It's not as hard on it as the truck pulls. That's really hard on the tranny."

"Maybe we should just get rid of it."

"Are you kidding? Hell no!"

"All right, all right. Let's just forget about it." Jeri sighed, nestling in the crook of Tom's arm.

"I can't get to sleep," she said after a few minutes, which brought no response from Tom other than his snoring.

THE TELEPHONE STARTLED her and awakened Tom.

"Who the heck is that?" she said. Tom, still half asleep, blindly reached for the phone on the nightstand.

"Hello?" He sat up on one elbow, now more awake and listening intently.

"Who is this?" he challenged.

He paused, listening. "What's going on?" Jeri interrupted. Tom held up his hand signaling for silence.

"How do you know? Who is this?" Tom said into the phone, beginning to sound angry. He hung up the phone. "They hung up."

"Who was it? What did they say?"

"I don't know who it was. They said we should be careful. They said we're under surveillance. That they have been watching us for a long time. They said now it's going to get worse because of what happened to the Weavers."

"What'd they sound like? We should tell the sheriff!" Jeri said.

"Not now. It was a man. He must have put something over the phone. His voice sounded muffled. Oh man, I can't believe this. I'm going to be wiped tomorrow," Tom groaned.

"You should stay home. We got to find out what's going on."

"I know, but I got the biggest orders of the week tomorrow. I have to go. I'll call my dad in the morning. You and the kids could go in to town to your mom's until I get back."

"What about you out on the route?"

"I'll be fine. When I stop at some of the other growers I'm going to find out what's going on. Maybe they know something."

"What would the cops be spying on us for?"

"How do we know it's the cops?"

"Who else could it be?" Jeri asked.

"I don't know. That's what I hope to find out when I'm at the other farms. I know there's some places down there that look a little strange. Some of those old farm houses way off the road. There's people living in them but I never really see them."

"You be careful. You call the minute you see anything suspicious."

"I will."

A FEW MINUTES BEFORE 6:00 a.m. Tom's delivery truck turned into the food service warehouse yard in the city. Usually the last one in because of the one-and-a-half-hour drive, on some days he had to wait for an open spot at the loading dock.

He closed his eyes and rested his head on his hands grasping the top of the steering wheel, barely hanging on with only two hours of sleep.

Inside the warehouse the loading dock foreman strode up, waving his clipboard at one of the drivers who leaned on his two-wheel hand truck chatting with another driver.

"Hey let's get a move on!" the foreman bellowed. "Enough bullshit already. Tomato's been waitin' for fifteen minutes. Get going so he can use this door!"

"Yeah, yeah, I'm going, I'm going," the driver replied. "Gotta make room for one of your really big accounts," he laughed. The driver climbed down the ladder from the loading dock and into the cab of his truck. Most of the big food service distributors used large tractor-trailer rigs marked with corporate names and logos.

The loud air horn blasted Tom from his momentary slumber. He saw the driver wave as he drove his truck away from the dock. Tom waved back. He started the engine on his International Harvester straight truck with the 20-foot refrigerated cargo box and backed into the dock.

The warehouse handled everything in meats, produce, and food service dry goods. Tom's orders consisted primarily of fresh produce from various growers all over the country and Mexico claiming the organic or natural foods label. Most of his fresh meat inventory came from five small farms scattered around the countryside around Buffalo Ridge.

The nickname "Tomato" took hold from Tom's first visit to the warehouse almost five years ago. Standing at the shipping clerk's office window he announced his name to pick up his first order.

"Tom Otto. Let's see…" the clerk paused, shuffling through a pile of orders. "Here we go. Tom's Fresh Meats and Produce, Naturally." He scanned down the order sheet and handed it to Tom. Should be over in Bay Five, Tom Otto. Hey, I like that name, Tom Otto, tomahto, tomato, tomahto," he laughed. "Have a good day," he waved, like brushing a flying insect away from his face. "Who's next?" Tom stepped aside for the next driver in line, who gave him an amused look.

Over the following week the name "Tomato" spread among the warehouse workers and drivers. It became part of the ritual hazing for newcomers, not to be cruel, but to test character and find a place for a new member of their tribe.

At first Tom became angry, but since he could do nothing about it, and once he became a member of the workplace tribe, he accepted it. Among the other drivers from larger companies, with larger trucks and orders, and being older, it would have placed Tom near the bottom of the pecking order. His clothing, blue jeans and t-shirts, also set him apart from the other drivers in their uniform shirts and work slacks with company names and logos embroidered or patched on the sleeves.

As time passed he stood his ground, returned their teasing with enthusiasm, and they accepted him, even admired him for his ambition toward success in his own business. They still called him Tomato, and that was the price he had to pay, which was bearable because it came from affection and acceptance, not ridicule. Tom still hadn't mentioned it to Jeri, preferring to leave the name behind in the city when he left each day on his route to the countryside.

Before leaving the warehouse and the city, he filled his thermal coffee mug from the large commercial coffee maker in the break room. Driving into the city early in the morning he beat the traffic rush. Entering the freeway in lighter traffic outbound from the city, he felt content going opposite the jerky, stop-and-start pile of commuters in the twice daily nuisance of big city life. He listened to the radio and sipped hot coffee, eager for another day. As the day progressed each contact with his customers seemed to build energy, which was fortunate considering how he often lacked sufficient sleep.

The day following Tulie's death and Stan's disappearance, the balance between energy and exhaustion would have been way off had it not been for his anticipation of talking about it with his customers, especially the other growers in the area who knew the Weaver's as well or better than he did.

On Tuesdays and Thursdays he made fewer deliveries because the route included stops at the small farms where he picked up much of his inventory. It varied almost every week. Tom surveyed the selection of fresh meat or produce available at the moment, decided what he thought his customers might buy that day or next, and hope that most of them did.

Once people tried it, they became sold on the leaner beef from cattle raised on pasture, on milk, and other dairy products from cows allowed to graze, and without hormone injections or excessive antibiotics. Some customers liked lamb, although sales remained steady compared with the growing popularity of bison, often mistakenly called buffalo.

Tom liked bison burgers on the grill. Very lean with a somewhat nutty flavor, they required lower heat and longer cooking.

Sitting in a lawn chair outside in the yard on a warm summer evening, gazing at the sky turning a soft blue and pink. The sweet scent of grass, leaves, and crops blendid with other greens and growing vegetation drifting in the air. Bison burgers on the grill, the kids playing on the swing set with their laughing voices among a chorus of birds, and Jeri carrying a salad and chips out to the picnic table, Tom savored the contentment for as long as it would last.

On this day Tom's thoughts still struggled to understand what happened to the Weavers and why. He turned the truck into the long driveway to the Daniels' farm. He needed to talk with someone, to exorcise the more strange mutations among his thoughts, make room for other ideas and perhaps new information through the eyes of another. Talking with Archie and Millie Daniels would help do that.

The Daniels raised corn and soybeans on 1,200 acres, barely enough to provide a modest standard of living. Each year production costs increased, crop prices stayed pretty much the same, and the weather provided a constant source of anxiety, as did the pressure to increase crop yields just to stay even.

After their children left home and started their own lives off the farm Millie returned to work full-time at the bank. The income helped, mostly to pay down past debt. Still, it wasn't enough to make room in the farm operation for one of their sons and his family to come back and farm with his dad. But it did allow them the luxury of buying fresh meat and produce, raised on small farms operated in greater harmony with nature, and without the use of pesticides and hormones.

Right after reading the flyer in the mail from "Tom's Fresh Meats and Produce, Naturally," Millie called and placed an order.

Tom rapped on the side door of the sprawling rambler even though he knew no one was home. Seeing the truck drive into the farm site, Duke, the Daniels' old, black Labrador retriever lying in the yard, merely raised his head off the grass, his tail managing a feeble wag. Had the visitor been any other stranger he would have stood and barked a warning.

Tom entered the big kitchen to put away their order: romaine lettuce, fresh spinach, tomatoes, and two whole chickens. The Daniels never ordered beef, but sometimes bison. Their beef came from another neighbor after processing at a small meat shop in Buffalo Ridge, and went into the big chest freezer in the back hall. They liked the fresh chickens that came from the Weaver farm.

He opened the refrigerator and there it was. Millie always left some treat, and today it was a big piece of German chocolate cake. Sitting at the kitchen table eating, Tom mused about the eating schedule on the farm. Although midmorning, this would be called lunch.

In the old days the morning started with coffee and a slab of bread or biscuit before milking the cows. Breakfast followed, then more chores with a lunch break at mid-morning. Dinner, the day's main meal, came at noon. Mid-afternoon brought another lunch, often sandwiches, and they sat down to supper at 5:30. Even though they sold all of their livestock eight years ago, which greatly reduced the amount of chores, Archie continued to eat on the old schedule adding more pounds than he needed to his large, beefy frame, like one of the ancient, gnarly oaks inhabiting the southeast shores of prairie lakes.

The cake gave Tom a brief escape from his thoughts and his fatigue. He faced the rest of the day with dread, of struggling to stay awake, of what he would encounter upon returning to the Weaver farm.

He thought about the little plastic salt shaker in the brown paper bag beneath the seat in his truck. It contained a few grams of a white, crystalline substance, but it was not salt. What would it hurt to try some? He knew it would drive off his need for sleep. Perhaps it would help him work even harder, enough to get his business off the plateau of just barely breaking even.

Jeri wouldn't have to know.

3 With the truck engine roaring Tom barely heard the ring tone from his cell phone nestled in the open ashtray. He turned down the radio and grabbed the phone.

"Hi Sweetie. How are things going?" Jeri usually called in midmorning after getting Jade and Trace to eat breakfast and outside to play.

"Hi. Okay I guess. I'm really wiped. I can't hear. You'll have to talk louder," Tom said, almost shouting.

"Where are you? Are you going to the Weavers?" Jeri said in loud voice.

"I just left the Daniels' place. Today Millie left me some German chocolate cake."

"That's nice. How's the truck running?"

"It's still running. Got my fingers crossed."

"What are you going to do about the Weavers? Don't you have to get some chickens there today?"

"Wait a minute. I can't hear. I got to pull over." Tom slowed to a stop on the edge of the gravel township road and shut down the motor. "What'd you say?"

"I just asked about the Weavers. Are you going there today?"

"Supposed to. I don't know what I'm going to do. I guess I'll have to try. I know where they keep the chickens so I could just get them. I'm sure they'll have the place roped off though. I'll just have to see when I get there. So what about that phone call last night? What do you think we should do?"

"I think we should tell the cops," Jeri said. "It's got to be part of the investigation."

"Yeah, maybe so. But I'm going to try talking with some people around here today. I'm going to the Hamiltons. They knew Stan and Tulie better than anyone."

"You be careful. You call if you see anything."

"Don't worry. I'll be fine. So what do you got going today?"

"I've got to head into town a little early for a union meeting. I'll take the kids to mom about two or so."

"You be careful, too," Tom said. "I hope you're doing the right thing, trying to do that. What if you got fired?"

"They can't do that. There's rules and laws and stuff against that. We're just trying to get some fair treatment."

"I know. Good luck. I got to get going. See you tonight. Love ya."

Tom pressed the 'end' button on the cell phone. He turned the key in the ignition. Instead of the motor starting up, he heard only the click of the starter solenoid. "Damn!" He cussed himself for shutting down engine. In recent weeks he had suspected that the starter motor was going. He put off replacing it, instead spending his time and money on the F350 Lariat.

He turned the key several more times. For a moment he sat there as if in a trance, hearing only the compressor motor kicking in on the truck's refrigeration unit. In his mind he saw all the doubts trying to creep in at the far horizon of his thoughts. He prayed, asking God for the strength to meet all the problems and challenges, for some sign that he was trying to do the right thing. Was he a fool trying to start his own business? Maybe he just didn't have what it takes. Maybe he should give up and get a truck driving job.

The image of Tulie lying lifeless on the floor in her own blood intruded on his thoughts and sent a wave of sadness, turning to fear and anger like surf breaking on the shore. Their poor kids. One minute they're safe, secure, and happy with loving parents in a country paradise. Now their lives are changed forever.

He felt worse having to call Jeri back.

Kids, c'mon! We're going for a ride in the truck!" Jeri hollered out the kitchen door.

She lifted Trace up into the Lariat. Jade climbed in on her own.

"We're going to see daddy! We've got to help him get his truck started."

She tried to sound excited, covering up the irritation she still felt after scolding her husband over the phone. She didn't blame him entirely for focusing his attention on the pickup and not the delivery truck. She worshipped the Lariat almost as much as he did. They could hardly wait for the weekend when they planned to enter it in the local stock class for the truck and tractor pull at the fairgrounds in Buffalo Ridge.

When he said it recently, Jeri didn't pay much attention to his casual mention of the starter in the delivery truck. She hoped it wouldn't take too long to help him get it started. He said all it needed was a pull to get it rolling and he would let out the clutch. Pulling it fast enough with the F350 Lariat would be no problem.

Tom thought he had given Jeri good directions. Sitting on the gravel township road that passed by the Daniel's farm, the truck still would be visible from the county highway nearly a mile away.

He leaned back, closed his eyes and tried to relax, listening to the radio. He knew it would take only about twenty minutes for Jeri to arrive. If he hadn't been too perturbed with himself he would have taken a short nap, soothed by the sweet, soft breeze drifting in the window and the melodic warble of meadowlarks.

He opened his eyes at the sound of a vehicle. In the side mirror he saw a pickup approaching from behind, leaving a cloud of dust in its wake, too soon to be Jeri.

An old 1970s vintage, gray Dodge pickup slowed to a stop alongside Tom's truck. The driver, a man looking to be in his sixties, leaned over and peered through the open passenger side window up at Tom.

"Howdy. You need any help?"

Tom thought he looked familiar. He had seen the truck before. He tried to remember the man's name. He wore blue denim bib overalls over a white T-shirt. An American flag hung across the back of the cab covering the back window and held in place by a gun rack bolted through the flag into the back wall. A Winchester 30-30 lever action rifle rested on the rack.

"Hi," Tom waved back. "No, I'll be fine. Thanks anyway."

"You sure? Can I give you a ride someplace?"

"No, that's okay. Someone's coming to give me a pull. The starter conked out. She'll start with a little pull."

"You got one of them cell phones?"

"Yeah, I called my wife. We got a big truck that can pull this."

"Damn things."

"What?"

"Them cell phone towers all over the place. You know all them waves and signals, you know what they're doing, don't ya?"

Tom looked at the old man wondering how to respond. He decided to try a diplomatic middle ground. "They work pretty good most places. That's what the towers are for. Don't know what we can do about it I guess."

"We'll see about that," the man said, surveying the landscape, his gaze fixing on a tower rising near a distant grove of trees. "All them signals in the air are messin' with our heads, you know. It's the government and phone companies. They're working on a way to control our thoughts."

He looked back at Tom, seeing the young man's face taking on a bemused look and dropped the subject, once again disappointed in the naïve and docile capitulation of most Americans, their blindness to what was really going on. "You sure you don't need a ride or something?"

"Nope. Help's coming soon."

"If you say so. But I'd be glad to help."

"Appreciate it. Thanks for stopping."

The man gave a little salute touching the bill of his cap with an eagle embroidered on the front and drove away. The pickup truck's box held a 50-gallon fuel tank with a hand pump, several smaller steel drums, an assortment of five-gallon pails, and an old, rusting V-8 engine block. Tom caught the wording on one of the numerous bumper stickers and decals: "The Second Amendment—Our Nation's True Homeland Security."

Tom thought hard trying to remember the man's name. He flipped through the small phone book that he kept in the glove compartment hoping the name would jump out. He knew most everyone in the area. When he first started doing the route he stopped at almost every home in town and around the countryside.

Because of their appearance he avoided some. They looked rundown, even spooky. They probably didn't have much money, and if they did, they didn't seem like good customer prospects. The old farm houses looked weather-beaten, the yards cluttered and overgrown. Old farm equipment and other junk lurked in the groves of trees. Some of the reclusive residents he had never seen. He wasn't sure if he seen the man in the gray Dodge pickup before.

LIKE SEEING THE CAVALRY ride to the rescue, Tom looked up at the big red truck far off, approaching from the opposite direction. He felt happy and disgusted, happy to see his family but embarrassed about dragging them out here because of his procrastination.

Jeri turned the pickup around and backed up to Tom's truck. Jade and Trace challenged her order to stay in the pickup enough so that she let them climb into their dad's truck. Tom got out and gave them all hugs. Jeri lifted the heavy tow chain from the pickup box, carefully to avoid marring the finish. Tom crawled under the front of the delivery truck and hooked one end to the frame. Jeri hooked the other end to the pickup hitch.

She drove forward slowly at first to take up the slack. Tom shifted the delivery truck in second gear, depressed the clutch, and waved at Jeri to start. Exhaust rumbled from the F350's twin tailpipes and the truck quickly gained speed. Tom let out the clutch with the ignition on and the big truck started right up. Jade and Trace laughed and bounced on the seat. "Yay daddy! Yay mommy!"

Tom lifted them from the cab and Jeri ushered them back into the pickup.

"Thanks," Tom said, lifting the chain into the pickup box. "I'll get that starter fixed tonight."

"I hope so. What would you have done if I hadn't been able to come out?"

"Somebody did stop. This weird old guy. He lives around here. Don't know his name. He seemed nice though."

"Where are you heading now?" Jeri asked.

"The Hamilton place. I'm still pretty much on schedule. Thanks for getting out here so quick. I'm going to see what I can find out about the Weaver's, too."

Jeri drove away with the kids pressing their faces into the back window and waving at their dad, still thrilled about the exciting and surprising adventure.

Driving onto the Hamilton's Sunshine Valley Farm Tom remembered to leave the truck engine running and hoped that the parking brake would hold.

The house, a three-bedroom rambler built in the 1950s, would have blended into any older, big city suburb. It replaced the original farm house that had been damaged beyond repair by a tornado. The twister also took a chicken coop and granary, but left the barn untouched. Now fifty years later the barn might have deteriorated from lack of use and upkeep, like they had on many other farms. When the Hamiltons bought the one-hundred sixty acre farm in 1978, reshingling the barn became one of their first projects.

Ron and Wendy Hamilton specialized in raising goats for their milk, most of which they processed into cheese. They strove to be self-sufficient and succeeded for the most part.

In the mid-1980s Wendy had to resume teaching school, which, along with the farm income provided enough for them and their four children to get by. The youngest, now a senior in high school, had no interest in staying around, planning to attend college in the city and stay there.

As more people learned about goat milk, especially if they were lactose-intolerant, the sales volume grew enough to make this a regular stop on Tom's route. He picked up milk and cheese, and sometimes dropped off fruit and vegetables, or beef from one of the other farms in their network that specialized in raising lean, grass-fed cattle.

As always, any visitor to the Hamilton farm first encountered Lily. The collie loped from the garage toward Tom's truck, announcing his arrival with loud barking.

Tom scruffed the soft, thick fur around her neck. The dog's welcome shaved off some of the edge to his apprehension of encountering the Hamiltons, about how they were coping with the fate, known and unknown, of their close friends. Anticipation also followed him toward the house, giving him hope for some answers and someone to talk with, whom he trusted and would not suspect him or ask anything of him other than to tell what he knew.

Ron Hamilton closed up the last case of the cheese delivery for Tom and walked out of the small, concrete block building between the house and barn. Despite the grief and confusion that washed over them when they heard the news on television last night, he had been waiting for the friendly young man in the delivery truck. Because of the nature of his work knew almost everyone in the area, mostly by observing their immediate surroundings, the condition of their homes, yards, what they ate, and how their characters were reflected in the behavior of their dogs and sometimes their children.

Ron and Wendy lived and worked as they did, inspired by the back-to-the-land vision from the 1960s and 1970s. Tom hadn't even been born when they moved on to the farm. Several times Ron tried to convey their ideals to Tom, thinking that his dream of creating a successful natural foods sales and delivery service arose from the same ideal.

It didn't, and eventually Ron understood that "the movement" as he called it might as well be ancient history to the younger man. But he still appreciated Tom's energy and pursuit of his own vision. He always looked forward to Tom's short visits on the route, and this day especially so.

Tom could almost see the veil of sadness over Ron as he approached. Tom wanted to know more about the Weavers almost as much as Ron needed to know what happened yesterday. Tom did not understand how deeply it had affected Ron until he approached, quietly, steadily right up to him, embracing him and seeming with great effort to hold back tears.

"It's terrible. I just can't believe it," Ron said, stepping back still resting his hands on the younger man's shoulders. Tom shifted his feet, discomforted with the close distance of the older man and unsure of what to say.

"We didn't know until we heard it on the news last night," Ron said. "They didn't say who it was but we knew when they showed the farm site. I can't believe it. Who would do such a thing?" Ron shook his head in bewilderment.

"I have no idea," Tom replied. "They even questioned me yesterday, like I was a suspect."

"You're kidding!"

"It gave me the creeps. I don't know. This BCI agent on the case is spooky. He just sits there staring at you like you're guilty or something."

"And there's no sign of Stan?"

"That's another thing. This agent acts like he thinks maybe Stan did it and took off."

"That's ridiculous!" Ron exclaimed. "Where are the kids? How are they doing?"

They walked back to the cheese-making shed. Tom described what happened as far as he knew. The Weaver kids had been taken to a foster home. Neighbors came over to do the chores.

Ron offered coffee, but Tom said he couldn't stay long because of the truck. He mentioned the starter problem and that he didn't want to use too much gas leaving the engine idling. He mentioned the old guy in a gray pickup who stopped to offer help. Ron said that must have been Newton Case. He chuckled as he described the conspiratorial and sometimes comical character. He said Newt went over the edge during the farm crisis in the early '80s, becoming one of those anti-government tax protester types. To this day he insisted on paying his property tax in cash and only to the town clerk, who in turn deposited it with the county auditor.

Tom said he had to get going and loaded the boxes of cheese into the truck's refrigerated compartment.

Normally, today he would not be stopping at the Weaver place. Pulling out of the Hamilton driveway onto the township road, today he would have turned right in the direction of his next delivery. By sudden impulse his hands spun the steering wheel left. A detour to the Weaver place wouldn't take too long, and he could continue his route from there. If the BCI's mobile crime lab was still there he would just drive on by. If only a deputy were there to secure the site Tom planned to stop, hoping it would be one with whom he was well-acquainted. He also rationalized that perhaps they needed help with chores.

A CLOUD OF DUST FOLLOWED Tom's truck along the gravel township road, part of a checkerboard network partitioning the vast fields of soybeans, corn and sugar beets. Two miles off he could make out the tree line along the creek through the Weaver farm.

Sometimes he would deliberately schedule his stops there around noon. Tulie always insisted that he stay for lunch. Like a traveling peddler Tom welcomed the food and company, and paid for it by providing news and conversation. He began adding small boxes of popsicles or ice cream bars to his orders at the warehouse, and gave them to children on his route. Stan and Tulie consented, although gently reminding Tom to use restraint, to understand their desire to curtail the consumption of sugars and processed foods.

A sheriff's deputy sat in a patrol car parked at the entrance to the Weaver farm driveway. Tom recognized the officer and braked the truck to a stop. The deputy got out and walked up.

"What do you guys know?" Tom asked.

"Not much. Probably not any more than you."

"They need any help, with chores and stuff?"

"Naw. Some guy was over earlier."

"Who was that?"

"Some Daniels guy. I think that was his name."

"Archie? Archie Daniels?"

"That might have been it. He was leaving when I got here. They were still out here this morning, the state crime lab."

"I was hoping I could come and get some stuff. I was supposed to pick up some chickens today," Tom lied.

"Weren't you here yesterday?"

"I think I left part of the order behind, you know, with all the distraction. I just wanted to check their cooler just to make sure."

Even though the deputy suspected Tom wasn't telling the whole truth, it was close enough and reasonable enough to consent, and he knew Tom well enough to believe that whatever he said and did there was good reason for it. He moved the patrol car farther off the driveway so Tom could get by with the truck. Tom waited for the deputy to park his car back in the middle and then climb into the truck.

"Don't take too long here," the deputy warned. "And don't touch anything. You got gloves? Use gloves when you're getting what you need."

In the cooler Tom found two cases of processed fresh chickens, which he thought he could sell with a little extra effort. After loading them he and the deputy walked around the farmyard speculating about what might have happened.

The deputy asked Tom if he knew anything about the meth lab suspects in the area. Tom had seen some unfamiliar cars around lately. A couple farm sites looked a little suspicious.

Tom asked if he could take a look at Stan's pickup parked under the lean-to attached to the garage workshop. The deputy's cell phone rang. Reaching for it he nodded at Tom and waved to go ahead, reminding him to keep his hands off. With the deputy on the phone, Tom walked over to inspect the pickup. He walked back to where the deputy stood, still listening on the cell phone. He noticed the way in which the deputy was looking at him, still listening intently on the phone.

The deputy flipped the phone shut. Now he seemed to be uncomfortable, unsure about what he should say. He did not want to offend Tom, but he had his orders.

"What's up?" Tom asked.

"Nothing. That was the sheriff. I guess he wants you to wait for a bit. He's coming out here. They just want to ask you a few more questions."

"Me? What for?"

"Well, you were the first one on the scene as far as we know. This investigation is just starting."

"I told them everything. I don't know what else to say."

"That was then. This is now. They've probably got a bunch of new questions. It's not an easy job to round up hard evidence in some of these cases. A lot of them, there's usually some connection. Sometimes people think stuff like this is random. Sometimes it is, but not very often."

"So I'm supposed to be connected somehow?"

"You're a primary witness. You know the Weavers. You know almost everybody around here. You're on the road a lot. You must see things."

"I told you, I've said everything I can think of. I hope this doesn't take too long. I got to get going." Tom regretted yielding to the impulse of returning to the Weaver farm when he didn't have to.

"It shouldn't. They should be here pretty soon."

"Who's 'they'?"

"Well, it's going to be the sheriff and the BCI agent. You talked to them yesterday."

Tom didn't mind talking to the sheriff. The BCI agent's demeanor gave him an unsettling feeling, a mixture of fear and helplessness. Trust ranked very high in Tom's world, and he could not detect any sign of it existing in the BCI agent.

"You know, you're still a suspect, too. You didn't hear this from me. That's just the way it is. Until this thing's cleared up they've got their sights on everyone with any connection."

"Why do you keep saying 'they'? You're one of them, too."

"Of course. I'm just trying to help you understand. I'm still a friend."

Tom felt some reassurance. A couple times they had gone off-roading with their four-by-fours, both with and without their families. At the county law enforcement center among the other officers the young deputy attested to Tom's character, despite their concern about the occasions when he drove a nearly 10,000-pound F350 four-by-four too loud and too fast. He still was a good citizen and could be a valuable observer in far corners of the county where regular patrols were infrequent.

The deputy tried to fill the long wait by asking Tom about his truck, about the upcoming truck-pull competition. The distraction drained off some of the tension until they looked to see the BCI agent arrive in an unmarked car followed by the sheriff in a patrol car.

THE SHERIFF WENT THROUGH the same list of questions as yesterday evening. Tom responded, sometimes curtly and feeling like he was being harassed.

"You sure you don't remember anything else?" the sheriff asked.

"Yeah. I'd like to know who called us last night," Tom said. "It was like one or two in the morning. Somebody called and said we should watch out. I don't know who it was. He didn't say his name and had something over the phone to muffle his voice."

Even before he had finished speaking Tom realized his mistake. He mentioned it thinking that somehow it would make him appear innocent, when in fact it offered some clue to the investigators leading toward the opposite.

"Oh really?" the BCI agent said, showing a raised eyebrow. "Now why would someone do that? What exactly did he say?"

Tom shifted his weight, growing nervous. "It was something like 'you better watch out, you're being watched'," he said.

"Sorry we got to do this," the sheriff said, trying to sound sympathetic. "We got to take a look at your delivery truck. It won't take too long. I hope you understand."

The agent was already walking toward the truck, removing his suit jacket and exposing his shoulder holster. He looked back at the younger deputy, motioning with his head telling him to join him in the search.

"What do you need to do that for?" Tom suddenly felt helpless against the sudden invasion. He wanted to shout something, to chase them down and stop them.

The sheriff sensed his panic. All along he believed in Tom's innocence, until now.

Seeing the agent and the deputy climb into the truck, Tom resigned, realizing he must face whatever truth they uncovered. He could deal with their discovery of his 9mm Ruger. Even though unregistered, it might be overlooked by those who knew him, and who also carried firearms, but not the meth. He had almost felt helpless, accepting it from a driver at the warehouse. He stashed it under the seat. At the time he couldn't think of anything else, and had almost forgotten about it since.

While the deputy and agent searched the truck, Sheriff Hank Schwartz asked Tom a few more questions. Tom asked how the Weaver kids were doing. The sheriff said fine as far as he knew.

They searched the truck for about twenty minutes. First the cargo box and then the cab. Hearing the cartons and bags of meat and produce falling to the floor, he felt angry and helpless. He protested to the sheriff, who only shrugged and even tried to sound sympathetic, saying he was sorry but that's what they had to do.

The deputy closed the cargo door and they moved the search to the cab. Tom's mouth grew dry. He did not worry so much about the gun. But when he remembered the little plastic salt shaker under the seat, he felt panic. He had never used any, and now he greatly regretted accepting the substance when it was offered to him.

The agent climbed out of the truck and approached, followed by the deputy. Tom saw something more than an ominous look on the agent's face. Instead of a serious, stony appearance it seemed almost sinister.

The agent stopped and motioned with his hand for the sheriff to approach. Sheriff Schwartz glanced at Tom and went to the agent. The sheriff blocked Tom's view, but they appeared to be looking down at something held in the agent's hand. The sheriff looked back at Tom, a worried look on his face. He turned back talking again with the agent, then walked back to where Tom stood. In one hand he held the Ruger, the other held something else, but Tom couldn't make out what it was.

"This registered?" The sheriff held up the gun.

"No."

"That's too bad. What about this?" The sheriff opened the palm of his gloved left hand revealing what looked like an egg. The Weavers also raised layer hens, and Tom sold fresh eggs, too. This wasn't one of them.

"Can you tell me about this?" the agent asked. He held it out close to Tom, who without thinking took it.

"It looks like an egg," Tom replied. "One of those plastic ones, you know, like with candy in them."

The agent took the egg back. "Yeah, candy, right." He acted amused looking at the sheriff and deputy. He twisted the egg, lifted off the top half and held out the bottom half. They all saw a white, fine granular substance. For a moment no one said a word.

"I know what that looks like. Do you know what that looks like?" the agent asked.

Tom looked up at the agent. He had never seen the white plastic egg before. He did not understand what was going on. They did not find the plastic salt shaker, unless they did without revealing it. Instinctively, Tom responded as if he were innocent.

"What is this?" the agent repeated.

"I don't know. It looks like salt or sugar. I never saw that before."

Tom noticed the agent wore gloves as he held the egg. Sheriff Schwartz and Deputy Randy Tollefson appeared grim and apologetic, but they did not reveal their surprise.

"You sure you never saw that before?" Sheriff Schwartz asked.

"Swear to God. I never saw that before," Tom said calmly, earnestly.

"That's funny, because we found this in your truck," the agent said. The deputy stared at him. During the search the agent never said anything about finding the plastic egg with about two grams of what looked like crystal meth. The deputy would've said something. He wanted to believe that Tom was telling the truth and easily could have. He thought he knew Tom well enough, that he would not be that stupid. He had seen what meth can do, and there was no evidence that it was doing it to Tom and his family. Right now he could not say anything.

The agent dropped the egg into a small plastic bag and put it in his suit coat pocket.

"Sheriff, you know what to do."

4

No one answered when Ron Hamilton called the county family services office a few minutes after 8:00 a.m. Wednesday. Wendy urged him to call and find out how the Weaver kids were doing. How were they holding up? Could the Hamiltons help? Right after hearing the story on the 10:00 p.m. news last evening Ron called the sheriff's department, wanting to know more, about what happened and about the kids. The dispatcher could not release any information because of the investigation. She said the children were safe and in protective custody. She asked if there were relatives or if they knew of any.

With their own kids leaving home the Hamiltons greatly appreciated any contact with the Weaver children. They took them for four days over the Memorial Day weekend so Stan and Tulie could get away for a few days, which they rarely did. At first little Jonathan cried, missing his parents. Anna and certainly Michael understood that they would return soon. They enjoyed helping Ron milk the goats.

Although only ten years old, Michael seemed older in some ways. With only brief instruction from Ron he quickly learned how to milk the goats. Ron knew he would, having seen the boy handle tools and tasks at the Weaver place at a level far beyond his years. On one occasion it surprised him to see Michael using a welder to repair a wagon frame.

Wendy couldn't help crying at the thought that the three young children would never see their parents again, Tulie for certain. They couldn't imagine what happened to Stan. To even think that he would harm Tulie and disappear was obscene. If kidnapped, they could hope that he would return unharmed. If something worse happened, if he never returned, little Jonathan would hardly even remember his father.

No one really knew much about the Weavers before they moved on to the old farm site eight years ago. They must have had some money. Raising livestock and vegetables on a small scale and hand-made wood products did not generate enough income to live on initially. They joined the group of organic and sustainable small farms in the area. Eventually they landed some contracts with restaurants and upscale supermarkets in the city. Tom Otto delivered the products of several growers to the city and served as their primary sales force in the local area.

If the Weavers hadn't come along the farm site would have been leveled. The barn was still in good shape, but toxic chemicals contaminated the house. The previous occupants now lived at the state penitentiary after the raid on their meth lab.

Old Mrs. Wegman, their landlady, thought the previous tenants seemed like nice people, and they could be when necessary. When she died without heirs the farm went on the auction block.

The farmer who owned the adjacent land coveted the eighty-acre parcel with its rich, loamy soil and level terrain. He already farmed more than two thousand acres in a checkerboard pattern of parcels around the area. He rented the eighty and became accustomed to paying a below-market-rate rent, which Mrs. Wegman thought was a lot of money. Having to farm around the old farm site annoyed him and on several occasions he asked her if she would let him level it, trees, house, barn and all, but she refused. She was born in the house as was her father. She didn't realize what it was worth now. She thought fifty dollars an acre for rent was a lot.

The farmer thought he could get a similar bargain at the auction. He backed down somewhat bewildered at the strangers who seemed to be operating from a different financial perspective.

Stan and Tulie Weaver were the highest bidders, even knowing what had been there and what they would have to do to make it habitable.

The extent of the clean-up surprised them. County hazardous waste technicians found alcohol, brake fluid, Drano, old batteries, lye, anhydrous ammonia, packages of cold tablets, and ether among the poisonous mess. Pails, pyrex dishes, coffee filters, plastic jugs, small propane cylinders, and hot plates littered the kitchen. A blender still contained chopped up cold tablets.

Sitting in the middle of the eighty acres near the creek, the farm site could be easily overlooked, and it was for the most part. Occasionally it aroused the Hamilton's curiosity but nothing more. As long as the tenants didn't bother anyone else, ignoring them came easy.

After the meth lab raid the Hamiltons felt somewhat embarrassed for not knowing better. That subsided after the Weavers arrived, cleaned the place up, and became new friends and colleagues in the organic and natural foods business.

SHORTLY AFTER RON'S CALL to the sheriff, someone from the funeral home in Buffalo Ridge called. The investigators had been able to contact Stan's relatives, but could find nothing about Tulie. With so many unanswered questions in the investigation, her body would remain at the hospital morgue indefinitely as far as they knew. Perhaps they could have a memorial service. They sought Ron and Wendy's advice. Could they come into town and help make plans at the funeral home? Ron said they would after they finished milking the goats.

When Tom stopped by later in the morning Ron asked him if he could accompany them going to the funeral home. Tom couldn't because of his heavy route schedule that day, but suggested that perhaps Jeri could. Ron called her and she agreed, but she would have to take the kids along.

This time, when Tom's cell phone rang and he knew it was his wife, he did not want to answer. He wanted to hear how the meeting at the funeral home went. To a greater degree he did not want to reveal the truth of what happened when he went to the Weaver farm earlier. Still, he needed to talk with someone he trusted about the search of his truck and the false accusation by the BCI agent about the plastic egg containing meth.

Although he had been able to avoid thinking too much about it, the realization gradually surfaced that sooner or later he had to tell Jeri about the other stuff, the two grams of crystal meth in the plastic salt shaker, which now sat in the small cooler that held his lunch, usually two sandwiches with whatever sandwich meat or cheese he could find in the refrigerator, an apple or banana, and a small bag of potato chips. Maybe it was the mysterious phone caller last night, but by some instinct, when he approached the Weaver farm and saw the sheriff's deputy's patrol car, he reached under the seat of his truck for the salt shaker and placed it in his lunch cooler.

Telling Jeri would affirm and likely reveal his guilt, which he dreaded. He convinced himself, just barely, of the greater hope that after the initial shock and anger she would support him and try to help.

"Hey babe, how'd it go at the funeral home?"

"Hi. Okay I guess. It was kind of spooky," Jeri replied.

"What do you mean?"

"I don't know. They had all these questions. I don't know why I had to be there."

"So what happened? When is the funeral?"

"We don't know yet. They've got to track down relatives. We're supposed to help with that."

"How do we do that?"

"We know them, the Weavers—you know them."

"Not that well. We know about them since they moved here. Stan talked a little bit about what he did before. You know all that as well as I do. Tulie's the mysterious one."

"I told them all that stuff," Jeri said. "Then they had us look at a price list. You wouldn't believe how much that stuff costs. When it's my turn to go just dig a hole out in the grove."

"If I'm still around then I probably wouldn't be able to. My back will be shot from sitting in this truck all day long."

"What makes you think you'll still be doing that?"

"What else is there?"

"If you don't start making money at this sometime soon there better be something else."

"Don't start up on that again. It just takes time. You just wait. I'm making money."

"But how much are you spending? You going to fix that starter?"

"All you think about is money. Let's quit this," Tom pleaded. "And besides, funerals aren't for the dead. They're for the living."

"So is the cost," Jeri replied. "They wanted to know how much money they had and where it was. Can you believe that? I mean, they were real nice about it and everything. It just seemed so weird. It seemed so unreal, sitting there and talking about that kind of stuff. I think it's just starting to hit me now, about Tulie and Stan."

"Yeah, I know. Me too."

"Ron tried to find out about the kids," Jeri said. "They're at some foster home. The sheriff wouldn't say who it was."

"Why not?"

"They said they could be in danger. Whoever did it might come after the kids. That's what they said."

"That's stupid," Tom said. "Why would they want to do anything to the kids?"

"I wish we could take them," Jeri said. "I'm going to talk to the sheriff. I know the guy who runs the county family services office. They should be with somebody who they know. Where are you now?"

"I'm just out on the route. I got a couple more pickups to make and then make the rest of the deliveries."

"Are you driving or stopped somewhere?"

"I'm driving now."

"So have you heard anything? Did any of the other farmers around there know anything?"

"Not really. Everybody pretty much thinks it was somebody who came to the Weaver's. A robbery or something. Nobody thinks it was a domestic or anything like that."

"Maybe it was one of those meth gangs," Jeri said. "That stuff is still around. Maybe some of them came back or somebody who used to know them went there thinking it was still like that. Did you go by there today? Did you see anything?"

"It wasn't on the route today. I went there, though," Tom admitted, realizing he had to, and probably wanted to, tell her about what happened, about the search of his truck. As much as he wanted to deny it, he could sense the current pushing him to confess the secret of the white substance in the little salt shaker.

He slowed the truck and turned into the parking lot at the gas station-convenience store-café at the intersection of the State Highway 19 and U.S. Highway 75. He almost by habit shut down the motor. With the engine idling instead of roaring he could hear much better.

"They had the driveway blocked off. You know that one deputy, the young guy that we know. Randy Tollefson, he was sitting there in his patrol car guarding the place."

Tom described how Randy allowed him on site to get some chickens. He vacillated about describing what happened next, the search of his truck and the BCI agent's accusation.

Sheriff Schwartz had doubted that the plastic egg containing what looked like crystal meth had come from Tom's truck. Against the agent's wishes he did not arrest Tom immediately. He could do that later if necessary. He knew where to find Tom and that he would not disappear. He had never known Tom to be a lawbreaker other than minor traffic violations and perhaps under-age drinking in the not-too-distant past.

Since he had not used any of the meth in the plastic salt shaker still sitting in his lunchbox, Tom persuaded himself that he had done no wrong. He stopped short of telling Jeri about the search.

They said good-bye. Jeri had to go to work soon. Tom was running a little late, but still hoped to be home by suppertime. Jeri said her mom was taking the kids to the swimming pool in Buffalo Ridge in the afternoon.

Right away that morning Jeri had called Anderson's Truck and Auto Service about getting a new starter for Tom's truck. They had one in stock, so that's what Tom would be doing in the evening, replacing the starter.

He appreciated her help in getting the part. If only she would stop using such occasions to question him about financial status of his business. He tried to keep a record of business revenue and expenses. Counting the income from customer payments and his checks for expenses was easy, but what remained didn't leave much for his time. Some months he could have earned more on a newspaper route for the Buffalo Ridge Banner.

Jeri also called the county family services director asking about the Weaver kids, if the Ottos could help in any way, stopping short, for the time being, of asking if they could take care of Michael, Anna and Jonathan. He sounded hopeful and said he would talk to the sheriff about it.

MOST DAYS TOM FELT CONTENT driving the truck on his route. Every day the weather provided a vast cinema of infinite variety if you counted the shapes of clouds, each one unique like snowflakes. Gazing up at squadrons of white, puffy cumulus clouds emerging from the far horizon, drifting along under an ice blue sky and casting shadows rippling over vast fields of corn and soybeans, Tom almost felt sorry for the people working in offices, factories, and meat processing plants.

On some days the weather brought many challenges, especially in the winter facing the occasional blizzards. The extra effort required to navigate the truck through white-out, icy conditions left a sense of accomplishment, which diminished if it lasted too many days. Twice in one winter he had to call for a heavy-duty tow truck to pull his truck from a snow-filled road ditch.

Today, after leaving the convenience store and the phone call from Jeri behind him, Tom's thoughts still carried the burden of what happened at the Weaver farm; the false accusation from the BCI agent, the threat of being arrested, and the secret in his lunch box. He had almost said something to Jeri, but could not do so over the phone. Eventually he had to tell her. It had to be face-to-face so she could see that he was telling her the truth, that he had never used any, and that it would soften the expected rebuke about being so stupid as to accept it in the first place.

His cell phone rang. He flipped it open to see the caller ID number. It read "Unknown call." He paused, debating whether not to answer or let it go to voicemail.

Tom answered. "Hello."

"Hello. Is this Tom Otto?"

"Hello. This is Tom."

"Hi Tom. This is Byron Swain, with the St. Paul Journal. How are you today?"

"Okay I guess."

"I'm a reporter with the Journal and I'm wondering if I could see you today. We're following the incident at the Weaver place."

"How'd you get my number?"

"I hope you don't mind. The story in your local paper today, it had some background about you, about your delivery business. You were the first one on the scene. You called it in. Is that correct?"

Tom hadn't seen the story until he stopped at the convenience store earlier that morning. Normally, he didn't read the Buffalo Ridge Banner. He and Jeri didn't subscribe. They got all the news they needed from friends, relatives, co-workers, and Tom's customers on his route.

He wouldn't have looked at it today, either, except for noticing the front page story about the apparent homicide. The four-column photo with the story didn't show much other than a panoramic view of the Weaver farm site, several vehicles in the distance, and a man wearing a dark suit looking toward the camera with his fist in the air.

Anger rose in his chest when he saw his name in the story and reading the comments that had been attributed to him. He didn't think much about it when the reporter from the Banner called him yesterday evening. He spoke about how he found Tulie and then the kids. The story included what he thought to be way too much background about himself, his business, and his family.

"I'm not talking to any reporters," Tom said.

Earlier, during the encounter at the Weaver farm, he had been sharply rebuked for talking to the Banner reporter. At the initial crime scene the BCI agent commanded him to refrain from talking to the news media. When the Banner reporter called, Tom said he wasn't supposed to talk about it, but started talking anyway. What irked him most was the erroneous statement in the story about his background. He did not work for a large food distributor in the city. "Tom's Fresh Meats and Produce, Naturally," consisted of just him and his truck.

"I just called around to some food warehouses in the city this morning. One of them gave me your number," Byron said. "Listen. I know they probably told you to not talk with the news media. I understand. They want to be in total control of the situation. But according to the law they have to provide basic information, you know, about what appeared to have happened, was anyone harmed, did anyone get arrested, things like that. It's in the public interest to know the basics of what happened."

"Don't you already know that? Why do you need to talk to me?"

"Because you were there, first on the scene. It's okay for you to describe what you saw. Not in grisly detail of course. The investigators won't say anything. Please, just describe in general what you saw."

"It's already in the paper. There really isn't much more to say. Why are you guys so interested? Don't you have enough murders in the big city to keep you busy?"

"That's not the point," Byron said. "Do you know much about the Weavers? How long have they lived there? Where did they come from? Things like that. Don't people in a rural area like that get nosey about their neighbors? Doesn't everyone know everyone else?"

"Not all the time," Tom said. "I know the Weavers a little bit. They supply me with fresh chickens mostly. I stop there at least once a week. We've been out there a couple times, my family and me, for supper."

"What were they like?"

"Listen. I got to get going. I'm trying to make my deliveries. Talking all day and letting my truck idle is costing me," Tom said, starting to get irritated.

"Okay. Okay. But maybe you might like to know something about the Weavers. We know some things about them that might interest people," Byron said.

"Like what."

"Their background, where they came from. I'm heading out your way soon. Maybe we can meet and talk."

"I'm really busy. I don't know. I've got to fix my truck this evening."

"I won't take much time. This is important, too. That's just tragic about their kids. What they must be going through. I can't even imagine. I've got two kids, six and eight, both boys. You have kids?"

Tom said yes. He told Byron he would be home around six and that he could stop by for a few minutes. He had to work on the truck in the evening, the starter for sure, and lately the compressor in the refrigeration unit had been making noises. Byron promised to keep the visit short.

Tom tried to imagine what there might be about the Weaver's that would attract the attention of outsiders to the community. The more he thought about it the more he realized that he didn't know much about their past, not that it really mattered to him. To some folks in the area it did. If you couldn't go back at least two generations in the area you were still considered a newcomer.

Tom took people at face value, and in the Weavers he could detect nothing of a suspicious nature that concerned him. He first met them when he attended a meeting six years ago of organic farmers in the area. The Weavers brought new energy and new ideas to the group. Up until then the others had only been loosely organized. They socialized, shared information, and helped one another with farm work when it was needed. For the most part, finding markets and selling their produce remained individual efforts. That changed when Tom Weaver brought in more than a dozen year's of experience as a former marketing executive with a large corporation in the food industry. Tulie had been a Web site developer, and in just two months after they settled on the old farm near Buffalo Ridge, the group's Healthfare Web site went online.

Tom had been trying to establish his own grocery delivery business. He had heard about the meeting and just showed up. They welcomed the young man as a key partner in transporting their produce directly to consumers in the area, and also to wholesalers and restaurants in the city. They appreciated his youthful energy and enthusiasm, even if he didn't quite grasp their vision of providing fresh, locally-produced meat and produce without the use of hormones or excessive use of pesticides, antibiotics and other chemicals.

Mostly by word of mouth, Tom's natural foods delivery service began to grow as more people became concerned about these and other alterations in mass-produced meats and produce. Local growers with whom Tom worked began to show modest profit. Ironically, they now faced a new challenge—from large, corporate food businesses beginning to develop and market so-called "natural" food products. The battle now focused on how that was defined.

In recent years the Weavers had become leaders among the genuine natural foods producers speaking out against standards becoming watered down. Two years ago Tulie drew national attention in the food industry with a passionate speech at the national conference of the NFPA—Natural Foods Producers Association—in Denver. Later, she testified before a Congressional committee against proposed revisions to the Organic Foods Production Act of 1990. Last year the Weavers led a small group of organic foods producers to Sioux Falls where they picketed outside a large chain supermarket that started selling what it claimed to be natural foods.

Not long after, a federal meat inspector arrived at the Weaver farm for an unannounced inspection. When he learned that it had been the site of a small meth lab, he threatened to shut the Weavers down unless they removed and disposed of all their stock and thoroughly scoured everything. They were forced to comply because not doing so would have jeopardized the local organic foods group's efforts to secure a USDA rural development loan to build a small meat processing plant in another nearby town.

JERI'S MOM CALLED TOM saying she was taking the kids over to her place for supper, to let him know why no one would be there when he arrived at home. Jeri called at 5:30 p.m. on her supper break at the poultry processing plant. They talked about getting the starter fixed on the delivery truck. Tom told her about Byron Swain, the reporter who said he would be stopping by to talk with Tom about the case. He almost said something about the search of his truck and the allegation by the BCI agent.

"Why did you agree to talk with him?" Jeri pressed Tom. "You know what they said. You're not supposed to say anything to anybody."

"I know, I know. I won't say anything."

"How can you talk to him and not say anything?"

"He knows all about it already. He says they've been investigating the Weavers anyway. He's just going to stop by for a few minutes. I told him I've got to work on the truck."

"You better. I'm not coming out somewhere again tomorrow with the pickup and rescue you."

"Don't worry. Maybe that old goofball will come by again to help," Tom tried to laugh. "You find out anymore about where the kids are?" he changed the subject.

"I did. They're staying with the Brocks. I called Amber and she said she wasn't supposed to talk to me or anyone. She said it's really been tough. Jonathan's so little he doesn't really know what's going on but he still cries. Being in a strange place without mommy and daddy. Anna cries all the time and Michael, he just sits there not doing or saying anything. That's what she said. I had to promise like everything not to tell anyone she talked to me. I wish we could get them."

"I got to go," Tom said. "Here comes that reporter. I'll get rid of him soon and get busy on the truck. Anything to eat in the house?"

"There's some tuna salad in the fridge. Don't let the kids stay too long at my mom's."

Tom said good-bye. He left the delivery truck idling in the driveway. A newer, dark-blue Nissan Altima entered the yard and stopped. Tom waved, but walked toward the shop to pull out the F350 pickup and park the delivery truck for the night.

Byron Swain's attempt at interviewing Tom didn't produce much. Byron revealed more information about the Weaver's than Tom ever knew. Stan left his well-compensated corporate job in Kansas City, left his wife, and started a new life with Tulie, eventually finding himself at the other end of the food industry spectrum. Going from a large corporation to a small "organic" farm, raising chickens, dairy cattle, vegetables, and an assortment of other farm animals.

He first met Tulie while on a hunting trip with some corporate buddies in the northern Rockies of Idaho and Montana. On their third trip he disappeared. Search parties and a helicopter scoured the rugged, mountainous terrain for more than a month.

"Why would he do something like that?" Tom asked. "I knew he had some big corporate job before. I didn't think about him having a family before. You know this for sure?"

"Stan Weaver wasn't his real name, either," Byron said. "And Tulie, we don't even know who she was, where she came from."

"Why is that such a big deal?"

"It's an interesting story," Byron said. "People want to read about it. This big corporate executive disappears, then years later turns up missing from a little farm out in the middle of nowhere." He sensed Tom's reaction to the last remark. "Sorry. I mean, to big city folks this is nowhere. I know there's a lot going on here. It's your home," Byron apologized.

"Anything else you can tell me about what happened yesterday, or today?" the reporter resumed questioning. Tom said no. He had to get busy working on the delivery truck.

Byron asked about the Weaver kids.

"We'd like to know ourselves," Tom admitted. "When I found them, that was really tough. Michael, he just stood there stone-faced. He knew what happened. Anna cried the whole time. The sheriff said they're in protective custody with some family. Jeri—that's my wife—she's trying to find out who. We wish we could take care of them. They've hardly ever been off the farm much. They had school at home."

Tom noticed Byron taking notes, but it didn't bother him. He didn't say anything. Talking about what he saw in the hallway yesterday morning was one thing. Compassion for the kids was another. Young children, so vulnerable and trusting, yet so often the victims of evil in the form of abuse, neglect, crime, poverty, or the weaknesses and ambitions of parents and other adults who should know better.

"Did they seem happy? Did they look well-taken care of?" Byron asked.

"Yeah, they had it really good," Tom replied. "Sometimes I used to think they were being isolated out there on the farm, not going to public school and everything. They always seemed like a happy family. Michael was in 4-H. They had kids out to their place to play a lot. Why?"

"Just wondering." Byron paused. "Did you ever think they were involved in any illegal activities? Drugs or anything?"

"Are you serious? I never saw anything like that."

"It's out there, you know. Marijuana plots hidden back in groves of trees. Small meth labs, things like that," Byron said.

"Right, but not at the Weaver's," Tom said. "Their farm place used to be a meth lab you know. They cleaned it all up."

"Now I didn't know that," Byron said. "Can you verify that?"

"It was in the paper a lot. Everybody knew about it. Some deputies that I know told me about how they had to clean it up. But that was a separate deal. That has nothing to do with what happened."

"How do you know that?" Byron asked.

"I just know, okay?" Tom began to feel even more irritated. Upon first impression the reporter seemed a little cocky, even arrogant. He wore one of those safari vests, a pair of blue jeans that had never seen manual labor, and Oakley shades perched above his wide forehead. When he first arrived, just the way he looked around the yard, at the trailer house, shop, trucks and assorted children's toys and outdoor furniture scattered around the weedy lawn, made Tom feel slightly offended. Toward the end he became irritated with himself for talking so much.

Tom looked at his watch. "Listen, Byron, I've got to get going on this truck. If I don't get it fixed tonight I'm in deep doo-doo."

Byron apologized for taking up his time. He gave Tom a business card. "Don't worry. You'll get that fixed," he smiled. "If you want to talk with someone about this any time just give me a call. We're just trying to get at the truth. We all want to know the truth."

They heard a vehicle and looked to see Lynn Meyers, Jeri's mom, drive her Buick into the yard. It had barely stopped when the rear doors sprang open. Jade and Trace jumped out and ran toward the shop toward Tom, not even noticing the strange man.

Byron politely introduced himself to Mrs. Meyers, knelt down and greeted the kids, and then left. Tom asked Lynn if she could stay and put the kids to bed so he could finish working on the truck.

Just before ten she went out to the shop. She was tired and wanted to go home. She loved being with her grandchildren and was happy to take care of them, but at the end of those days she felt like she'd just run a marathon. She hoped Tom was finished. She waited until he tightened the last bolt and tried the new starter. It worked fine.

Tom thanked her for staying so long. He had just enough time to clean up and get something to eat. He had forgotten to eat all evening. He sat in the kitchen eating tuna salad with a beer and watching television. He looked forward to seeing his wife when she returned from work soon. He wanted to tell her about the day's events, about getting the truck fixed, about the pushy reporter. He avoided thinking about what he would say about what happened at the Weaver farm that morning. He had to say something. It would be a lot worse if a deputy came to the house with a warrant for his arrest and she didn't know.

A shiver rippled down his spine when a thought flashed in his mind, that he would be arrested, tried and convicted of drug possession and possibly even transport. It could destroy his life, his family. He looked out the window seeing the headlights of the old Crown Victoria entering the driveway.

5 Working inside, unable to enjoy mild and mellow summer evenings with her family, proved to be the toughest part about the second shift at the poultry processing plant. At one time Jeri said she would rather work the night shift. Then she could be home in the evening, reading stories to Jade and Trace and tucking them into bed before going to work. On the night shift she wouldn't have to work the line, but performed cleaning and maintenance duties instead.

Working the second shift meant that in the mornings she spent most of her time doing housework and taking care of the kids. She hardly ever got enough sleep, getting to bed past midnight and getting up early with the kids. Lately, she had been able to stay in bed, falling back to sleep after being awakened by the sound of clattering bowls, rustling cereal boxes, the opening and closing of the refrigerator, and Jade's voice issuing commands to her younger brother.

It was hard to leave them in the early afternoon with her mother and go to work. Considering employment options in and around Buffalo Ridge the job wasn't too bad. Following an almost successful union organizing attempt several years ago, the company began to offer some employee benefits. With the employees carrying a large portion of the premium cost, the health insurance coverage was slightly better than nothing. And since Tom was self-employed it was their only option.

Most evenings Jeri returned from work tired, relaxed and glad to be home. Some nights it felt lonely entering a quiet house. Immediately she went to check on the kids, gently caress their sleeping faces and re-tuck the blankets. She checked on Tom, glad to see him sleeping because he needed it, but missing his company.

Tonight she was glad to see him still up, although she knew two late nights in a row would make him overly tired the next day. She had to talk to someone about work, about the relentless pressure of the production line, about the behavior of some co-workers, and the union meeting earlier in the day.

"Ever since that Clymer guy showed up the place has been crazy," Jeri said, chewing the words in a mouthful of tuna salad.

Tom had already told her more about the visit from Byron Swain, the big city newspaper reporter, about how the BCI agent and Deputy Randy Tollefson searched his truck. On the verge of telling her about the meth they claimed to find, he paused.

Jeri patiently had listened long enough. Now it was her turn, and she wanted to vent.

"They've sped up the production line like crazy," she said. "I used to be one of the fastest workers in our section. Now I can hardly keep up."

"Don't worry about it. You're one of the best workers they've got and they know it."

The Prairie Pride chicken processing plant in Buffalo Ridge provided jobs paying $10.23 an hour and a meager list of benefits for about two -hundred fifty employees. In recent years, as the farm wives who had comprised most of the work force gradually retired, the worker population began to show increasing diversity, mostly Latinos from Texas and Mexico.

Lyon Clymer arrived three months ago as the new assistant plant manager. One day a week he actually worked on the production line at various stations. Wearing the tall rubber boots, white smock, hairnet, and gloves he blended in with the other workers. Even a casual observer could see that he could not keep up with the others, cutting or trimming only half as many hanging carcasses passing by. But at least he tried.

He laughed and joked with the employees. He persuaded the manager and company CEO to allow him to provide employees with donuts and pastries during the first break of each shift.

Jeri would return home from work in a good mood. At last, a manager who actually cared about the workers. The suits in the office wouldn't last half a shift, standing for hours on the cold, damp production floor. Their hands and arms ached from grabbing and cutting as fast as they could under a shower of glaring neon lights, and the clattering racket of the machinery burrowing through each eyploexees' ear plugs.

Mr. Clymer was different than the others. They spent most of their time in the office. Once or twice a day they walked through the production areas, sometimes taking notes. Clymer seemed to take a genuine interest in the line workers and their relentless, repetitious jobs.

"I thought you liked him," Tom said. "Doesn't he still work on the line once in a while?"

"Hardly anymore. It's just been a couple times this last month."

"Do you guys still get free rolls at break time? That's a good deal."

"Oh yeah, we still get the rolls. It's like he's buying us off or something. I won't take any. Sometimes it's hard to resist though. They've got these glazed donuts with chocolate frosting. They just melt in your mouth."

"I thought you said you didn't take any."

"Well I did once or twice. But they're so fattening. It's pure lard. I don't know where they get them. It's some little bakery. I think it's the one in Kasota Creek. The grocery store bakery here doesn't make anything that good. I think the real reason they hired him was to go after our union committee. That's mainly why I won't take any. He's been watching me and Hector and the other guys on our committee. I'm just waiting for him to do something. It's like if we just look at each other he comes over and asks what we're doing."

Although Tom had advised against it, Jeri had called the number on the cards that someone from the Teamsters union had been handing to workers as they left the plant late last winter. Jeri didn't get one of the cards herself. The man had been escorted from the property before she left. Later she got a card from another worker.

The last organizing attempt four years ago by the meat-cutters union actually went to a vote. It was close, forty nine percent in favor for and fifty one percent against. A combination of threats and a few additional benefits chilled any tentative support among the undecideds, fearing for their own job security. The tactics worked especially well among those employees whose IQs fell below average, or entered the world with other developmental limitations. They had very few employment options to choose form.

When the union issue resurfaced, Jeri wavered among the undecideds. That lasted until the day Clymer announced that the workers in her section soon would be using a newly-designed knife. He showed them the prototype. When the knives arrived in bulk, the first hour of the next shift would be used for demonstration and training.

When she saw the knife prototype Jeri's face burned. Anger rose in her chest so much that she wanted to scream and run away. She glared at him, muttering to herself "that son-of-a-bitch."

Apparently, Clymer neglected to honor the company's policy of rewarding employees for their ideas and innovations.

From her experience working the line, Jeri had thought of a new design for the knife blade. To someone unfamiliar with their work it wouldn't look like much, just a slight curve and twist of the blade. She believed it would help them make the cuts more quickly and with less twisting of the wrist. It could reduce the prevalence of carpal tunnel syndrome—the inflammation of tendons pressing painfully on nerves in the forearm that afflicted so many of her co-workers. So far she had managed to get by aided by daily doses of ibuprofen.

She hadn't told anyone about the idea until the day Clymer happened to be working alongside her on the line. At first she hesitated, feeling embarrassed. It was so simple. Why hadn't anyone thought of it? What if they had and it hadn't worked?

Walking back to the line after a break, during which Clymer ate two frosted long johns, Jeri asked him if he wanted to hear about the idea. He said yes and she told him. She heard nothing more about it, until that day when he called the workers together before their shift started and showed them the prototype knife.

Like the sudden blast of a cold front moving in sweeping across the prairie it blew her off the fence to the union side.

"I told you that would happen," Tom said. "I told you not to call that union guy. They could just fire you right now if they wanted to. I don't know what we'd do if that happened."

"You could get a real job, one that actually earned some money," Jeri said with weary sarcasm. Even before he finished speaking, Tom realized what her response would be. His elbows resting on the table, he massaged his forehead, rubbed his eyes, and said nothing.

"So it's all my fault," he replied.

"I'm sorry. I'm just so frustrated," Jeri said. "I know something's wrong, at work. Somebody's got to do something. It didn't used to be this way. We used to get along really well. Now it's like nobody trusts anyone."

"How's that going to change if you get a union?" Tom asked. "Then nobody will trust anyone ever."

"But at least we'll have some clout. At least if they try firing someone for no good reason, or harass someone until they quit, the union could back us up. At least we have a contract. We'd probably get better pay."

"Yeah, but if you have to go on strike you'll eventually lose. And then there's union dues," Tom said.

"That's the price you have to pay to get some power. That's what the union guy says, to get collective bargaining or whatever."

"Sounds to me like they're just trying to get money and power for themselves," Tom said.

"It probably won't happen anyway," Jeri said, looking discouraged. "Most of the Hispanics don't seem like they would go for it. Hector is different. He's like the main force on the union committee. You know him, Hector Vasquez. He's trying hard to get the other Hispanics to go along. He talked about that at our meeting today. He says it's not part of their culture. They don't trust anybody outside their family and friends. They see the union as just another kind of government that's out to screw them. They're making a lot more money here than they did back home. They get health benefits. They like the schools here. They're getting used to our winters. Hector says all that makes it hard for them to go along with a union."

"So why even try?" Tom asked.

"Don't even say that," Jeri said, sounding irritated. "We've gone too far. If we quit now we'd all be screwed forever. And Clymer, he pisses me off like I don't know what. Remember that time I told him about my idea for a better knife? I should have gotten five hundred bucks for that. The bastard said he had been thinking about it, too, so I didn't qualify for the money. I'll never forget that."

"I know, I know. We've heard that a hundred times before," Tom said. "Just forget about it."

"I wish we had Ted back. He was a lot better than Clymer."

"I thought you were glad to see him go."

"I was, at first. He was trying to stop the union, but at least he was decent. You could still trust him, sort of," Jeri said. "Clymer comes in like this nice guy, real friendly. He's a snake, that's what he is."

OVER THE PAST TWENTY-TWO YEARS Ted Durand had worked his way up at Prairie Pride from shipping foreman to plant manager, reporting directly to the CEO. At fifty-three he suddenly found himself unemployed. Prairie Pride had been founded and locally-owned by a small group of farmers and businessmen in the Buffalo Ridge area.

Three years ago they sold out to one of the largest poultry corporations in the nation. The former owners each walked away with several million dollars. But they paid a price, too. Any sign of conspicuous consumption in the small town and they would feel the cold draft of jealousy and resentment wherever they went. Many of the workers at the plant felt betrayed. They received nothing from the sale except new masters. If they had any complaints about the previous ones, at least they knew what to expect. From the sale of the plant all they received was uncertainty.

Not long after his fiftieth birthday, Ted began to worry that his job might be in jeopardy. After several years had passed with the new ownership and things seeming to be going okay, he gradually became more confident and felt more secure in his job. He thought that he and the CEO, Raymond Morris, always got along well.

He never saw it coming.

He arrived at the plant as usual at 6:00 a.m. on that Monday in early March. Just after 9:00 a.m. out in the main plant he heard the announcement over the PA system. He was to report to the Morris' office. That in itself was not unusual.

Ted left his hard hat and white smock in the changing room, removed his tall rubber boots, stepped into his street shoes, and went to the office. It bothered him when these encounters dealt with relatively minor matters, ones that could be addressed later. Everyday brought problems and decisions. It could be anything: a personality conflict between two employees, an equipment breakdown, explaining why a production goal that had not been met, and a report from the federal meat inspector that required immediate attention.

Confident in his experience, Ted entered the office ready to handle anything thrown at him, yet annoyed at the waste of time having to come in off the production floor for something that could have waited until a more appropriate time.

Had he been more alert Ted would have detected the distress billowing up in the chest of his boss, the taut, dry throat, trying to swallow the stress of what the CEO had to do; being forced to do.

This time the words hit Ted like the front grille on one of the company's Mack semi-trucks barreling down the road at sixty-five miles-per-hour. He just sat there, stunned. Then numb. It wasn't really happening, like in a dream. He would get up, go back to the plant floor and go about his work.

"I'm asking you to resign," Morris said, without any prelude.

Every so often over the years the thought emerged from Ted's unconscious mind that he could be doing something else with his life. He loved his work, the plant. He knew everything about the business. He loved his family and worked hard to provide for them. Even when he tried to think of doing something else for a career, he couldn't. He gave all the best years of his working life to that company.

Ted sat quietly, feeling as if he were floating somewhere in space.

"What? What are you talking about?"

"We're asking you to resign," Morris repeated. "It's time for a change. It's not all my decision, but that's just the way it is. You'll be fine. You're a good man. You've got a lot of experience. We just need to go in a new direction. We'll be fair in giving you a severance. Pretty soon you'll be back in stride."

Ted sat paralyzed, not hearing a word as Morris went on babbling for fifteen minutes. Although unspoken, it became clear that the company was launching a vicious campaign against the union organizing effort. It viewed Ted Durand as being too cozy with the employees. The company could cut him loose with no liability other than a severance package, which to them was no more than a pittance. It could replace him with someone they controlled completely, and who had no qualms about doing whatever it took to prevent the workers from forming a union. They couldn't care less about Ted's future.

Tom yawned and glanced at the clock on the stove approaching 12:30 a.m. He felt sadness from their little argument hovering around the small kitchen table, and anxiety arising from uncertainty. He knew his delivery business wasn't making much money. He kept hoping that someday soon it would turn up enough profit to make it worth his time. He avoided thinking about how much he actually earned at an hourly rate.

He remembered the last time Prairie Pride employees tried to organize a union and what happened to the employees when it failed. Harassed by the company and eventually seen by other workers as outcasts, one by one they quit.

Right now Tom felt too tired to talk about it anymore.

"I got to hit the sack. These past two days have wiped me out." He rubbed his eyes with the palms of his hands, then laid his head on the table.

Jeri reached over and felt his hair, letting the shorter layers sift through her fingers and flop back to the longer layer falling across his neck and shoulders. "You need a haircut. Just tell him to be more careful and not to cut too much of off the back.

"How are the kids? My mom didn't mind coming back again?" she asked.

"Naw. No big deal. She ragged on me a bit about that reporter. That's about it."

"I think I'm going to stay up awhile," Jeri said. "I'm too wired right now to go to bed. I'm going to watch TV."

"Just keep it low." Tom got up from the table, stood behind his wife and kissed the top of her head. "Don't worry," he said softly. "I'll make it work someday. You can quit that place. Then you can get that dead chicken smell out of your hair."

Jeri sat on the couch watching a show on the Travel channel about Gibraltar. She smiled watching the antics of the Barbary apes begging for food from tourists. Two baby apes looked so cute nestling in their mother's lap.

Ever since they bought a satellite dish Jeri often watched the Travel channel. She longed to travel to some of the exotic locations it featured. Once, when she was fifteen, she traveled with her parents on a jet airliner to Washington, D.C. Tom had never been on a jet. Not long after they were married she tried to persuade him to take a winter trip to Cozumel. He didn't want to go.

After Jade was born they no longer had the time or money for a vacation. So Jeri watched the Travel channel almost every night after work, always learning something new. She had not known that Britain owned Gibraltar, not Spain.

THE RINGING PHONE STARTLED her, bringing her back to the older mobile home nestled in a grove of cottonwood and box elder trees on the Midwestern prairie, about five minutes after 1:00 a.m. on a Thursday morning in June.

"Hello?"

Whoever it was didn't speak immediately.

"Hello? Who is this?"

"I saw the light still on so I thought it would be okay to call now," said a muffled, male voice.

"Who is this? Where are you calling from? What do you want." Her initial worry transformed into fear, then anger. Who was watching their house, and why?

"That's not important. Don't worry. I'm on your side. I want to help you."

"On our side for what? Help us for what?"

"There's things going on that you don't know about. No one does."

"What things? Are you the one who called last night?"

There was a slight pause in the wake of her challenge. He finally spoke, but as if in retreat. "I'm not saying anything more, except that you shouldn't trust anybody in the investigation about the Weavers, and watch your back at the plant."

"So what else is new?" Jeri almost laughed. "Hello? Hello?"

He had hung up.

Jeri wondered if she should have awakened her husband. *That's just what they need now, prank calls,* she thought to herself sourly. It had happened before. Breathers. Perverts.

One time, a former male co-worker started calling them at home. He was obsessed with the young, attractive woman. Eventually Tom tracked him down at a bar in Buffalo Ridge and the calls stopped.

It was different now with the kids. Sometimes she worried about Jade, especially after hearing the occasional news stories about children being abducted and molested. Jeri could take care of herself. Harming innocent children was the worst of all crimes. Every time she thought about such things or saw the news stories on TV, she boiled inside.

She decided to let Tom sleep. She could tell him about the call tomorrow. She hoped he wouldn't become too angry for not telling him. She could never tell for sure what might set off his temper.

What could they do about the call right now anyway? Waking him now would only rob him of sleep, she rationalized. The voice on the other end of the line even though muffled didn't sound dangerous. If anything it sounded sincere, although it was hard to tell.

She tried to think happy thoughts. Last weekend she had casually mentioned the truck and tractor pull this coming weekend. Tom had been talking about going off-roading in the big pickup this weekend in the river bottom. He said the truck took less of a pounding doing that than it did trying to pull a heavy sled as far as it could until the tires started spinning on the dirt track going nowhere.

Twice before they had entered the F-350 in the stock pickup class at the truck and tractor pull at the Harrison County fairgrounds. In terms of spectator attendance, the event approached that of the demolition derby. As many as 1,500 spectators crammed into the grandstand for two hours, watching souped-up trucks and tractors of all sizes. The sound of engines roaring and wheels spinning, struggling to pull a weighted sled the greatest distance.

On his first attempt Tom took fourth in his class. In the next event at the Harrison County Fair he took second.

His father finally persuaded him to stop. They still had more than four years of payments remaining on the truck. The pulling events gave the truck too much of a beating.

This year, when she learned that the organizers had announced the addition of a powder puff class for women drivers in the stock truck division.

She sat quietly on the couch, staring at the TV and thinking about how she would try one last time to raise the subject and get Tom's consent no matter how tentative it might be. They needed something fun to look forward to, something beyond the ordinary weekend activity.

She sat on the couch beginning to feel sleepy. She alternated massaging her forearms and hands, which ached in pain. Before falling asleep she took another six-hundred milligram dosage of ibuprofen.

The union representative from the Teamsters Union office in Rochester said they needed to be doing a lot more work before setting an election date. The company had been bearing down on having a vote as soon as possible, believing that it would be to their advantage.

The union guy told Jeri and the others on the committee that they had better get going with more meetings and personal contacts with their co-workers. Jeri understood and agreed. She wished she had more time. Working full-time, taking care of the kids, and all the other things going on, it was becoming overwhelming. Sometimes she just wanted to quit the union work. She knew that if she said this to Tom he would agree.

She knew that if she quit now it would be even worse. They had come too far. Everyone at the plant who supported the union effort looked to Jeri and Hector for leadership. At first she didn't understand what it really involved. She felt the burden daily when making decisions and taking responsibility that affected the livelihood of others.

A few years older, Hector Vasquez had worked at the plant nearly ten years. His wife, Martina, worked in housekeeping at the county hospital in Buffalo Ridge. They had four children all under the age of ten.

"Hector, you still up?" Jeri apologized for calling at this hour, but she had to talk with someone.

"Hey Jeri. Yeah I'm up. What's up?"

"I just got this phone call. We got one last night, too."

"What do you mean 'phone call'?"

"An anonymous phone call. Some guy but I couldn't recognize the voice. He had it muffled or something."

"What'd he say?"

"Not much. He just said we shouldn't trust anyone in the investigation about the Weavers. He said he was trying to help. He said to be careful at the plant, too. Then he hung up. I asked him if he was the one who called last night but he didn't say anything after that."

Hector searched his memory for any clues about who might have called the Ottos. He knew what was going on at the plant and couldn't imagine anyone doing something like that. It was either someone who really wanted to get caught, or really wanted to help but remain anonymous.

"I have no idea who it is. What did Tom say?"

"He's sleeping and I didn't want to wake him up. It was kind of weird. I didn't really feel scared. Like this guy really wanted to help. I probably should tell him because if I wait 'til later he'll really be pissed for not telling him right away. Do you think it was somebody from the plant, trying to scare us or something?"

"I don't see anyone doing that, but I wouldn't put it past them. They've got all kinds of dirty tricks. They'll do anything they have to, to beat us."

"Clymer, that slime bag," Jeri seethed. "You should see the way he's been watching me at work. He's just waiting for any little chance to pounce. Anytime I talk to anyone on the line he's right there trying to listen."

"I know, I know. We've been through this. You need to settle down and get some rest. We got to finish strong. We can't get distracted by this Weaver thing, either."

"You ever wonder how those kids are doing?" Jeri asked.

The incident at the Weaver farm had been a primary topic of conversation and speculation all day long at the plant, before and after work and during breaks. Everyone wanted to hear about Tom's involvement, so much that Jeri refused to talk about it anymore.

"What?" Hector was expecting to hear something more about the union. Immediately he regretted even mentioning the incident.

"Those kids they had, the Weavers." Jeri said. "I'm trying to see if we can get them. See if they can stay with us."

"Don't you think you've got enough to do already? We need to stay focused. If you do that it'd be too much. We're in the home stretch to the vote. We can't let up now."

"We won't. I can handle it."

"Don't worry about the kids. They're being taken care of. You've got your own kids to think about. Just think about it. They're going to double our part of the insurance premium and add a co-pay. It's going to cost you more every time you take the kids to the doctor. They're adding more work and speeding up the line. If this keeps up they're just going to suck us dry 'til we're all worn out and bring in new working stiffs just like us."

"You know where they're coming from," Jeri said. "You guys come up here and think ten bucks an hour is great. That probably helps keep the pay low."

"Hey, it's not my fault. We got to live, too. Besides, your people don't want these jobs anymore. You're too good for that. You want your kids to be working the line when they grow up?"

"Sorry. It just really pisses me off, what's happened with the company since those new owners took over."

"I think everything will work out okay in the end," Hector said.

"I hope so."

Jeri said good-bye, turned off the TV and went to check on the kids. Breathing softly, they looked so sweet and adorable. Trace had been a little hellion the past year but lately had been becoming a little more sociable. It didn't help that Jade tried to boss him around, although even that was subsiding and they seemed to be getting along better.

Jade and Anna, each five years in age, could become real friends and playmates if they had the chance, Jeri suddenly thought. She looked forward to seeing the Weaver kids Friday at the memorial service for Tulie, if she could get the time off from work.

6

Sheriff Hank Schwartz led FBI agent George Saunders toward the elevator. The morgue in the lower level of the Buffalo Ridge hospital held six refrigerated compartments. Sometimes Hank wondered what they would do in a big disaster with more corpses than the morgue could handle. Some would have to go to nearby counties.

He still couldn't imagine why the feds were interested in this case. The agent had said something about a case twenty years ago. A federal marshal had been killed in a shootout with a group of radicals in the mountains of western Montana. Most were eventually rounded up, and several escaped. The investigation remained open and they have been looking for Tulie ever since. The search rekindled when Tulie resurfaced at a convention and spoke for the Natural Foods Producers Association.

When her fingerprints matched a set taken from the Montana case the FBI sent an agent to Buffalo Ridge. They found her, but they weren't going to get the information they were seeking. The FBI wanted to see her just to make sure.

Hank didn't know a whole lot about the Weavers. Being apart of the small group of organic and sustainable farmers in the area, they kept to themselves and didn't cause any trouble. Hank thought they seemed kind of snooty. They seemed like liberals, almost radical sometimes. Every so often they sponsored programs and events on liberal topics like the environment, global warming, organic farming, and free-trade coffee, whatever that meant. They paid their taxes and revealed no evidence of drugs. Hank was happy to see them clean up the meth lab at the old Wegman place.

"Hope you guys don't take too long," Hank said, opening the door to the morgue. "I'd still like to know what this is all about."

He rolled out the slab and unzipped the shroud far enough to reveal Tulie's face and shoulders. Stringy and matted, her long, dark hair coiled in a bunch behind her neck. The cool air drifting up from the shroud carried a slightly sour, pungent odor emanating from the pale form that looked more like wax than flesh.

The FBI agent put on surgical gloves, lifted the shroud and peered in at her torso. The shotgun blast left a dark, grapefruit-sized, ragged crater just to the left of the lower part of the sternum.

"I presume you took x-rays and retrieved the BBs?" The agent spoke softly, looking up at the sheriff.

"Of course we did, the coroner did," Hank said feeling slightly irritated at what he perceived as a condescending tone, like these hick, small town cops were way over their heads on a case like this. "This is nothing. You should see some of the homicide cases I've had over the years."

"I'm sure."

The sheriff zipped up the shroud and rolled the slab back into the compartment.

"When did death occur?" the agent asked.

"Probably just before we got there. A combination of the shock and blood loss. That's what the coroner says."

"You've got everything covered, weapon, possible motives, right? And you don't think it was her husband? Stan, correct?"

"Nobody we talked to could even imagine it was Stan. One of the kids, the little girl, Anna, said something about a vehicle arriving at the place. Tulie here shooed them down into the cellar so they didn't see anything. And the oldest kid, Michael—he's ten—he won't talk. Won't say a damn word. I won't say it's random, but it's got to be someone not from around here coming on to the place."

"Well, we've got to find Stan," the agent said.

"You never did really explain why the feds are on this case," Hank said on their way out of the hospital. "We've got the state guys helping us. We can handle it."

"Things are different now. You ought to know that. Ever since nine eleven."

"What does that have to do with this?"

"Maybe nothing. Maybe something. What some of those folks did back in the '80s, they were terrorists, too, only home-grown. Oklahoma City, Waco, Pine Ridge, in the mountains out west."

"Are you serious? I think you guys are getting a little carried away," Hank said. "These guys today, they're not some Muslim radicals. The right-wing wackos, they're super patriots or at least they think they are."

"It's not the ideology or even the religion," the agent said. "Even if some of them really think that, it's not. It's just a cover, a cover for money and power. It's some antisocial sickness. You think you're isolated from all that out here in the middle of nowhere. They call this the heartland. Maybe that's what they're doing, going for the heart. On a world scale the U.S. has been the Number One power so long we think it's natural. We take it for granted. More people than you think are out there trying to knock us off. We have to be ready for any possibility. You ever heard of bio-terrorism? Can you imagine what would happen if somebody got some deadly virus into our food or water supply? You've surely heard about bird flu. You got all these chickens, turkeys, and hogs around here, almost all of them in these big confinement barns. What a target for terrorists, home-grown or otherwise."

Hank didn't have a good answer. He wasn't too worried about it. Any suspicious behavior by anyone new coming into the area soon would be noticed. The Weavers were responsible, law-abiding citizens as far as he was concerned. The feds, the people in Washington, they're the ones who were really isolated. They come out here thinking they know everything. It was bad enough having to deal with the BCI agent messing up the investigation. This FBI guy was way off base.

HANK TOLD THE AGENT to meet him at the office, then left in his dark gray, unmarked Crown Victoria police cruiser. The agent wanted to look at the county plat book and locate the Weaver farm site and some of the other organic growers. He wanted to look around the Weaver place and then go see their kids.

He wanted to see any personal effects and documents the local and state investigators had retrieved from the Weaver household: bank statements, property tax records, deeds, federal and state tax forms, insurance policies, investments, marriage license, and Social Security numbers.

"This Tulie, where's her Social Security number? And I didn't see a marriage license, either," the FBI agent said, dropping the large manila envelope on Hank's desk.

"I don't know. What do you need that for?"

"As far as the federal government is concerned she doesn't exist. No Social Security number. No marriage license. No birth certificate. Her name's on their property deed and some insurance forms. That's about it."

"So what are we supposed to do about it? It don't make any difference now anyway. At least she'll have a death certificate."

"You guys have any idea how much money comes in around here from meth?" the agent asked. "Do you know where that money is going?"

"What? What does that have to do with this?"

"Don't know for sure. Where do you think some of these terrorists get their money? We intend to find out."

"Yeah, we've got meth around here, but not like it used to be. We got rid of most of the local cookers. We know it's coming in but it's not out of control," Hank said, becoming annoyed.

"You ever think some of these so-called farmers, those old hippies out there, you think they're really making a living selling a few fresh chickens or vegetables? You ever think they might have another business going on?"

"We'd know about it if they did."

"You don't seem to know much about this Tulie Weaver."

Hank thought he saw a little smirk on the agent's face. It annoyed him even more. He opened the county plat book and flipped to Patterson Township page. He pointed out a small, black square in the middle of one of the sections. "There. That's the Weavers."

Hank made a photo copy of the page. He was glad to see the agent leave.

FBI AGENT SAUNDERS WENT first to a house in town. He left his car in a Casey's gas and convenience store parking lot and walked a block to the two-story brick and stucco house. A small porch covered the front door. A woman in her forties answered the doorbell.

George introduced himself and presented his FBI credentials.

The woman, a special education teacher with the local school district, had been dividing her time with the Weaver children between school lessons and psychological counseling. With little Jonathan it was mostly trying to keep him entertained, fed and rested. Protected by the wall around his thoughts and feelings Michael could not be reached. Anna believed it when they told her everything would be fine and to not worry. The lie became reinforced when she repeated it to Jonathan.

"I'm sorry. I can't let you see the children," the woman said.

"I just need to see them, just talk with them a little bit. We need their help. It's very important to the investigation. I know how to talk with them. I won't upset them."

"Too late for that now. Some guy was already here and took care of that," the woman said crossly.

"Who was that?"

"From the state, the Bureau of Criminal Investigation. I don't remember his name. He left a card. Wait here. I'll go get it."

She handed agent Saunders the card. He looked at the name and put the card in his coat pocket. "Thank you." Saunders decided to back off. He could talk to the kids later. He had read the initial reports. He could wait until the other agent arrived from Sioux Falls. Together they would examine the scene at the Weaver farm and visit the other farms in the organic foods cooperative.

Saunders met the other agent at the truck stop just outside Kasota Creek, a smaller town west of Buffalo Ridge. They opened the front door of the adjacent café, which otherwise stood as a barrier between the fresh morning air only slightly tinged by scents of gasoline and diesel fuel. Inside the stuffy café, the air flowed with scents of bacon, eggs, and hash brown potatoes sizzling on the heavy griddle.

Moving quickly among the tables trying to keep up with the orders, the waitress immediately noticed the two men wearing suits. These two seemed different, not like the businessmen on the road. They seemed almost too polite, a façade of humility concealing something she couldn't quite interpret. She nodded when Saunders smiled and apologetically asked if they could sit in the drivers' section. They passed near her toward the open tables. She could tell the suits were not expensive and needed dry cleaning.

The waitress stopped at Tom Otto's table and re-filled his coffee cup.

Tom stopped there two or three times a week depending on his route for the day. Sometimes he drove out of the way for one of their saucer plate-sized cinnamon rolls. If the timing was right they still were soft and warm.

He enjoyed the light-hearted banter with Holly, the regular daytime waitress.

"Don't look now but I think those guys are cops, FBI maybe," she whispered.

Tom looked up and smiled. "Oh you think so?" He looked up at Holly but his attention focused on his peripheral vision, which registered two men in their late thirties or early forties wearing dark suits. "So what am I supposed to do about that?"

"Just watch your back I guess."

"Isn't that a little paranoid?"

"Well I've never seen them before. Maybe they're in on the investigation."

Like a hummingbird hovering briefly and darting among flowers, Holly left Tom abruptly and stopped to take the agents' orders. They ordered coffee. Agent George Saunders nodded in Tom's direction. "I'll have one of those rolls over there. That a cinnamon roll?"

Holly looked over at Tom and back to the agents. "Yes, that is. A house specialty."

Their glances made Tom feel self-conscious. He started to think about the meth that the sheriff and BCI agent claimed to have found in his truck. It made him feel guilty. He told himself they certainly wouldn't be after him for that. Maybe they were just passing through.

He watched Holly leave their table. The other agent looked over in Tom's direction making brief eye contact. Tom looked down at his plate. His cell phone rang and almost in unison other nearby customers looked over at him, including the two agents.

"Tom, I got to talk to you. Where are you?" Jeri's voice carried more than the usual tone of urgency. Tom said he couldn't talk right then. He would call back right away.

"You should've seen ol' Newt tear out of here when those guys came," Holly said, taking Tom's money at the cash register. You know him? Newton Case?"

Tom told about how he stopped when the truck broke down. Otherwise he didn't know too much about the old man.

"He sure don't like the government," Holly said. "He comes in here sometimes and starts ranting and raving, it's not like he's dangerous or anything. He's just different. He smelled out those guys the minute they walked in the door."

Back in the truck Tom called Jeri. "Hey, what's up?"

"That state BCI guy, you should've heard what he did." Jeri's anger hadn't subsided much since she got off the phone with Amber Brock, the foster mother at home with the Weaver children.

BCI agent Harmon Leuten arrived at the Brock home just after nine a.m. In his late thirties, standing five feet six inches, and wearing his light brown hair combed back, he looked like a salesman or a teacher, except perhaps for his large moustache. He wore a dark suit that made him seem larger. He presented his badge and asked to see the children. Mrs. Swanson, the school social worker, answered the door. She agreed as long as she could be present. He preferred being with them alone, but shrugged his assent.

Leuten picked up Jonathan and tried to amuse him. The toddler fixed on the agent's moustache, reached to grab it. Anna giggled. Michael sat with no discernable expression, except for his eyes that bore into the man holding his younger brother.

Leuten's conversation drifted to questions. Did the children see anyone Tuesday? What did they hear? Anna began to cry. Michael remained mute, expressionless. Mrs. Swanson said that was enough. She insisted that Leuten leave immediately. He stood up abruptly and dumped Jonathan on the couch next to Anna. He walked over in front of Michael, glaring down at the ten-year-old.

"Listen you little shit. I'm getting sick of your stonewalling. If you want to find your old man and who did your mom you better talk."

Mrs. Swanson jumped up, grabbed Leuten by the elbow and ordered him to leave. He jerked his elbow away.

"You better work on him," the agent snarled. "He hasn't said a thing the whole time. He knows something." He walked out, leaving Mrs. Swanson trying to comfort Anna, and then Jonathan who began crying because his sister was. Michael stood up to look out the window at the man getting into his car. Dust shot out from the rear tires as it sped off.

Holding the cell phone to his ear, Tom climbed into the truck. "So what did he do now?"

"I just talked to Amber," Jeri said. "That BCI guy stopped over there this morning and started picking on the kids. He was asking them questions and they started crying. He called Michael a little shit and everything. That's what she said."

"That's ridiculous, he has no right to harm the children like that."

"I wish we could get them. I mean, Amber and her husband are really nice. Those kids just aren't used to living in town. They need to be outside, out where they can run around."

"Let's keep trying. Let's talk to Mrs. Swanson and that county social worker that you know."

Jeri said she would call as soon as they got off the phone. Tom closed the cell phone and jammed the truck into first gear. The same feeling of helpless anger started to resurface.

And what if the two guys back in the restaurant really were FBI agents?

Tom steered his truck heading west on the Highway 19. A southeast breeze had picked up earlier in the morning foretelling rain. Clouds began moving in from the west, muting the bright green colors of the lush crop canopy that gradually covered thousands of acres of farm land. Neat, endless rows of cornstalks stood almost knee-high. A green carpet of soybean plants covered fields where last years corn stood tall. As long as the approaching storm didn't bring hail, the rain would be welcome.

He hoped the weather would be nice on Sunday; Father's Day. He wanted to take the big four-by-four off-roading in the river bottom. Jeri wanted to enter the truck-pull competition Saturday and if there were no breakdowns, the Sunday excursion seemed likely. Rainfall beforehand would create a copious amount of mud on the trail. The day would end with the truck covered in mud, which took some getting used to for Tom and Jeri when the truck was newer. Washing off the mud became part of the fun, like seeing the bright red F-350 shiny and new all over again.

Tom drove onto the farmyard. The white SUV parked in the driveway matched the farmhouse only in color. Otherwise the large, shiny vehicle stood in sharp contrast to the chipped, weathered paint and rotting eaves of the old house. Built a few years either side of 1900, the main part stood two stories, a brick chimney on each end, each strapped with a four-foot lightning rod. A one-story kitchen with a covered porch jutted from the side. No one answered the door when Tom knocked. He drove away. A quarter-mile down the gravel road he turned the truck into a field approach next to a drainage ditch. A row of cottonwood trees lining one side of the ditch shielded the truck from the view of anyone at the farmhouse. Tom got out of the truck and crept along the tree line to the end of the soybean field where it met a cornfield. He walked between rows of tall corn to the edge of the grove of trees surrounding the north and west sides of the farmyard. He carried a 9mm Ruger stuffed in the back of his jeans. Hidden among the rows of corn Tom peered through the trees and tall grass in the grove. Rusted hulks of old farm machinery poked through the grass. Seeing no movement, no people, Tom darted from the cornfield to the grove. He crouched behind the remains of a 1932 Chevrolet four-door sedan. The wood-and-fabric roof had rotted away years ago. Shreds of fabric dangled from the seat springs. He heard footsteps from the direction of the house, crunching through the tall grass. Two men entered the shelter of the grove, stopped, and looked around. One carried a small, heavy canvas bag encased in a sturdy plastic storage box, the cover sealed with silver duct tape. The other carried a shovel. He pointed over to the Chevrolet and the other man nodded. Tom ducked below the hood, his heart pounding. The men approached the car and stopped on the opposite side. They spoke in low, raspy voices, Spanish, which Tom did not understand. He pressed into the empty right front wheel well, every muscle tense. The men went to the front of the car and one started digging. Waiting, the man carrying the box walked around toward the other side of the car. The man's eyes barely registered the crouching figure when it flew at him. Tom drove his fist into the man's midsection just below the sternum. The man doubled up gasping for air. The butt of Tom's Ruger smashed into his temple. The other man charged at Tom thrusting the shovel out like a spear. Tom fired the pistol into the man's chest. He collapsed mortally wounded. Regaining consciousness the other man rolled to his knees and reached into his jacket. Tom kicked him in the face. He fell back and Tom stomped on his gut.

THE DAYDREAM VANISHED, followed by a flush of embarrassment. He had developed the habit of trying to trace his thoughts back seeking the initial thought that triggered the fantasy, marveling at curious and sometimes bizarre linkages.

Not this time.

Instead he tried to imagine what he could have done had he arrived at the Weaver's earlier on Tuesday morning if he hadn't stopped at the café beforehand. What if he had been at the Weaver's when the assailants arrived? Seeing Tom's truck perhaps they would have stayed away. If not, Tom imagined being in the house with Tulie and the kids defending themselves, himself with the Ruger and Tulie with a shotgun. Even Michael with an older, single-shot .22-caliber rifle.

When Michael turned eight Stan took him hunting for pheasants in the cornfields, road ditches, and tall grass fringes of sloughs. They would also hunt squirrels and rabbits in the grove.

Last fall not long after Michael's tenth birthday they stalked deer in the river bottom. They sat for two hours perched on a wooden platform twelve feet high in a basswood tree. An eight-point buck stepped into a clearing about twenty five yards away. Stan nodded to Michael: Take the shot. Michael slowly raised his twenty-gauge shotgun, a single slug shell in the chamber. He sighted down the barrel to a point just behind the foreleg and squeezed the trigger. The buck lurched, trying to flee until its forelegs buckled. It struggled back to its feet, trying again to flee whatever caused the searing, crushing force that tore into its side. It stumbled and lurched a few more yards crashing off the deer trail into the brush, then collapsed.

"Woo-hoo!" From somewhere off to the right, Tulie, who had been walking through the brush and trees hoping to drive the buck near the tree stand where Stan and Michael sat, whooped and hollered, hurrying toward the kill.

Tulie handled a twelve-gauge shotgun as if it was something she did every day. She helped gut the deer and together they dragged it back to the pickup.

A drifting image of Tulie's body lying on the floor in the hallway of their farm house re-surfaced in Tom's thoughts. *What did she see? What did she think and feel the moment before slipping away into unconsciousness? Was death really like passing some threshold or emerging from a dark tunnel into a bright light, enveloped in a warm and secure sense of peace?* At church it was never really made clear. If you were born again you would go to heaven when you died, simple as that. Except for what the Bible said about heaven the exact details were hard to come by. There were moments when Tom felt peace, relaxing in a lawn chair in the yard in soft summer twilight, watching the kids tussling with the dogs and each other on the grass, Jeri cleaning up in the kitchen before coming out to join them. Fleeting moments that fled before the return of pressures and worries of life. If heaven were an eternity of something close to the former, Tom could live with that.

As far as he knew the Weavers didn't attend any church. Tulie's memorial service was scheduled at the funeral home, and not being a church, cast some doubt on whether or not she would have gone to heaven. What the Bible said about hell was something too uncomfortable to even think about. Sometimes you couldn't avoid it when the preacher occasionally warmed to the subject during a Sunday sermon at the Gospel Tabernacle Church. Even if it wasn't actually burning in flames for eternity, being forsaken by God would be bad enough, shunned forever, like a child rejected, cut off from a parent's love. Tom recoiled from even questioning such a thing. By every earthly measure that Tom could think of Tulie certainly qualified for admittance to heaven. He prayed asking God for such consideration.

And Stan, what happened to Stan? Maybe he was kidnapped. Tom stubbornly hoped Stan would be found okay and return. The kids still would have their father.

CARRYING TOM AND HIS THOUGHTS the truck traveled a distance much shorter than eternity to Kasota Creek, about two miles away, and up to the back door of the Home Bakery.

The bakery stood one block off the main highway through town. Every month Tom delivered bags of flour. The bakery somehow defied the economic decline that plagued many smaller towns. For many, most of the retail business had gravitated to regional centers, which Buffalo Ridge had been growing into. Population in the smaller towns remained stable except during work days when traffic flowed toward jobs in Buffalo Ridge. Before and after work the commuters bought their groceries, clothing, and other goods at the large discount stores in

Buffalo Ridge. Back home in their small town they were lucky to have a small grocery, café, and hardware store. All that some of the small towns had to offer was a gas station-convenience store. Many still had a local bank or branch of a larger bank. Often, it was the newest, largest, and fanciest building in town.

The Home Bakery in Kasota Creek still hung on because of quality and variety of its products. Passing through town some folks would turn off the main highway and stop at the bakery.

Its fortunes improved even more when the Prairie Pride poultry processing plant in Buffalo Ridge began placing regular orders for pastries. They paid the asking price even though they could have received a volume discount. Their only request was that the bakery use a certain brand of flour. It was delivered by a young man driving a truck labeled "Tom's Fresh Meats and Produce, Naturally," who made regular trips to the big city warehouse.

Whenever Tom felt sorry for himself for having to start his workday so early, he could count on the understanding of Home Bakery owner Mel Torgerson. Mel was already heating up the vats of cooking oil and mixing dough when Tom's alarm buzzed at 4:00 a.m.

Twice a day Mel or his wife delivered twenty dozen assorted donuts and pastries to the Prairie Pride plant, before 9:00 a.m. and again at 3:00 p.m. After a month, the novelty, and for some workers, skepticism, had been replaced by a conditioned expectation of soft, fresh rolls and donuts. Still, it was not the same as trust or respect for the new plant manager, Mr. Clymer.

Mel talked about Clymer like he was the best thing that had ever happened to the plant and Buffalo Ridge. His energy, enthusiasm and new ideas were good for the whole area. Mel said to not tell anyone, but Clymer told him he was thinking about running for the county board of commissioners.

That was one part of Tom's job that he kind of liked, hearing bits of news and gossip from people on his pick-up and delivery route. He generally used discretion when repeating anything, except for telling Jeri when they talked over Sunday morning breakfasts or late at night if he was still up when she came home from work.

At the plant when she told Hector Vasquez the rumor about Clymer, they both agreed that the free donuts at break time for the plant workers must be part of his campaign strategy until Hector thought some more and realized it couldn't be true: Most of the workers didn't vote anyway so what would be the point of bribing them with donuts?

Mel said it would be good to get a businessman on the county board, someone who looked to the future and would be a force for more economic development. Clymer knew what it took to run a business and make a dollar or two. Sometimes you had to take a risk, to invest and put some money on the line. The farmers on the county board did that every year when it came to their own farms, but not with the county budget.

Tom felt encouraged every time Mel talked like that, about working hard at your own business, taking some risk and becoming successful. He thought it would be nice to have a big customer or several like Mel had with the Prairie Pride plant.

He carried the bags of flour into Mel's storeroom. Mel patted Tom on the shoulder, leaving a white imprint from his floured hand, and handed him a small bag of fresh donuts for the road.

A BARRAGE OF RAINDROPS splattered on the windshield. Tom thought he heard thunder rumble off to the west.

Most thunderstorms occurred later in the afternoon after the day's heat rose up in thermals ahead of a cooler low pressure system drifting in from Canada, colliding with higher air pressure and heat over the Dakotas. This time occurring earlier in the day it might clear out later in the afternoon, leaving a freshly washed landscape. The leaves and crops glistening as the sun emerged making the clouds departing off to the east, appear dark gray.

The rain intensified and Tom turned on the windshield wipers. Jeri would be keeping Jade and Trace indoors, underfoot while she worked on household chores. He had three deliveries to do in Kasota Creek and four more in the country before returning to Buffalo Ridge. Jeri told him to stop at the Hamilton's to see if they knew anything more about the memorial service for Tulie. Was it going to be Friday or Saturday? He hoped Friday although that meant he would have to adjust his schedule and Jeri might be late for work, which would be another mark against her as far as Clymer was concerned, being unlikely that he would approve time off so she could attend.

7

Despite the heavy rain in the mid-morning thundershower, Newton Case drove his pickup without switching on the headlights. He knew the roads well enough so it wasn't necessary to light the way, but only to be seen by other motorists. Now, he did not want anyone in other vehicles to see him, even from a distance.

He followed the full-sized sedan that he had seen at the café. A second sedan that arrived there later remained behind, the driver now riding in the first vehicle.

Newt stayed at the café just long enough to get a look at the two men, whom he did not recognize except for their appearance and type of vehicle. His observations, instincts, and beliefs clearly announced the presence of the federal government. They left the café immediately after Tom Otto pulled out on to the highway in his delivery truck.

Down the highway when Tom continued straight ahead and the sedan slowed, turning south on a county highway, Newt hesitated. For a moment he couldn't decide if he should follow Tom or the sedan.

The rain from the passing thunderstorm began to let up.

Ignoring the warnings from his experiences many years ago, at the intersection Newt turned to follow the sedan. He told himself that unless they were looking specifically for him he had nothing to fear. It had been almost twenty years since he had anything to do with Posse Comitatus. He had been caught up for several years now on his federal and state income taxes. He trusted and respected Sheriff Hank Schwartz, who along with the county board of commissioners and the Constitution represented the only government that he truly believed in and saw as being necessary. All the federal agencies and departments, particularly law enforcement, stood as threats to the will of the people and their right to own property and do with it as they pleased.

Newt followed the sedan until it turned on to a gravel township road. Approaching the long driveway into the Weaver place it slowed and turned in. Newt passed by, noticing in the distance a sheriff deputy's squad car in the farmyard along with what looked like Archie Daniels' pickup. Or was it Ron Hamilton's? Newt chuckled to himself at the thought of Archie and Ron working side by side. Although not too far apart in age, their beliefs and practices regarding agriculture diverged by at least a generation if not a century.

Archie sold off his small dairy herd, about forty cows, years ago. Too much work day after day, week after week, year after year. He and Millie hadn't taken a vacation, hardly even a long weekend, for more than ten years. The couple times they did get away for two or three days he worried constantly that the neighbor back home doing the chores might not be doing everything the way Archie would have liked.

YIELDING ONLY FIVE OR SIX pounds of milk per day, goats could only be considered a hobby, Archie firmly believed when he first learned of the Hamiltons' venture. Early on they did need outside income, Wendy's teaching job, which confirmed Archie's opinion that they could not be considered real farmers. That status required more land for various crops and heavier equipment.

Ron Hamilton raised crops mostly for feed, using smaller, older equipment that didn't come with a price tag in six figures.

How the Weavers earned a living was even more of a mystery to Archie. Neither Stan nor Tulie had a job off the farm. Why they used the rich, level ground bordering the creek as pasture for their sheep instead of corn or soybeans he could not understand, although he had to admit the return on corn was far less now than it used to be. Somehow the Weavers seemed to get by on selling chickens, eggs, lamb, and hand-made crafts. They cultivated almost half an acre for a garden, its produce filling rows of quart mason jars with preserved tomatoes, peas, beans, corn, beets, peaches, pears, and who knows what else. The warm climate fresh fruits came in crates delivered by Tom Otto. What farm implements the Weavers had—tractor, hay baler, plow, hay rake, manure spreader, and old combine—were long paid for and not much to begin with since most were bargains at farm auctions. Most equipment of similar vintage now sat in the back row of the used equipment inventory at the implement dealer's, abandoned in a grove, or somewhere in a salvage yard. Stan took good care of his equipment and it still was sufficient for an eighty acre farm.

Acquainted for years, Ron and Archie met at the Weaver farm that morning knowing reasonably well what to expect from each other. They knew what needed to be done, quickly divided up the chores and began working immediately, motivated more so because they had other things to do at their own farms that day.

Still, there was time for talk. Working long and often solitary hours in the field or around the farm yard many farmers more than made up for it during chance encounters at the grain elevator, café, or implement dealer. With their kids grown and gone and Millie off working at the bank, Archie's need for conversation exceeded that of Ron, whose life still revolved around kids at home and tending a hundred dairy goats.

At ten they met back at the Weaver farm house for a lunch break, conveniently timed, allowing them shelter from the rainfall. Ron had brought a thermos of coffee. Randy Tollefson, the young sheriff's deputy was present to protect the crime scene.

NEWTON CASE CONTINUED PAST the Weaver farm toward his own place although not taking a direct route. Were it not for all the law enforcement around he would have wanted to help out with chores at the Weavers. He would have worked alongside Ron Hamilton, occasionally having to show him how to do things right. That was the one thing he had in common with these so-called "organic farmers," their belief in small, sustainable, and diversified farms. But they hadn't fully learned how to do everything the way it was done in the old days, like using enough herbicides and pesticides. That part was the only thing he agreed on with Archie Daniels. Had he known Archie was there he would not have stopped to help even without the cops present. He still resented Archie for outbidding him on the quarter-section that abutted Newt's farm and would have fit nicely into his holdings.

FBI AGENT SAUNDERS set the box of fresh cinnamon rolls on the kitchen table in the Weaver farm house. Introductions followed, and George thanked Ron and Archie for taking care of the chores.

Deputy Tollefson started a pot of coffee in the drip percolator on the Weaver's kitchen counter.

"We better wait for Hank and Harmon before we go any further," Saunders said after a few minutes of small talk, mostly about the thunderstorm and rain now subsiding.

Out the kitchen window they saw two sets of headlights coming down the long driveway.

Sheriff Hank Schwartz and BCI agent Harmon Leuten walked together toward the farm house. The sheriff had already briefed the state agent about the interest in the case shown by the federal officers.

In the kitchen they pulled up extra chairs and took places around the table except for the deputy, who leaned against the counter holding a cup of coffee and keeping the driveway in view through a kitchen window. Sheriff Schwartz briefly reviewed the case mindful of the presence of two civilians and alert for sometimes not so subtle cues from Leuten about what he should and should not say. Their objectives for the meeting were to interview Archie and Ron again, assure that the farm work was being taken care of, and find out what the FBI agents wanted. They had worked with Saunders before. The other agent was new to them. He didn't say much, letting Saunders do most of the talking, which left Leuten feeling even more uneasy although he would never show it, hiding it well behind a façade of brusque authority.

For the agents' benefit Schwartz gave a brief history of the farm, how it had been used for a small meth lab by some local dirtballs, then purchased and cleaned up by the Weavers.

Among the toxic mess they found a two-year-old boy. Emaciated, barely covered by filthy, ragged, poop-stained clothing. A green-and-yellow bruise about the size of a small egg splayed out between his left eye and temple. He just sat quiet in a playpen, which looked to be smeared with streaks of dried, crusted excrement, and stared up at the giants wearing uniforms and heavy belts loaded with handguns, handcuffs, mace, and flashlights. As they carried him from the house he saw other giants entering, looking like some kind of snow monsters in white Tyvek coveralls, thick rubber gloves, and bulbous respirators.

After the raid and toxic clean-up, the Weavers bought the farm, and ultimately adopted the toddler, who had been removed from the custody of his apparent mother as part of a plea agreement.

BEFORE WE GO ANY FURTHER here we need to remind these gentlemen here that anything they say is on the record," Leuten said, nodding toward Ron and Archie. They said they understood.

Saunders proceeded to question Ron and Archie about the Weavers. How long had they been acquainted? Did they ever notice anything about them that seemed unusual? Did the Weavers ever talk about their past, before settling on the farm near Buffalo Ridge?

"What's this all about?" Ron asked. The direction that the interrogation seemed to be taking was beginning to chafe on his normally trusting nature and cursory respect for authority. "I thought the criminals were the ones who did this. You make it sound like Stan and Tulie are the criminals," he said with a temperate measure of sarcasm.

"What was Tulip's last name, before she married Stan?" Saunders pointedly directed the question at Ron. "If you know someone well, were such good friends, don't you usually learn something about their past?"

"I guess it just never came up. It's not a big deal. We never asked," Ron said.

"As far as we know she never had a last name, at least anywhere on paper," Saunders said.

"So?"

"She doesn't have a Social Security number. They weren't legally married. As far as the federal government knew she didn't even exist. And what the hell kind of name is that anyway? Tulip. If you want to know, she came from one of those hippie communes back in the mountains out west," Saunders said.

"Listen, all I know is that they were good people," Ron said. "It's none of my business where they came from. Look at this place. It's a country paradise. They both worked hard. Their kids are great. They were wonderful people. Isn't that right, Archie?"

Archie Daniels nodded in agreement.

"Sometimes you can be fooled by appearances," Saunders said.

Leuten decided to re-direct the proceedings. He wanted to know more about the FBI's interest and if it could be useful. He tried another angle.

"How often does this Tom Otto stop at all your places?"

"Who's Tom Otto?" Saunders asked.

Leuten looked at him like he didn't hear what he just heard. "You don't know? Didn't Hank tell you?" He gave a questioning nod toward the sheriff. Hank said nothing.

"He was the first one on the scene. He found the woman's body and called it in," Leuten said, almost sounding embarrassed. "He's this kid with a food delivery business. 'Tom's Fresh Meats and Produce' or something like that."

"You forgot the 'Naturally'," Ron said.

Leuten looked sourly at Ron. "Don't be a smartass."

The ominous response far exceeded any notion of perceived disrespect, and particularly because it was not intended to sound that way. Ron glared at Leuten. "It's natural foods. You know, organic. No chemicals. It's a lot healthier. He delivers our produce to some big city restaurants and fancy grocery stores. And a lot of folks around here, too. It's a growing business, no pun intended."

Archie gave a little laugh, trying to ease the tension. "We get stuff from him. It seems silly don't it? Here I live on a farm, have all my life, and I have to have fresh food delivered. My grandpa would think we were nuts."

Leuten's glance at Archie said 'who the hell cares?'

"And what else does he deliver?" Leuten continued.

"What are you getting at?" Ron asked.

"A couple times a week he goes into the city. He delivers food like you said. Then he goes to a couple of warehouses and picks up food and brings it back."

"No shit? Wow, you guys are really on the ball," Ron shot back.

"Now fellas, that's enough," Hank Schwartz interjected. "Listen, Ron. We just can't say anything more. You understand. We're trying our best to solve this case. We have to find hard evidence. We have to find a motive or motives. We need to know what you can tell us."

"You know what they call him at one of the warehouses? They call him 'Tomato'," Leuten smirked. "Tom Otto, tomahto, tomato. He just hates it. Some of the other drivers even chipped in and got him this shirt with a big red tomato on the back."

"I don't know what you guys are trying to do. All I know is Tom's a great kid. If you're insinuating that he's somehow involved in some kind of wrongdoing you're way off base," Ron said. "Hank here says you guys need hard evidence. Sounds to me like you're trying to build a case on circumstantial evidence."

Along with most of the coffee and all of the cinnamon rolls, the initial atmosphere of friendly cooperation had drifted off perilously close to the edge of some deep precipice off the edge of civility. Sheriff Schwartz thanked Ron and Archie for helping out with the chores. He felt a little embarrassed asking them if they would be interested in sticking around to help with the search party. They had already spent several hours doing chores and had agreed to continue doing so.

Since yesterday afternoon volunteers had fanned out from the farm site. They tramped through the grove, the pasture along the creek, finding no signs of Stan's whereabouts or any other possible clues.

Now in its second day the search expanded to the surrounding area. Searchers walked along drainage ditch banks, across corn fields, through groves of trees, and along sloughs. Still, it would have been easy to miss something. In tall grass you could walk within two feet of something even as large as a human body without detecting its presence. But even the K-9s couldn't find anything human.

After the rain the water in the drainage ditches flowed almost bankful, tugging at the roots of now submerged weeds and grasses bending gracefully downstream. Pulled along by gravity the water flowed in a current that would carry some small floating object almost five miles in an hour if there were no obstructions or constrictions, which occasionally there were, but in theory all the way to the Gulf of Mexico. Some culverts under township roads offered a diameter insufficient for such a volume as this and earlier rain storms had provided. Although eventually relentless, the water slowed and pooled behind the bottlenecks. The searchers scanned the surface and would have been able to see most any large floating object were it to be out in the open.

THE SHERIFF AND OTHER investigators waited patiently and quietly as Ron and Archie rose from the bench at the kitchen table and departed. After they went out the door and out of earshot the discussion continued, more at the insistence of FBI agent Saunders.

"Before I came out here I stopped in town. I was hoping to talk with the Weaver kids," Saunders said. "Somebody beat me to it. Seems like whomever it was left them pretty upset. The social worker there insisted that I let them be and I had to agree. She gave me this card." He flipped Leuten's business card on the table. "What the hell do you think you were doing?" He looked hard at Leuten, contempt dripping from his words.

Leuten's nervous habit of stroking the left side of his moustache did not escape the practiced observation of the two federal agents. Those untrained in deciphering body language would have taken his assertive verbal response at face value. "Of course I was there," he said. "These kids could be key witnesses, what they heard or saw. Why am I telling you that? This is our case. I still don't really know what the hell you guys are here for."

"Just because you guys have eradicated a lot of the local meth labs doesn't necessarily mean you've solved the problem," Saunders said.

"So you're saying these folks are part of a meth trafficking ring?" Sheriff Schwartz asked.

"We're just investigating every possibility, that's all," Saunders said.

"So how did the Weaver's get on your radar screen?" Leuten asked.

"They fit one of our profiles."

"Which one is that?" Deputy Tollefson spoke up for the first time.

Saunders looked at the young man, and like a father teaching his son how to hunt or fish, began to describe the characteristics of various profiles federal agents used in tracking illegal activity, especially that considered to be subversive and a threat to the political and economic stability of the nation, particularly the part embodied in the federal government. Drug trafficking was a major source of revenue for terrorists. Through a complicated chain of transactions people in the U.S. who used illegal drugs such as meth were helping to fund terrorist activity, homegrown and foreign. And the blossoming of the World Wide Web had virtually dissolved national borders and geographical distance so that even the nation's heartland was on the front line.

THE FBI's INTEREST IN TULIE dated back to the early nineteen eighties. Although just a child then, she bore the radical reputation that had been assigned to her parents and the hippie commune they lived in, irregardless of whether or not it was deserved. Settling in an abandoned old mining town in the mountains of western Montana, the commune wandered into the crosshairs of the federal government, more so for its disregard for the Internal Revenue System than for the marijuana they attempted to grow.

Never legally married, Tulie's father and mother spent some time in federal prisons, after which they drifted apart leaving their past behind including a young daughter. In the extended family of the commune she lived in various households, none of which ever became home. At sixteen she hit the road moving from job to job and from one boyfriend to the next. She bought a fake driver's license and created her own Social Security number when necessary to fill out a job application.

Working as a freeway truck stop waitress she homed in on any male that fit her notion of a likely prospect: not too many years either side of her age, the more handsome the better, traveling alone or in a group other than a family, the confidence of monetary abundance, and offering feedback to her overtures that suggested further interest.

Returning from a hunting trip in Idaho, Stan Weaver's banter with the young waitress at the truck stop began to probe deeper, beyond her name, where she was from, and where she now lived. He noticed that she wasn't wearing any rings. He asked if she had a boyfriend. She acted embarrassed and laughed when he asked about her life's ambitions and dreams. As for Stan they primarily were achieving a sufficient measure of acceptance of his failed marriage and beginning the search for a new relationship.

Stan received a severance package amounting to two year's salary when he left his corporate job a few months later. He called Tulie. She remembered him and was all excited about going with him to a little farm on the Midwestern prairie.

Stan had been doing much research on organic or natural foods and sustainable farming. He had been searching the internet for farm auctions. It took Tulie some time to adjust to living on a relatively flat, prairie landscape. Whenever she saw low, dark blue or gray clouds on the horizon she imagined them to be mountains.

An FBI agent attending and surveilling the annual conference of the Natural Foods Producers Association convention two years ago in Denver took note when, during her speech, she told about her background growing up in a commune in the mountains of western Montana back in the 1980s, which he remembered because he was there.

Now, he stood alongside agent George Saunders in the Weavers' kitchen. From what he had seen so far there was no evidence that they were in any way connected with the meth trafficking from Mexico that had been on the rise in the Midwest ever since state and local law enforcement had come down hard on local cookers around the countryside.

But the state investigator, Harmon Leuten, continued to insist that they were. He even alluded to the possibility during an interview with a newspaper reporter, which rekindled the interest of the FBI agent who knew of her past. He called Saunders and they decided to check it out. It was unfortunate that they could not interview Tulie. They still had hope for Stan, but their experience and instincts made it seem remote. Experience also suggested that any involvement with large amounts of crystal meth trafficking by the Weavers was unlikely, although there still could have been some link considering the past history of the farm site.

SAUNDERS THANKED THE SHERIFF and Leuten for their cooperation and assistance. They spent a few minutes browsing through files on the Weavers' computer and found nothing that aroused their suspicion. Saunders said they were going to take a look around the farm site. They asked Leuten and the sheriff to let them know if any major developments occur, shook hands and departed.

"Good riddance," Leuten muttered, watching the FBI agents walk toward their car.

"You better be careful," Hank chuckled. "They might have bugged the place." He turned serious. "What was that all about, with the Weaver kids? What was he talking about?"

A look of irritation moved Leuten's usual arrogant countenance toward insolence. "I stopped by there again earlier this morning. Where they were staying at that foster home in town. You know we haven't gotten squat out of the older one, Michael. He's old enough to know something, to have seen something."

"There's still time. They need some time," Hank cautioned. "They've been through a lot and the worst is yet to come. Can you imagine what that must be like for a little kid? It just makes me sick to my stomach. That's the worst part about this job. Seeing what happens to little kids in some of these cases. Like that Michael kid. You don't know all he's been through before. This is like round two."

The sheriff recalled the scene eight years ago in the same house, the same kitchen. The filth, the stench, the toxic chemicals. Somehow the little two-year-old boy had managed to survive. He still showed scars on his hands and arms from crawling around on the floor, hungry and desperate for food. Fortunately, a bottle of lye spilled, the venomous liquid burning his hands releasing the bottle before he could bring it to his mouth.

"When the Weavers took him they did a super job," Hank said. "They cleaned this place up. They provided a loving, stable home. Sure, they were a little different, but they were good people."

"Those are the ones that can fool you," Leuten countered. "I just don't trust that kid. I know he's only ten but he knows something."

Hank saw no value in discussing it further. He disagreed with Leuten's approach. He now wished the state agency hadn't become involved. Had the crime been domestic in nature it would have been fairly simple to investigate and solve, the only complexity being in the family's internal dynamics and all the psychological, emotional, physical, and economic variables comprising it.

The sheriff said he had to go check on he search party. Leuten remained at the farm to check in with the mobile crime lab crew, which was nearing completion of its crime scene forensics.

FROM HIS ABOVE-GROUND BUNKER camouflaged inside the farm's concrete-stave silo, Newton Case peered through a telescope at the surrounding countryside. The silo looked no different than most others, except for the openings concealed in the checkerboard pattern of black-and-white staves decorating the circumference near the top. Moving his telescope from one to the next gave Newt a three-hundred sixty degree view of the surrounding countryside.

Although too far away to see the Weaver farm, he was just able to see vehicles and figures walking through fields and ditches. He still hadn't decided for sure what he would do if searchers came on his farm. If they were local people that he knew he probably would have to go out and meet them, talk with them.

Of greater concern were the two men in dark suits driving full-size sedans that he had seen at the café.

Newt had to consciously resist panic when he saw the sedan kicking up a cloud of dust on the gravel township road approaching his driveway. Should he rush back to the house, try to conceal his fear and animosity, and talk to them? Or should he remain in the bunker hoping they soon would leave after finding no one at home, hoping they would not start snooping around the farm site?

It had been a lot of hard work, the tunnel system. Now he was thankful that he did it. If the car turned into his driveway Newt could climb down from his perch in the silo, scoot through the underground tunnel to the house, and be at the kitchen door by the time they parked in the driveway. Another branch of the tunnel connected the silo to the barn, and from the barn to an exit concealed in the grove.

About the only thing Newt didn't have for independent survival was his own source of electricity. Despite their politics, he admired the Weavers for their self-sufficiency, particularly their wind-powered electric generator. He also admired Stan Weaver for his skill in producing corn liquor.

That was the solution to his dilemma.

If the car stopped and the men were federal agents, and if they questioned Newt about the case, Newt would tell them about Stan's home-made still. As far as he knew the investigators had not discovered it, camouflaged as an old water pump in the little pump house next to the barn.

When he saw the car turn into his driveway, Newt climbed down the ladder in the silo, quickly for a man over sixty, scooted through the tunnel into the house and sat waiting at the kitchen table for whoever these men were, with anger and fear in competition for his primary acknowledgement.

8

LIFE HAD BEEN GOOD. It changed a lot when Jade and Trace came along, for the better. Although there was no training for becoming a parent except for the example, good or bad, of your own parents or those of your friends. Tom's parents had divorced when he was about Michael Weaver's age. Jeri's parents had been able to maintain a comparatively stable, caring, and loving relationship until her dad died when she was in high school.

Like many children of divorced parents Tom carried for years the guilt and sadness that somehow it was his fault. He tried hard to prevent it from remaining on the surface to rot, decay and foul his life. He covered it piling on work, ambition, big toys, and the dream of a happy and loving family of his own.

Tom would never forget the day his mom told him that dad was going to live someplace else and with someone else. Remembering that was the only concession he made to the past, more of a yielding because it couldn't be erased, but its intensity had subsided as time passed and he matured. His parents had tried to shield him from the arguments, arising mostly upon his father's return from business trips. His mother did not believe him when he insisted that he had remained faithful despite the temptations offered occasionally by female business associates and sometimes hookers. And until he found out the truth later in his teen years all that time Tom felt compelled to take the blame.

Tom loved his own kids so much. He couldn't comprehend how his own father could leave. Every day he came home from the route, tired and sometimes anxious. The kids came running toward him laughing and shouting, 'daddy, daddy'. He couldn't think of a value high enough to describe the pure joy he felt when he scooped them up and carried them back to the house. They would be laughing and talking, telling about the day's adventures and misadventures. He could not imagine ever leaving, but stopped short of thinking to make it a vow.

The young couple still hadn't recovered from the financial hit brought by having children. Before kids they had money left over at the end of the month. Now they barely made it paycheck to paycheck, which varied according to Tom's variable income, and more and more of it going to pay minimum balances. Like a silent, deadly, cancerous growth the credit card balance crept up well into four figures. They still had three more years of payments on the four-by-four.

Although he still rode it occasionally, the ATV parked in the shop no longer held the same level of excitement that it once did, which at first helped to rationalize the monthly payments. Payments on the loan to build the new shop were higher than those for the old farm site and buildings. The original house, deteriorated beyond repair, had been demolished. Its replacement, a 1970s vintage mobile home, and a few old outbuildings weren't much but at least had been purchased before the big run-up in real estate prices in recent years.

Despite the accumulating responsibilities and burdens, life had been manageable. The sense of fulfillment in being a parent to your children, working hard to develop your own business, and sharing life with your wife made it all seem worth it. Tom felt that he was really becoming a man now, confident in his abilities and sufficiently seasoned by experience.

On some days it was just plain stubbornness that kept him going toward his goal: Selling and delivering fresh, natural foods. If he didn't have bills to pay it would have been enough to just be able to be out on the road each day and seeing his customers. He couldn't imagine sitting in an office cubicle all day staring at a screen, or standing on some production line doing the same thing minute after minute, hour after hour, with someone else telling him what to do.

So far his ambition to be his own boss had been working out. He still remembered the good luck that opened the door: Ron Hamilton's classified ad in the Buffalo Ridge Banner:

Driver Wanted: Area organic growers seeking pickup and delivery of fresh produce in region and metro area. Refrigeration unit required. Opportunity to develop sales and expand market.

The contact information in the ad included a phone number for HOPE, which Ron Hamilton said was the acronym for Harvest Our Prairie Ethically, an organization of area farmers trying to avoid the use of chemicals and factory farm technology. Some had jumped through all the bureaucratic hoops to become certified organic farms.

THE WEAVERS WERE TRYing to do it by the book. They grazed their livestock, supplemented with organically-raised corn and soybeans. They did not routinely administer antibiotics and growth hormones, using medications only for illness. They had fulfilled all the requirements for achieving the official organic certification bestowed by the U.S. Department of Agriculture under the Organic Foods Production Act of 1990. It would have been granted except for the inspector's discovery that the farm site previously had been used as a meth lab.

Tom recalled the day Tulie told him about the inspector's visit. She cried. It just wasn't fair. They had done all that was required and more. Not a trace of the past could be found except in the prejudices of the inspector and some local authorities with whom the inspector had consulted. Tom tried to console her saying that he understood, and she understood what he meant. Maybe the inspector was right. Maybe they did clean up the chemicals, practically gutting the old farm house. The toxic wastes had been hauled to the county hazardous waste facility for proper disposal.

All this—Tom's work, ambitions, and family responsibilities—would have been enough for a reasonable measure of life's challenges and rewards. But events over the past couple days threatened to tip the scales toward the former, leaving Tom unsettled and beginning to doubt.

If and when Jeri found out about the meth, that which Leuten claimed he found in Tom's truck and was actually there, Tom feared the consequences would be far greater than anything the law and courts would impose, considering what she had been through and how she might react. The times he awoke in the night hearing her quietly sobbing had been becoming fewer. She still carried Michael's picture in her billfold, a felony conviction on record at the courthouse, and scars on her body, mind, and soul.

She went nuts when Amber told her how Leuten badgered Michael when he tried to question the Weaver kids. That she couldn't do anything about it only made it worse.

The whole situation began dredging up the past. They had worked so hard to leave it behind. Regarding Michael the effort sometimes was almost more than she could bear. It had become easier with the mellowing effects of time and especially now since he was older. At first, the pain came in equal measure from missing him, her own son, and from the nightmare during the first two years of his life, what she could remember of it.

SEVERELY ADDICTED TO METH, living in the toxic squalor on an old farm site in the countryside, an eighteen-year-old girl was arrested along with three older men in the custody of officers raiding the suspected meth lab at the old Wegman farm. Jerilyn Meyers did not know for sure which one of the men was Michael's father, nor did she care. As the boy grew older she couldn't stop herself from thinking which one he most resembled. The thought that someday he would want to know frightened her. She had been trying to erase those years from her memory, much of it buried in her subconscious. Sometimes in the early moments of a new day, while darkness still held open the door to a glimpse of the past, she awakened in time to hold back images groping their way from the nightmare that had been her life in those years, and back into her thoughts.

She had accepted the consequences, the most difficult being that as far as Michael was concerned, Tulie Weaver was now his mother.

Even though he knew Jeri's role in his life, whenever the Otto's visited the Weaver's, Michael seemed no more concerned than if she had been some distant relative whose connection did not go beyond the lines connecting names on a family tree. The neglect, occasional swats because he was crying, hours spent alone in a darkened room, and scars from painful burns suffered during the first two years of his life were nearly healed in the nurturing love of his adoptive family. He was too young to remember enough that would cause him to blame her now. If anyone or anything came too close he withdrew into a numbing inner sanctuary, a refuge for survival that served him even before he was old enough to understand.

During such retreats brought on in later years by meeting people outside the Weaver family or some unexplainable inner momentum, the Weavers tried to understand. They gave Michael the space he needed to wait out the storm.

After meeting Jeri and getting to know her better Tom Otto did the same. She told him about her past and he accepted it. They agreed to leave it behind them. Family counseling and Jeri's treatment for chemical dependency helped them look to the future, aiding them in their quest for peace. It helped Jeri accept that Michael would never see her as his loving mother, but it would never stop her from loving him. And it could not erase completely her bitterness about those who took advantage of her teenage rebellion, who chained her to the white powder and crystal, dragging her into a blurred existence of flying high then crashing with hardly any demarcation between day and night.

EVERYTHING CHANGED TUESDAY. Jeri couldn't stop thinking about some chance to regain her son, which made her feel even more guilt about what happed to Tulie Weaver. It wasn't Tulie's fault that Jeri screwed up her life. She should be thankful that Tulie accepted her with gracious understanding, allowing, even welcoming, the Otto's to visit the farm and giving Michael the chance to at least become acquainted with his birth mother.

She wondered if the Weavers had any relatives who might be in line to get the kids unless Stan suddenly showed up. Her intuition suggested that did not seem likely.

As much as she disliked leaving Jade and Trace in the afternoon and going off to work, her job provided more than the pittance that it paid. It provided structure, stability, and social contact. It gave her an escape from chores at home, and now from the approaching turmoil stirred up by what happened Tuesday at the Weaver's.

LIFTING HER TIME CARD from the rack to punch in, she wondered what the sticky note attached to it was all about.

"Jeri, please go to Mr. Clymer's office immediately."

She punched the card automatically. She shrugged off the question whether or not whatever ensued should be on the clock. She had never set foot in the production manager's office since Clymer replaced Ted Durand.

Occasional meetings with Ted, even though they usually involved union activity, had always been cordial and productive. They resulted in meaningful communication and understanding of the other's viewpoint. That all ended when Clymer arrived and the company strategy changed to hardball tactics.

Approaching the office this time Jeri felt dread, along with irritation. Was it something about the union committee? Did she do something wrong? Was she going to be fired? When Clymer first arrived, while still feeling sorry for Ted, she tried to believe in a positive outcome of change. Clymer seemed friendly and sincere. The free pastries at break time surprised and pleased almost everyone.

It didn't take long for the harassment of the union organizers to begin. When Clymer betrayed Jeri by refusing her credit for the improved knife design, any hope for future conciliation vanished.

The office door was closed so she knocked.

Jeri did not expect to see two men in the office. Someone wearing a suit sat in a chair next to Clymer, who sat behind his desk. The man's smile, which at another time might have seemed cordial and even a bit diffident, sent a cold chill down her back. He motioned with his open hand toward the chair in front of the desk.

"Jeri, this is agent Harmon Leuten," Clymer said. "He's with the state Bureau of Criminal Investigation." Clymer looked at the agent. "This is Jerilyn Otto."

"Nice to meet you," Leuten said, holding out his hand.

His pale, soft palms looked as if they would turn red and raw in less than an hour on the cutting line. At least the chewed fingernails would not collect fleshy tissue, which somehow seemed to show up in the oddest places no matter how diligent the production line sanitation regimen.

"Hi," Jeri said. "So what's going on?"

Clymer's gaze bore into Jeri's face as if he were searching for any clues that he had missed, that might have told him more about her past, which Leuten had been doing before she arrived in the office. There was nothing about it in her personnel file. Clymer's predecessor, Ted Durand, believed in leaving the past behind as long as a person was trying hard to do the same. Jeri's criminal record and subsequent treatment for meth addiction remained buried in the bureaucratic maze of the district court records system. Clymer had been digging into her background looking for anything, any skeletons or vulnerabilities that might be useful in destroying the union organizing effort. This could be very useful, and he could hardly believe his good fortune.

At first, when Leuten called and asked to meet in his office, Clymer hesitated. He thought it was too risky. He agreed when Leuten convinced him that the investigation at the Weaver's would provide more than enough cover. As the spouse of the first witness on the scene, questioning Jeri, even at her place of employment, could be justified. Leuten didn't say so, but he also wanted to visit Clymer and the plant in person. They had met a few times in private and talked on the phone. But Leuten still felt uneasy. It was like doing all the planning and providing materials for a house, then turning everything over to someone you didn't fully trust, and never seeing it get built, or providing ingredients for a recipe but never seeing it created.

Leuten had felt confident that the meth he had planted in Tom's truck, the Weavers' mysterious background, and the meth lab history of the old Wegman farm would be more than enough to build a case leading to an indictment. In some cases society didn't really care whether or not true justice was served, only that someone would be convicted and punished. That was not his plan for Tom Otto. He only intended to create enough circumstantial evidence to generate enough suspicion that it was all part of a larger meth ring. That would put the perps beyond reach, reduce the pressure for solving the case, and eventually the public would lose interest.

It was unfortunate that the situation had gotten so far out of hand, but he had always been very adept at working his way out of a jam. When Sheriff Schwartz told him about Jeri's past it reinforced his belief that criminals could never be fully rehabilitated, never worthy of complete trust. Her past would provide another argument supporting the outside meth ring theory, and that somehow the Weavers got caught in the crossfire.

After dozens of talks to student and church groups in recent years, Jeri could recite the speech almost word-for-word from memory. Describing the impact of meth in lurid detail drawn from her own experience she could mesmerize an audience, especially the younger teenagers who were as much titillated by the details as sobered by the message. At times her own composure crumbled when she told about the little boy who does not think of her as his real mother, whom she can only watch grow from a distance and have occasional visits to his adoptive family. The speech remained basically the same except for occasional statistical updates. Even those told only part of the story.

Standing in front of a high school class or church youth group Jeri tried to describe the effects of meth without making it sound appealing. Looking at some of the kids in her audiences she sometimes had doubts about the success of that effort. She could see herself ten or fifteen years ago, looking for some excitement, rebellion, and a older crowd of peers. When one of them offered her a beer the illicit thrill that she felt overpowered her knowledge of right and wrong. Then one of them convinced her that a little snort of a white powder would really give her a rush. *No, it wasn't heroin or cocaine. Meth was harmless.*

That was in her senior year of high school. She made it through graduation. Her plans for attending nursing school died when she started hanging around with an older crowd trying to numb the awareness of their otherwise purposeless lives with alcohol and drugs. Some held jobs—machine shops or truck driving. A few made careers of producing, transporting, and selling the white powder. They moved around a lot, finding old farm sites or old houses well beyond their prime years sheltering hard-working, functional families, who took good care of their homes.

The roots of her rebellion remained a mystery. Perhaps it was no more complicated than a lively, adventurous personality, losing its way during the roiling years of late adolescence that test the boundaries of reason and rules. Only later did she understand the pain it caused her family when she pushed too far, becoming trapped in a world where all of their values meant nothing. She tried her best to convey this to young kids. She felt confident that most received the message and understood as best they could, but in the eyes of some she saw skeptical, even cynical attitudes, seemingly amused by the phony attempt by just another dorky adult trying to tell them what to do when they already knew everything.

It left Jeri feeling as though she had failed, although she never stopped trying.

"AS YOU KNOW, JERI, we're investigating the apparent homicide and kidnapping at the Weaver farm Tuesday," Leuten said. "I'd just like to ask you a few questions. Mr. Clymer said it would be okay to talk here. That way we don't have to bother you at home or go to the law enforcement center." He paused for a millisecond wondering if he would detect any reaction in her composure at the mention of the latter location, any recollection from her past.

"What do you want to know from me? Tom was there, I wasn't," she replied, resisting a defensive tone that would betray a mirage of guilt. "You already questioned him."

"Yes, we did. Now it's your turn. We have to talk to everyone connected in any way," Leuten said.

"This is bullshit." Jeri's back stiffened, her eyes like flamethrowers. Clymer's office suddenly felt like a room in one of those horror movies where the walls began moving slowly inward. "You've questioned my husband already. I don't have to take any of this bullshit."

"Is it?" Leuten replied, straining to hold back a threatening tone, oozing from contempt, rooted in fear, which he did not consciously acknowledge. He waited for a response.

Jeri sat stiff, frozen, silent, and quivering perceptible only to herself. Leuten half expected her to jump out of her chair and rush out the door. She sat paralyzed, the numbing poison tainting more than usual the atmosphere in Clymer's office. Leuten relaxed and switched to a more patronizing strategy.

"You know, in most of these cases the motive is fairly evident. A lot of them are domestic, but there's almost always some connection. Sometimes it's not easy to find right away. We have to consider every little shred of evidence."

It made sense. Maybe this didn't have anything to do with the union committee. Now two days later the initial shock of what happened to the Weavers had begun to wear off, its place being taken by Jeri's growing understanding of the deeper, long-term consequences. Mostly, what all this would mean for the Weaver kids, Michael especially, and Tom's route business. She had no inkling about what she heard next.

Clymer leaned back in his chair relishing the show, counting up the ammunition this would provide in the company's war against the union attempt and one of its main leaders. Intensely annoyed by this feisty adversary, he took great pleasure in watching her teeter back on her heels from Leuten's interrogatory assault. Leuten leveled his eyes toward her and decided now was the time.

"Jeri, we know about your past. We know it's behind you. You've paid your debt to society, more than enough. I hear you're still paying, giving talks to kids about what happens when you get hooked on meth and other drugs, that's great."

Jeri's sudden glare ricocheted between Leuten and Clymer. "What's that have to do with this? What are you trying to say?"

"As far as we know that has nothing to do with this," Leuten said calmly. He looked at Clymer as if warning him to be ready for whatever might happen next.

Leuten reached in his pocket and withdrew a small plastic bag containing an oval-shaped, white object. He held it up.

"We found this in your husband's truck yesterday."

"What is it? It looks like an egg," Jeri said, almost with comic relief.

"It's one of those plastic eggs. You want to know what's in it?"

Jeri's fire from the preceding verbal combat flickered, then became extinguished by a cold draft of uncertainty.

"What?"

Leuten reached in his other pocket, withdrew a pair of plastic gloves and put them on. He removed the egg from the bag, twisted it open and held it out close to Jeri's face. She looked at it, tentative and foreboding. She smelled the venomous odor that erupted in a deluge of buried memories from the nightmare that had been her life a decade ago.

What was this all about?

"I think you know what that is," Leuten said smugly.

Jeri stared back, wavering between dread and disbelief.

"You know anything about this?" Leuten asked quietly.

She looked at him and then at Clymer. She stood abruptly.

"That's it. I'm outta here."

Jeri went for the door and then stopped halfway. Clymer's face showed surprise. Leuten leaned back in his chair with the same smug smile.

"Where do you think you're going," Clymer asked, failing in his effort to sound authoritative. He had thought that the trap was secure, that she would crumble under the accusation. Leuten knew better. Learning about her background he suspected that she knew the system as well as anyone. "That's okay Lyon," he said. "We all know what we need to know now."

"Maybe for you," Jeri shot back. She couldn't believe Tom would do that, after what they had been through, what she stood for now. But she was helpless against doubt and her eyes burned holding back tears. "Tom would never do such a thing. That's bullshit," she nodded toward the plastic egg still held in Leuten's hand.

"Ol' Tomato," Leuten said, smiling. "We'll see."

Jeri gave a curious look. "What?"

"I suppose he hasn't told you that, either. That's his nickname at the warehouse in the city. Tom Otto, tomahto, tomato. I think it's kind of cute," Leuten looked at Clymer with a little laugh.

"What in hell are you talking about? You're a sick bastard," Jeri snarled. She rushed out of Clymer's office, ran down the hall and out the door toward the parking lot.

CLYMER LOOKED WARILY at Leuten. He now wondered if that had been such a smart thing to do, agreeing with Leuten's suggestion to question Jeri at the plant. An event such as this, her rapid, distraught departure from his office, certainly would be noticed and launch the gossip machine into high gear. Now he had to come up with some explanation, which wouldn't be all that difficult considering their already-strained relationship arising from the union issue. He didn't need any more complicating details. He had already given up some control to Leuten, and feared that it might get out of control. It wasn't supposed to be this way.

"Now what?" Clymer's words almost sounded plaintive. "What was the point? Did you find out anything new?"

"No, but I think you did," Leuten said. "Why don't you just fire her?"

"In my dreams," Clymer said. "Right now that would just add fuel to the union fire."

"Didn't she just walk out of here? I think she's on the clock but I don't think she went out into the plant. Isn't that enough?"

"Maybe under normal circumstances. This is anything but, no thanks to you. Why'd you have to bring up the 'tomato' thing?"

"It keeps 'em off balance. I didn't think that he had told her about searching his truck yesterday. Now I know for sure. What else is he hiding, or both of them for that matter?"

"Well, I can't fire her, at least not right now," Clymer said. "That would just create sympathy for her and the union bunch. And if people believed when she told them about our little chat here, that'd make it even worse."

Leuten stood up to leave.

"Is that really true, the meth in that little egg thing there?" Clymer asked. "You think he's transporting the stuff?"

"It's all part of the investigation," Leuten said. "You'll find out along with everyone else when the time is right."

"You just keep me out of it. Don't come around here anymore. This was stupid in the first place."

"I'll go where I please, whenever I please. If this blows up it's your ass that's gonna get cooked, not mine," Leuten said with an ominous smile. He put on his sunglasses and stood up. He headed for the door, poked his head out and looked cautiously both ways. The side door opened toward the loading dock in back where he had left his car. Leuten drove slowly through the employee parking lot looking all around. He saw Jeri sitting in her car. It looked like she was wiping her eyes.

Leuten turned his car into an open parking space and turned off the engine. He took a bite from one of the fresh, glazed donuts Clymer had given him before he left.

He watched, wondering what she would do. Soon he saw the backup lights of her car. He smiled to himself watching it tear out of the parking lot. He enjoyed trying to imagine what would happen when she got home, if that's where she was going, and if Tomato was there.

9

FEW PEOPLE EVER CAME TO THE FARM of the old recluse, Newton Case, which is what he seemed to prefer. The few who knew him knew better. When he stopped to offer assistance at Tom Otto's disabled delivery truck Wednesday it might have seemed like a coincidence. When Tom told him that his wife, Jeri, soon would be there but thanks anyway, Newt drove off reluctantly. He scanned the roads in all directions out to the horizon, and behind him through the pickup's rear view mirrors looking for the big red F-350 pickup.

He truly felt sorry about what happened to the Weavers Tuesday. Their naive belief that basic goodness prevailed in most people, that the political system would protect them from evil, could not be successfully defended in all cases. The evidence presented itself every day, most clearly in the financial and commodity markets, and the growing gap between the super-rich and everyone else.

The presence of two federal agents confirmed what he already believed. They weren't working only for the government. Like they controlled everything else in the farm and food business, giant corporations were trying to take over the organic or natural food producers. With their tentacles deep into the federal government, in this case the Department of Agriculture, they sought to discredit and even destroy competitors, just like they destroyed Newt, his farm, and his family.

Until the boom and bust in farm land back in the eighties Newt, owned and farmed more than four-hundred acres. Caught in the squeeze of a huge debt load from buying much of the land at an unheard of price, followed by a thundering crash, Newt barely hung on. He found support in a clandestine network of farmers and other anti-government factions waging an economic and political struggle with banks and the government. One still remained in a federal prison, convicted of shooting two bankers to death who went on to his farm to deliver foreclosure documents. Newt lost all but eighty acres including the farm site, and his family.

When he built the aerial bunker in the upper reaches of the seventy-foot-tall silo next to the barn twenty years ago, he did not consider the future, the inevitable decline in kinetic abilities from biological decay later in life. The same lesson could be taught every year to anyone who observed and reflected upon the cycle of life among the grasses, leaves, and crops. A tree gave life to leaves in the spring, sustained them during the heat of summer, produced seeds of the next generation, shed them in fall, dried and shriveled to be carried off by the wind, and awakened in spring with a new generation.

Now, after twenty years Newt climbed the ladder to the bunker with thoughts about the next twenty years. Back then the way things were going, he did not believe he would survive into his fifties. Now in his early sixties thoughts of making some final stand, even to martyrdom, had diminished. Except for the loneliness, life had not been all that bad in recent years. Connected by satellite dish to the Chicago Board of Trade and other commodity markets, Newt discovered an aptitude for competing with the big city wheeler dealers at their own game, and weighing gains and losses earning barely enough to get by.

He climbed the ladder inside of the silo, but almost not fast enough when he saw the two men in dark suits that he had seen at the café turn their big sedan into the driveway and park by the house right next to his pickup. He now wished that he had parked the truck in the garage. Not seeing a vehicle they might leave thinking he was not there.

A 1953 Studebaker, which Newt acquired recently at an auction and had been tinkering with lately, currently occupied the single garage, crammed in among a complicated jumble of garage stuff: work benches, tools, oil cans, a wood stove, old license plates covering half of the side wall. A collection of old batteries covered the floor along the back wall beneath shelves full with a display of automotive and internal combustion engine history enough for a small museum.

At the last second, looking out the kitchen window and seeing the men, Newt changed his mind. He thought they might have been investigating the Weaver case, but why would they want to talk to him? Suddenly, he didn't want to find out. Newt hurried down the basement. He swung back the hinged shelf concealing the entrance, and stepped quickly in a crouch through the subterranean passage to the barn, strings of Christmas lights connected end-to-end twinkling from the ceiling.

FROM THE WINDOW in the shed connecting the barn and silo he saw them still knocking on the kitchen door. He climbed up the ladder gasping heavily on each rung. He could hardly push open the trap door into the bunker. His chest burned, lungs bellowing unable to keep up as they once could.

"Look at all this shit," the agent from Sioux Falls said. He knocked on the door again.

"It might look like a mess. You'd be surprised what some of this stuff goes for these days," agent Saunders replied.

They waited at the door, looking around the farm yard. Virtually every piece of equipment brought to the farm over the past century never left. When a tractor, plow, threshing machine, car or truck became obsolete or quit running, it remained right where it sat or had been dragged into the grove.

Saunders pounded on the door again. He looked at the other agent. "You didn't think he'd actually come to the door."

"Oh, he's here. That's his truck. Let's look around. This is amazing. Let's look at some of this stuff."

"We really don't need to be here," Saunders said. "We've learned what we need to know about the Weaver case. This guy doesn't know anything. This doesn't have anything to do with what happened back then."

"I'm not so sure about that. All the equipment he's got here, it's almost as sophisticated as the spooks at the CIA," the Sioux Falls agent said. "He could have seen or heard stuff."

"So where is it? Let's get a search warrant," Saunders said.

"Don't worry. It's here. He's got a big satellite dish somewhere around here. He may look like some crazy hermit, but he's not, I mean, he's probably crazy and is a hermit, but he's plugged in more than you know. Let's just look around a bit. You're not worried about an ambush, are you?"

"I'm always worried," Saunders said. "That eliminates anything happening when you're not expecting it. You ought to know that."

"I know him better than you. Let's just look around. I'd love to get my hands on some of this stuff."

Newt stepped off the ladder into the bunker and stooped over taking deep gulps of breath. Thirty seconds passed and his breathing began to slow. His heart rate took longer. What would he do if he had a heart attack? He hadn't much questioned the belief that such things would never happen to him. The increasing frequency of newspaper obituaries for his contemporaries occasionally overpowered his stubbornness, causing him to at least consider briefly the possibility.

Not this time, energized by the shot of adrenalin aroused by the intruders.

He looked out one of the narrow openings camouflaged in the silo wall, watching as the two men stepped back from the kitchen door and stood talking. They started walking toward the barn. He could take them out so easy they wouldn't know what happened, at least the first target. He wondered which of the two would have the slower reaction and make a better second target. At that range and with his sniper rifle he knew such large targets would be much easier than the squirrels, cans and bottles that he used for practice.

He prayed they would not detect any clues leading to the aerial bunker in the silo.

IF THEY WERE SO CLEVER, where were they ten years ago? He knew all about the activities at the old Wegman farm. Every day he looked through his telescope, seeing more in fall and winter through the brush and branches stripped of leaves. The attempted theft of anhydrous ammonia from a neighbor's place confirmed what he believed. The unusual traffic, the trash around the farm yard, no other visible means of support all added up to a rural meth lab. When he tried to tell the sheriff about the scumbag meth heads renting the place, Schwartz did little more than say they would check it out. Against his principles Newt even placed anonymous calls to state and federal authorities.

Nothing happened as far as he knew until the day two years later that he would never forget.

EVERY SO OFTEN on Sunday mornings Newt made surreptitious visits to the county landfill. One such morning in late January the sun rose above the flat horizon casting its glow through quiet air, softening the sting of ten degrees below zero. With fewer farm equipment auctions in winter, Newt found a surrogate junk fix in scavenging at the landfill. Except for the cold and snow it was actually easier in winter. It slowed the bacterial decay and reduced the stench.

On the backside away from the main highway he turned his pickup into a field approach and parked it among a clump of box elders. As the sun rose he would hike about two hundred yards to the fence around the landfill, peel back a section of chain link and drag through a long, plastic toboggan. He didn't spend much time in the mixed solid waste area, typical household garbage, scanning around for anything that looked interesting while he continued on to the appliance and construction demolition sections.

His contentment warmed with the morning sun and still, peaceful air, void of blowing dust and screeching gulls that plagued the landfill outside of winter. If he found an appliance that appeared to be repairable he would sometimes return during regular hours and negotiate its release with the landfill operator, with the promise that he would take it back if he failed to get it working again and that he would not try to sell it for personal gain. Among Newt's neighbors, many lake cabins, hunting shacks, and in some cases even households had been equipped with stoves, washers, dryers, and refrigerators that he had salvaged. He would not accept cash payment, but if they left something in trade he did not object.

This particular morning he hit the jackpot, a stack of old computers sitting outside the main equipment shed. Small enough to carry in the plastic toboggan, four computers disappeared from the stack. After years of disassembling old computers and rebuilding them, knowledge gained through his hands, manuals at the library in Buffalo Ridge, and via the Internet, Newt had equipped and connected his remote farm to the world.

Returning from the landfill, driving along the gravel township road he squinted through the windshield into the morning sunlight trying to see what looked like a bulging figure stumbling along the shoulder.

"What the blazes? Who's that?" he muttered. The dog saw it even before he did. Harvey, Newt's old beagle, braced his front legs on the seat bench against the forward motion of his own momentum as the pickup slowed to a stop.

A woman of undetermined age carrying a bundle, unusual enough in itself at this particular time and place, walked barefoot in a stumbling dance over small pebbles and patches of snow and ice on the frozen road. Harvey's breath left a moist film on the side window after Newt pushed the dog back against the seat trying to get a better view. "Harv, I think you might be riding in the box the rest of the way." Newt thumped the beagle on his chest.

SHE WORE YELLOW SWEAT PANTS, rumpled and stained with what looked like blood. At first it appeared that she was trying to ignore the pickup, while at the same time giving wary glances. Whether from recognition or desperation she stopped. She approached and her face became more visible behind loose ropes of long, greasy, light-colored hair glinting in the early morning sunlight. He could see now that she was young. Her eyes peered from dark craters in her pale face smudged with dirt and streaks of old makeup. Newt leaned over and rolled down the passenger side window.

"Mornin'. You okay? You need a ride someplace?" Newt said in a friendly tone that attempted to avoid any acknowledgement of the otherwise unusual circumstances. "Ain't it a bit chilly to be runnin' around out here like that?" Harvey poked his head out the window trying to detect a scent.

"I need a doctor. I got to get to a hospital." She spoke in a low, quavering, determined voice.

"What you got there?"

"The dog bit him, my little boy. I got to get to a doctor. He's bleeding."

Looking at Harvey to keep a safe distance, she held out the bundle to where Newt could see a large, dark blue towel wrapped around a small figure, discernible only by the tufts of light hair protruding from the top, and one bare foot hanging out the bottom.

A sudden thought about his own children compounded his compassion. He missed them intensely, not so much their physical absence, the youngest still living with their mother in another city, but that he had almost become a stranger to them as the emotional distance had grown over the years. Sometimes in the evenings alone at the farm he would drag out the photo albums filled with pictures taken when they were very young, holding the images to his chest, closing his eyes trying to remember those early years.

Newt left the truck idling in neutral, set the brake, and stepped out. "C'mon Harv. Out." The old beagle paused, looked back at the strangers, then turned toward the open driver's side door, jumped out and grunted on the heavy landing. He followed his master to the back and accepted some assistance in climbing into the pickup box. Newt closed the end gate and went around to the other side of the truck.

"What happened? How bad is he hurt?" he asked. He opened the door. The young woman's expression remained frozen. He could now see fear, pain and terror in her eyes, which he had seen before in the eyes of wounded soldiers in Vietnam. He took the bundle from her arms, a small child, one or two years old. He couldn't tell for sure. The girl climbed in the truck. Handing her the child Newt saw through the opening at the top of the towel the ragged lacerations on the boy's head, coagulating blood on his hair and in streaks down the side. His eyes looked up at the stranger who now held him. He made no sound, showed no expression.

"The dog attacked him. Please get me to the hospital."

"What's your name?" Newt asked as they drove away. She told him. She pointed toward the farm site where she had been living, the old Wegman place that Newt had been surveilling since the new tenants had moved in awhile back. She looked thinner close up than she did far away through the telescope.

"What kind of dog was it?" Newt asked. She said it was a pit bull, they had two. One was okay. For some reason the other perceived the young child as a threat or a vulnerable target. This wasn't the first time. The dogs ran loose outside and in the house wherever they pleased. When the one dog started going after the baby, Jeri did the only thing she could think of when she was lucid enough to think. She left the baby in a playpen in one of the bedrooms with the door closed.

RIGHT AFTER HE WAS BORN, Michael received much attention from Jeri and most of the guys. After a few months the novelty wore off. The meth highs grew more intense and so did the crashes. It became more convenient to keep the baby out of the way as much as possible, and when the dog attacks started, the seclusion seemed to be justified, to the extent that anything needed to be. The white powder and crystal, the money, the weapons became the only justification they needed.

Instead of evoking the devotion that compels new parents toward intense focus attending to a tiny infant, its cries brought angry shouts and attempts to stifle the piercing noise by any means short of infanticide. Despite Jeri's erratic efforts to sustain the child, neglect was moving the situation in that direction.

Newt knew her name. Up close he could now recognize her, barely. He knew the depths to which people could crash, pushed over the edge by physical, psychological or financial trauma. In many cases the circumstances made it understandable even if not justifiable. When people consciously and deliberately ingested substances that led to such a descent, it was another matter.

Newt took one look out the back window to make sure Harvey was settled in the back of the pickup next to the old computers and a tall wooden stool that someone discarded for no apparent reason visible in its appearance or condition. Harvey lay curled up on an old rug Newt kept there for that purpose.

"How bad's he hurt?" Newt repeated.

She did not respond, her composure succumbing to sobs.

He wanted to ask her for the boy's name. He knew who she was. He wondered how she came to this, growing up in what seemed to be a loving, stable family. He could almost imagine Jerry and Lynn Meyers' pain, their bewilderment about how their child ran off with a bunch of depraved dirtballs who wasted their lives on a rollercoaster of addiction to the white powder, the crystal. She met them in the summer after high school graduation. She moved in with them in the fall and not long after became pregnant.

The injuries Michael received from the pit bull healed leaving scars mostly concealed by his hair after it grew back. The scars on his face and arms from acid burns receded as well although remained visible up close.

While at first the dog attack seemed a terrible thing, Jeri's family and former friends grew to believe it was God's way of bringing her back from an existence so sinful and depraved that it provided overpowering evidence of Satan's power in the world as if they needed any, and to their families excruciating evidence that sometimes moved them to question their own faith.

Even worse, they felt the shame of having failed as parents. It followed them around town, at work, everywhere. After the raid on the meth lab at the old Wegman farm, Jeri was arrested along with the others. Although prosecutors didn't really need more evidence, they asked Newt to testify, to tell about the activity he observed.

At first he refused. Entering a courtroom would expose him to whatever tricks and harassment the judges and lawyers cared to impose. It happened before and it could happen again. If they wanted him to testify they would have to issue a subpoena delivered by the sheriff himself.

He relented when Jeri called from the county jail pleading for his cooperation, hoping that he would be able to describe how he found her out on the road trying to go for help, that somehow it would persuade the judge and county family services she truly cared for her child and was fit to be a mother. They believed the first part. Evidence of the second part did not emerge until a year or two later, but by then it was too late. In the negotiations for her parole Jeri agreed to give up her parental rights. At the time everyone thought it was the right thing to do. Paternal rights never came into question. Jeri had a hunch which one it might have been. No one else really cared.

As far as Michael was concerned, it was happening all over again. Stan and Tulie Weaver had become Michael's parents and the only ones he really remembered. Now they were gone, Tulie for sure.

If only Newt had seen something going on at the Weaver farm Tuesday morning. He no longer spent much time watching through the telescope as he once did. Driving by the Weaver place on his way in to the café he paid little attention to Tom Otto's food truck in the yard. Approaching the main highway he pulled to the side yielding to the sheriff deputy's patrol car speeding by with red lights flashing. His curiosity almost moved him to turn around and follow. Later he regretted not doing so. It might have weakened what became circumstantial evidence that put him on the list of suspects. He believed that he survived the interrogation fairly well, until the FBI agents showed up.

Newt watched the agents' movements until they went out of range of the security camera, one of four that he had strategically placed around the farm yard. What would he do if they discovered the bunker high up inside the silo? Well-stocked with food and water, it also left him trapped like medieval monks in a stone tower surrounded by warring heathens. With no escape route he had no choice but to make a final stand, unless he could clamber down from the silo and escape unnoticed into the tunnel system. He regretted not being able to fetch Harvey and lift him up on the platform that he used to hoist supplies and equipment into the bunker.

"There's nothing here," agent Saunders said.

"He's here," the other agent said.

"He's not what we're looking for," Saunders said. "What happened twenty years ago is over. Besides, that was nothing compared to what's happening now. Let's not get sidetracked here."

"I know, I know. I just like looking around at all this shit. He could turn this place into a museum."

"Let's go. We saw the local report on his interrogation. It didn't look to me like they missed anything," Saunders said.

The Sioux Falls agent looked out the back door of the barn. A small pump-house beckoned from about thirty feet away. Six feet square, its weathered white paint camouflaged solid construction and a newly-shingled roof. With modern submersible pumps on most farms, pump houses had become obsolete and most had disappeared. Newt stared at the monitor for the security camera on the machine shed, which viewed the back of the barn including the pump house.

This is it.

His chest tensed holding his breath as if any infinitely obscure sound would betray what the pump house concealed. He had analyzed every precaution to make it inconspicuous. The tunnel from the barn to the grove passed beneath the pump house so Newt could enter without wearing a path to the door. Instead of using wood to fire the boiler as Stan Weaver did, Newt used propane supplied from buried copper tubing. Under Stan's tutelage he had become quite good at operating the homemade still.

Not quite ready to drift away to the east, the morning thunderstorm opened the gate to one last burst of rainfall. The FBI agent remained in the doorway of the barn looking up at the sky. His vision made a final sweep across the yard. He stepped back into the barn and closed the door.

Newt muttered a silent, thankful prayer. He watched the men hurry to their car through the rain, already beginning to let up.

"That was a waste of time," agent Saunders said.

"What do you mean? Checking out all this stuff, I want to come back and see if he'd sell some," the Sioux Falls agent said.

FOR SEVERAL YEARS FEDERAL AGENTS had been investigating drug money laundering in the Midwest. FBI, IRS, and ATF agents had been looking for evidence of cash being siphoned from all corners of society, all economic and social levels, by dealers in meth and crack cocaine. Investigators believed the money was finding its way back into circulation through investments in large factory farms, ethanol plants, wind turbines, and other bio-energy projects.

Using profits from his growing expertise in making transactions on the Chicago Board of Trade and the rising energy markets, Newt Case had made substantial investments in the booming agro-energy industry, unaware of the scrutiny that his investments had attracted. In terms of the law his only real crime was the backyard still. At least he was not addicted to its output, his obsessions being fulfilled instead by his privacy, paranoia, Tulie Weaver, and Jeri Otto.

Out in the field agents from the various departments met on occasion and shared information. Not long after the Department of Homeland Security took control over everything causing the informal channels of communication among the various agents to wither. And with the specter of agro-terrorism added to the existing investigations, the truth became buried even more deeply among the false perceptions, private agendas, and bureaucratic blunderings.

10

Thursday morning's thunderstorm moved off to the east leaving the landscape fresh and moist. Vistas of corn and soybean fields spread out in all directions, the crops' young stalks and stems silently drawing sustenance from the freshly-tilled soil. The torrent of wind rushing into the cab of Tom's truck smelled sweet and clean, but he did not savor it.

No matter how hard he tried it seemed as though it were happening all over again. His childhood ended too soon when his parents split up, now almost twenty years ago. Twice during the lonely, haunted years of high school he embraced thoughts about ending it all. One final act would expose the pain to the world and bring it to an end. On two occasions that he knew of during those years the precedent had been set. After the second incident kids listened when the high school counselor visited every home room class to advise them that deliberately ending one's life was a misguided and selfish attempt to gain attention to one's suffering. It neither ended the pain nor gained attention. The pain permeated every day and night of surviving loved ones the rest of their lives. It was a big price to pay if the motive was revenge. In the two cases the attention did not materialize in a big story in the Buffalo Ridge Banner, or an auditorium filled with sobbing people. And revenge hurt the perpetrator more than anyone, unless punishing yourself was the true motive. If that were the case, then the only hope would be that God's grace and mercy counted on either side.

He would have used carbon monoxide from his car idling in the closed garage, not a noose like one of the kids did. Perhaps it was more cowardly, but he felt queasy imagining strangulation by a rope clinched around his neck.

In one of their long talks when they first started dating he confided some of these thoughts to Jeri. She believed him when he said he never would have done anything like that. She had her own story and in some ways it made Tom's burden seem routine. It's just that the thoughts sneak up on you sometimes when circumstances occur that seem to be so painful and complicated as to make every second, every breath of life seem almost unbearable.

Tom silently chastised himself when the thought flashed in his mind of jerking the steering wheel to the left pointing his truck at the grill of a Kenworth, or a Peterbilt or White Freightliner. Any one would work just fine. It would be over in an instant. But maybe not. He'd been the first on the scene of several highway crashes before. It never happens like in the movies.

He drove the truck into the long driveway to the Hamilton's farm site.

Soon after they moved on the old farm back in 1978, Ron planted a row of Black Hills spruce flanking the driveway on the north side. Across the driveway on the south side stood a row of black walnut trees. Shed of their leaves in winter they allowed the sun a chance to melt the snow cover on the driveway, while the evergreens held back much of it in the first place. Almost everything the Hamiltons had done to the farm had been planned for energy conservation, ease of maintenance, and aesthetic appearance, guided by a well-thumbed copy of the Mother Earth catalog.

Now more than thirty feet tall the spruce evergreens stood like sentinels making directions to the farm an easy task.

Until Ron told him about all the trees he had planted, Tom had never thought about doing the same. It seemed that it would take an eternity for a tree to grow to useful maturity. The saplings of ash and birch, the potted evergreens, and shrubs at the nursery in Buffalo Ridge seemed inconsequential compared with forty-foot-tall spruce or columns of fully mature elms along the boulevards. Their high branches reaching out over the streets forming leafy arches in the long-established neighborhoods. The nursery stock seemed so small, making it difficult to comprehend that it held within a steady, slow, unstoppable force of growth, much too slow to appease the urgency and impatience of youth.

During a visit to the Otto's not long after Tom started providing truck transportation for HOPE, the area organic and natural food growers, Ron observed that planting more trees around the Otto's trailer house and shop might be a good idea. Many of the box elders and cottonwoods in the old grove served well in years past, planted around early farmsteads for their rapid growth. Each passing year brought more protection from the persistent prairie winds. With the hardships faced by the early settlers, especially the blizzards in winter, they could not be blamed for planting fast-growing, soft-wood trees that rarely lived beyond a century. Ron said he felt the same impatience years ago as Tom did now. Plant the trees and if not entirely for yourself, for your children and others who follow.

Ron had called Tom earlier in the morning. He had another shipment of goat cheese ready for delivery to the warehouse in the city, and if Tom didn't mind running the truck's refrigeration unit during the night and until delivery, could he swing by in the afternoon for an unscheduled pick-up?

Halfway into the Hamilton's driveway Tom's cell phone chirped.

"Where are you?" It was Jeri.

"Hey what's up? How come you're not at work?"

"I was. Where are you?"

Her words came with a tone that he did not remember hearing, or it had been so long ago that it faded into distant past.

"I'm just turning into the Hamilton's. What's going on? Everything okay?"

"No, everything's not okay."

"What do you mean? Are the kids okay? C'mon. What are you doing?"

"I got called in to a meeting with Clymer and that BCI guy, whatever his name is. Herman something."

"Harmon Leuten?"

"Yeah."

Tom stopped the truck. He stared straight ahead listening intently, not so much for the words as the tone. "So what did they want?" The conversation so far added up to a somber realization that unpleasant facts were about to emerge. Did Jeri get fired because of the union activity? She would have said that right away. The timing of her call didn't fit the usual pattern. "Did you get fired?" Immediately he regretted asking the question.

"Heck no! What would I get fired for?"

"Well what is it then?"

"They asked me more questions about the Weavers and what happened."

"Why'd they do that? What did you say?"

"Don't lie to me." Even over the cell phone the sound of her voice trembled. "This Harmon or Herman showed me something that he found when they searched your truck. That better not be true."

Tom couldn't find the words to answer right away, and if he could they would have become stuck against the sudden dryness he felt in his mouth. He regretted not telling her immediately about the meth, or what Leuten claimed was meth that he claimed to have found during the search of the truck. They really hadn't had much chance to talk since yesterday. Once the first moment passed, the urgency waned allowing the denial about the real meth given to him by another driver at the warehouse to resume control.

"What are you talking about? What was it?" Even he was partially convinced by the innocence with which he tried to cloak his response.

"A little plastic egg? With meth inside?"

"Did he show you that? That was a plant! He must have put it there. You better believe me. I never saw that before Leuten showed it after searching the truck yesterday. I think he's trying to frame me or something. Swear to God!"

"Why didn't you tell me? What's wrong with you? I can't believe you didn't tell me!"

"I was going to. I didn't have a chance. Please, I'm sorry. This is all so screwed up."

"Okay, okay, I want to believe you. Maybe he's trying to frame me."

"Why you?"

"He knows about my past. The bastard told Clymer all about it. Maybe he's one of those types who think people can't change. God knows I've paid my debt. If he drags that stuff up I don't know what I'm going to do. Where are you?"

"I said, at the Hamilton's. What are you going to do? Maybe you should go back to work."

"I can't. I just don't think I can right now. I just feel sick to my stomach. I'm going to call in sick. I got hit by the flu. You wait there at the Hamilton's. I'm coming out."

"What do you have to come out here for? Jeez, I got to keep going," Tom protested. "Can't you just go home? I'll be there soon."

"I'm not going there. I don't want to upset mom and get her asking all kinds of questions. Is Ron there? Let's talk to him."

Tom lowered his forehead, resting it on his arms across the steering wheel. He could deal with having to explain the meth that Leuten planted. He had tried to avoid thinking about the other meth in his lunch box. He wished now that he had said something right away. r He shifted the truck in gear and drove into the farm yard.

RON HAMILTON POKED his head out the cheese shed door and waved. Tom backed the truck up to the shipping door. The herd of goats standing on their muddy hooves in the corral surrounded two sides of the barn, turning in unison to stare at the rumbling truck.

"What's the rush?" Ron asked, tossing the last case up to Tom in the truck. "Thought maybe you might want to take a break. It's almost time for a beer. This last batch is really good."

Under normal circumstances Tom would have accepted the offer and downed one or two. He looked at his watch trying to judge when Jeri would arrive, debating whether or not he should hurry to leave before she got there, not to only avoid her, but to prevent an embarrassing encounter in the presence of the Hamiltons. He turned down the offer.

Ron looked intently at the younger man. "Anything wrong?"

"It's just this investigation and everything that's happened. It's a real mess."

"I know. It's just starting to hit me now. What happened to Stan and Tulie. I still can't believe it sometimes. Last night it woke me up. It seemed like a dream. Then I just laid there thinking about what might have happened to Stan. And we still have to figure out what's going on for a memorial service for Tulie. You heard anything more about how the kids are doing?"

"I guess that Leuten, the BCI agent, went over to where the kids were staying and tried to question Michael. Jeri said he was verbally abusive, cussing at him and stuff. She just went nuts when she heard that."

"That really sucks. What an asshole."

"And then they searched my truck yesterday," Tom said. "Leuten and Randy Tollefson, the deputy. Leuten pulls out this little plastic egg with some meth inside and says he found it in my truck." Tom hadn't intended to say anything. It just came out. It would come out soon anyway when Jeri arrived. It was too late now to escape. It felt better to get it out.

"What?"

"I think they're trying to frame me or something. Like I'm transporting the stuff."

"Why would they think that?" Ron's automatic response came from his knowledge of Tom. He felt uneasy about the unexpected notion of suspicion that came with it. Immediately he felt embarrassed at the thought, but still he couldn't shake the idea that circumstantial evidence could be found that might cast doubt on Tom's innocence. His regular trips to the city, his frequent stops around the rural countryside and small towns. But what happened to the Weavers? That was unthinkable. "That's just nuts. Don't worry. We'll vouch for you."

"I'm not worried. I didn't do anything." Tom tried to sound unconcerned. The threat of pending charges gnawed at his gut. He didn't know how they could afford a lawyer. It felt like an invasion of something ominous and evil, threatening to take control of his life. He looked at the goats with envy. They spent their days wandering around the corral and out on the pasture, grazing on grass and hay with plenty of company, their only real labor being a few minutes in the milking parlor and the nannies. The young bucks got shipped off to HOPE's cooperative meat processing plant just outside Kasota Creek. The same fate eventually befell the milk goats; at least they all had a clear purpose for their lives, which they did not question nor worry about.

RON AND TOM TURNED toward the sound of a vehicle approaching down the long driveway. Ron checked his watch.

"That must be Wendy." She usually arrived home around four after getting off work. Tom looked up wondering if instead they would see Jeri in the old Crown Vic. Wendy drove all the way over to the cheese shed, stopped and rolled down the window.

"Hi Tom. Nice to see you. Hi Hon. Was Jeri supposed to be coming out here? I'm sure it was her car I saw out on the highway. It was pulled over by the highway patrol."

"Oh jeez," Tom groaned. He turned and looked away, aiming his exasperation toward the open fields across the road. A speeding ticket would cost a hundred bucks or more. Usually she observed the speed limit, if that's what it was all about.

Ron looked at Tom. "Really? Isn't she usually at work right now?"

"She called and said she was coming out here," Tom admitted. "She's pretty upset. I guess her boss called her into his office. The BCI guy was there and they questioned her some more about the Weavers."

"That seems strange," Ron said. "But maybe not. This morning Archie Daniels and I were questioned again. We were over at the Weaver's doing the chores. I know what you mean about Leuten. I can understand they need to try nail this thing right away. But his questions really got bizarre. It was really threatening."

"You didn't tell me that." Wendy said.

"Sorry. I suppose I could have called. I think we all need to step back here a little bit and think things through. Maybe when Jeri gets here you guys might as well stay for supper. Jeri's mom is with the kids, right?"

Ron's invitation sounded reassuring. Tom hoped Jeri would agree. Although younger and not quite on the same philosophical and political plane as the network of folks operating the small, organic farms in the area. The Ottos liked the business relationship and enjoyed the occasional social invitations. At first, when the conversations shifted from farming and the weather to politics, economics, and sometimes religion, their divergent views created some tension. It became evident that the knowledge and beliefs of the Ottos did not measure up to the depth and breadth of their hosts. At least it did to Tom and Jeri. The Hamiltons and others did not seem to judge the younger couple. In time their subtle mentoring had broadened the Ottos' intellectual horizons. A nice dinner and a few beers with Ron and Wendy promised a comforting oasis, amid the turmoil.

Wendy returned to the house to start dinner. In other circumstances Ron and Tom would relax outside on the deck sipping beer between threads of conversation. Instead they drove in Ron's pickup in the direction where Wendy last saw the car that looked like Jeri's.

"How have things been?" Ron asked casually, looking at Tom sitting on the passenger side and staring blankly out the window. "Everything okay otherwise?"

"What do you mean?"

"Oh, I don't know. Your delivery business, you and Jeri, the kids, just life in general I guess."

"We're fine. The money's a little tight. What else is new?"

"You making any profit with the truck?"

"I think so. Jeri keeps telling me I got to do a better job of accounting. I try to write everything down but sometimes I forget. Then I get behind and just give up."

"You let us know how it's going," Ron said. "Maybe we can do something about our shipping rates. Maybe we can try harder to market our produce. You're doing a great job and we need you."

"Thanks. I wish it would be enough so both of us wouldn't have to work all the time. My days are long. When I get home she's already off to work. About the only time we get to be together is on weekends. It works out okay with the kids and daycare. At least we don't have a big bill there. Jeri's mom helps out for the time between when Jeri goes to work and I come home. We get along okay. She's good with the kids."

"It's too bad things have to be that way," Ron said. "It's tough on families when both parents have to work outside the home full-time. You can thank our post-industrial corporate oligarchy for that. They move their factories and headquarters to other countries so they can pay less taxes and use cheaper labor. Or they actively recruit cheap labor and bring them here. The income gap just keeps widening. I guess the world has always been that way. The only difference is that centuries ago they called it slavery."

"It's not that bad," Tom said.

"I know. I just get a little carried away sometimes. Maybe I'm even being a hypocrite. It's those wealthy investors and corporate executives who are buying our produce at those fancy food stores in the cities. And then our consumer society, everybody works all the time so we can buy all this stuff we don't really need. Except for food, of course. Everybody's got to eat. And the organic stuff is getting more mainstream. I think the future looks really good for what we do, you included."

"I sure hope so."

THE CONVERSATION HELPED dull the edge of anticipating what they might encounter in finding Jeri, except for the mystery about her meeting with Clymer and Leuten, and her sudden departure from the plant.

They saw a car approaching, a boxy, older full-size sedan. Jeri didn't immediately recognize the Hamilton's pickup passing by in the opposite direction despite Ron's waving and flashing the headlights. He made a U-turn and followed the Crown Vic back to the farm. They caught a glimpse of Jeri driving past looking straight ahead, stonefaced, both hands gripping the wheel.

"It's just probably a speeding ticket," Ron muttered.

Tom wanted to say, 'no, it's more than that', but he didn't.

Wendy was standing by the car talking with Jeri when the men drove into the yard. The officer said he clocked Jeri at eighty-four. The one-hundred forty two dollar fine would take almost two day's wages at the plant. Wendy begged her to stay for dinner.

"I can't." Jeri wouldn't look at Wendy, averting her face trying to conceal smudged mascara around her eyes and down one cheek. She felt embarrassed. If they didn't already know, what would they think when they learned about her past? How could she confront Tom about Leuten's allegations in front of the Ron and Wendy? She now regretted going there.

"Listen, I don't know what this is all about. We don't have to know. But you can still stay and have dinner with us," Wendy pleaded. "This whole thing has been tough on everyone, not to mention the Weavers. Let's just have a good meal and try to relax. We've got to stick together."

Ron let Tom out and drove the pickup into the garage. Wendy went into the house to start dinner. Tom approached Jeri still sitting in the car. She looked up, capturing him in a steady gaze.

"Just tell me it's not true," she said through clenched teeth, her eyes showing more hurt than anger. "Just tell me."

"You mean the stuff Leuten said he found in my truck? That's bullshit. He had it all along. He comes back out of the truck and says he found it there. I don't know why."

"Why didn't you tell me?"

"There just wasn't time. I was going to. I didn't know what to do. We've hardly talked since Tuesday. It just seemed so unreal. I thought they were just kidding. I'm sorry."

"He laughed and said they call you 'Tomato', at the warehouse in the city. You never told me that, either."

Tom rolled his eyes, thankful that she believed him about the meth that Leuten planted in his truck. The embarrassment of the nickname seemed much less than he would have anticipated, perhaps so in comparison with the meth allegation. With some relief he explained how it all started.

"I think it's funny."

"You would," he said trying to sound exasperated.

"Tomahto, tomato, tomahto, how's that song go?" Jeri even laughed a bit, then turned sober again. "Okay. I believe you. So what do we do now? Are they going to arrest you?"

"I don't know. I always thought once you did something they had to file charges in twenty-four hours. It's probably past that now. That's what scares me. Maybe he's got something else up his sleeve."

"From what I saw today I wouldn't be surprised," Jeri said.

RON HOLLERED FROM THE DECK. Dinner would be ready in half an hour. They should join him for a beer or wine. Jeri gave in to the temptation of a good meal and conversation with the Hamiltons.

The twelve-by-sixteen-foot deck jutted out from the south side of the rambler between the kitchen and dining area, shaded by a row of ash trees along with several maples and a large birch clump. Although it required more maintenance and needed to be stored in a shed during winter, they would have nothing other than sturdy oak deck furniture crafted by the hands of Stan Weaver.

Wendy carried out a salad—romaine lettuce and klamata olives generously sprinkled with crumbly goat cheese, and drizzled with olive oil and red wine vinegar. She declined when Jeri asked if she needed any help in the kitchen. "You just sit and relax. You've had a rough day."

Jeri sat back and took another sip of raspberry wine, one of the several varieties home-made by Tulie Weaver, and it suddenly occurred to her that this would be the last.

"You two just stay put," Ron said, getting up to help Wendy. Jeri and Tom sat quietly savoring the fresh, sweet-scented air, a slight coolness in the leafy shade over the deck filtering out the sun still high this late in the day approaching the summer equinox. The melody of robins chirping in the trees or an occasional bleating goat from the corral barely intruded on what little they could hear from their own breathing and heartbeats.

"This is some of Stan and Tulie's chicken," Wendy said setting the casserole of chicken tetrazzini on the table. Ron carried out a basket of crusty bread.

Jeri felt compelled to ask if she could ask a blessing on the food, and the Hamiltons respectfully consented. "Dear God, thank you for this food and bless it to our bodies. Thank you for your love, grace and mercy. Help us through this time of trouble and sorrow. May you embrace Stan and Tulie Weaver, and especially the kids. Amen."

"Amen," Tom added. "Amen," echoed Wendy.

"This looks delicious," Jeri said. "Thanks." Under normal circumstances she would have continued the conversation, introducing whatever subject that stood out in her thoughts. Instead they began to eat in silence that soon became noticeable without the sounds of words to mask self-consciousness or dissipate any tension, which quickly grew beyond tolerance.

"So what happened at work today?" Wendy asked. "You said the agent questioned you again?"

Jeri looked at Tom wondering how much he told them before she got there, how much they knew in the first place. He picked up on the cue. "I just said you left work and were coming out here. They've been questioning everybody."

"Did you tell them what they told me about you? You might as well tell them. Everyone will find out soon enough anyway," Jeri said.

Tom looked at Ron. "I told you." Ron nodded, indicating that Wendy also knew. "We just can't believe it. Why would they do something like that?"

Tom now relaxed as he described again how agent Leuten and deputy Tollefson searched his truck the day before. Ron and Wendy listened intently sometimes shaking their heads in dismay, wishing their sense of disbelief would turn out to be true.

It felt good to talk about it. If only that would be enough to make it go away.

"Did you tell them about your nickname, from the warehouse?" Jeri teased.

Tom felt his face become flush. "C'mon, why'd you have to bring that up?"

"I'm sorry. I just think it's cute."

"I hate it."

"That's okay. We already know," Wendy said. "Ron called the warehouse not too long ago looking for you. The guy who answered hollered to someone to check if Tomato was there." She looked at Ron. "I thought you might have said something."

"I thought I'd just leave it alone," Ron said. "We should appreciate everything you have to put up with doing what you do. It's hard work and the days are long. Sometimes I worry about you driving tired."

"I suppose I shouldn't get so mad about it," Tom said. "Sometimes it seems like they just like to pick on me. I just try to shrug it off."

He looked at Jeri. "Did you want to tell them something too?"

"What?"

"About Michael?"

She stiffened and glared at him. Maybe they already knew about Michael's past. It always bothered her that she never really knew how much the Weavers might have said to anyone. As close as they were to the Hamiltons they must have said something. Why did he bring that up now?

"We know about Michael," Wendy said quietly. "I hope he gets through this okay. And the little ones, too. I wish we could help."

"We're going to try get him. Anna and Jonathan, too," Tom said. "Maybe you could help us do that." He looked at Jeri wondering how she would respond.

Although she never talked about it over the past eight years, every now and then the longing would emerge in her dreams. A few of those times Tom heard her speak Michael's name. They never talked about it, except for the times they visited the Weaver's. Later at home Jeri would make some comment about something that Michael did or how he looked, which as he grew older began to show some resemblance.

"You never said that. Do you think we could?" she replied, hope rising in her voice.

11

Byron Swain's story appeared Thursday morning on the front page of the state and regional section of the St. Paul Journal. The story angle focused on drugs as the likely motive behind the apparent murder of a woman on a farm near Buffalo Ridge, a small town about one-hundred twenty five miles southwest of the metro area. Investigators found no evidence that money or property had been taken; the only thing missing was the victim's husband, Stan Weaver.

Most copies of the big city paper circulating around Buffalo Ridge came from vending machines sitting outside cafes, grocery stores, and gas stations. Thursday morning they had been cleaned out by eight a.m.

Sheriff Hank Schwartz set the paper down on his desk. He just got off the phone with the Buffalo Ridge Area Chamber of Commerce director. He called wanting to know how the investigation was going. He complained about the outside news coverage. They never report on the good things going on. But when there's a murder or something bad happens they come out from the big city and do a big story. It makes people in the city think small towns and rural areas are full of drug-crazed hill-billies.

Hank listened politely, saying there was nothing he could do about that. "It's been on the front page of the Buffalo Ridge Banner for two days now, too," he said.

"I know, I know, but that's our paper," the Chamber director replied. "And besides, it doesn't go all over the state. And the TV news! Did you see Channel 10 last night? They had their chopper flying around taking aerial shots. They made us look like a bunch of idiots. I bet if I called them to come out and do a story on our Dairy Days festival next week they'd laugh and hang up in my face. One year they came out only because we had the governor in the milking contest, but otherwise forget it."

"Why don't you call them? Don't take it out on me," the sheriff replied. "We're doing the best we can. If we can manage the information the news coverage can be helpful in the investigation. Whoever did this could be far away. Maybe the outside news coverage will bring in some tips. Happens all the time."

In this case he was not optimistic, a thought he did not share with the mayor. If what he suspected were true the chances of finding the killer or killers were less than fifty-fifty.

Hank leaned back in his chair staring at the Les Kouba framed print hanging on the wood-paneled wall across from his desk, an idyllic interpretation of a hunting shack among the trees near a slough in November, lighted by a golden setting sun in the background, firelight flickering through the windows, a thin column of smoke whispering up from the chimney toward a dark lattice of bare tree-top branches. Tiny arrows of dark paint against the golden twilight suggested a distant V-shaped formation of geese. He often gazed into the painting when pondering some dilemma or another, or simply seeking escape, hoping to survive into retirement and spending more time hunting, fishing and traveling. Only four more years.

He searched his mind for clues that might lead to possible motives. The thought of any terrorist connection amused him. He grew irritated at the feds running around the countryside and sticking their noses in the case. Dealing with Leuten was bad enough. And the two FBI agents had no reason to be here. Hank had even heard that the Drug Enforcement Agency and IRS were snooping around, although no one had contacted him directly.

It used to be the Communists. Now it was terrorists who were the big bogeymen in the national obsession for some kind of "ist" or another to blame things on. If the county would just take care of the home front first we would be a lot stronger in facing up to any external threats, Hank believed.

The real threats to peace and prosperity could be found in the households wrecked by poverty, lack of education, injustice, and illness—as much mental and emotional than physical. In almost every case that Hank had seen, alcohol and drugs, especially meth, played a major role. It affected so many children. They enter the world so innocent, vulnerable, needing love and nurturing, promising so much potential. Most are lucky enough to be born into reasonably successful families, but too many suffer from neglect or worse, abuse.

After the Weavers took over the Wegman farm the change went from night to day. Over the past eight years they transformed the place from one of the worst cases of rural meth labs he had ever seen into a clean, quaint family farm right out of a Norman Rockwell painting.

Finally, rural counties were beginning to turn the tide against the meth epidemic. Hundreds of small labs mostly in rural areas had been discovered and eradicated. Pharmacists helped by noting suspicious behavior among any customers trying to buy cold pills containing pseudoephedrine.

Unfortunately, the work didn't stop there. Hospitals, jails, the court system, and family social services had to deal with the aftermath. Hank estimated that meth figured into the cases of almost one-third of the prisoners next door in the county jail.

He still had a hard time believing what Leuten claimed, that Tom Otto was using and transporting meth. And even if he did, what connection did that have with the Weavers?

He had sifted through the old case file several times looking for clues. The three men and one woman who had been convicted on drug charges stemming from the meth lab at the old Wegman place had already served their time, but as far as he knew they were not back in the area. The young girl, Jerilyn Meyers, was the only one who had any roots in the area.

THE COUNTY SOCIAL WORKER'S TESTIMONY during Jerilyn Meyers' court hearing, definitely helped her case. It came at a high price in terms of trying to present a respectable image to the community.

Among all the gruesome cases Hank had dealt with in his nearly thirty years as Ames County sheriff, what he saw in Jerry Meyer's garage still flashed before his mind's eye from time to time. Little clumps of bloody tissue and grayish, pudding-like matter splattered on the window and wall behind the chair in which he sat, shoving the shotgun barrel into his mouth.

The official explanation seemed to be sufficient. He had been extremely depressed and suffering from alcoholism.

When Jeri ran off at eighteen with the older men to get caught up in drugs and alcohol, petty thievery, and become pregnant by one of them, only those who knew the nightmare of her middle teen years understood.

IN MOST CASES the sheriff tried to avoid thinking too much about the personal lives of law-breakers and their victims. Most of them deserved what they got, thrashing around in the social and economic garbage pit of the local community. He wanted to believe most could climb out and become respectable citizens if they really tried. If they did, he and his deputies would have a lot less work to do, which some days would seem like a good idea. His faith that growth in proper education and home life would bring improvement to the general population dissipated years ago. There seemed to be a never-ending supply of socio-paths, perverts, and general dirtballs.

The light sentence for Jerilyn Meyers eight years ago at first made him furious. Just because she came from a supposedly good family we shouldn't give her get-out-of-jail card. It always bothered him that there was a different standard of justice for people who had connections in the community.

At least the little boy survived and ended up with a good family. The children they often found in the toxic debris of the meth houses were the real victims. For Jerilyn maybe having to give up her son for adoption was punishment enough.

Everyone rejoiced when Jeri and Tom Otto were married and later became parents. The community connections of the Ottos continued, even growing stronger. The Gospel Tabernacle Church enveloped them in Christian love and support. They had steady jobs and children to support. That's what life was all about once they got past those somewhat turbulent years before emerging into young adults.

Hank hoped that Tom hadn't done anything to derail their seeming success as a family, as productive and law-abiding citizens. His bias caused him to resist Harmon Leuten's badgering to arrest Tom. He deflected the pressure saying that he first wanted to meet with FBI agent George Saunders. He hoped the feds knew something else, something that pointed to a possible motive and suspects from elsewhere. Hank knew that since most of the local labs had been shut down, meth dealers from outside the area were moving in. The crystal meth coming in from industrial-sized yet clandestine labs in Mexico were much more potent and dangerous.

The new players were in a different league, professional in a perverse sort of way, no ambivalence about using violence but only when necessary, and carrying gobs of cash along with their arsenal of handguns and automatic weapons. In recent years it was becoming increasingly difficult to pick them out among the faces and vehicles in the area's changing population.

Still, the circumstantial evidence pointing to Tom could not be ignored, his regular trips to the big city in a truck easily capable of transporting a few pounds of chunky powder concealed in some ingenious manner.

Hank didn't know what to do. He needed to talk things over again with Deputy Tollefson. The young deputy and Tom Otto seemed to be buddies. Similar in age they shared a passion for tearing around the countryside on ATVs or four-by-four pickup trucks. Hank checked the work schedule. Randy was supposed to be on duty this morning at seven. Hank decided he would try to meet with Randy before the FBI agent was scheduled to stop in around nine, after which they all would head back out to the Weaver's.

RANDY SAT DUTIFULLY in the wooden arm chair in front of the sheriff's desk, his elbows on the armrests and hands together on his lap.

Hank went immediately to the point.

"Randy, do you think there's any way Tom Otto is connected with this, other than being first on the scene and calling it in?"

"You mean the meth that Leuten said he found in the truck?"

"I mean more than that. I don't know. For some reason Leuten didn't sound all that convincing. He gives me the creeps anyway. I mean do you think that Tom knows more than we think? You ever have any reason to think that he actually might be involved in, say, transporting the stuff, or maybe has some just for his own use? You guys hang around together sometimes, right? Riding ATVS and stuff. You ever see or notice anything that might be a little bit suspicious?"

The young deputy shifted his elbows back on the armrests and refolded his hands. He sometimes wondered how Tom could seem to have so much energy on some weekday evenings when they took the ATVs or four-by-fours out for a few hours. Jeri was at work, her mom agreed to watch the kids a bit longer, and Tom's day had started before four a.m. Randy never really thought about it, but would have assumed that the energy simply arose from Tom's characteristic enthusiasm for his passions, from off-road riding to his family.

"When we were searching the truck, I never really saw Leuten actually find the stuff, that little plastic egg. I mean, he showed it to me right away but I was on the other side."

"What'd he say when he found it?"

"I don't know. It was like 'just what I thought, our boy Tom is going to get some egg on his face' or something like that," the deputy replied.

"What I'm going to ask next does not leave this room. Understood?"

Randy nodded soberly.

"Do you think he could have already had it and just pulled it out of his pocket?" Hank asked.

"Oh man, that's heavy. I could hardly believe it at first, you know, Tom hauling the stuff. But even I've been around here long enough to not be surprised anymore at all the weird shit that goes on. Why would Leuten do something like that?"

"I'm not saying he did. But I've been around long enough to pay attention to your gut feelings. Why are the feds snooping around? We know the stuff we're seeing now is coming in from the outside. To do that it takes more than a few scumbags cooking the stuff out at some old farm house and selling what they don't use themselves. The stuff coming in from Mexico takes a lot more organization, and it's stronger stuff, too. It all boils down to the law of supply and demand. We get rid of the local supply, so the stuff starts coming from elsewhere. There's always a demand. That's the whole problem. Even among some of our so-called law-abiding citizens. You get enough of them wanting to have a little toot now and then, and you get the demand. This mention of Leuten, you just keep that under your hat, okay?"

"You got it, sheriff." The feeling of importance arising from the sheriff's taking him into confidence helped to assure the deputy's solemn assent.

"We'll see how things go out there today," the sheriff said. "You head out there and get the search party organized. I'll be at the farm after I'm through with the FBI agent here. He wants to look at the past files and see the body. Who the hell knows why? Then I got to decide what to do about Tom."

RANDY LEFT AND HANK refilled his coffee mug before getting back to finishing the news story in the Buffalo Ridge Banner and going through the rest of the paper.

The second day story seemed okay so far. It told more background on the Weavers and came with a front page photo of the search party. The story continued on an inside page along with a photo from the news conference Wednesday. It showed him standing in front of the law enforcement center speaking into a microphone with Harmon Leuten immediately to his left. The photo captured several television cameras from the big city, which were mentioned prominently in the news story. It was also news in the local paper when the big city news media came out to Buffalo Ridge to cover a story.

Hank might have lingered on the photo longer, considering that the low angle and his expression made him look authoritative and even a bit handsome, with the low angle concealing his bald spot.

Instead, his eyes focused instantly on story jump headline on page three: 'Autopsy reveals possible fatal knife wound.'

For someone accustomed to total control over a situation, including any information that became public, Hank's shock flowed into anger. He grabbed for the phone almost knocking over his coffee mug. He caught it just in time, moved it back, and punched the numbers for the county coroner.

The Ames County coroner, a local doctor nearing retirement, long ago had figured out how to avoid much of the medical profession's stress by mentally blocking out any sense of urgency. When someone approached him in such a state he responded to their need immediately if he could, or ignored them if he couldn't.

When the reporter from the Buffalo Ridge Banner called him around nine last evening asking if he could have a copy of the autopsy report, the coroner, who was still at his office, agreed. The reporter rushed over, returning to the newspaper office in time to revise his story by the 10:00 p.m. deadline. Over his protest the editor decided to bury the new information farther down in the story, saying it still could be speculation.

According to the coroner's report, while the shotgun blast probably would have been fatal eventually, in the doctor's opinion Tulip Weaver still could have been alive when rescuers arrived. Probing organs adjacent to the wound the pathologist who the coroner had brought in from a nearby regional hospital found what appeared to be a linear puncture wound in the heart, which he presumed could have been caused by a knife or some other sharp object, stated so in the report.

Hank slammed down the phone. The coroner was making rounds at the hospital.

Hank's call to the newspaper office also went unfulfilled. Working late into the night six nights a week, the reporter and editor at the paper would not be in until ten. Frustrated, Hank decided to not say anything when FBI agent George Saunders arrived soon to review the files unless the agent already had seen it in the paper. Hank hoped that the newspaper had it wrong.

Early on in their professional relationship Hank reminded the young reporter from the Buffalo Ridge Banner of the old adage: Burn me once, shame on you. Burn me twice, shame on me. The paper should have contacted him last evening.

They should have called him. It would have been worse had they called him and published the information anyway. He could understand poor judgment, but the effect of that on their relationship would probably be the same as a loss of trust.

Things had been going fairly well with the Banner. They dutifully published information provided by law enforcement, and sometimes withheld information that might jeopardize an investigation. The latter helped to weed out the crank calls that usually followed news coverage of major crimes. In a few cases unbalanced minds sought some kind of redemption in offering a false confession. More likely, an anonymous caller trying to get revenge on some foe would call with false information.

The sheriff's office had received about a dozen calls so far about the Weaver case. Hank knew which one came from Newton Case, as much by the attempt to disguise the voice as anything else.

The caller he assumed was Newt didn't really offer any information. The muffled voice let loose a diatribe about the group of radical organic farmers moving into the area. "The Weavers deserved what they got. They don't farm like they're supposed to with proper equipment, fertilizer, chemicals and genetically-improved seed. How is America supposed to feed the world, and now supply ethanol for fuel, without the latest techniques and technology? These old hippie so-called farmers raising a few goats, chicken, and vegetables with so-called organic methods so a few rich people in the cities can feel good about their food, it's just not the American way."

Hank listened for a minute and hung up. Long ago he accepted that Newt, if that's who it was, never would let go of his grudge against the sheriff for conducting the foreclosure sale at Newt's farm twenty years ago. Over the years some of Newt's calls actually turned out to be helpful. Hank conceded that he should have listened and responded immediately when Newt told him about the goings on at the Wegman place after old Mrs. Wegman went into the nursing home. None of their children had stayed in the area, so they managed her affairs from a distance, which included renting out the farm house to a succession of tenants, and the eighty acres of cropland to Archie Daniels.

Hank allowed his prejudgment of Newt to interfere with obvious signs of a connection between the new tenants and an increase in break-ins and thefts, particularly from equipment storage sheds and shops at area farms. He later recalled the incident where a young man arrived at the hospital emergency room suffering severe burns and lung damage from anhydrous ammonia, and he didn't look much like a typical farmer. Most of them Hank would have been acquainted with anyway. He could no longer deny the changes occurring, bringing in more outsiders to the area and who knows what. Back in the days of dealing with indigenous crackpots and backwoods tax protesters now sometimes seemed tame compared with drug and meth crowd.

Another caller Tuesday evening who spoke in a low, soft voice, said something like, when they cleaned up the meth lab at the Wegman place eight years ago before the Weavers took over, they didn't get everything, and hung up. Hank had supervised the cleanup and couldn't imagine what they missed. Surely, Stan and Tulie Weaver would have said something.

Hank re-read the news story in the Banner. This time he paid more attention to the actual wording, that the autopsy on Tulie revealed only the possibility of wound to the heart by a knife or sharp object. His initial anger subsided. He would deal with the newspaper and the coroner later.

IT WAS NOW FORTY-EIGHT HOURS since the 911 came into dispatch reporting a possible homicide at the farm of Stan and Tulie Weaver about five miles from Buffalo Ridge. Clues and evidence remained scarce. Several people had reported seeing two vehicles Tuesday morning traveling at a high rate of speed on a gravel township road in the vicinity. They concurred that one vehicle was a pickup truck. Descriptions of the other vehicle varied from a light-colored van to a silver SUV. The pickup could have been Stan Weaver's. When officers arrived at the farm it was sitting in its usual spot under the lean-to next to the garage.

He believed the statements of Tom Otto. Nothing in his intuition from long experience with people in stressful situations told him otherwise. If only they could elicit some testimony from the boy, Michael Weaver. As far as Hank knew the boy had not spoken a word now for two days.

12

The battery indicator on Tom's cell phone showed a weak charge, so he asked to use the Hamilton's phone. He needed to call the customers who would not be getting their deliveries Thursday afternoon.

His route for the day ended at the Hamilton's when Ron popped open a couple of home-made brews when Jeri arrived. He hoped to make up the difference Friday, although the way things were going his doubt increased with each revelation of what might come next.

Calling the customers took some of the burden off his thoughts. They had no problem waiting until Friday. Several sounded sympathetic asking how he was doing and if he had heard anything new about the Weavers. They knew only what had appeared in news stories.

The additional deliveries would make Friday a long day, with the only doubt being the possibility that something related to the investigation would intervene, even to the point of preventing his usual routine altogether. At least the way it looked now, the memorial service for Tulie would be Saturday and not Friday.

The white powder in the salt shaker in his lunchbox had been no more than an afterthought, a bump in the road, until now.

The food and a few more glasses of Tulie's wine gradually mellowed the questions and uncertainty of the moment. A sweet breeze riffled through the leaves of the red maple shading the Hamilton's deck. They sat back in the wooden chairs so artfully crafted by the skilled hands of Stan Weaver, soaking in the peaceful, mild summer evening.

Jeri returned from making a call to check in with Lynn and the kids. Her mother wanted to know more about why she was not at work. She backed off when Jeri explained where they were and what they were doing, although the subject of planning a memorial service so far had remained unspoken. Under normal circumstances Lynn disagreed whenever her daughter used sick leave for other purposes. This time it was different.

"The funeral home called again. They were wondering about when we were going to have the memorial service," Wendy said.

"I still don't know why it's up to us," Ron said. "Why do they care? They don't even have the body yet."

"Sooner or later they will. They're still trying to locate relatives. Tulie doesn't have any that we know of. Stan might somewhere but he never said anything. I guess we're it, for now anyway. They need somebody to pick up the tab."

"Well it's just a memorial service, right? I mean, they're going to keep the body for awhile so it's not going to be a funeral and burial."

"We could see about having it at our church," Tom said.

"That would be nice," Ron replied. Wendy looked at him trying to interpret the response between automatic and sincere. They believed the sincerity of Tom's offer, which made it more difficult to decline and offer another alternative although they didn't really have any.

THE HAMILTONS WERE MEMBERS of a small congregation of people around Buffalo Ridge who generally accepted the notion of some kind of supreme being, mostly because science can't explain all the phenomena in the universe. A high correlation existed between their mailboxes and a handful of subscriptions to The New Republic or the Utne Reader sorted through the Buffalo Ridge Post Office.

Once a month except during summer they presented programs at 5:00 p.m. on Saturdays. Guest speakers gave talks on social, economic, and political topics. Invited by the Weavers, the Ottos attended once to hear a professor from the university talk about child labor in third world countries, which enables large corporations to get rich while still offering consumers low-priced products.

On the drive home, comparing it with the Gospel Tabernacle Church, the Ottos concurred how they felt awkward, sitting in pews in a building that resembled a church, without any acknowledgement of the rituals, beliefs, and sacraments of Christianity. There had been an invocation at the end offered by Ron using short excerpts from the writings of Erasmus of Rotterdam. He prefaced the first saying that it related to the program's topic:

THE VAST MACHINE THAT IS THE EARTH WAS CREATED TO SERVE YOUR ENDS. HOW NARROW-MINDED AND UNTHINKING NOT TO USE IT AS A MEANS BUT TO BE ENTRANCED WITH IT AS AN END.

The second excerpt came closer to some acknowledgement of God:

IT HAS NOW BEEN SUFFICIENTLY DEMONSTRATED THAT WHATEVER WE ARE AND WHATEVER GOOD WE POSSESS IS ALL DUE TO THE DIVINE MERCY. THIS IS WHY WE ARE PROTECTED FROM MENACING EVILS, SAVED FROM OPPRESSORS, MADE BRAVE AND CHEERFUL DURING ILLNESS, GUIDED TO REPENTANCE, TRAINED IN PERFECT VIRTUE, AND FORGIVEN OUR FREQUENT OFFENSES.

The mystery of the sixteenth-century philosopher, the restrained reference to God, and absence of an "Amen" at the close left the Ottos mildly bewildered.

The Hamiltons' perception of the Gospel Tabernacle Church in Buffalo Ridge derived mostly from conventional knowledge based on stereotypes prevalent among the intellectual elite and reinforced while flipping through cable channels showing occasional glimpses of sweating, gesturing television evangelists preaching vehemently in Carolina accents under the glare of studio lighting.

"That's nice of you to offer," Ron said. "Would there be enough time? Maybe it would be easier at the funeral home. Maybe we could use our church. All we would have to do is unlock the door and turn on the lights."

"Who would conduct the service?" Jeri asked. "I think our pastor at the Gospel Tabernacle would do it. That would be okay wouldn't it?" Jeri looked at Tom.

"Why not? At least we could ask."

Wendy saw the opening.

"They didn't really attend any church you know," she said with a hint of embarrassment. "Don't you think that might be a little awkward? Don't you have to be a member of your church for something like that?"

"It's kind of late now," Jeri joked.

"Maybe we should stick with having it at the funeral home," Ron said. "It's not the same as a church I suppose. It might be easier for some of the people who would be attending."

Jeri shot Tom a searching look. Didn't he understand the opportunity of the moment? What an opportunity to witness for Christ? If the Weavers weren't born again at least they might have been part of God's plan to reach others in their community.

Her conscience suffered watching Michael grow up outside the church. Every day she prayed for his salvation. Now she felt guilty thinking that the Weavers' misfortune might bring him back. She could understand that a parent might make such a sacrifice, but she never could fully accept that the Weavers were his parents even though his behavior indicated that to him they were. Accustomed to seeing an event or situation in the possibility that it may be part of God's plan, she understood, and even more, hoped.

"Can we at least ask?" Tom replied. "Everyone would be welcome."

Ron offered a compromise that seemed to blunt the edge of tension seeping in and threatening to sour the mellowing effects of the wine and beer. They would enquire with their respective groups and hope that a relative could be found, and if not, request that the county social services decide a course that would be best for the children.

WENDY RETURNED FROM THE KITCHEN with another bottle of Tulie's wine, which emptied into four glasses even though Tom normally didn't care for it. They listened to Ron describe the morning doing chores with Archie Daniels at the Weaver farm. Ron had offered to join the search party looking for Stan, but the sheriff said helping with the chores was plenty enough. Ron still felt a bit like he should help even though doing the chores provided enough to ease his conscience, which also grappled with ambivalence arising from the image in his mind of tramping through tall grass along some ditch bank and stumbling over Stan's body. He didn't know which would be worse, that, or finding out later that Stan had something to do with Tulie's murder and took off. Even the mention of that possibility angered him when investigators, mostly Harmon Leuten, grilled him and Archie that morning sitting in the Weaver's kitchen.

"I still can't believe it, them thinking that Stan may have done it and took off," Ron said shaking his head slowly. "It just doesn't make sense. They don't know the Weavers like we do. You'd think we would have noticed something.

"They even questioned me and Archie like we were suspects. We come in from doing chores this morning and that's the kind of thanks we get. I can understand how you felt talking with that Leuten and your boss," Ron acknowledged to Jeri.

"You got that right.," Jeri said.

"This is serious," Ron said. "A law enforcement investigator claims he finds meth in your truck. No one else actually sees him find it. What did you say? One of the deputies was helping him search but didn't see it until the agent shows it later outside?"

"That's what Randy said, the deputy. He didn't see Leuten actually find it."

"Right now it's your word against his. I think you should get a lawyer right away. And as far as they're concerned you still might be a suspect although I don't see that continuing. Still, you should get a lawyer. If you need some money we'll help out."

Wendy sat with her elbows on the table and hands covering her face. She was crying.

"I'm sorry. It's just starting to really hit me. I miss her so much. Not knowing about Stan is even worse."

Ron reached over and massaged the back of his wife's neck. "I know. We all do. We'll just have to get through this."

"I was just thinking about the fair," Wendy said. "Tulie was the main force behind that. Even if we keep it going it won't be the same without her."

"We will," Ron said trying to sound confident and reassuring. Like Tulie, Stan provided the kind of quiet, stable leadership that made things happen without anyone realizing how it all happened.

IN THE EVENING OF THE LAST NIGHT of the 1998 edition of the fair Stan and Tulie sat on a bench outside the poultry barn watching the people, the carnies bantering with kids waiting in line for rides, teenage boys and girls clustering in courtship rituals, the muffled, phony carillon music of the merry-go-round filtering through the brash undercurrent of noise rumbling from the generator truck, and the glaring rainbow colors of neon lights dissolving into the deep purple evening sky.

At 10:00 p.m. they would begin packing up the display in their booth in the commercial exhibits building. They would have preferred to have had their display in the poultry barn. The county public health inspector denied their request to display and sell natural and organic foods in a livestock barn.

"I'm tired," Stan said. "I think it went well. What do you think?"

"We were busy, that's for sure," Tulie replied. "Ask me how well it went after I balance the books."

"Well I know we didn't lose money."

"Right, but what about our time? That's money, too."

"It's also an investment, in marketing. The more we get people around here to know about our products, the better chance we have of increasing sales. You know what they say, marketing is getting the ducks to land, sales is shooting the ducks."

"Where did you hear that?"

"Pretty folksy, huh? This old guy at the newspaper. Been selling ads since Gutenberg. I think he knows more about sales and marketing than I ever did, me the big shot corporate marketing executive."

"Well you get the ducks to land and I'll shoot 'em," Tulie said.

"We're a helluva team," Stan grinned, reaching his arm around her shoulders and drawing her close.

"This is kind of romantic," Tulie said.

"Really? That was easy."

"No, I mean the whole scene here. It's such a beautiful evening. All these kids running around intoxicated by hormones and pheromones. It's like there's some electricity in the air."

"Oh. Sorry. So it's not me then." Stan feigned a pout.

"Oh come on. You know better," Tulie chided. "I'm just feeling a little wistful I guess. I see all these kids here, they look so, I don't know, they look so happy, excited, innocent, full of life. I know, I know. That sounds really corny. I just never got to experience that growing up, a normal family life, whatever that is."

"I think 'normal' really should be defined as a 'median'," Stan said. "If 'normal' is the median, then most people fall someplace on either side, so in reality very few people grow up in a normal family. But we go through life acutely aware of our own problems and thinking everyone else is normal. It just isn't true. Look at those kids over there. I bet if you could see into every home situation you'd find all kinds of weird stuff."

"That's encouraging. So much for my romantic reverie."

"Sorry. I'm just trying to say you don't have to feel disadvantaged for growing up the way you did. You had a lot of positive experiences, too. Things these kids may never learn. You learned the hard way, but I think it's paying off."

"Okay. That makes me feel better." Tulie leaned over and left a soft kiss on Stan's cheek, just above his close-cropped beard beginning to show flecks of gray. Woven in the dark hair around his temples the graying filaments made him look distinguished, which helped immensely when they sought a mortgage at the bank in Buffalo Ridge to cover the remainder of the Wegman farm purchase price above what he had left from his sizeable severance package. After a merger left him at forty-two fighting for his job, he finally gave up and took the buy-out. His pals thought he was crazy to hook up with the much younger waitress they had flirted with on one of their hunting trips, but Stan saw something different right from the start. He looked her up and launched the new relationship even before leaving his wife and home, with a divorce not far behind.

"Sometimes I wish that there had been somebody around when I was growing up who cared once in awhile," Tulie mused. "At least I can make sure that our kids know that they're loved. Sometimes I worry that they're sheltered too much on the farm. Maybe I'm being overprotective."

"I don't think so," Stan said. "I think we're teaching them lessons that will help them cope better than most. I think your home-schooling idea is great. You'll be the best teacher they could ever have and not just because you're their mother. You've seen and experienced a lot more about life than most people."

"I suppose. If you say so. I hope the kids behaved themselves at the Hamiltons."

When Ron and Wendy hesitated upon hearing Tulie's idea for a booth at the county fair with food displays and samples from the organic and natural food producers, Tulie asked if they would at least let them stock some of the Hamilton's goat cheese and other produce. The Weaver's would handle all the arrangements, and if it were successful, perhaps the HOPE members would participate next year. The Hamilton's also offered to baby sit Michael and little Anna.

"I hope we made some money on this venture," Stan said. "I doubt most of these people around here will ever pay more for organically-produced food."

"We have to at least try. Wouldn't that be fantastic if we could sell more locally and not have to ship it all to the city? We still have to get somebody to haul it there on a regular basis. It's just not working out with you and Ron and the others to take turns."

"We'll find somebody. I'm going to put an ad in the paper after this is over and really get going on that," Stan said. "It's actually kind of ironic."

"What?"

"All these people in the country eating the mass-produced, processed food shipped in from who-knows-where. Their ancestors who settled here probably would gag on the stuff we have now. It's so bland and limpid. People today look at brown-shelled eggs like they're some kind of mutation. The pioneers ate fresh produce grown right on their farms. It wasn't pumped full of chemicals. It's just so stupid. You buy a package of cookies in the grocery store and look at the label. It's made half way across the country and then shipped all over. If we made all that stuff here it would provide more jobs, save on fuel, and be a lot more fresh."

"That's society's failure," Stan said, gazing pensively at the carnival midway scene.

"What?"

"The social order. The political and economic system. We've allowed corporations to dominate everything from government, education, health care, and agriculture. We're just little ants working and consuming."

Tulie listened without paying much attention, having heard Stan's speech many times. She believed, too, but at the moment still savored the perfect summer evening surrounded by the warmth and sense of belonging in a community.

"A lot of ants have a stake in all that you know," she said. "Stocks and mutual funds, pension plans. Some of the same people who complain about low wages, cheap labor, and the widening income gap are the ones benefiting from the corporate growth and profits."

"Well, I sold all my stock. Now it's all in the farm."

"And you did pretty well, too. Somebody might say it looked an awful lot like insider trading the way you sold the stock in your company before it tanked."

"It dropped because I left," Stan laughed.

"Yeah, right." Tulie leaned over and rested her head on his shoulder. "It's been going good here though. I'm glad we made the move. At first I was a little apprehensive about taking Michael. Now I can't imagine being without him. Little Anna has a ready-made big brother."

"Time will tell. How it works out. Remember, they said it affected his early development, his physical development."

"I think he's recovered a lot."

"I agree. And the scars seem to have become less noticeable. It's just his emotional and behavioral development that worries me sometimes. Irritable. Short attention span. It's one thing with a toddler. It's something else when they're teenagers."

"You sound like a pessimist."

"Just being realistic."

"How'd we get talking about this anyway?"

"You started it."

"Well I think it's going to be okay," Tulie said. "I think it changed a lot for the better when Anna was born. He just loves her so much. He tries to be so helpful. And he's not bossy with her like some older siblings. The age difference helps."

"At first I was a little concerned that his birth mother would have major regrets," Stan said. "I worried that she would start hanging around. That still could happen. That could get complicated."

"She just had a baby not too long ago, a little girl. I saw it in the paper. She married some local kid."

"That's good," Stan said. "I hope they're happy."

"I didn't tell you this, but they called the other day wondering if it would be okay if she could visit Michael occasionally."

"Who called?"

"The county. Family services."

"What do you think?"

"I'm not sure. I'm kind of leaning that way," Tulie said. "I feel sorry for him in a way. You know how I was raised. Out there in that so-called commune sometimes I didn't know for sure who my mother or father were. They were so spaced out half the time."

"You know as well as I do there can be consequences to letting our emotions sway decisions. We could be opening a can of worms if we agree to letting her visit Michael."

"You make it sound like all emotions are bad."

"Aren't you worried that we might lose him? That he might want to stay with her?"

"Of course not. I don't think he even remembers her. There's nothing legal she could do. We're not just foster parents you know."

"What a mess."

"What?"

"All this happening because of people getting trapped and destroyed by meth and other drugs," Stan mused. "So much pain and tragedy. So much effort to repair the damage. I guess it's okay with me. If you want we can let her have visits. If you feel secure about it. Maybe it will be a good thing in the long run. Family, relationships, that's what life is really all about anyway, right?"

Other vendors had already started dismantling their displays in the county fair exposition building when Stan and Tulie returned. A few cheese samples remained on the tray at their booth. Stan ate them. They packed up and left for the farm, their thoughts racing with ideas for improving the display next year and recruiting other HOPE members to participate. The kids fell back to sleep almost immediately after being picked up from the Hamilton's. Tulie decided that she would call family services in the morning and agree to allowing Jerilyn Otto visit Michael. She looked forward to having guests at the farm, which almost always was a special and rewarding occasion.

Jeri leaned her head back on the chair and gazed blankly at the leaves screening out a clear view of the pale blue, early evening sky. Savoring the feast of colors and textures offered by nature at a time of day that normally placed her on the line at the processing plant. In a little while her co-workers would be taking their second break, which came between the six-thirty lunch break and 11:00 p.m. quitting time.

Under the circumstances she did not feel guilty taking the day off. Every other summer evening during the work week at the second break she felt imprisoned inside the plant and thinking about home where Jade and Trace were getting ready for bed, Tom reading them a story, and nighthawks swooping and screeching across the summer twilight.

"You kids okay to drive home?" Wendy asked. "You could stay here. We've got plenty of room."

"Oh jeez, no, we got to get going," Tom said. "We'll be fine." Jeri looked forward to getting home in time to read a story to the kids at bedtime.

They thanked the Hamiltons for their food and hospitality. Jeri led the way in the Crown Vic and Tom followed in the truck down the driveway.

13

Spending most of a warm afternoon at the municipal swimming pool in Buffalo Ridge burned more than a normal day's worth of energy for Jade and Trace Otto. Even with the setting sun extending daylight late into the mid-June evening the children easily could have fallen asleep, and would have until grandma Lynn told them that mommy and daddy soon would be home.

"Mommy here!"

With grandma busy helping Jade get out of the tub and into her jammies, and no one near to prevent him, Trace dragged a chair from the kitchen table over to the counter. Sitting on the edge of the sink with his feet over the drain he could see out the window and down the driveway. "Mommy here! Daddy home!" he shouted, laughing and pounding his pudgy hands together.

Jeri hurried into the house, hoping the kids were still awake. Hugs and kisses, a bedtime snack, and two stories brought a good measure of peace and contentment to the end of a troubling day.

Lynn had zeroed in on the speculation reported in the Buffalo Ridge Banner that drugs provided the motive for the murder of Tulie Weaver and disappearance of Stan. Meth in particular. Something had to account for what had happened to her own family and for her it was illegal drug use and abuse. Every morning she still awoke to the nightmare that crashed in on their lives a decade ago. She prayed every day for her daughter's recovery. She cursed the devil and all his wicked tools.

She could not shake the thought that Stan may have had something to do with it. How else could they buy the Wegman place, fix it up, and seem to make a good living off eighty acres? Others farming eight hundred acres still needed another job to make ends meet. Stan and Tulie coming into the area from nowhere with little known about their background, what were they hiding? She couldn't completely erase the thought that they still manufactured meth or distributed a supply brought in from elsewhere.

"I just don't get why people have to use that stuff," Lynn said. "It just ruins their lives. They end up in jail or in the hospital and we get stuck with the bill."

"I don't get it, either," Tom said, his agreement true although not accompanied by a feeling of strong conviction, and wondering if she sensed it.

"It's a plague on the land. God is punishing us for the sinful ways of the world today," Lynn said, with a grim, slightly sorrowful expression in her face.

Tom didn't quite see how someone using meth was God's doing. He recalled hearing something similar in one of Pastor Gabe's sermons not too long ago at the

Gospel Tabernacle Church. Drug and alcohol abuse were modern day plagues sent by God to punish a sinful world and bring people back to Him. Tom believed drug abuse was something some people did on their own. If anything, it was more Satan's fault. It may have been a poor decision when Tom accepted the couple grams of crystal meth at the warehouse. Now he felt embarrassed for caving into the peer pressure and threats. What's done is done. As far as the revelation had progressed with the meth allegation from Harmon Leuten, he was beginning to accept the possible consequences.

Jeri entered the kitchen overhearing the conversation. Although very outspoken in public about the evils of meth and other drug abuse, she usually tried to avoid talking about it at home, especially around her mother.

"I wish I could do that every night," she said. "Sometimes when I'm at work and think about them getting ready for bed I get so jealous of you guys." Any response would have been awkward and pointless so she did not wait for one.

"What makes you think the Weavers were cooking and dealing?" she asked looking at Lynn. "Tom's there a couple times a week. Me and the kids have been out there. If they were doing anything we'd sure know."

"Well I can't think of anything else why that would have happened," Lynn scowled. "The paper said it wasn't robbery or anything like that. What if those guys are back? What if it was them?"

"What for? They're long gone. I hope they're long gone." Jeri grasped for something to avoid triggering an avalanche of sorrow and regret. Helpless against it in recurring dreams, she did not want the memories spoiling her days. She looked at Tom, tensing about what she felt compelled to reveal.

"You should tell her. It's better coming from us than reading it in the paper."

Tom slumped back in his chair, turning the bottle in his hands and staring at the label. His uncertainty about what her response to the meth allegation might be far exceeded Lynn's annoyance of the beer, which she ranked highly among Satan's many weapons.

"It's bogus. You have to believe me on that." He looked at Lynn. "Yesterday they searched my truck. They said they found some meth. I know it was planted or carried in there by that investigator."

"What?" Furrows across her brow deepened, her eyes and face turned rigid.

"They searched his truck," Jeri repeated. "They said they found a little plastic egg with meth in it. They showed it to me in Clymer's office today."

Lynn paused while the revelation settled in. "Why would they do something like that?"

"Who knows?" Jeri replied.

Tom sat quietly still turning the beer bottle in his hands and staring at the label. He felt the urge to get another one. At least her initial reaction indicated that she believed them.

"That's terrible. What are you going to do?" Lynn asked.

"Ron says we should get a lawyer," Jeri said. "Those calls that we got, maybe they're right," she looked at Tom who still sat quietly.

"What calls?" Lynn asked.

"The last two nights we got these anonymous calls. The voice was disguised. They said we should be careful about the investigation."

"You should have told me."

"It didn't feel threatening. It seemed sincere like they really wanted to help. Not like some of those other prank calls we've gotten."

"Why didn't you tell me? Did you tell the sheriff?"

"Not yet."

"Why not? You should have told the sheriff right away."

"We will. We will. Don't worry about it."

"I'm not worried about it. I just think you should have told him right away."

"I'll talk to Hank about it tomorrow," Tom said.

IF IT DIDN'T COMPLETELY ELIMINATE Lynn's concerns, Tom's statement sufficed to end the interrogation. By now she had to admit that on balance her son-in-law was turning out okay. When she first met him eight years ago her initial reaction only saw the outward appearances, the insolent slouch, the t-shirt with in-your-face slogans, the loud pickup truck, the mullet hairstyle all permeated with sour cigarette odor. At least he had a job although it was far from the professional career that she had envisioned for the future husband of her daughter as she was growing up.

Moving to Buffalo Ridge from the even smaller town where he was born and raised, Tom Otto initially spent his work days in the shipping and receiving department of a small metal fabricating company. If his educational and career ambitions didn't quite meet the standards of Lynn Meyers, she at least sensed that the young man was stable, hard-working, ambitious in his own way, and really cared about her daughter. After what they had been through, Lynn could not imagine how she could cope with any more strife and the pain that it caused. At least after they were married they would not be running off to the big city, and she still could keep them under close scrutiny in Buffalo Ridge. The two grandchildren and her role in caring for them had become a blessing greater than she had ever imagined possible. The busy days with visits to the park and municipal swimming pool, afternoon snacks, and reading stories blotted out memories of their past nightmare, most of the time.

She became most unsettled about the monetary behavior of the young couple. When Tom decided to build the big shop, her opposition was ignored. Whenever their cash flow dried up she commented pointedly about all the expensive tools in the shop, the four-wheeler, and especially the big Ford F-350 four-by-four pickup. She had believed that the mobile home in which they lived would only be temporary. "What do you think is going to happen?" Lynn asked.

"I'm innocent. It wasn't my stuff. They can't arrest you for something you didn't do."

"What do you mean it wasn't your stuff?"

Tom felt his face flush. He strained to keep it from affecting the tone of his voice.

"I just meant they must have put it in the truck without me knowing about it. I'm sure it was that Leuten. Randy Tollefson was in there too when they searched the truck. He looked at me like something weird was going on. He doesn't think it was in there. That's what he told me but don't tell anybody this because he'd be in big trouble for talking about it."

"Well I'm going to talk to the sheriff and find out what's going on," Lynn said, tersely trying to suppress the fear of resurrecting the tribulation of the past. They had not talked in recent years, but she knew that she could walk into his office and pick up where they left off.

"Mom, don't do that," Jeri pleaded. "Let's just get a lawyer first."

"And who's got the money to pay for that? Do you know how much they cost?"

"Ron Hamilton said they would help if we needed it," Tom said quietly still staring at the beer bottle in his hands.

"Well at least I'm going to talk to pastor," Lynn said. "I think I should call him right now. We should pray right now, too. I've been praying all along."

"Me too," Jeri said. "If you call him ask if we could have a memorial service for Tulie."

THE REVEREND GABRIEL EVANS led the small flock of the Gospel Tabernacle Church in Buffalo Ridge with the engaging personality of a politician and theology of abundant grace for the born again, more than enough to overcome the daily onslaughts of Satan. The rescue and salvation of Jeri Otto ranked among the highest of his accomplishments. He accompanied her many times on her speaking engagements at churches and schools in the area about the evils of meth and how God saved her and brought her back to abundant life. Her recent involvement in the union organizing effort at the Prairie Pride plant had been generating some concern in the congregation, and he prayed privately that God's will would lead toward some other less confrontational resolution. Gabe graciously accepted her husband as a work-in-progress.

After hearing Jeri's complete story, Gabe's real concern focused on Michael Weaver. How could God allow her first-born to be taken away and raised in a household that did not attend church or show any evidence of being born again Christians? He wept along with Jeri when she sat in his study gushing the whole story about her years as a young meth addict out at the old Wegman farm. She left the office spent and resigned to the hope that with God everything would eventually work out.

Lynn's phone call to the Evans' residence went to the answering machine: "Hi. Pastor Gabe and Tami aren't home right now. Please leave a message and God bless." Every time she heard Tami's chirpy voice Lynn wondered how the young mother of five children could always seem so upbeat and cheerful. How she maintained a trim figure must have been a miracle. At least her auburn hair in a meticulous, shiny bouffant could be explained by frequent visits to Haley's Hair Harbor in downtown Buffalo Ridge. Gabe matched her style with crisp shirts, dark blue suits and swept-back light brown walnut-colored hair, all glistening and shiny, suits included. Lynn and Jeri decided they would visit Pastor Gabe Friday morning. Tom said 'good night' and headed off for bed. He looked in on Jade and Trace sleeping soundly, peacefully.

WHEN HE TALKED TO GOD, which he tried to do on a regular basis, it required a conscious effort of faith. Pastor Gabe's sermons made it seem like an easy thing to do, and if it wasn't easy then it was your fault somehow. And with the little bit of meth in the salt shaker in his lunchbox it became even more difficult. Knowing that it was there how could God even listen to him? When the other driver offered it to him he accepted it unthinking. He then ignored it and tried to forget about it. Not until now did he realize that it planted an evil seed that suddenly grew out of control and soon would blossom into some sinister, powerful force that would destroy the life they had been building.

The other meth or whatever was in the plastic egg that agent Leuten revealed only made Tom angry. Angry and bewildered like the look on Randy Tollefson's face when the sheriff's deputy and Leuten emerged from searching the truck. Angry that it was such a lie and that he was helpless against it.

Although tired well beyond the point of the ordinary yet considerable stamina of a young man, Tom felt anxious about going to bed, because even if he could drop off to sleep, the nightmare would roar back at his first conscious moment early in the morning. With all the extra deliveries and the uncertainty of consequences from the meth allegation he did not look forward to Friday as he usually did.

He turned on the small television in the bedroom to catch what remained of the ten p.m. news. He already had a good idea about the weather forecast. The cooler and drier air would continue for another day or so after the big thunderstorm yesterday morning. With the broadcast still in a news segment the lead-in to the next story made Tom stop and listen.

The newscaster tried to sound more serious switching from a fluff story about offbeat Father's Day gift ideas to a follow-up on the continuing search for the missing farmer near the small town of Buffalo Ridge and the investigation into the apparent homicide of his wife. Authorities said they have questioned "a person of interest."

Tom looked back toward the kitchen where the television on the counter showed the same newscast. Jeri and Lynn had stopped talking to watch and listen.

"Tom, come in here and listen to this." Jeri spoke loudly in an urgent voice. "They're talking about the Weavers. Did you hear that? About the person of interest?"

He returned to the kitchen.

"Who do you suppose that could be?" Lynn asked when the broadcast switched to an ad automatically elevating the volume in the process.

"I'll give you one guess," Jeri replied with a small bit of faux sarcasm in her voice. Looking at Tom her face showed sympathy. "Where are you going?"

Tom had paused to watch, then walked toward the door. "I can't sleep. I'm going out for awhile."

"What for? Where are you going?" Jeri rose from her chair and followed him, concerned. "Don't you have a lot of extra deliveries tomorrow? It's going to be a big day."

"No kidding. I'll be back soon. I'm just going to go for a little ride." He went out the door toward the shop, quickly trying to break free from the gravitational pull of Jeri's questioning.

"Where's he going?" Lynn asked.

"I don't know." Jeri looked back toward her mother sitting at the table, then at Tom walking across the yard, not sure what she should do. "He's got to get some sleep."

The big, eight-cylinder engine in the red four-by-four pickup rumbled backing out of the shop, its decibels drowning out the chirping of crickets and frogs, normally the only sounds in the late summer night.

"Is he going somewhere?" Lynn said rising from the table and looking out the window above the sink. "Why is he going now? Maybe you should follow him?"

"What good would that do? That would just make him mad. He does this sometimes. Sometimes he just has to go out and drive around. I don't know why. He drives around all day anyway. He'll be back soon. I just hope he can get some sleep for tomorrow."

Lynn's face took on a worried look. "That can't be him that they're talking about, can it? What does 'a person of interest' mean anyway? You don't think they think he's a suspect? That's ridiculous. He should be a hero, finding them and calling the sheriff and helping take care of the kids. Whoever did it certainly wouldn't hang around like that."

"I don't think they think he did it. Maybe they just think he knows something about it. I can't even imagine what. I think that state agent is up to something, that's what I think. You saw him when he came over to question Tom again on Tuesday night. Didn't he seem kind of creepy to you?"

"I don't know. I thought he seemed nice. He was real nice to the kids."

"That creeps me even more. Were you there when he questioned Tom? If it was like when they questioned me again at the plant today you probably would've tried to strangle him."

"No, I guess not. I took the kids outside when they were talking. Sheriff Schwartz was there, too."

They returned to the kitchen table. Jeri buried her face in her hands trying to conceal the tears squeezing from her clenched eyelids. Lynn reached across and held her shoulder.

"Don't worry, hon. Everything's going to be okay. I'm really sorry about Tulie. And Stan, too. We'll just have to pray real hard. You know everything is part of God's plan."

"So murder and drugs and all this bad stuff is part of God's plan?" Jeri said sourly.

"You know what I mean. You know, like pastor Gabe says, the devil is powerful, too. There's always been a war between good and evil. God will win in the end. But in the meantime we have to fight evil, in the world and in ourselves."

"But what about disease and accidents and all that stuff? What about tornadoes and hurricanes that kill people?"

"That's the old question 'why do bad things happen to good people?' Why does God let things like that happen? Like Gabe says, we can think of all those things as being a part of evil. Sure, God created a perfect world. The devil messed it up and a lot of that done by humans. The only thing we can count on is that God will help us when these bad things happen. He sure helped us get through all the things we've been through. Maybe some good will come out of this."

"How can you even say that? Look what's happened. If something good does happen it's a big price to pay."

"I used to think that, too. We always focus on the negative, the bad things. If we put our energies into our strengths and finding solutions we'll be a lot better off."

"That sounds like one of Gabe's sermons again. Sometimes all this goody-goody feel-good stuff gets to be a little much."

"That doesn't sound like you. You pretty much say the same thing he does in your talks to high school kids. God knows we don't have to look too hard to find problems. No matter how careful we try to be they find us. So much of the time we run around looking for problems—mostly in other people. When we see them in others we use them against the other person. It's a sure-fire way to keep up the supply of problems, just like the devil wants. I know we get criticized for all this Pollyanna stuff, and like if you have problems you're not being a good Christian. But it's not really like that. We try to focus on solutions and we rely on God to help us. It's not all that complicated."

"I suppose. It's so easy to dredge up the past but sometimes you just can't help it. I feel guilty even saying this because of Tulie and Stan, but I can't stop thinking about Michael. What's going to happen with him and Anna and Jonathan?" Jeri asked.

"That the first thing I thought about, too."

"I wish Tom would come back. It really bothers me when he does that. Just takes off when he gets mad or upset." Jeri could feel the emptiness coming on like it did in the years following her decision—not entirely hers—to allow Michael's legal adoption by the Weavers.

AFTER STARTING A NEW FAMILY with Tom the void filled with Jade and Trace, building a home, working at the plant, public speaking, and her recent efforts with the union at the Prairie Pride chicken processing plant in Buffalo Ridge. Over time she adjusted to the reality that Michael would grow up if not a stranger, a remote acquaintance a generation apart as far as he was concerned. On their occasional visits with the Weavers she secretly longed for any sign of connection or affection. He had her dark blue eyes and high cheekbones, but his hair was dark brown, and cut short looked like a round brush. Since Tuesday she could not stop thinking about where he would go if something bad happened to Stan, which by now seemed likely.

"I'm sure Tom will be okay," Lynn tried to sound reassuring. "He's been under a lot of pressure, too." She pushed aside memories of Tom's earlier years when he would return home at two or three in the morning, intoxicated but not overly so, and very infrequently. Once engaged to Jeri and both of them engaged by Pastor Gabe's marriage counseling, Tom seemed to mature sufficiently to act like a responsible adult in a healthy relationship and caring for a family, despite his continued stubborn attachment to outward appearances and artifacts of a rebellious young man.

"I just hope he doesn't do something stupid," Jeri said, wiping her nose with a tissue. "You know him."

"You want me to stay for awhile?" Lynn asked.

"No. I'll be fine. He'll come back before too long. He knows he's got a long day tomorrow. We'll be okay. I just can't wait for the weekend. I hope they find Stan. I really do. They were such nice people. I guess that's partly why I could get over everything about Michael. They really loved him. He's probably had it so much better growing up there on the farm, especially one like theirs. I guess I should be glad about that, that he's had such a good life there."

Lynn said good-bye. Jeri watched the Buick pull out on to the county road. She looked in both directions hoping to see another pair of headlights approaching. She looked in on the sleeping kids, then switched the television to the Travel Channel and flopped on the couch.

14

THE BROCK HOME SAT ON A CORNER LOT two blocks from the Buffalo Ridge business district. The backyard sloped down to a small stream about twenty feet wide at normal flow that meandered right through town, although mostly invisible from the streets screened by shrubs and trees. Motorists crossed the necessary bridges rarely looking to either side, oblivious to the flowing water below.

Despite his preference for Chicago, Jon Brock agreed to the move after much persuasion from Amber. She had always wanted to be closer to her parents and siblings. After settling in, Jon discovered that practicing law in a small Midwest town could be very rewarding in ways other than financial stability. On most days he walked to the office that he and his partner shared in a space carved out from the old movie theater.

Initially, Jon's and the landlord's perceptions of the rental rate diverged immensely. Coming from Chicago Jon could hardly believe the five-hundred-dollar-a-month rent, not much more than what had been his average hourly rate for corporate clients. The building owner suppressed his glee when the city slicker lawyer accepted the offer without hesitation. Although Jon knew that his income would be less than in Chicago, the reality took some adjusting to. In time, when he learned what other tenants were paying he found other reasons to appreciate the value of his side of the deal, such as the short walk across the street to the courthouse.

At first Jon resisted, then relented, realizing that the extra money would be needed. Amber's work in the county's foster care program would make a significant contribution to the family income. After adding and subtracting all the numbers Amber realized that what the county paid for foster care fell short of actual expenses, at least to which the Brock's were accustomed. The county paid $356 a month per child in foster care. Actual and in-kind costs almost always exceeded. Unless it became an issue, she decided to keep the information to herself. It was an important job. Too often, children in foster care bounced from one family to the next, compounding their problems. The Brocks would not allow that to happen. She became determined to make it work by reducing household waste and judicious spending.

Even if he detected the actual impact on the family budget, Jon instead expressed concern about any influence on their own children from young intruders who might exhibit improper or even dangerous behavior. But in time he had to agree with Amber that Ashley and Hunter, now thirteen and eleven, possessed strong and stable personalities enough to resist such negative influences, and possibly even contribute to a healthy family role model.

In time he became supportive and actually enjoyed the role of a foster parent. In some cases he felt rewarded to be seen as a positive adult male role model. Sometimes he felt a little guilty about the amount paid by the county for such service. He was shocked and dismayed at the extent of the need, even in a small, rural town. Most resulted from families battered and broken by poverty, often handed from one generation to the next as surely as DNA. Unless through persistent and passionate individual and community effort the cycle could be disrupted and the young lives set straight.

But this was the first time such circumstances as the crime at the Weaver farm brought foster children to their door, and none of the typical circumstances applied to the Weaver children. From what Amber and Jon could see in the first two days, they seemed well-adjusted, well-educated, and exhibited social skills beyond their chronological ages, causing the Brocks to reconsider their opinions about the pros and cons of home schooling, particularly that on an isolated farmstead.

However, with the shock of the tragic circumstances still present although diminishing, it had remained unspoken. The Brock's had begun to realize Michael Weaver presented a challenge beyond the ordinary cases, which were challenging enough. Not so much because of any physical danger from violent behavior; most often the children acted subdued, even though sometimes seething and unsettled beneath their appearances. With concern and compassion the Brock's strove to dismantle the walls even the very youngest had developed attempting to withstand assaults, physical and emotional, from parents, relatives, even animals—particularly pit bulls.

So far Michael's walls had been impenetrable against the Brock's gentle approaches. That he sat mute yet obeying any request, worried Jon and Amber the most, as if he suddenly would erupt into some threatening, violent, physical behavior. Amber instinctively remained close by him at all the times, more for the protection of her children than anything else.

ON THE DAYS THAT HE COULD, **Jon** walked from the office which is four blocks from home for lunch, sometimes leaving a little early to stop in the law library at the courthouse.

Stepping inside from the early summer scents of fresh-cut grass and glistening leaves flickering glints of late-morning sunlight, Jon could still smell history in the musty wood and stone interior, quickly permeating all the new paper being generated in the various offices. With much cleaning and repainting he and his partner had been able to eliminate or at least mask much of a similar odor in their office across the street.

Before coming home for lunch Amber had called and asked him to research case law on child custody that might have a bearing on the Weaver case. She had told Jeri Otto that she would do anything she could to help her regain custody of Michael, but she also cautioned Jeri that the court and family services would try to keep the children together since they still were so young.

How'd it go? What did you find out?" Amber asked.

Jon set his briefcase down and gave his wife a little hug. He asked how the kids were doing.

"The way things look right now I think there might be a good chance the Ottos could get Michael," he said. "It all depends on the whereabouts of Stan, of course. Each passing hour makes his return less likely if you ask me. The two little ones, I really don't know. That would be a big responsibility for the Ottos. I think they could handle it, and it would be good to keep the kids together. How'd things go this morning?"

"All right I guess. The novelty of staying in a different place is wearing off, especially for Anna. I've been able to keep them busy most of the time, but now I'm starting to wear out. At that age two days is an eternity. Two hours is an eternity. Jonathan's constantly asking about mommy and daddy. Ashley's really helped out a lot with him, but when she has to leave for something it gets tough. And Michael. There's something really serious going on there. I don't know what it's going to take to get him to open up. Hunter tries to talk with him and stuff, but without any response he gets frustrated and just gives up. And that investigator coming over yesterday sure didn't help."

"I wish I would have been there," Jon said shaking his head. "That guy is out of control. I don't trust him one bit. I've heard some things about him from someone I know in the AG's office. It sure doesn't help to prosecute a case when you have to work with evidence cooked up by some rogue investigator. Thinking about that sometimes makes me thankful I didn't win the county attorney election. It might have been good for our budget, but I don't know if I could take all the grief."

Jon helped Amber set the table and serve lunch for the Weaver children. At the Brock's the lunch menu often consisted of leftovers, or else a can of soup. Amber stood at the counter tossing a salad of fresh spinach, tomatoes, and goat cheese; delivered earlier that morning by Wendy Hamilton. She had said she was just heading over to the Gospel Tabernacle Church to meet with Jeri Otto and Pastor Gabe Evans about the memorial service.

I THOUGHT I'D JUST STOP BY and drop this off," Wendy said, handing Amber the small plastic container of goat cheese. "I know the kids really like it on a salad. How are they doing?"

Amber said they seemed to be okay under the circumstances. She didn't say anything about Michael. She didn't express her surprise that the Weaver kids, the older two, actually requested a salad for lunch. In some ways they seemed more mature than most kids she knew. They liked to read and be read to. The Brock's felt much better when they discovered that Jonathan settled down quickly when someone read him stories at bedtime, which Ashley discovered enjoyment in doing.

"I don't think they watch much TV," Amber said. "Do they even have a TV?"

"They do, but I don't think they watch it much. They don't have a satellite dish or cable. The only channels they get come from the UHF tower."

"It's not like I'm one of those parents who park their kids in front of the TV. But sometimes it's okay," Amber said, showing a slightly embarrassed smile. "I mean, Sesame Street and public television are good, right?"

Wendy smiled. "You don't have to apologize to me. Look at your kids. Active and engaged, well-adjusted. You should be proud."

"We try, but still it's a lot of luck. Although I have to admit that being home-schooled doesn't seem to have hurt these kids. Tulie must have done a really good job. Stan, too. They're probably one or two grades ahead of the kids in public school. It's just the socialization part. I think they're at a disadvantage when it comes to relationships, dealing with all kinds of people."

"I used to think that, too," Wendy said. "I think sometimes what we're really talking about is competition. What tricks we can learn to manipulate others and climb to the top of the heap. I'm not saying you and Jon are like that, but you should see some of the parents I have to deal with at school. Arrogant, pushy, aggressive. We try so hard to instill cooperation, but it's tough when so many just focus on competition. But I still cling to the hope that competence prevails in the long run. That's what I've seen in the Weaver kids even as young as they are—cooperation and competence. Sorry. About getting on the soapbox."

Before she left Wendy asked if she could see the kids. She tried to sound reassuring telling them that they would find Stan and eventually things would turn out okay.

Talking softly to Amber on her way out the door, she tried to explain that Michael typically was quiet. He would open up before too long. With the shock of what happened it was understandable.

"Just give us a call if you need anything. We'll let you know what we, Jeri Otto and I, find out after we meet with Gabe Evans. I don't know what you think, but I'm not real comfortable with that, with having a memorial service at that church," Wendy said. "The Ottos are really pushing it. I think it could just as well be at the funeral home. I suppose we could have it at our church, but we're not too good at that stuff," she said sounding slightly embarrassed.

AMBER THANKED WENDY for stopping by with the goat cheese. They parted, each feeling enriched by the opportunity to talk with someone else from same demographic in a rural population that sometimes seemed bereft of people who appreciated education, the arts, social and economic justice, and community involvement.

Wendy approached such meetings and activities with purpose and enthusiasm. This time, steering her Toyota Avalon into the parking lot of the Gospel Tabernacle Church, instead of those forces she felt apprehensive. She had met Gabe Evans just once, not long enough to look past the shiny suit, glistening swept-back hair, and broad face with ice-blue eyes and a seemingly eternal smile, which struck her at the time as forced and phony.

Wendy reminded herself again to approach the meeting with Gabe and Jeri with an open mind. Arriving deliberately about fifteen minutes late, she felt a mixture of relief and tension in seeing the big, red Ford F-350 already in the parking lot. She wished now that she had asked Ron to accompany her.

"Welcome. Thanks for coming. Come on in," Pastor Gabe said through an earnest smile, extending his hand to hers and ushering her in the door. "Nice to see you again."

Wendy forced a smile and followed him into the study. The plain exterior of the simple structure followed through to the interior. Blank white walls, casement windows of clear glass, round globe lighting fixtures, folding chairs instead of pews in the sanctuary, and in Gabe's small office, used steel office furniture. A large, wood cross on the back wall behind the pulpit provided the primary visible evidence of being a church.

Gabe's suit and tie, on the other hand, stood out like a neon sign—shiny, iridescent dark blue fabric over a sparkling white shirt and bright yellow tie.

"Hi," Jeri said softly. Her eyes showed a reddish hue. Smudged mascara told she had been crying.

"Jeri said they had a real nice time having dinner at your place last night," Gabe said. "Sounds like you have a nice place there. You raise goats for cheese and milk among other things? I know someone who can't drink regular milk. What do they call it, lactose intolerant or something? But they can drink goat milk just fine."

After several minutes more of small talk Gabe asked if he could pray before they addressed the purpose of the meeting.

Otherwise mildly amused at the naïve belief of those who interpret a supreme being in terms of human characteristics. Wendy listened without judgment to Gabe's earnest words to a personal God. At this point anything was worth trying. He asked for God's help in the search for Stan and the investigation, for the well-being of the Weaver children, and for the soul of Tulie.

"Jeri's asked if we could hold a memorial service for Tulie here at the church," Gabe said looking at Wendy. "We'd certainly be open to doing that."

"That's nice of you to offer," Wendy said. "We talked about it yesterday. With Jeri and Tom when they were out at our place."

"I hope you don't mind," Jeri said, sounding somewhat apologetic. "We could have it someplace else, too. It just kind of popped into my mind."

"Maybe we should consider what they would want. I know that sounds strange," Wendy said.

Gabe stopped himself from saying that they should consider what God wants. Earlier in his career he would have jumped all over it with unquestioned zeal. He now knew that such displays of certainty could seem threatening, even offensive, to people like the Hamiltons and Weavers.

Although not part of his nature, he consciously tried to choose words that conveyed a more analytical, objective approach to the situation, which to him included God's word in the Bible.

"I'm not quite sure how to say this without it sounding demeaning about the Weavers," he started out. "But you know in the Bible Jesus didn't hang out with the high and mighty or the super religious. He focused on ordinary people, often standing up against the powers that be to defend them. Tax cheats, prostitutes, sinners... now hold on, I'm not saying that about the Weavers. I guess what I'm trying to say is that if Jesus were here today he'd be more than happy to hold a memorial service for them."

"That's kind of what I was trying to say last night," Jeri said. "They don't really have to be a member of our church." Gabe nodded in assent.

"Well I don't know if this makes any difference, but I do know they were very spiritual. You could just tell sometimes from the things they said," Wendy said. "I don't know if they read the Bible or anything like that. Maybe they did. I'd say their actions spoke louder than anything. The way they cleaned up that old farm and all that meth stuff. Then they took little Michael and that was a big risk."

Jeri's head jerked up as if she'd been poked with a sharp stick.

"I'm sorry," Wendy pleaded. "I didn't mean it to sound like that. I just meant that Stan and Tulie always seemed to care about others. That's just the way they were."

"I know what you mean," Jeri said. "Looking back it probably was the best thing for him at the time. I was in no shape to be a good mother."

"I'm going to say something that I hope doesn't get misconstrued," Gabe said. "You've heard this before, Jeri. It's what got me into trouble with the main church body. We're a totally independent congregation here," he said addressing Wendy. "A few years back I questioned some things at one of the conferences. They considered me some kind of heretic and we were expelled from the organization. Some of our members left because of that, but most stayed. Now we're on our own."

"What did you say that was so bad? I don't remember all that," Jeri said.

"How can I say this without making it sound really off-the-wall," Gabe said, eying Wendy. "Nobody talks about sin anymore. Or Satan or the devil if you will. The church, our denomination anyway, focuses so much on this upbeat, feel-good stuff. You've seen those worship services on TV. Music and praise are good, but if your life wasn't going good it left you feeling like a failure. I just basically said that we should have a very broad definition of sin. It should include disease, accidents, or natural disasters. It's more than just human behavior. That sort of answers the question about 'why bad things happen to good people'. The weather, for example. We need the sun and rain, but not hurricanes, floods or tornadoes. And things like meth. It's just a chemical formula, but misused it's extremely harmful. The Weavers got rid of it at their farm, but Satan brought it back. That's right, isn't it? They think it was some meth gang behind what happened Tuesday?" Both Jeri and Wendy nodded. Gabe continued, "Satan is powerful, too. Even aging and death could be considered the result of sin, not always because of what we do, but because of Satan. But as Christians we believe that God through Jesus conquered sin and death. And when bad things happen to good people, God helps us deal with it."

He sat back in his chair, waiting for some response.

"That's an interesting perspective," Wendy finally said. "I don't think I have a problem with it. That's what I like about the universalists. You can pretty much believe what you want to. But I'm sure among our group some would have a problem with the 'through Jesus' part. That gets into all that about the eastern religions, the Muslims, everyone who lived on earth before Christianity... just a few people."

"I have some thoughts about that, too, that also helped get me in trouble with headquarters," Gabe said smiling.

"You guys are getting too deep for me," Jeri said. "We got to decide what we're going to do here. Are we having a service here or not?"

"We might as well," Wendy said. "No one else is stepping up, other than at the funeral home."

"We could have it there and I'd still be happy to officiate," Gabe said.

"Let's have it here," Jeri said. "That way we'd get some people into a church who haven't been there for awhile, if ever."

Gabe agreed, reminding them that they had work to do to if they hoped to let people know. Someone would have to get an announcement in the newspaper, and they would have to start making phone calls. They decided that eleven a.m. Saturday would work the best for the memorial service, followed by a light lunch.

JON BROCK TOOK DELIGHT in the walk back to the office after lunch at home with Amber and the kids. He waved at several acquaintances driving past. The sun at its apex directly overhead felt warm and fresh, much more comfortable in the less humid air after the cleansing thunderstorm Thursday, followed by a cooler, drier, high pressure weather system.

He arrived at the office feeling good. The tone of his secretary's voice quickly changed the mood.

"Amber called. She said Michael's disappeared. She wants you home right away. She already called family services."

15

Ashley ushered the Weaver kids into the family room to read a story, mostly for Anna's benefit. Jonathan fussed a bit. He and everyone else would benefit from his taking a nap instead. Michael followed dutifully, hanging back as he usually did.

Ashley promised to take them outside later. She wanted to take them to the municipal swimming pool three blocks away. She thought it would be silly if the police would not allow them off the Brock property. She conceded when her mother sternly explained why, even pointing out the unmarked private security car parked across the street about a half block down. The children could still be in danger and must be kept under protection.

On the way to the family room Michael stopped in the bathroom.

A cast-iron, claw-foot bathtub sat below a small casement window on the outside wall of the main floor bathroom. Set higher on the wall the window brought in light without compromising privacy, yet was large enough for a smaller-than-average-size ten-year-old child to crawl through.

About ten minutes later, when the call came into law enforcement center dispatch, the dispatcher listened intently to Amber Brock's frantic report, which conveyed fear about her failure of duty almost as much as about the safety and well-being of Michael Weaver.

Only his will power kept Michael from breaking into a run. He sensed that doing so might make his behavior appear suspicious.

Even though he could not explain the impulse that drove him, instead of running from the foster home he ran toward something, toward his missing parents, the farm, the animals, and two of his best friends, Pee Wee and Henry, the Weaver's dogs.

During the past two days fleeting thoughts of trying to escape from the foreign place that had been his prison danced like shadows in the back of his mind. At first, the shock of all that had happened so quickly seemed to paralyze his thoughts and actions. He withdrew, feeling numb and then anguish when Anna cried and Michael fussed. Wanting to protect them as he had in the past, this time he could not explain to them what had happened. He could not assure them everything would be okay.

Once through the open window and outside running across the backyard toward the stream the pent up stress transformed into energy, until the question of where to go brought him to a stop along the streambank under a bridge.

He stopped, catching his breath. He heard the murmur of water riffling around a rock in the stream, and felt his heart pounding in his chest. He gripped a handful of tall grass on the streambank and dug in his heels to keep from sliding down. He decided that the difficulty of moving along the steep slope of the bank exceeded the benefit of concealment from the surface. He stepped down into the water. He walked slowly, stumbling on slippery rocks for half a block. Unable to move fast enough, he climbed out of the streambed. Water squished from his shoes on the climb up the bank.

Few vehicles traveled on the quiet residential streets on a weekday afternoon in summer. Michael peered over the edge of the bank and through a curtain of bushes to see if he could climb out without being seen.

AMBER HUNG UP THE PHONE. She ordered Ashley to stay with Jonathan and Anna in the family room and ran across the street toward the security car. The man inside looked up in hopeful anticipation that some action might end the long hours of boredom.

"Michael's disappeared. I think he just ran away. I don't know how. I'm so sorry," she cried.

The security officer, holding up his hand and nodding at her, listened from the radio ear-piece to the alert from the law enforcement center dispatch. He said something into a microphone and then clicked off.

"We're on it right away," he said looking up at Amber. "Don't worry. We'll find him. He can't go far on foot."

Amber listened with relief and hope beginning to soften the hard lines of her worried face. "Would you like some coffee or something?" She met him once, briefly, when a detective introduced the security guard and explained his assignment to the Brocks. "It must be boring sitting out here day after day. Just call us if you need anything. Thanks for doing this."

"Hey don't worry about it. I'm getting paid. I read and listen to music. Sure, it gets boring, but once in awhile there's some excitement. I retired from the post office a couple years ago. I got bored sitting around and trying to find things to do. I figure you gotta do something worthwhile as long as you can. I don't do this full-time or anything like that. Sometimes the hours get a little long, like now, but it's okay. That's too bad, what happened about that farm family. Did you know them at all?"

"Not really. We would get food from them sometimes. We didn't see them much though because it was delivered by Tom Otto."

"Yeah, I heard about him. He's the guy who found the body, right? I heard they're taking a close look at him. I think it was one of those meth rings. It's coming up from Mexico. Some pretty nasty characters I hear. I don't think they're ever going to find the husband, at least alive. That's what I think."

"I've heard that, too," Amber said, reacting with a barely perceptible recoil.

"Sorry. I probably shouldn't have said that."

"Listen, I have to get back," Amber said. "You let us know if you see anything."

The security guard said he would. He watched her cross the street, then stepped out of his car to walk around and stretch a bit after sitting for hours. He felt only slightly guilty about not elaborating on all the details of his assignment. If the protection of the Weaver children were the main objective, it most likely would have been handled differently. Sheriff Schwartz and the Buffalo Ridge police chief questioned Harmon Leuten about his request, more like an order, to hire a private security company to keep watch over the Brock residence. Lacking a clear line of authority, which Leuten used to his advantage, resulted in the security guard looking to him for some inkling of what he was supposed to do. Whenever Leuten called him, which occurred several times a day, the guard reported descriptions, times, and any other pertinent observations of anyone entering or leaving the Brock residence. His descriptions of a young woman who drove either an enormous, red Ford F-350 pickup or an ancient, beat up Crown Victoria, or two men either side of forty driving a late model Taurus, which they parked a block away, seemed to be received with interest by the BCI agent.

JON TOOK THE CALL FROM AMBER on his secretary's phone without going into his office. "A lot of good that rent-a-cop did," he said.

Amber's voice trembled. "But he was parked on the street a ways down from the house. Michael got out the back. He crawled out the bathroom window. He couldn't have seen Michael."

"I don't know whose idea that was," Jon said. "No one except those who need to, know where the kids are. This rent-a-cop guy probably attracts more attention than anything."

"You know what they said. If the bad guys are part of some big meth ring they can be real nasty," Amber said. "Like the mob or something."

"I don't think that's the case around here. This town's small enough so anyone like that would be easy to spot."

"I wouldn't be so sure."

"Just don't worry so much. We weren't negligent." Jon tried to sound calm and reassuring. "He'll be found soon. We did everything necessary in a reasonable manner. If they suspected that he would flee they could have placed him at the juvenile detention center."

"A ten-year-old in that place? That's a little much, don't you think? Anyway, splitting them up like that would be tough on the two little ones."

"I know, I know. I'm just saying it's not our fault. It's not your fault. Ashley was with you, right?"

"She was taking them into the family room. Michael just stopped to use the bathroom. Without him ever talking we just have to take cues from his actions and behaviors. It hasn't been easy."

"I know. Don't worry. We'll find him. I'm going over to the law enforcement center and see if I can find the sheriff or police chief. I'll call if I find out anything. I really don't think there's anything to worry about from a safety standpoint. The boy just ran. He wasn't abducted. Whoever did the crime is long gone. I'm sure of it."

STOPPING TO CATCH HIS BREATH and survey his surroundings, thoughts about possible consequences returned. He feared retribution if he were caught, but at least he no longer would be alone. The panic remained, forcing him to move whether or not he willed it.

Instinct drove him to try locating his position in the town in relation to his home; wherever his father might be. He could comprehend no other possibility than finding him back at the farm. And if what had occurred Tuesday was only a dream, his mother, the only one that he remembered, would be there also.

After the Weavers installed satellite Internet service about three years ago, Michael spent as much time daily as his parents would allow browsing such data, especially the satellite photos, topographic and soil maps.

He could visualize the meander of the stream through Buffalo Ridge and out into the countryside. There it became an engineered ditch with a ruler-straight channel and banks set at a forty-five degree angle, designed to quickly drain water from the surrounding farm land, and bypass the bends and oxbows of the natural streambed for the benefit of large tillage equipment.

The ditching, which had been done in the 1950s, ended about a mile upstream from the Weaver farm, where the stream resumed its natural meander. If he could reach that point, trees and vegetation would provide cover. If only he had one of the kayaks leaning against the side of the barn.

Michael ducked down below the rim of the bank, unseen by the officer passing by in the squad car. He clambered along the steep bank heading west, grasping for whatever vegetation he could to keep from sliding down. Farther away from the street, between the backyards of large houses built almost a hundred years ago by prospering local merchants, doctors and lawyers, a majority of owners among later generations such as the Brocks proved competent in maintaining the structural integrity, architectural style, and interior grace of the woodwork. Their detached garages sat back on the lots.

Looking up from the stream Michael saw the back of one garage with a wooden rack jutting out from the gray stucco siding. It held three kayaks.

He scrambled up the bank and looked around for any pursuers. He lifted the forty-two pound fiberglass watercraft from its perch and slid back down to the water. He did not see any paddles and did not take more time to look for one.

Floating along in the bright yellow kayak through the open ditch portion without much cover, he would be much easier to spot by pursuers along the banks or from the air. But it was much easier and he could not think of anything else.

The current carried the kayak along at four miles-per-hour. It was a nice kayak, light, durable, stable, about a 12-footer, he thought. He had always wanted one like it, superior to the cheap, rigid plastic ones that Stan bought at the big annual canoe and kayak auction held each May in Minneapolis.

WITHOUT A PADDLE TO CONTROL the craft he stroked his hands in the water attempting to keep it from turning broadside in the current. Going sideways into a rock it could capsize.

Beyond Buffalo Ridge the stream kept its natural meander for about a half mile. In town property owners kept the bank mostly clear of downed trees and coarse woody debris. Away from urban interference and lined with a dense cover of trees and grass it presented a new challenge encountering deadfalls and strainers across and into the water. With a paddle, skill, and a little luck he easily could knife between branches of fallen trees. Without a paddle he tried to keep the kayak somewhat straight and hoped to make it through.

He saw the small branch partially torn from the tree trunk just in time to grab and twist as the kayak slipped beneath the deadfall. Trailing behind it served as a rudder of sorts and did not compromise forward motion too much. Approaching the next obstacle Michael could steer and keep the kayak pointed downstream. It carried him toward the farm, although the total distance measured about twice as far in river-miles than by road.

Beyond town where the creek became the engineered ditch void of trees along its banks the danger of being seen replaced the hazards of downfalls and strainers. At least with the latter, if he were wearing his lifejacket with the folding knife in a front pocket, he could cut himself free from ensnaring branches. Out in the open he could not hide from anyone along the ditch bank or on road crossings.

He saw the man on the bridge first. He tried to slow the kayak and steer toward the bank. The v-shaped channel moved the water deep and fast. The man saw Michael before he had time to tip out of the kayak and try swim to the bank.

The man smiled and waved. Within earshot he shouted, "Where's your paddle?"

"I lost it," Michael shouted back.

The kayak scooted under the bridge ending the brief encounter. Floating away on the other side Michael looked back. The man had walked across the bridge deck to the other side. He waved again. Some of the sheriff's posse carried only cell phones and not two-way radios. The man on the bridge did not hear the radio alert from dispatch about the missing boy.

Michael waved back as the kayak floated downstream.

After three days of searching for Stan Weaver, Sheriff Schwartz decided to scale back.

More than a hundred volunteers helped officers tramp through fields and groves a mile or more in all directions from the Weaver farm. The sheriff posted members of the volunteer posse at strategic points such as major road intersections and bridges. He instructed waitresses at truck stop cafes to be alert for any clues about the whereabouts of Stan Weaver.

In states where the Weavers previously lived, FBI agents checked out former addresses, businesses, and acquaintances.

Early Friday morning BCI agent Harmon Leuten returned to his office in St. Paul. He would continue working the case there over the long weekend. He left instructions to call his personal cell phone immediately about any new developments in the case. He had been looking forward to an early start of the weekend as a guest on a friend's twenty-six-foot cabin cruiser on the Mississippi River south of the city. He anticipated few if any developments in the investigation. So far he had seen no connection to any locals. It had to have been someone coming in from the outside. The likely possibility of an intrusion by a professional drug ring caused him great concern.

His friend steered the cruiser away from the marina and started heading south downriver, keeping a safe distance from a gang of barges plowing upriver. Harmon sat in the chair next to the captain, sipping a beer and savoring the river scenery.

His cell phone rang, ending the reverie. He glanced at the signal indicator before putting the phone to his ear.

"Hello?

"Harmon. This is Schwartz. Hello? Hello?"

"Who is this? I can barely hear you."

"This is Harold. In Buffalo Ridge. The kid ran just a bit ago. Michael Weaver. He took off from the safe house. We're on it looking for him."

"Hello? Schwartz? I didn't catch all that. I heard something about Michael." The signal wandered in and out.

"Michael... Weaver... ran... today..." Schwartz repeated loudly, slowly.

Wind noise buffeted the faint, erratic sound waves with only bits and pieces making it into Leuten's ears.

"What happened to Michael? Is he okay?"

He heard nothing more. He felt perturbed switching the phone service to Roam. It picked up a strong signal. He called Harold back. The sheriff explained what had happened.

"A lot of good that rent-a-cop did," Schwartz said.

"I knew that kid was going to be trouble. I just knew it," Leuten said.

"Well it's not your problem. We're the ones who have to find him. Maybe if you had gone a little easier on him this wouldn't have happened. He's just a little kid for cryin' out loud. Imagine what it's like for those kids, what they're going through."

"Listen, Harold. I didn't rough him up. You weren't there. He doesn't know what rough is." Leuten ignored the questioning glance from his friend at the wheel. "I know the kid knows something. I guess I'll just leave that up to you to find out."

"I wasn't there but I heard about it," Harold said.

"From who? Brock? I told you that was a mistake, letting them take care of the kids."

"You're wrong on that, Harmon. They're great people. They know the system. Anyway, I'm just letting you know what happened. You have a nice weekend. We'll be here working through it. We'll find him."

Leuten flipped the phone closed and shook his head. He knew better than to leave things in the hands of the locals, but had decided to go on the long weekend boat ride anyway. As far as county sheriffs go, Harold was one of the better ones, which also added to his concern. On the other hand, maybe it was good to get away for awhile. Too much oversight might generate unnecessary intuition among the local investigators back in Buffalo Ridge.

Most Friday afternoons, especially on such warm, clear sunny days, Jeri counted on the force of willful duty to leave for work. She hugged the kids and kissed them good-bye. Trace no longer fretted to see her go, understanding that she would return, which greatly eased her anguish. Lynn said she might take them to the municipal swimming pool in Buffalo Ridge.

At the Prairie Pride plant and dressed in the white coveralls, hairnet, boots, and gloves, the relentless pace and physical exertion gave Jeri some relief from the current turmoil.

Lyon Clymer looked up from his desk, surprised to see Ray Morris, CEO of the Prairie Pride plant.

"Ray, what's up?"

Morris sat in a chair facing Clymer. "What do you know about Michael Weaver?"

"What?" Clymer looked surprised. "Uh, I don't know. He's one of their kids, the Weavers. Why?"

"Did you hear what happened a bit ago? He's run from the foster home. They're all out looking for him."

"So? I mean, that's too bad. I didn't know that. What's this all about?"

"I was thinking we should tell Jeri Otto."

"Jeri? What for?"

"You know he's her kid. They've had some relationship with the Weaver's in recent years. I know she's not his mother legally. But I think she'd still like to know what happened."

"You mean you want me to go out there, pull her off the line and tell her?"

"I think that would be in order."

"I'd just as soon not do that. I think it would just get everybody all worked up again. Production would take a big hit. It's bad enough on these nice Friday afternoons."

"I just think it's the right thing to do. I'll take full responsibility for any little blip in production. That's all it would be if anything."

The dilemma angered Clymer. He toyed with the idea of defying Morris, even telling him to go out on the floor and talk with Jeri himself. He usually tried to conceal his contempt for Morris, but not his arrogance. A holdover from the previous owners, who Clymer believed by their ineptitude in keeping Morris around were driving the business into the ground, he considered and sometimes acted on opportunities to undermine the CEO. With Morris gone Clymer believed he would have a clear shot at the top job.

"I think it's a mistake. But if that's what you want I'll go get her. You know this for sure? You'll stay here and tell her?"

Morris said he would.

"If we tell her I don't think she should be allowed to leave work," Clymer challenged. "This is different than if the kid was legally hers and living at home. They're out looking for him. He'll be found okay. Few people know about the connection anyway. We've got enough problems with absenteeism the way it is. We do this and it sends the wrong message."

"We'll see," Morris said. "It depends on her response. If she becomes really distraught it would be better if she left."

Clymer shrugged and started for the door.

Morris stepped over to a table holding several large boxes of pastries.

"You know, is this really such a good idea?" he asked, peering through the clear cellophane cover at the assortment of glazed donuts, long johns, and bulging doughy apple fritters. "These things are terrible for you. Full of fat. Should we really be providing these to our employees?"

The digression caught Clymer off guard.

"Those? They're real popular. It's a nice gesture, I think. They burn enough calories anyway. I thought you approved."

"Let's just say I didn't prohibit you from doing it," Morris said. "Mind if I have one?"

"By all means, go ahead. I'll go get Jeri."

Clymer decided to go in person rather than use the loudspeaker throughout the entire plant. Plant noise often covered those messages anyway, and he wanted to avoid distracting the workers.

After hearing the news from Morris, her only request was to call her husband. Clymer offered his phone. She called Tom, appearing unconcerned about the others' presence. They didn't hear much anyway because Tom did most of the talking.

"Hey, how's it goin? What's up?"

Tom sounded too ebullient at the end of a long, stressful week, and hardly any sleep the two previous nights. He sounded too confident when she described the situation with Michael.

"Hell, I'll go find him. We'll get him," he laughed. "Those county mounties couldn't find their own ass. He'll be all right. Don't worry."

She advised letting the authorities handle the situation. She urged him to finish his route and get home safely to Lynn and the kids. She returned to work feeling hopeful and unsettled. She would do anything to bring Michael home.

16

"What was that all about?" Hector Vasquez walked over from his work station, impatient to know why Clymer took Jeri up to his office.

"It wasn't anything about the union. It was nothing." She tried to shrug it off.

"It had to be something. C'mon, you can tell me."

"It was about Michael. You know, the oldest kid at the Weaver's."

"What about him?"

"He ran away. They're out looking for him."

"What's that have to do with you? I thought our pal Clymer was getting you for some union thing or to chew you out for something. You've been acting a little weird lately if you don't mind my saying so."

"It's a long story."

"Are we still meeting tomorrow?"

"I don't know. I don't know if I can make it. There's too much other stuff going on right now."

"This is not a good time for that, you know. We're in the home stretch with this thing. If we let up now we're cooked. The union's done for."

"I'll still be at the meeting. Don't worry. They'll find Michael. But if he's still missing, I can't promise about the meeting."

"Why are you so worried about this kid? Did you even know them?"

"A little."

Hector searched the look on Jeri's face for any clues. This was not like her, to look so worried, so reticent to speak what was on her mind. He decided to back off.

NEWT GENERALLY TRIED TO AVOID meddling in other people's business, other than observing their activities as much as he dared. He knew that the three men and one young woman, and later her infant child, who occupied the old Wegman farm site, did not make their living on farming, nor on any regular employment as far as he could tell. The chance encounter with the young woman and her injured child on the township road confirmed his suspicion, enough to pay even more attention to their activities but not yet enough to alert the sheriff, which he believed would not be taken too seriously anyway and would only draw more attention to himself.

But when peering from his aerial bunker in the old silo through a night-vision scope early one morning in March, he saw irrefutable evidence of their activity.

He had deliberately left the five-hundred-gallon ammonia fertilizer tank near enough to the road and along a field windbreak of evergreens. The signal from the remote motion-detector hidden near the tank set off a beeper on the dresser next to his bed. It awakened him just before two a.m. He dressed quickly, went from the house and climbed up into the bunker. Through the night-vision scope he saw a blurry, greenish pantomime of two human figures furtively moving around the tank. He saw what looked like hoses leading to a smaller tank.

This time he punched in nine-eleven on the phone.

"Nine-eleven emergency how may I help you?"

"Okay, this is Newton Case. I live at thirteen hundred forty six eighty seventh avenue southwest. I'd like to report a theft on my property." He had rehearsed several times, hoping that he sounded respectable, credible, and normal.

"Could you repeat your name and address?"

"Newton Case. Thirteen hundred forty six eighty seventh avenue southwest."

"There's been a theft at your property? Can you tell us what kind of theft? When did it occur?"

"It's going on right now. Someone's out there taking anhydrous ammonia from one of my field tanks. I'm a farmer."

"Are they still there?"

"That's what I just said. They're out there right now. How long will it take to get a deputy out here?"

The dispatcher said a deputy would be sent out immediately. "Can you give me any description?"

"I know who they are. I don't see a vehicle. They might have walked across the field from someplace else."

It took almost fifteen minutes for the sheriff's deputy to arrive. During the wait Newt's anger and frustration grew. The men would be gone, the deputy would find nothing, and his reputation as a crackpot would be reaffirmed.

Forty-five minutes later the deputy drove into Newt's farm yard. The beam from his spotlight caught Newt walking from the barn to the house. Newt felt trapped by the light, but relieved that he had left the silo bunker before the deputy arrived.

Through the night scope Newt had been watching the deputy search the scene. When he saw the squad car leave and head in the direction of his farm, Newt climbed down from the silo as quickly as his creaking joints and stiff muscles allowed.

He did not find out until later in the day that the deputy, after leaving Newt's farm and driving back toward Buffalo Ridge, encountered two men walking along the road. They explained that their vehicle had run out of gas. They went to a nearby farm and got some gas and were taking it to their vehicle. They declined an offer for a ride.

The deputy observed their muddy shoes and jeans. They acted almost too casual. Running out of gas in the middle of the night on a deserted country road, most people would seem more distressed and surely would have accepted the ride. He could smell ammonia.

He let them go on their way, and then called for backup. Ten minutes later the men were apprehended, arrested and taken to the jail in Buffalo Ridge where they were booked on charges of theft and manufacture of methamphetamine. Later that morning officers went to the farm where they arrested the third man and the young woman. County social services took the young child.

MILLIE DANIELS GLANCED out the kitchen window and wondered why Tom Otto was stopping on a Friday. *His truck pulled up in the driveway a little too fast*, she thought, when he stopped five feet from the garage door. Tom jumped down from the cab and hurried to the side door into the kitchen.

"Hi Tom. C'mon in. What brings you here today?"

He swept in the door, grabbed a chair at the kitchen table, spun it around and sat with his arms rested on the chair back rest.

"How ya doin' Millie. You heard the news?"

"No, I haven't. Would you like some raspberry coffee cake? I just made it. Sorry I don't have a fresh pot of coffee though. I wasn't expecting you today."

"You know that kid, the oldest one at the Weavers? He's gone. He took off somewhere. I'm going to go out looking for him. If you see anything give me or Jeri a call."

"My goodness, no, I hadn't heard. That's too bad. I hope they find him soon. And his father, too. That was such a tragedy. Have you heard anything more about who might have done it?"

"Some of 'em think I did it," Tom said, tossing his head back with little laugh.

"Are you serious?"

"Not really. I mean they've grilled me a couple times. They searched my truck. I think they've been following me around. I'm going to find Michael."

"You said that."

"I know where he is. I think they took him, the guys who did this. I think I know where they are. I just need to figure out how to do it."

Millie gave the young man a worried look. He always seemed sure of himself, and tempered with good judgment, he demonstrated confident action that promised eventual success. But it was not like him to seem almost arrogant about something that sounded very risky.

She offered him a piece of raspberry coffee cake, the familiar, nurturing action providing a lull in the discussion that to her had become very disconcerting.

"I'm sure the authorities are doing all they can to find Michael," Millie said, handing Tom a small plate with a two-inch-wide chunk of the cake. "I have some old coffee from this morning still in the pot. Would you like me to heat some in the microwave?"

Tom declined the offer with a head shake, stuffing cake into his mouth at the same time.

"You look tired," Millie said. "This must have been a long week. Are you about done for the day, or do you have many stops left?"

"I only got two left, then I'm going to find Michael."

"Would you like Archie to go with you? He should be home soon. I could fix you boys some supper. It'll be light until almost ten o'clock so you'd have plenty of time to look."

"He can go out looking if he wants to. Let him join up with the deputies. Hey, thanks for the cake."

"You're welcome." Millie felt vaguely unsettled. If Tom didn't have a delivery there today, and if he wasn't looking for Archie, he had no reason to stop at the Daniels' place. To the extent that she knew him from his delivery stops and occasional encounters around town, he could seem brash sometimes, even fearless, but she attributed that mostly to his comparative youth. She sensed something in his behavior that aroused concern about what he intended to do.

"You be careful. Maybe it would be best to check with the sheriff first. I would guess that the boy just ran off somewhere. I'm sure they'll find him. Probably already have."

"I think somebody took him, that's what I think," Tom said. "I know a couple places around here that look like something's going on."

Millie saw that continuing to push back would further entrench Tom's delusion, and perhaps even generate anger.

"Here, take some cake with you. Let me heat up some coffee." Tom took another chunk of raspberry coffee cake and thanked her.

Jamming the truck into reverse and stomping the accelerator much more than necessary, he paid no attention to the worried look on Millie's face as she stood in the doorway watching the truck tear down the driveway.

Millie went back inside and started to fix supper, baked sirloin from one of their grass-fed Black Angus steers, drenched in Campbell's cream of mushroom soup, baked potatoes, and a can of peas.

Thinking about Michael as she started working on supper, Millie decided the news met the requirement of the phone tree.

ORGANIZED BACK IN THE EARLY 1950s during a polio scare in the area around Buffalo Ridge, the structure had survived for more than fifty years, quickly spreading news about urgent school news such as closings due to blizzards or mechanical problems with heat and water systems. Only the names changed although a few dated back to the beginning, women now in their eighties who wanted to keep in touch by remaining on the list. Millie joined more than thirty years ago and remained for the same reason.

MILLIE ALMOST CHANGED her mind, thinking that people already knew about the missing boy, that it really was none of their business. But she had to tell someone.

Still looking at the dust cloud hovering over the driveway stirred up by the truck, Millie called the neighbor at the top of the phone tree list. She relayed the message about the missing boy. The neighbor had not heard the news and agreed that it should be sent out. Millie mentioned her news source, but no more about his stated intention because at that point, that's all she hoped it was. At least she felt comforted knowing that virtually every rural residence in a twenty-five-square-mile area had been alerted and would be on the lookout for a small, ten-year-old boy who had gone missing.

EVEN WITH THE SMALL board that he used as a paddle, found among the pile of twigs, leaves, and general debris snagged by deadfall lying halfway across the creek, a burning ache ascended in Michael's arms.

Looking downstream he saw danger in a huge cottonwood toppled across the water.

His strength waning, Michael willed his arms to back-paddle against the current, trying to slow down before reaching the strainer of tree branches, like a huge comb blocking his path.

He saw a small opening barely the width of the kayak and tried to steer toward it.

The prow caught a small branch turning the kayak sideways in the relentless current, smashing it against the branches. He reached up to grab the tree trunk. The kayak tipped sideways into the current and water poured into the raft. The weight of the water and current pulled the kayak under the strainer leaving Michael hanging from the trunk, helplessly watching the water-filled craft float downstream.

His burning muscles found enough strength to pull his body up on the tree trunk. He sat for a moment to catch his breath. He did not know his exact location.

For as long as he had been traveling downstream Michael thought by now he would have reached the farm. Stan had told him that stream and river miles cannot be compared with the engineered lines of roads and rails. Despite Stan's patience in trying to explain such things for Michael, the experience now became the more effective teacher.

He crawled up the tree trunk toward the higher bank where the roots had torn away. He climbed off the upended sprawl of roots, clawing his way up the fresh wound in the soil at the edge of the stream bank where the tree once stood. At the top, peering around at the landscape he did not immediately recognize any familiar landmarks. Then he saw the cell phone tower that stood several miles southeast of Buffalo Ridge.

It meant that during the entire afternoon he had made it only halfway back to the farm. The kayak had been his chance for returning to the farm, clinging to the hope that he would find it as he had always known it, reuniting with his parents, Anna and Jonathan, Pee Wee and Henry.

Suddenly he felt very alone, alone and hungry.

He brushed the soil off his jeans and wiped his hands on grass. He scanned the surrounding area. Trees crowned the prairie hummock that caused the stream to turn where it did. He sat awhile, allowing the high afternoon sun to warm his body and dry his soaked clothing.

NEWTON CASE SMELLED the smoke first. Checking the wind direction he looked in the direction of the source.

"What do you think that is, Harv?"

The beagle sat up in on the passenger's side of the old Dodge pickup. Newt stopped along the gravel township road. Harvey stuck his head out the window taking in a full whiff of smoke, which, had he possessed a greater vocabulary, he would have been able to identify as old, dried branches from an oak tree.

Tinkering in the shop back at the farm, Newt heard the chatter among deputies on the scanner, searching for Michael Weaver. He heard something about a kayak and wondered what that was all about. He summoned Harvey and they hopped in the pickup to begin their own search. On foot the boy couldn't have gone far. Newt headed the pickup toward Buffalo Ridge.

Now and then over the years the memory resurfaced of their first meeting eight years ago on that cold January morning on the deserted, gravel township road. He still felt some paternal responsibility without ever having the chance to express it.

Finding the boy superseded the search for Stan Weaver, now in its third day. Newt participated in the organized search on the second day, but stayed home Thursday when the thunderstorm rumbled through, listening instead to the radio scanner traffic and intercepted cell phone conversations. He had already determined that Stan never would be found alive.

Newt steered the pickup onto the grass bordering the narrow gravel road. He helped Harvey down from the seat.

"Okay boy. Let's see what you can find."

The beagle's upturned nose sniffed again. His drooping eyes looked up from overhanging eyelids looking for a cue from his master.

"Go on. Let's go for a hike. I bet it's those trees back there." Newt started walking on the narrow passage along the edge of a corn field, barely wide enough for a pickup. He considered trying to drive in, deciding against it in favor of stealth over mobility. He briefly reconsidered, realizing that being in the pickup could provide some protection if at the source of the smoke he encountered possible danger, he decided to carry the 12-gauge shotgun.

THE THICK, CURVED BASE of the broken glass bottle worked as he thought it would. He found it reflecting sunlight in a grassy area that had seen occasional visitors, mostly teens socializing away from the adult world.

Michael lay on his stomach propped up on his elbows, holding the glass in his right hand. Finding the correct focal length he directed the pinpoint of magnified sunlight on a tuft of dried moss. When smoke appeared he blew gently on the tiny, glowing filaments, growing them into a small flame ascending to a miniature tipi of dry, matchstick-sized twigs. They took up the flame spreading it to a succession of larger sticks.

He sat back feeling the warmth from the growing fire and sunlight soaking into his soggy clothing.

17

Tom drove away from the Daniels' farm thinking about Sunday and becoming more deeply convinced that he should be the one who made the call on what they did on Sunday.

Approaching the intersection of the road that passed by the Weaver farm he felt drawn to it, mostly out of curiosity about any investigative activity that might still be occurring, and the chance that Randy Tollefson might be on guard duty.

Near the entrance to the long driveway he saw the yellow crime scene tape fluttering in the breeze, wrapping part way around the little school bus shelter. Whether or not it had torn loose or was deliberately removed did not concern him.

He drove onto the farmsite, hoping that the sheriff patrol car belonged to Randy and not one of the other deputies.

Randy rose from the kitchen table. The vehicle noise sounded like a large truck, so it couldn't be Sheriff Schwartz or one of the BCI investigators. He opened the kitchen door and stepped outside.

Tom walked over from the truck. "Hey Randy. How ya doing?"

"Not too bad. What brings you out here?"

"I was just driving by and saw the car. Thought you might be here. You heard about the kid? The Weaver kid"

"Michael? He'll turn up soon. How'd you know?"

"Jeri called me. They told her about it at work."

Randy wondered how the news would have traveled so quickly. "We've got a lot of people looking for him. You keep your eyes peeled and let us know if you see anything."

"Don't worry about that. I think I might look around a little bit myself."

"Why don't you leave that to the pros? Nobody's supposed to be here anyway. If Hank came out now and saw you here I'd be in trouble."

"I'm the one that's in trouble. They still think I had something to do with it?" Tom waited for a response. Randy remained silent.

"You should probably go," Randy finally said. "Sorry, but I just can't take any chances." He tried to form a thought that would help him better understand something he sensed in Tom's behavior.

"Okay, be that way," Tom said, affecting a sulky expression. "Are we still taking the trucks out Sunday?"

"I'll have to see. It's Father's Day you know."

"I know. That's why I thought it would be okay. Why's everybody getting so cranked up about that?"

"Who's getting cranked up? Maybe some of us are."

"What do you mean by that?"

"By what?"

"Some of us are getting cranked up."

"You don't want to know."

"What do you mean I don't want to know? What's going on?"

"Nothing."

Tom stepped back from a line between their friendship that he had never experienced before, and it took him by surprise when he apparently stepped over it. Many times Randy had described circumstances of cases or investigations without naming names or providing other identifying information, although knowing the context often led to fairly accurate speculation. It did not occur to him that this was any different.

"Man, I mean it," Randy said. "You got to go. If Schwartz or Leuten came by we'd both be in deep shit."

"Leuten's gone anyway," Tom said.

"How do you know? What do you mean 'gone'?"

"He took the weekend off."

"I know that. How did you know?"

"Jeri told me. When they called her in to Clymer's office today she thought maybe he would be there again. She asked about him and Clymer told her. So what?"

Randy decided to let it go. The longer Tom stayed the greater the chance someone would see him there.

"Where are you heading now?" Randy asked, trying to keep his growing irritation from infecting his conversation.

"I was going to grab a bite to eat and go look for the kid. The truck's about empty. I just unloaded a bunch of broilers with Millie Daniels. She ragged on me again about the food shelf."

"Millie? That don't sound like Millie."

"What's it sound like then?" Tom replied.

Randy realized that anything he said likely would not be understood as he intended, and surely fail to dissuade Tom from his intention of searching for

Michael. In fact, it might even intensify the tension between them, perhaps inciting Tom to overstep the bounds of sensible and law-abiding behavior.

"Well, I wouldn't waste my time looking for the kid in the country."

"Why not?"

"I don't think he could have gone too far. Outside of town he'd be easy to spot anyway. If I tell you this, you got to swear never to say where you heard it."

"What?"

"We've been watching a house in town."

"So?"

"That's all I'm going to say."

"C'mon, that doesn't tell me anything. What does that have to do with the kid?"

Randy searched Tom's reaction for any clues, then responded with a plea. "Hey man, let's just forget all this. Really, at some point if you don't I'm going to have to say something. That wouldn't be good."

Tom stood looking back at him, silent. He felt like cussing him out. He turned around and went to his truck, muttering 'asshole', barely loud enough that maybe he heard, but not loud enough to be certain, and enable Tom to deny it later if necessary.

Then he remembered the money.

SHORTLY AFTER THEY MOVED on to the old Wegman farm, Stan and Tulie Weaver heard the legend about a large amount of cash hidden there somewhere, a legacy of its days as a rural meth lab. They even searched now and then. Eventually Stan characterized the story as a local legend. With the passage of time and the farm's transformation under the hard work and stewardship of the Weavers, the story began to fade.

Tom stopped and turned half way around toward Randy. "Did you find the money? When you guys were searching all over the farm did you find it?" he asked with a half smirk.

"What? What money?"

"The drug money. You know the story. There's a pile of money supposed to be buried here somewhere, from the old meth lab days."

"I never heard that."

"You ain't been around here long enough."

"Well nobody's been looking for any money. Nobody's found anything like that, that's for sure."

"I bet." Tom couldn't help his tone of sarcasm, and it made him feel uneasy, even sad because it had been directed toward his friend. "I'm still going to look for the kid. I was the one who found them Tuesday. That was a tough deal, finding Tulie like that. The kids all crying, except maybe for Michael. Seems like nobody cares about them. What if I hadn't come along when I did, they still might be there cowering in the basement. Ever think of that? Instead they make me out to be a criminal."

"You got nothing to worry about. And the kids, they're being well taken care of."

"Here it is Friday already and no suspects, no real clues. What's the matter with you guys?"

"C'mon Tom. Knock it off. Why don't you just chill and let us handle this?"

"So you don't want any help from us good citizens?"

"I didn't say that. Just don't do anything stupid."

"Thanks a lot. I got to go. So, we still going out with the trucks Sunday?"

"We'll see."

JERI HURRIED TO THE CAR parked at the far end of the employee lot at the Prairie Pride plant. She took the mobile phone from the glove compartment and called home. No one picked up. She didn't leave a message.

Lynn must have taken Jade and Trace somewhere. She did that sometimes, drive into town to McDonald's, or perhaps to stop at her apartment for some chore, or to check on the cat.

No one answered when Jeri called her mother's apartment. She then tried Tom's cell number.

"Yeah." He sounded agitated.

"Hey babe, how you doing?" She tried to sound upbeat.

"What are you calling for? Why aren't you at work?"

"I said I was going home sick. I don't care if they believe me or not. I just couldn't take it anymore, thinking about Michael."

"Why don't you give it up? It's over. We got our own family to worry about."

The retort stung Jeri like a wasp. The aftershock quickly transformed from sorrow to anger. "What's with you? Don't you even care about him?"

"Yeah, I do. In fact I'm going to find him. But you gotta stay at work. If you keep missing and getting in Clymer's face all the time your ass is cooked. You keep causing trouble and pretty soon nobody around town is going to hire you."

"What? You wanted us to push the union thing. Don't blame me for that. And as for Michael and the Weavers, you know that story. You think you know what meth can do, how bad it is, but nobody really does unless they've been through it. I think drugs or meth or something like that is behind what happened to them. You know that. Besides, I got some sick leave left. And I wasn't feeling good."

"What are you doing now?"

"I was trying to find Mom and the kids. They didn't answer when I called home. I'm going to check in town and head home. What did you mean 'you're going to find him'?"

"I'm going to look for Michael."

"I thought you didn't care," Jeri said, consciously measuring just the right amount of sarcasm.

"I just think I know where he might be."

"How do you know that? I want to come with."

"I don't want you coming with. You should go find your mom and the kids."

"What's with you anyway?" Jeri replied, now becoming irritated.

"Nothing. I'm okay. I got to go now." Tom closed his cell phone.

WADING THROUGH TALL GRASS and weeds, stepping over deadfall branches made the going much more strenuous for Newt than for Harvey. Even with his short legs the beagle wove through the underbrush leaving a tell-tail ripple following behind in the tall grass.

Newt didn't need the dog to tell him what to expect. There could be no other explanation for wood smoke in a grove of trees next to the creek, yet far from any habitation, than the presence of someone. Fires didn't start on their own unless by spontaneous combustion in a pile of damp hay.

Despite the logical unlikelihood that a ten-year-old boy could have traveled such a distance from town in a short time, Newt had a strong hunch he knew whom he might find. He contemplated possible reactions from the boy, although he did not worry about any physical confrontation. The boy was hardy and robust, but still no match for a man even though in his sixties, except in a foot race.

The thought occurred to Newt that the shotgun might detract from having a peaceful encounter. He briefly considered setting it down before going any further, but it was something his instincts and past experience would not allow him to do.

If he had been pheasant hunting, Newt would have commanded Harvey to stick close, no more than fifty feet ahead. He decided to allow the dog to range farther. Perhaps the boy might think the dog was alone. Being a friendly sort, upon meeting a stranger Harvey most likely would find encouragement instead of fear or anger.

If his hunch about the source of the fire proved correct, Newt hoped he would be able to observe the encounter with Harvey yet remain unnoticed. He stopped about thirty or forty yards from the column of smoke drifting up from a fire near the rim of the streambank.

Michael's head whipped around toward the sound of movement in the tall grass above. Acute apprehension quickly rousted the hunger that had occupied his thoughts shortly after he got the fire going.

He stared in the direction of the sound, all senses intensely alert. It might have been a rabbit or perhaps even a woodchuck.

He paused, then relaxed momentarily when the small, brown and white dog with long, floppy ears and short legs emerged from the grass about twenty feet away.

"Hey boy, who are you?" Michael's attention captivated by the dog, he did not at first consider whether or not it was alone.

"Come here." Michael motioned with his hand, beckoning the dog to approach. It felt good to speak out loud.

Seeing the dog suddenly made him think about his own dogs, Pee Wee and Henry. He missed them almost as much as his parents and siblings.

Harvey lowered his head in a hopeful, submissive posture and tentatively approached the boy, apparently forgetting to alert his master with a bark.

No longer able to see Harvey, and hearing no sounds, Newt slowly walked toward the smoke, now slightly apprehensive about what he would find. It was not like Harvey to remain quiet.

"Hello there young fella," Newt announced when he saw the boy sitting by the fire, petting Harvey.

Michael whipped around and stared at the man.

"You Michael Weaver by any chance?" Newt tried to sound friendly.

After a slight pause, Michael nodded.

"Are you okay? How'd you get out here anyway?"

If it hadn't been for the dog, Michael might have tried to flee. He turned his attention back to Harvey, who sat beside him and tried to lick his face.

Newt hadn't really thought beforehand what he would do if he found the boy. He had been fairly certain that would happen during the search in town. Something restrained him from calling nine-one-one on his cell phone right there.

"Would you like a ride somewhere? However you got here, it looks like the only way out is to hoof it."

Michael looked down at the creek.

"You came down the creek? In a boat?"

"I had a kayak," Michael said.

Newt felt some relief that the boy had spoken. "Why don't you come on with me? You can ride in the truck with Harvey. He'd like that. You know who I am?"

Michael nodded.

"I'm Newt. Newt Case, your neighbor."

He knew that the boy knew who he was, but identified himself anyway as a reinforcement and to eliminate any possibility of doubt.

"I'm real sorry to hear about your folks," Newt said. "I know things are pretty tough right now. But trust me, we'll all get through this. Things will get better."

Michael returned his gaze toward the fire, his right arm draped around Harvey's neck.

NEWT HELPED MICHAEL EXTINGUISH the fire. They stomped on the coals and spread out the unburned portions. They pulled surrounding grass leaving a perimeter of loose soil, even though the fresh, green vegetation and recent rain reduced chances of rekindling.

"Sorry about the shotgun," Newt said. Walking back to the pickup he retrieved it from where he left it leaning against a tree. "You never know. You might see a rabbit or something. I make a real good rabbit stew."

Michael remained silent except for calling Harvey to follow along, for which the dog needed no encouragement. The mention of food reminded him again of his hunger.

Back at the truck Newt still hadn't decided what to do. He wasn't sure where the boy had been staying. He feared drawing attention to himself if he brought Michael to the sheriff's office.

He decided to drive past the Otto's. Even if Jeri was at work, Lynn would most likely be there with Jade and Trace

"You probably don't remember, but this is the second time I've given you a ride somewhere." Newt glanced at Michael wondering if he would detect any response. Most everyone knew the story, and Michael was old enough now to have also heard and understood to the extent that a ten-year-old could.

"We're going to stop by the Otto place first, if you don't mind."

Michael continued to pet Harvey and stare blankly out of the passenger window.

"You can use the bathroom there if you have to. Maybe get a snack. You must be getting hungry by now. How long did that take, getting all that way in a kayak?" Newt still questioned the explanation but at the moment could not think of a better one. Michael remained silent and looked back toward the front windshield as if in a trance. He shifted in the seat, beginning to feel itchy in his damp clothing. He looked down at his shoes and wanted to take them off.

Newt noticed his discomfort. "Maybe we could get you some dry clothes there," he said, though he doubted the Ottos would have any in his size.

DRIVING INTO THE YARD and not seeing Lynn's Buick, Jeri felt disappointment, although at times the opportunity for some solitude was not entirely unwelcome. She glanced at the note taped to the door, knowing the kids were in town with Lynn. Had it not been for the disappearance of Michael or contentious phone conversation with Tom, she could have relaxed, savoring a few moments of peace and quiet.

Lynn's note said she took the kids to the municipal wading pool in Buffalo Ridge and they would return at about five. Jeri grabbed a cold Sprite from the fridge and went down the hallway to the closet.

Reaching behind a stack of towels, she took out a plastic storage box with the words 'old baby clothes' neatly printed on the cover with a blue felt-tipped marker. She removed the lid and lifted out a layer of folded infant and toddler outfits. Beneath them were eight sets of clothing, each set for a boy ranging in age from three to ten.

No one, not even Tom, had suspected that each year on Michael's birthday she bought a nice polo shirt and slacks or shorts, sized and styled appropriately, and hid them away. She purchased the most recent outfit two months ago when Michael turned ten.

18

Sheriff Schwartz leaned back in his chair and glanced at the wall clock showing about ten minutes before five. He had just hung up the phone after telling his fishing buddy that he couldn't drop the anchor Saturday morning at one of their favorite spots on the river.

With the search for Stan Weaver now on autopilot and with Harmon Leuten temporarily out of the way, he still might have been able to go fishing without too much repercussion. Over the weekend his two investigators could handle the Tulie Weaver homicide case, if that's what it was. Now with Michael Weaver missing, Hank could not leave his post until the boy was found.

After more than three hours of searching, Hank began to worry that the situation was something different than a runaway child.

When Amber Brock called it in there seemed to be no evidence of abduction. Hank knew the possibility had always been there. The boy was the only person close to being any kind of a witness that they had, and required some protection. If only they could get him to talk.

Hank at first opposed Leuten's request for a rent-a-cop to watch the Brock residence. He relented when Leuten said the state would pick up the tab, despite knowing the promise may not be fulfilled.

Hank felt confident that he had made the right choice to have the Weaver kids stay with the Brocks.

Even if their parents projected a competent and stable image to the community, attempts to cover up faults could be exposed by the behavior of their children. From what he knew of Ashley and Hunter Brock, he saw no evidence of discrepancy between the image and their actual home life. He especially appreciated the absence of arrogance, which sometimes tainted attitudes and behavior among the town's upper professional and business classes.

Hank decided to call the only other person he could think of who had some connection to Michael, who might be able to help in the search. He suspected that when he called the Prairie Pride plant and asked Clymer to tell Jeri about the missing boy, she would not go back to work. He half expected her to call him wanting to know more details, and offering her advice and assistance.

Hank also wanted to talk with her about Tom, but without making it seem as if he still were a suspect under surveillance. And he was curious about Tom's late Thursday night-early Friday morning travels.

A deputy on patrol reported seeing Tom driving around about 3:00 a.m. in the big, red F-350 pickup truck. The deputy heard it first, the rumbling exhaust growing to a roar as the truck accelerated out of town. The deputy considered pursuit, deciding instead to follow at a distance. He saw Tom return home.

At home Tom went in to the house for a few minutes to use the bathroom and put on a clean shirt. He glanced at Jeri sleeping on the couch, refraining to act on an urge to kiss her good-bye. He left the house quietly, climbed in to the delivery truck, and drove away for the city.

JERI TURNED OFF THE TELEVISION. She sat in silence at the kitchen table, tuning out the white trash squabbles passing as entertainment on the afternoon television court show, feeling the weight of the Otto's own real-life tribulations.

The phone rang. She replaced the cover on the box of children's clothing and reached to answer the call with a mixture of dread and relief. She felt guilty hoping that it wasn't Tom.

Hearing Sheriff Schwartz' voice restored reason and objectivity in her thoughts, and sparked a faint hope that he might be calling with some encouraging news.

"Hi Jeri. This is Hank. Hope you don't mind me calling you at home."

"Hi. No, that's okay. What's up?"

"I figured you might head home after hearing the news about Michael Weaver. I'm hoping that maybe you could help us find him."

"Sure. I don't know what I can do. Whatever I can I guess."

"I have to admit we're stumped. Most cases like this we would have found him by now. Lyon said you probably were headed home, so that's why I called. I have to ask if you've seen him, or know anything of his whereabouts."

"Of course. Sure, I'll help any way I can. I haven't seen him. If I had I certainly would've called."

"Good. I appreciate that."

"Listen. There's somebody coming into the driveway," Jeri said. "It's probably mom and the kids. I'll call you back if I find out anything."

"Okay. Just one more thing, real quick. How's Tom? You heard from him today?" Hank asked.

"We talked on the phone earlier. He's fine. Why?"

"I was just wondering. He's out there driving around the countryside. He's helped us before where he's seen people and things we've been looking for. Does he know about Michael missing?"

"I called and told him, sure. He said he would keep an eye out for anything."

Jeri listened, looking out the window. She recognized the old Dodge pickup. Newton Case emerged from the driver's side. She felt a lump swell in her throat when the other door opened and Michael stepped down, followed by Newt's beagle, Harvey.

"Good." Hank replied. "Again, sorry to bother you. Hope you have a good weekend."

Hank waited for the customary reply. For a moment Jeri felt paralyzed. Her throat constricted, holding back an immediate response. She swallowed hard.

"Okay, thanks. You too." She hung up the phone.

HURRIEDLY, SHE CARRIED the plastic clothes box back to its closet hiding place.

Newt's rapping rattled the aluminum outer door, sending waves of anticipation and apprehension tumbling over Jeri. Without waiting for a welcome he opened the door and ushered in the young boy.

Jeri stared at Michael.

"Hi Jeri. Hope you don't mind me bringing him over here. We were close by. I thought maybe he needed to use the bathroom and get some clean clothes."

Jeri sat down and looked away, her left hand covering her mouth. When she looked back Newt saw lines of moisture glimmering along her lower eyelids.

"No, I'm glad you did," she replied, willing back her composure. "Where was he?"

"I found him by the creek. He said he had a kayak. Looks like he got tipped over and it got away. Otherwise he hasn't said much of anything."

Jeri went over to where they stood standing by the door.

"I hope I didn't scare him too much," Newt said. "The way I look. But ol' Harvey and him made friends."

Jeri placed her hands on Michael's shoulders. "Hi Michael. Are you okay?" He nodded, 'yes'.

Newt saw in her eyes, her face trying to hold back tears, a longing to embrace the boy. "Been a long time," he said.

"What should we do?" Jeri asked.

Newt gave a questioning look. "They're out looking for him. I suppose it makes sense to bring him in."

"Why didn't you just bring him in?"

"I was hoping you could do that. It would look better if you did. They think I'm a crazy old man. I don't want them thinking I'm a pervert, too.

"Oh come on. Nobody thinks that."

"Besides, you and him got something in common I guess. Anyway, I'd just feel better if you did. You can say I found him and took him here first. He could use some clean clothes. Maybe something to eat. You hungry, you want a snack or something?" Newt addressed Michael. He shook his head 'no'.

"I have some clothes that would fit him," Jeri said. "Would you like to put on some clean clothes?" She looked down at the boy. Their eyes met for the first time. He nodded 'yes'.

"Thanks for doing this," Hank said. "I s'pose I better scoot."

"There's no hurry," Jeri said. "If you don't mind I'd prefer if you could wait until we go. You want something to drink? Pop, a beer? I could make some coffee."

"No thanks. I'll be fine. I guess I can wait for a bit. Maybe Michael would like can of pop."

Jeri offered Michael diet Sprite, apologizing for the lack of other choices.

Newt sat at the kitchen table and waited while Jeri fetched a box of clothes from the closet. He worried if Tom should suddenly arrive home. Although everyone know about Newt, few had ever talked with him at any length, much less invite him into their homes. Recalling Tom's brusque brush-off of Newt's offer of roadside assistance the other day didn't add to his confidence.

He surveyed the messy family room, the toys strewn about the floor and on the furniture. He began to wonder if that's what the homes of his own grandchildren looked like. He shut down the thought before it took hold, evoking the regrets of past conflicts that had estranged him from his own family.

Jeri and Michael returned to the kitchen, the boy wearing a bright green Chaps polo shirt and baggy khaki expedition shorts.

"Well that sure looks nice," Newt said.

"Okay, we're going now. Thanks for waiting."

"No problem. Are you going to call first?"

"I think we'll just go in. I think I'll take him to the Brock's. That's where he was. I don't want to go in to the law enforcement center."

"I know what you mean," Newt said with a slight smile. "Do you want me to follow along, at least in to town?" He didn't say what he was thinking, that if the boy ran once he might do so again.

"I don't think that'll be necessary, thanks," Jeri said.

Outside Newt called Harvey and helped him up into the passenger's seat and they drove off.

Watching them leave, for a moment Jeri wondered if that had been a mistake. Newt seemed to have had some rapport with the boy, to have gained some trust. Faced with Michael's silence alone, the situation began to feel awkward.

FOR YEARS SHE HAD FANTASIZED about it, that by some miracle he would be restored in her life, picking up from where it left off, from what she could remember of it. He just stood there quietly, showing no indication of any connection between them other than the few occasions when the Ottos had been guests at the Weaver farm, which had meant much more to her than to him. The children had enjoyed each others' company, particularly Anna and Jade being the same age. Michael went off with the younger children to play, oblivious of the gazes directed at him from Mrs. Otto.

He obediently followed her outside and they climbed into the F-350 pickup.

"You ever been in one of these before?" Jeri asked.

She felt rewarded when he shook his head 'no'.

"It don't look much bigger than the one-fifties. You can tell the difference, though, when you're hauling or pulling something. Sometimes we take it to tractor and truck pulls. We were thinking about doing that this weekend, until all this happened."

Jeri recoiled at her own insensitivity in alluding to what happened to Tulie and Stan. She looked over and saw no reaction in Michael's expressionless face.

Instead of heading directly into town Jeri turned the big pickup truck south on the county road. Michael would be back with the Brock's soon enough, and it gave her more time to be with him.

In five miles they would pass by the Weaver farm. A mile past there the road intersected with an east-west county road. She planned to head east where the road gained elevation ascending the ridge east of town, and then turn north and then west back toward Buffalo Ridge. The circuitous route wouldn't take much more than half an hour. It passed by the Hamilton's, and she considered stopping there to see if Wendy could accompany them on the trip in to town. Ron and Wendy were almost like uncle and aunt to the Weaver kids. They had sought temporary custody, but the sheriff wanted the children to be kept under surveillance in town during the initial investigation.

Jeri did not think much about how Michael might react when passing by his home. By the time the thought occurred to her it was too late. They were approaching the entrance of the Weaver driveway. A sheriff's deputy sitting in a squad car waved at the big red pickup rumbling by on the gravel township road. A flash of panic gripped Jeri, who feared the deputy might have seen the boy in the truck. She looked in the rear-view mirror and saw no movement of the squad car.

Michael remained still, without any discernable expression.

Newt followed along in his pickup, turning into his own driveway after passing the Weaver farm. Jeri continued on.

Jeri noticed Michael looking at her intently until she realized he was looking past her. Straightening up and leaning forward to see past Jeri out the driver's side window, about a hundred yards upstream from the bridge Michael saw a yellow object in the grasp of a gray-limbed, leafless fallen tree lodged in the creek.

Jeri followed his gaze. "That your kayak?" Michael nodded. "Where'd you get it?" He shrugged slightly and remained silent.

Jeri decided against stopping at the Hamilton's. Michael would associate with Wendy and Jeri's time alone with him would end sooner than if she continued on, even though their level of communication was not developing as she had hoped.

THE F-350'S POWERFUL ENGINE barely noticed the grade ascending Buffalo Ridge, the geological formation and not the town, so named by early settlers who found hundreds of bison skulls and bones, either exposed and sun-bleached, or unearthed by plows where the soil seemed sufficient for tilling. Most of the soil was thin and strewn with rocks, making crop production a dubious enterprise.

"You ever get up here much?" Jeri asked, now resigned to simply making one-sided conversation in an attempt to overcome the heavy silence. Michael shook his head 'no', which affirmed some communication, but far from that necessary to breach the wall Jeri felt between them.

"Up here is Buffalo Ridge. That's how the town got its name. That's where you were born. Of course, you don't remember that. I hardly do, for that matter."

Jeri let out a sigh.

"Don't worry. We'll be back in town soon. I'm just taking the scenic route," Jeri smiled. "It was nice to have you see our place. It's not much, but we like it. The house ain't much. We got all our money tied up in that big shop, this truck and all those other toys. Not like your place. It's really something how you all fixed that place up. I don't blame you for wanting to get out of town and back there."

She almost said 'home'. Instead she said 'there'.

The same thing happened earlier when offering her condolences about the tragedy. She almost said 'sorry about your mom and dad'. That implied flesh and blood, so she substituted the word 'parents'.

THE OTTOS OFTEN TOOK weekend rides up and along the ridge, especially on summer days such as this one. Almost a thousand feet above the distant prairie spreading out to the southwest, the wind blew constantly as if the turning of the earth kept it going even when the weather didn't. Sometimes they would stop the truck at the highest point and hike out among the prairie grasses rustling and bending in the wind.

"You want a candy bar or something?" Jeri asked. "There might be one or two in the glove compartment."

Michael looked at her, hesitating. "Go ahead," Jeri smiled and nodded.

He opened the cover, reached in and sifted through a jumble of paper—flyers with pizza coupons—a Phillips screwdriver, a Leatherman all-in-one tool, two cellophane-wrapped fortune cookies, and the remnants of a take-out meal from the Orient Express restaurant in Buffalo Ridge. Touching another metal object, he paused. His fingers detected a small handgun. He pulled his hands back and looked at Jeri.

"What'd you find?" He reached back in, took out the fortune cookies, and showed them to Jeri.

"Is that all? Jeez. How long they been in there? Go ahead and have them if you want. I don't think it'll kill you or anything." Again she winced, catching herself again making a casual comment that under the current circumstances took on a greater meaning.

Michael opened the wrapper and split open one of fortune cookies. "What's the fortune say?" Jeri asked. He held up the tiny slip of paper for her to see. "I can't see it," Jeri said, exaggerating her concentration on driving. "Can you read what it says?"

Michael looked at the fortune.

"What's it say?" she repeated.

He stared at it for a second, and then spoke: "A confidential tip clues you in to a great financial deal."

"Oh that's good," Jeri said, smiling at the sound of his voice. "You heard any clues from anybody lately? We sure could use a great financial deal."

Jeri savored the communication breakthrough. His words came out clear and strong, and although still a boy's voice, it carried the promise of developing into fine young man in the ensuing years, and it made her feel proud. She smiled looking straight ahead so that her joy might not seem so obvious.

Michael held up the tiny slip of paper, his eyes questioning what he should do with it.

"I know some clues about money," Jeri said. "Rumors, more likely." She looked at him still holding the paper. "Anyone ever tell you about the money that's supposed to be buried somewhere on the farm, your farm?"

Michael shook his head 'no'.

"I don't think your parents ever believed it. I told Tulie once and she kind of laughed. I know they had some money back then, the guys who used to live there before Stan and Tulie bought the place. I don't know how much."

Jeri stopped short, holding back what she almost said next, her speculation about who committed the crime Tuesday and why. She hadn't mentioned it to anyone, although Sheriff Schwartz had dropped some hints indicating that he had similar thoughts. Jeri clung to denial in fear that the possibility would dredge up all the turmoil in their lives eight years ago.

"That's where I lived then," she said, looking over at Michael. "That's where you were born."

She looked back toward the road ahead and continued on in silence.

THE ROAD CRESTED THE RIDGE and began the northeasterly descent down the opposite side. Jeri debated continuing to the next primary county road, which would take them farther away from town than she had originally intended, or backtracking and going there directly.

"Lord, what should I do?" She spoke as if she were addressing someone. Michael glanced over wondering whom.

Jeri slowed the truck, pulled over to a stop, and flipped open the cell phone. She prayed Amber Brock would answer.

"Amber. This is Jeri. I've got Michael. I'm bringing him to your place."

"Oh thank God! Is he okay?"

"He's fine."

"How did you find him?"

"You know Newton Case? He found him by the creek a few miles south of town. He took him to our place and now we're on our way in. Sort of."

"I'm so relieved you just don't know. I'll call the sheriff right away."

"Could you wait a little bit? We're a ways out yet. I just want to bring him in without a posse all around. You know what I mean?"

"Jeri, I don't think I can do that. Now that I know where he is I can't wait. He's been our responsibility. I think Jon would really be upset if we didn't call right away. What if something happened?"

"Nothing's going to happen." Jeri felt irritation at Amber's attempt to assert her authority. "What if I call in? I—me and Newt—we found him."

"I know. But right now we're his legal guardians. That puts me in a tough spot." Amber hoped she could dispel the resistance she thought she heard in Jeri's voice.

"We'll be in soon. I'll call," Jeri said brusquely. "I think my phone is running out. I got to save some juice. Okay, bye."

She flipped the phone shut and stared grimly at the road ahead, feeling angry and guilty. She liked Amber and trusted her. Jeri thought she had outgrown the stubborn rebellion and poor choices of the past.

Jeri steered onto the shoulder and stopped the truck. With Michael casting a questioning glance, she opened the cell phone and punched the numbers for the sheriff's office. She avoided using nine-one-one even though she knew the regular number would be answered at dispatch, the same as a nine-one-one call, and be recorded as well.

Sheriff Schwartz was unavailable to take the call right away. Jeri could have reported to anyone there, but she saw an opportunity for further delay, and she could say that she had not lied to Amber when she said she would call. She left her cell phone number, and said she would call back if the sheriff didn't call first.

"Have you heard from your husband?" the dispatcher asked.

"Tom? I talked with him earlier today. Why?"

"One of the deputies found his delivery truck. Apparently abandoned someplace outside of town. At least Tom wasn't there and no one that we know of has heard from him."

"What? When did this happen? No, I haven't heard from him now. Why didn't somebody call me?"

"We just started trying. It wasn't all that long ago. We left messages at your home. We called the chicken plant but you were gone. We've alerted all the city and county officers to look for him as well as the boy that's missing. If you know anything be sure to call."

"Okay, I will."

Hearing about Tom's truck at first seemed like just another inconvenience. It probably broke down again and he was walking to get help. But he would have called instead, unless his phone was dead.

Jeri turned the truck around, deciding to backtrack toward the area she thought Tom might have been making deliveries. Now she began to worry. It was probably just the truck, she told herself. It provided an excuse for not returning to town immediately with Michael.

"How you doin' kiddo?" She glanced over at Michael and smiled, consciously trying to seem purposeful and confident. "We're going to take another little detour. We're going to look for Tom on the way in to town. That okay with you?"

Michael shrugged his shoulders. He was beginning to enjoy riding in the big truck. Despite feeling badly for Anna and Jonathan, he did not want to return to the Brock's, and Jeri was beginning to fill the void left by the absence of his parents.

19

FINDING TOM OTTO'S DELIVERY TRUCK broken down somewhere wasn't particularly unusual, even up on the ridge. Deputy Tollefson rolled to a stop behind the truck and switched on the light bar, not that he expected much traffic. He anticipated encountering Tom, with more than a hint of curiosity running through anticipation of the camaraderie of a friend.

Walking from behind toward the truck cab he could not see Tom's reflection in the side mirror. He opened the door and saw the keys still in the ignition. His thoughts ran through all the possibilities he could imagine, some of them not good. He placed his hand on the tread of the left front tire; it felt warm. He climbed in, turned the key, and the engine started right up.

If the truck broke down Tom certainly could have called for assistance, unless he didn't have his cell phone or the battery was dead. The nearest residence nearly two miles south fell within reasonable walking distance. Perhaps he hitched a ride, although with the truck apparently drivable, none of that made any sense. Maybe he stopped to take a leak. If that's all it was he must have hiked a ways from the road to find some cover.

Randy had been patrolling along a county road that took him up on the ridge northeast of town, thankful to be relieved of guard duty at the Weaver place acquiring basic necessities they could not produce on their own.

Randy welcomed the break from the tension from the Weaver case infusing through the department, and now the search for the boy. While it meant missing out on some possible action, he didn't mind because he knew that the sheriff liked to have at least one deputy far away from any major activity, just in case some dirtball saw an opportunity, even if it were just speeding at eighty or ninety on a county road. Sometimes being in reserve encountered even more action.

Without an intersecting township road due to the rugged terrain, at least in comparison with the prairie floor, Randy could not be sure about the exact location of the county line.

THE ROCK OUTCROP THAT OFFERED some protection from the wind also kept the old farmhouse unseen from the county highway.

More out of curiosity than anything Tom felt the urge to check it out. He turned the truck off the highway onto one of the few gravel township roads on the ridge. Approaching slowly he surveyed the distant farmstead, reminiscing about the late night parties that high school kids held there, the frequency fluctuating with the level of intrusion by parents or sheriff's deputies. Mostly the latter since many parents clung only to the illusion of discipline, and some having relinquished responsibility for the behavior of their teenage children.

Tom wondered if the house was even still there, and if so, in what condition it might now be. He stopped at the driveway entrance.

The two-story frame addition reminded him of a ghost, the exterior a once-white shell reduced to chipped and fading paint, completely gone in patches exposing weathered wood; smashed windows looked in on a dark, empty interior. Tall weeds and grass covered the yard. An old granary listed to the right waiting for a west wind strong enough to flatten it to the ground. The upper branches of a young box elder tree emerged through a missing section of roof on the chicken coop. The metal frame of the windmill barely projected above the treetops, the blades missing after decades of almost incessant wind.

Through the open barn door Tom saw what appeared to be a vehicle parked a ways inside. It looked like the back of a light-colored SUV or van.

He continued driving down the road trying to think who that might be, and what to do. If anyone suspicious he couldn't imagine them being missed by the investigation. Although up on the ridge and at that remote farmstead, the small thought of its possibility grew.

A quarter mile past he turned into an access road leading into a wind tower site, he turned around and drove back past the farmhouse and out to the county road.

Even though it was almost suppertime he was not ready to go home. Lynn would be fixing something for him and the kids. Maybe Jeri would be there. Right now he did not want to see them, or have them see him.

He left the truck parked on the highway shoulder.

Climbing over an old fence he caught a finger on the barbed-wire, tearing open a little flap of skin that just kept bleeding. He licked at it until the blood ceased to flow, leaving a warm, slightly salty taste on his tongue.

Crouching in the tall weeds at the top of the rise he looked down on the farmstead rooftops visible between upper tree branches of the mostly cottonwood and box elder grove. He had to move in closer in order to see anything, anyone.

He thought about going back to the truck for the gun, which amid the commotion at the Weaver farm Wednesday, had not been confiscated. Then he remembered. He took it with him in the pickup last night. Half way into the city warehouse this morning he realized that he forgot to put it back in the delivery truck. He'd never used it anyway other than to shoot beer cans; he could get along without it.

Whoever was there, if forced to, he felt certain that he could take them on. Especially if they had anything to do with the Weavers. Constant thoughts about finding Tulie's body, the kids, the disappearance of Stan, added up to an irresistible momentum heading toward action without an astute evaluation of the possible consequences.

THAT JUDGMENT VANISHED along with a pinch of white powder from the small, plastic salt shaker in his lunchbox. It hit him like the rush he felt in the F-350 in four-wheel-drive roaring up a steep hill, only this was ten times times more intense.

It happened just past noon, desperation breaching the defenses of his vow to Jeri when they first met that he would quit drinking hard liquor, cut back on beer, and never, ever use meth or any other illegal drugs.

He had fallen asleep and came within seconds of crashing the truck into another vehicle or into the road ditch. The loud buzz from the tires hitting the narrow band of grooves bordering the pavement jerked him back to consciousness.

It wasn't the first time that had happened, only this time it seemed worse, like it really could happen, sending a chill of evaporating sweat erupting over his back and forehead.

He had been making deliveries around several towns south of Ames County. He turned off the highway onto a county road looking for a place to stop, an inconspicuous place. He remembered a vacant farmsite about a half mile west on the first township road. The truck rolled to a stop in the driveway, narrowed by overgrown weeds and brush.

"What am I doing?" he muttered.

The voice of his conscience intruded.

STOP. DON'T DO THIS.

Despite the persistent voice he could not stop. He felt ashamed being engulfed by a rising tide of rationalizations. What if the truck had crashed and he were killed or seriously injured? Without any comprehensive or collision insurance they would not have enough money to cover the loss. He believed other drivers used it. Long hours on the road justified using something more effective than caffeine. Jeri wouldn't have to know. And if she found out she would understand if it meant saving his life, at least from a crash. If God gave man the ability to create such things, it must be okay if they are put to good use.

Tom opened his lunch box. He opened the plastic salt shaker and looked at the white powder.

For a moment he considered closing his eyes for a short nap. He did that sometimes and it seemed to help, even only ten or fifteen minutes. Most times, which could be almost every day, he kept on going, fending off fatigue with coffee and will power.

But he was getting tired. Maybe just a little bit wouldn't hurt and it could help.

How do you even take this stuff, he wondered?

He wet his finger and dabbed it into the powder. He raised it to his face, looking at it as if it were some tiny insect or grain of sand. Curious about its odor he raised it to his nostrils. He felt something trying to hold him back. Its grip failed and he pressed the powder into his right nostril, pressed a finger against the left and inhaled sharply.

He sat back and waited.

See, it wasn't so bad. You'll be fine. There's nothing wrong if you don't abuse it. It could save your life. He thought.

He turned up the radio. He took a stick of jerky from the bag on the seat and started tearing and chewing on the spicy, dried, leathery beef. He began to feel a force surging through his body and his thoughts.

He backed the truck out onto the road and stomped on the accelerator with each gear shift, ready to tear through the afternoon deliveries.

Later in the afternoon before leaving a neighboring town and returning to Ames County he snorted another pinch, and he felt great, almost invincible. Maybe this was the answer for getting through the twelve-to-fourteen-hour days.

His cell phone rang. He looked at the number calling; it was Jeri. *She should be at work. Why is she calling now?* Tom thought to himself.

DEPUTY TOLLEFSON DIDN'T KNOW what to do. The detective who took the fingerprints didn't have any good ideas, either.

"Should we search the area?" Randy asked.

"Probably, but who? Everybody and his brother's out looking for the kid, for Stan. And the homicide, it's like nothing happens and then everything happens at once."

"Ain't that the truth," Randy said. "I could probably look around here a little bit."

"Anybody call his home?" the detective asked.

"I already did. Jeri's at work. Her mom probably had the kids with her in town."

"No she's not."

"She's not what?"

"Jeri's not at work," the detective said. "She took off when they told her about the missing kid. I didn't know why they told her until Hank told me."

"About Michael? So you know he's really her kid. Until she gave him up for adoption. Yeah, that was awhile ago, before you came here."

"I should have known. I mean, there was just something about the kid that didn't quite fit in with the Weavers. You know, looks, mannerisms. Now that you mention it I can see a resemblance with Jeri Otto. So who was his father?"

"It had to be one of the meth heads she was hanging out with back then," Randy said. "They got her hooked on the stuff and they all had a piece of her. She was only eighteen. She wasn't even out of high school. What's worse is what it did to the kid. You know, you've seen them. Edgy, undersized. Just an innocent kid and he gets dealt a lousy hand right from the start. That's the part of this job that makes you sick."

"Don't worry. We'll get them. We'll find their sorry asses and haul them in," the detective said.

"Yeah, right. They do a little time and they're out doing the same shit all over again. Hell, they don't even stop when they're locked up."

"Oh, this will be different, I can assure you. It's not just a drug crime, you know. They really screwed up when they took out Tulie Weaver."

"Sounds like you already know who they are," Randy said.

"We've got our sources."

"You got somebody inside? How come I didn't know?"

"Well, now you do. And now I know you know, so if word starts to get around I'll know where it came from."

"Hey, c'mon. Aren't we all on the same team?"

"We are, but we all play different positions. And we have different rules about working with informants."

"It can't be one of ours, otherwise I'd know," Randy said.

"Of course not. They have to move around, no local connections."

"I suppose. Did you see the Bibles?" Randy asked.

"Bibles? What about Bibles?"

"He started selling Bibles awhile ago. I found a box in the back." Randy mildly savored the detective's surprise, taking some of the sting away from his exclusion from the informant loop.

"Did you look through them all?" the detective asked, unable to conceal completely his surprise.

"Of course. They're clean."

"At least for now."

"No, I think he's sincere about it. You know that church they go to, kind of holy-roller."

"I'd keep an eye on it just the same."

THE DETECTIVE TOOK OFF. Randy called dispatch and said he was going to drive around a bit.

"We just talked with his wife and told her about the truck," the dispatcher said. "She's out driving around, too."

"Did we call her?"

"She called us."

"Maybe I'll see her."

"I think she's in their big pickup, the red one."

"Can't miss it," Randy said. "Anything else?"

"That's all I can say now. Call in on the cell if you need to."

Randy removed the key from the ignition of Tom's truck. Leaving it there was illegal anyway. In case Tom showed up later Randy knew he always carried a spare in his billfold.

He waited several more minutes, still hopeful that Tom would appear. He called the Lakota County dispatch about the abandoned truck just inside its county line. The dispatcher said she would alert a deputy in the area to be on the lookout.

He left the scene to enquire about the truck at the next farm house, two miles farther into Lakota County where the ridge began its gradual descent to the northeast.

A dozen or so chickens scattered noisily away from the path of the deputy's car rolling down the driveway. A 1974 Caprice parked by the house appeared drivable, although he couldn't imagine who would want to. An assortment of dents, rust, and a chipped finish made it appear similar to the old house. A few pigs, horses, a llama, and ostriches assembled in separate corrals around the barn and other outbuildings.

Randy checked for dogs before walking to the house and knocking on the door. If no one were home, dogs certainly would have appeared to confront any intruder. All clues indicated that someone was there.

After a few minutes with no response he left. Just another eccentric recluse, made even more so by the sight of a sheriff's deputy. Sometimes driving around on patrol he forgot the impact of uniformed officers in marked vehicles. He drove back toward Buffalo Ridge, passing Tom's abandoned truck.

He remembered the old abandoned farm site just off the county road. Just past the truck he turned left on the gravel township road to check it out.

He drove slowly into the driveway, eyes scanning the overgrown yard, grove of trees and old buildings, looking for any sign of human presence. He noticed tire tracks in the driveway ahead. Fresh tire tracks left sometime after the thundershower Thursday morning.

IN THE GROVE ABOUT FIFTY YARDS from the house Tom froze, then slowly moved behind a box elder tree. A man walked from the house into the barn, closing the door behind him. He did not get a good look at the man's face.

The man wore a white tee shirt and jeans. His short, dark hair showed a large head, his face either well-tanned or naturally light-brown.

Tom rummaged around in his memory for any recollection of who this might be. Definitely Hispanic.

Another man left the house for the barn, entering a side door. He looked Anglo. A faint glimmer of recognition stirred in Tom's thoughts. Dark hair, almost black, shoulder-length. A slender build. If only he could get a better look at the man's face.

It must be them. Who else could it be? Why are they still hanging around the area?

He didn't know what to do. If he called the sheriff they might leave before deputies arrive.

Something else held him back. He tried to convince himself there was no way they would know. All those years of accompanying Jeri on her speaking engagements, he knew all the behavior clues. He did not know how well he would be able to avoid them. He had never understood or been fully convinced about the effect that it could have, until now.

It felt good. He felt an urge to rush in and take them all on. He was young and strong. Invincible.

Even if they had weapons, which they surely did, he had the advantage of surprise. He would disarm and subdue them. He had done it a hundred times in daydreams on the road. Now it would be for real.

It was not just a coincidence that he found them. God had led him here, to the deserted farmstead up on the ridge. The perpetrators would be captured and punished.

The wind sifted through the grove, a constant hissing from fluttering leaves smothering any sound from his footsteps moving among the trees. He crept closer heading around the perimeter of the farmyard toward the back of the old chicken coop and barn intending to look through a window on the backside.

Still behind the chicken coop he stopped to listen. He heard a faint sound, like tires crunching on driveway gravel. He crawled through a broken window into the chicken coop, stepping around rusting water cans and disintegrating roosts to a front window. He paused, looking curiously at the young tree, trying to calculate its age from the four-inch-diameter trunk. The hole in the roof must have occurred first. One of thousands of seeds fluttering through took hold in the dirt floor.

Keeping low he crept to a window in front, its glass amazingly intact although coated with crusty grime and flecks of feather.

A sheriff's patrol car sat in the driveway by the house. Deputy Randy Tollefson emerged, his eyes slowly scanning around. He wondered why they hadn't checked out this place before. Maybe someone had done so and he didn't know about it.

Randy looked briefly at the old house, then started toward the barn.

Tom watched. He realized that if he tried to signal Randy through the window, the deputy would not know it was him. Depending on how Randy reacted, it might betray both. If only Tom had his phone, perhaps he could have called.

The men in the barn must have seen the car by now. It was too late to alert Randy without being noticed. Tom decided to stay hidden, for now.

20

"This isn't Nuevo Laredo. You can't just kill him."

"We can do whatever we want. What do you care? Why are you such a chicken shit?"

The four men watched from the barn as the deputy stepped out of the patrol car. He walked up to the house and looked in a kitchen window. He pounded on the door, waited a moment, and turned around. He stood on the porch looking around the farmyard, then went back to the patrol car and used the two-way radio. He started walking toward the barn.

"We shouldn't have come here," the long-haired Anglo said. "A big mistake."

"It was your idea," replied the Latino with the large head. "To try find the money. Yes, that was a big mistake. There is no money there. And I think you are the one who is going to pay."

"What do you mean? I just told you about it. You decided to come here. I know there was money there. We didn't get a chance to look. If she hadn't come out with that shotgun we could have stayed long enough. I know where it was hidden."

"*Suelta.*"

"What?"

"I think we have to do some weeding." Large head looked at the others, two men in their thirties, one Anglo, one Hispanic. They held the long-haired Anglo in a steady glare of accusation, as if the matter already had been discussed and a decision made.

"What the hell's that mean?"

"Why is the cop here? How did he find this place? It's you. We've been watching you. They bought you out of prison. The story about the money is a big lie. You are *suelta, traidor, informante.* Understand? How much are they paying you? I should have known."

"Bullshit."

"Okay. You can prove to me that you are not. You take him out. You don't have much time."

The one they called Weed again looked out the barn window. The deputy approached from the patrol car, warily scanning the farm yard.

"He's called in to dispatch. We'd never get away with it," Weed said.

"You know him, that's why. You son-of-a-bitch *suelta*," snarled the other Latino.

Large head, their leader, smashed the butt of his assault rifle across Weed's face. His head snapped back and he staggered, cursing. The leader hurried toward the broken window on the left side of the door, raising his weapon to firing position. The other two men reacted too slowly to prevent Weed from recovering like a cat and running to the door. He pushed it open.

"Get down! Randy... look out!"

Randy dove to the ground, reaching for his weapon on the way down.

The leader's finger twitched on the trigger, hesitating. He must solve this without killing a cop, at least for the time being.

"Don't move or you're dead!" he shouted through the window. The other two had pounced on Weed landing vicious blows until he collapsed unconscious. One grabbed two large zip ties from a gear bag and bound his feet and wrists.

Randy lay still on the ground.

"Let me see your hands!" the leader shouted.

Lying on his belly, Randy slowly moved his arms out in front. Somehow he knew they had killed before. He prayed for deliverance. Hope, however minute, flickered in knowing that someone had tried to warn him, that more than the usual amount of division and mistrust existed among them, whoever they were. How did one of them know his name?

"Come to the door and turn around, pronto!" the leader shouted. "Now!"

Willing himself to stifle fear, to resist accepting defeat, Randy slowly rose to his feet, his thoughts a swirl of panic and possibilities. All he could do now was to obey their commands. The powerless, helpless feeling grew painful, much worse than the death grips of the martial arts instructors during training. His stomach churned. Sweat grew clammy under his Kevlar vest.

"Turn around! Walk backwards!" The harsh voice coming from the barn window carried no hints of uncertainty.

Tom tensed, fighting the urge to rush out of the chicken coop, until he saw what looked like the barrel of an assault rifle poking out a barn window.

Seeing Randy slowly get to his feet, hands up and walking backwards toward the barn, Tom waited for his chance. He would try get to the patrol car and call in. He would try to release the shotgun clamped upright in a rack attached to the middle of the dashboard. He would sneak around behind the barn. If only he could hold them off until officers arrived.

If only they believed him when he called in. After the questionings, after being confronted with the plastic egg containing meth, after actually using some today, after finding him at the same location with the four men in the white SUV, Tom believed his only choice was to take them out now, proving which side he was on, and making himself a hero.

His shaking body compromised his balance stumbling over the chicken coop debris. He reached the back and stopped, hoping they hadn't heard the clatter of a wire egg basket that almost tripped him.

He ran back toward the grove and circled around the front of the house trying to keep it between him and the barn. Not seeing any movement from the barn he dashed from the front of the house and crouched behind the patrol car. Slowly, he raised his head above the trunk, trying to see anything through the windshield. With the patrol car at a slight angle to the right, he crawled along the right side, hoping to find the door unlocked. He took another look toward the barn, then opened the door. Clamped in the locked rack, getting the shotgun looked hopeless. He reached for the two-way radio microphone.

"Hello? Hello? Calling dispatch."

He waited several seconds for a response.

"Hello? This is Tom Otto. Randy's in trouble. I think it's them. Hello?"

"Who's calling?" A female dispatcher's voice responded.

"This is Tom Otto…"

Bullets ripped into the patrol car shattering the windshield, some tearing through the seat backs.

"They're shooting! Hurry!"

Two men rushed from the barn, one firing another volley from an assault rifle. Tom lunged out of the car at the other man. A gun barrel smashed into the left side of his head. One of the men jerked him to his feet, jamming the gun barrel into his back.

Randy lay on his belly on the dirt floor of the barn, a thick zip strip clamping his wrists behind him. Duct tape wrapped around his ankles and his face tightly over his mouth.

He tried to look toward the other man in the same predicament. A fierce, swift kick slammed into his ribs.

"Keep your head down! Move again and it will be your last!"

The sharp pain recurred with every breath. Nausea began to curdle in his throat. He fought with his instincts to follow his training. Do not resist. Stall. Cooperate. Wait for assistance. He did not believe, no one did, that something like this would ever happen. He fought to maintain inner control against the power of the helpless feeling.

Keeping his head still, he moved only his eyes looking to his right, toward the other man. He lay still on his back, arms bound beneath, blood oozing from a swelling, ragged gash on his cheek.

"That your buddy?" taunted the man, his voice revealing a Spanish accent. He stood between them pointing large handgun at Randy. "I'm sorry but we are going to have to kill you both. Him too, the guy outside. You are messing with something way out of your league. You should know better. I know. It's not your fault. You're just doing your job. We all are. I am very sorry for your family, I really am. But we have families, too. But you gringos take everything. You expect us to do your shit work and pay us nada. Some of us die, too, doing the shit work. So it will be with you. God will take care of you. And your family, too."

The lethal distractions did not prevent Randy from flipping through a mental image of mugshots. He couldn't see the other captive well enough to get a good view. His peripheral vision detected long, dark hair, a large nose, leather-like skin, a slender build. He could not see the eye color.

It had to be him, Randy thought, the informant mentioned by the detective. If they had someone inside why hadn't they grabbed these guys earlier?

THE BARN DOOR OPENED. With the man guarding them looking away, Randy slowly turned his head just enough to see. Two men roughly dragged in Tom Otto, dropping him on the floor about ten feet inside the door.

The one with the large head spoke, as if he wielded some power or authority over the others. "Take him. Leave the other two. Let's go!"

"We can't leave them here," another said. "We'd never make it. Just kill them."

"No. Then we'll take them with us. Dump them along the way. Let's go, pronto!"

Two of the men wrapped duct tape around the captives' heads tightly covering their eyes. They opened the back of the Escalade, dragged Weed over and shoved him in, using their feet to push his limp arms and legs close to his body, stuffing him in like a bag of garbage.

They lifted Randy and Tom by their bound feet and armpits, tossing them in. They opened the barn door wide and the leader climbed in to the driver's seat.

The captives lurched sideways as the vehicle lunged forward.

Tom poked his elbow against one of the bodies, testing for a response. He felt a slight nudge, then heard some type of motion followed by grunt, the kind inflicted by a sudden painful blow and not exertion.

The noise turned the head of the man sitting in the backseat to watch the captives. Randy's head exploded in pain from the pistol barrel smashing into the side.

Tom could only hear the movement and another grunting noise. His body felt on fire, from the power and energy that seemed to follow when he first took the meth, now helplessly constrained. As if possessed by some demon his body began to twist and writhe free from its bonds, kicking his legs in fury. His mouth sealed by duct tape, he could not gasp for air. Panic brewed as he fought to inhale deeply through his nose. It was not enough and his lungs began to burn.

A cold, metal object jammed painfully into the side of his head.

"I said don't move!" the man in the backseat shouted, reaching to hold the forty-five's barrel against Tom's head. "You move again and you're dead!"

Randy tensed in terrifying uncertainty, waiting for an ear-splitting blast. If only his thoughts could speak directly to Tom's. *Tom, you idiot. Stop! They will kill you!* Pain throbbed through his head; he felt a trickle of blood.

He wondered if Tom had been able to call for help. That was their only hope. But bouncing around in the back and not belted in, the end result of a high-speed chase would not be good. All he could do was pray and hope that Tom was doing the same.

He grasped the faith that help would arrive. When it did, how it all played out became the greater uncertainty. With their heads and faces covered, the drug dealers could not be identified from mug shots, which under the circumstances gave Randy additional slight hope that he and Tom would survive.

One of their own, the one they called Weed most likely would not be so fortunate.

"We can't go on the main road," the leader said. He turned left out of the farmsite driveway heading east on the narrow gravel road. It appeared to go higher on the ridge among hills where rock formations poked through a carpet of prairie grasses.

"We'll dump them along the way, about a mile apart," he said. "The cop and the other guy first. Weed goes last."

He expected to find an intersecting gravel road and turn north, planning to take back roads until far enough away to take a main highway. He became angry at the thought of ditching the Escalade and finding another vehicle. He cursed himself for getting sucked in by the foray into the foreign countryside in search of a hundred thousand cash, which most certainly was a lie planted by the TRAIDOR. He would make sure that Weed departed this life after an hour or so in agony from a forty-five caliber gut shot. It would be delivered with great vengeance, building from the growing suspicion about Weed's loyalties, other than power and money. Not like when the final breath left the woman on Tuesday.

He did not feel sorry for the woman.

He no longer felt sorry for anyone. If he ever did, by now he was forever incapable, except on occasion for his people, the ones who tried to play by the rules just enough to get by, who worked like slaves in foul, low-paying jobs. And those thoughts occurred only after a visit from a priest, who went to the prison everyday to pray and grasp for the souls of men who many would say had none. But that was years ago and never really taking root, long forgotten.

The woman did it to herself when she grabbed a shotgun and pointed it at him.

Awareness of the fact that they were there to take something that did not belong to them could no longer exist in their minds; they took what they wanted, did what they wanted, with the only constraint being the practices necessary to avoid the attention of law enforcement and any probable cause for its intervention.

THEY DROVE INTO THE FARMYARD Tuesday morning under the pretense of purchasing fresh chickens, which people often did. If people didn't already know, the large sign at the end of the Weavers' driveway by the road boldly announced the sale of chickens, crafts, and hand-made furniture.

Tulie Weaver saw nothing to concern her. Many customers came from the area's growing Latino community, many of whom disdained the pale, processed chickens at the supermarket in Buffalo Ridge, preferring the firm, robust flesh of the chickens raised by traditional methods, without routine antibiotics, able to roam between an open pen and a large shed.

Even the expensive SUV, while it caught her attention, no longer could be considered highly unusual. An increasing number of Latino families were trading in their old pickups for more costly vehicles.

When she saw four men exit the white Escalade, caution instinctively infused Tulie's readiness to welcome customers. She remained in the house, slightly ashamed at the thought of staying near the double-barrel twenty-gauge shotgun behind the door of the small closet between the main floor bedroom and the kitchen.

She thought about Stan out in a far section of the alfalfa field, mowing behind Zelda and Ernie, the team of Percheron draft horses.

Whenever he used the old farming methods, he did not take his cell phone with him. But knowing he was out in the field on a sunny morning in June, sitting on a sickle mower, the powerful horses plodding steadily through the second cutting, their occasional snorts punctuating the clattering rhythm of the sickle blades and meadowlark songs, she understood.

Only now, despite her usual self-reliance, she wished that he were nearby.

Normally, when a vehicle carrying several people drove into the farmyard, only one would walk up to the house or over to the small sales shed next to the barn, and then signal to the others.

Seeing four men, two Anglo and two Latino, approaching the house, impassive expressions on their faces betrayed by darting glances in all directions, Tulie looked back at the children around the trestle table finishing their breakfast.

"Kids! Get down in the basement! Right Now!"

"But mommy, somebody's here," Anna said, not perceiving the fear in the urgent intensity of her mother's voice. "They want to buy chickens!"

"Let's go! Now!" Tulie almost shouted.

Anna searched her mother's face trying to understand. Tears filled Anna's eyes.

The men had almost reached the kitchen door. Tulie jerked Jonathan from his high chair. "Michael, take your sister," she ordered.

"C'mon Anna. Do what mom says!" Michael urged.

"Why," she whined. "I want to see the people."

"They might be bad people. C'mon!"

Tulie felt a slight twinge of guilt. Having the thought was bad enough. Hearing it spoken made it real. Her reason intervened. There's nothing to worry about. Now she felt ashamed, yet her instincts prevented her from changing the course of action already under way.

Michael took Anna's arm, trying to be firm and gentle at the same time. "Let's go. C'mon. We can play hide and seek."

"But I didn't finish my breakfast," Anna whined.

"You hardly do anyway," Michael countered. "Mom says go, let's go."

Tulie carried Jonathan to the hallway closet. In the back, a door opened to a steep stairway leading to the cellar, which the Weavers had added since the only previous access to the cellar of the old house was on an exterior wall. Michael followed holding Anna's hand, her voice still whimpering.

"Be quiet!" Tulie commanded, looking sternly at the children huddling at the bottom of the cellar stair. "Everything will be fine." She closed the cellar door. Backing out from the closet, she moved the shotgun from behind the door and leaned it against the closet wall, out of view but accessible.

The sound of knocking on the kitchen door sent a shock streaking through her body.

She prayed for Stan to appear.

Slowly, stopping once to listen for any sound from the kids, she went to the kitchen door.

This is silly. What am I thinking? There's nothing to worry about. Willing a smile, she opened the door.

GOOD MORNING." He appeared to be mid-thirties, stocky build, about five-eleven, Latino, with a somewhat large head that would have looked even larger had he not worn his dark hair slicked back, long enough for a pony-tail about six inches long. The other three stood behind him, all of them smiling and seeming to be friendly.

"Morning," Tulie said in a clear, firm voice, and forcing a smile. "How are you folks today?"

"Very well, thank you. We would like to look at some of the tables and chairs that you make. They seem very nice."

"My husband makes them. He's around here somewhere."

"Mind if we take a look? At the furniture?"

"Sure. I think it would be best though if you talked about it with Stan. I don't know much about it. If you're looking for chickens, I can help you with that. Rugs, too."

"We like chickens, too."

"C'mon Rafe, enough of this BS," Weed interjected. "Just tell her why we're here and get on with it."

Rafe turned his head glaring at him. He turned back toward Tulie and smiled. "It's nothing."

"What's this all about?" Tulie asked, choking down a growing sense of fear.

Rafe shot another ominous glance at Weed. He paused, then turned back to Tulie and smiled again. "We believe there is some property here, left here before you came, that belongs to us."

"What kind of property? What do you mean?"

"It's not really property, like furniture or tools or anything like that. You didn't even know it was here."

"There's nothing here that we don't know about. This whole place was stripped bare and cleaned out before we moved in."

Tulie moved to step back inside the screen door.

Rafe grabbed the handle, preventing her from closing it. He pulled it open and stepped inside, the invasion pushing Tulie back into the small enclosed porch leading to the kitchen.

"Ma'am, we just want to take a look around, not in the buildings. In the back, among the trees."

Tulie tried to regain her composure. "In the grove? There's nothing out there. We cleaned out most of it. There might be a few pieces of junk. I know there's an old car body. That's about it."

Her thoughts bounced back and forth between fear and reason, between grabbing the cell phone and calling nine-eleven, or accommodating the visitors and seeing them on their way.

She stepped backwards into the kitchen, giving way to Rafe's slow, measured approach with the other three close behind. He looked back at them with an unspoken message in his eyes that they seemed to understand. He turned slowly back toward Tulie.

"All right. Go ahead and look. But you won't find anything," Tulie said.

"We would like you to help us," Rafe said. "Go with us and everything will be fine."

"Why is it not fine? Why don't you just leave?" Tulie felt her voice quaver, her body, too. She moved farther into the kitchen near the refrigerator, not far from the closet between the kitchen and bedroom. Rafe and the others followed.

He looked at the table, the cereal bowls, toast, glasses of juice. "Where are your children?"

Tulie repressed saying that was none of his business. "They're with their father. Out in the barn. I'll go get my husband. He can tell you about the furniture." Tulie took several steps backward. She thought about rushing out the front door. But Stan was too far away, and she could not leave the children.

"If that man way out in the field with the horses is your husband, he is too busy, too far away. Please go with us and no one will get hurt," Rafe said in a pleading, almost gentle voice.

"If anybody's going to get hurt it's going to be you," Tulie blurted.

Rafe smiled, looked down and slowly shook his head. He did not anticipate such resistance. He looked back at the others. "Okay, tie her up."

Tulie darted back to the closet and grabbed the shotgun.

Rafe whipped around facing her. He leaped forward. His hand flashed out, knocking aside the barrel, grabbing it and yanking the gun away. Tulie's finger caught on one of the two triggers. A thunderous blast shot a pattern of BBs into the wall by the door, barely missing one of the men.

She lunged at Rafe, grabbing for the gun. Her hands gripped the barrel trying to pull it away. His finger on the triggers, the shotgun fired a twenty-gauge shell with number six shot, striking her midriff. She grunted and fell backward to the floor in the hallway.

Rafe knew she would not survive, but he did not know how long it would take. The remote chance that anyone would find her still alive and able to identify them made it necessary, and it also would end her suffering.

He pointed the double-barreled shotgun at Weed. Even though empty, it emphasized the command. Rafe could have pulled out his forty-five and would have done so had it been necessary.

"Finish it!" He nodded toward the wood block on the kitchen counter holding six sharp knives. "Up into the heart! Now!"

IN THE CELLAR, MICHAEL HAD TOLD Anna and Jonathan to look for spiders, quietly so as to surprise them. Seeing them occupied, he crept up the stairway.

Peeking from the door he saw his mother holding the shotgun, talking with men whom he could not see. It did not occur to him to intervene or distract her. Whatever was happening, she would take care of everything.

His eyes saw the struggle, his ears heard the blasts. He could not move, transfixed by images occurring so quickly that he could not immediately comprehend their meaning. His childhood so far void of violent video games and movies, seeing firearms used against humans did not register.

Or blades.

Guns and knives were used for hunting and occasionally on disabled livestock.

He saw the man, the slender one with long, dark hair, bend down and thrust a kitchen knife into her body, up toward the heart. He heard objects crashing to the floor in the living room.

They were gone.

Slowly, he opened the door and stepped quietly to his mother. She lay on her back, still, blood oozing from a ragged mess of flesh just below her chest, the wooden handle of knife protruding.

His throat tightened. He gently placed his hand on her forehead.

"Mom? Are you okay? Mom?"

Tulie's eyes stood half closed, unblinking. He could not see any sign of breathing, any movement.

Where was dad? He had to find Stan. He started for the kitchen door. Hearing Anna's voice and footsteps on the cellar stair, he hurried back to the cellar door in the back of the closet, carefully stepping around Tulie's body.

"Anna! Stay there! Don't come out!"

"Why?" she whined. "What happened? I want to see mommy! Where's mommy!"

Abandoned at the bottom of the cellar stair, Jonathan began to cry. On his hands and knees he started up the stairway toward Anna.

Michael reached the door, blocking Anna's view and holding the door as she tried to open it.

"Michael! Don't do that! Let me out!"

"Anna! We have to go back downstairs. We can't come out yet." He squeezed through the partially-open door and closed it behind him.

"Some men were here. I'm going to get dad. You and Jonathan can't come out yet."

"I'm scared. Where's mommy?"

Michael took Anna by the arm down the stairs into the cellar, grabbing Jonathan's arm on the way.

"Anna. Do you have your phone? I'm going to call dad."

Since receiving her own phone for her birthday, she always carried it. She reached in a pocket and handed it to him.

Stan did not answer.

Michael left a voice message. "Dad. Something bad has happened to mom. Some men were here. Please get back here." He flipped the phone shut, lowered his head and clenched his eyes, struggling to stem the flow of tears.

21

THE DOWNPOUR DURING THURSDAY MORNING's thunderstorm left deep gullies in the narrow gravel road climbing higher on the ridge. Jeri shifted the truck into four-wheel-drive.

"You ever been off-road in one of these things?" Michael looked at her, shaking his head 'no'.

"We've got time for a little detour before we head into town," Jeri said. "Pull that seatbelt tight and hang on."

Instead of circling around back toward town on the county road, she steered the truck onto small gravel road ascending the ridge. Alongside stood a small sign: "Minimum Maintenance Road."

"It's a dead-end road," Jeri said. "I don't know why they don't put a sign about it back there. It don't go anywhere. It just ends. People just have to turn around I guess, unless they have a truck like this. We don't need a road. We'll just go across the ridge on our own. That sound like fun?" she smiled, looking at the boy. "Let's just say it's a little short-cut."

"We'll just head over the top and pick up the road on the other side. What do you think? Ain't this kind of fun?" She looked at him and consciously affected a grin.

Michael shrugged, mostly noncommittal with any remaining intent teetering between resignation and temperate approval. What he really needed was some place to pee. The fullness grew not long after he drank the diet Sprite. At every jolt of the bucking truck he clenched his teeth trying to hold it back, and he felt too constrained to ask her to stop.

Over the past three days he had almost forgotten the sound of his own voice. A long time had passed since he had been awakened by nightmares. Comforted by his parents and a growing sense of security, the demons that had tried to invade nearly a decade ago had been beaten back by his parents and a family's love. The shock of being torn from them was wearing off. Whatever the cause, it was making him angry.

WHO IS THAT?" Jeri stopped the truck and sat forward gripping the wheel, as if moving ahead one foot gave a better view. "Michael, look. There's a white truck up there."

He turned his head away from gazing out the side window. About a hundred yards away, a white SUV sat tilted toward its left side. Two men appeared to be at the front pushing. A third sat in the driver's seat.

"Who the heck is that?" Jeri looked curiously at Michael. He shrugged.

"Can't you just say something?" It slipped out through a crack in her resolve to remain calm. After a quick glance trying to read her expression, Michael looked down at the floor, then out the side window.

"Oh jeez, I'm sorry. Okay? Everything's going to be okay. I suppose we better go see who that is. See if they need any help."

She tried to ignore a flicker of apprehension. No one else around on the desolate terrain. If they went to offer assistance, they could be at the mercy of strangers. The cell phone sat ready, except that help would be too late. Jeri paused, then accelerated the truck forward, coasting down a small gully and powering up the other side.

Closing in on the stalled vehicle they saw the three men inside. They must have climbed back in when Jeri and Michael were in the gully out of view. Faint caution lingered until they saw the men smiling and waving.

It must be okay. For whatever reason they happened to be there, all they needed was a little help getting unstuck.

Jeri quickly identified two Latinos and one Anglo, probably somewhere in their thirties. The driver, a good-looking Latino, wore a dark-green polo shirt and his dark hair in a pony tail. The Anglo sat in the front passenger seat, the other Latino in back.

She steered the truck alongside about thirty feet away, avoiding rocks near the other vehicle.

"Hi," the driver said, smiling and waving, his voice loud enough to carry over the wind.

"Hi. Looks like you guys could use a little help," Jeri shouted.

"That would be great." He shrugged and gave an embarrassed look. "The road just ended. We thought we could make it anyway."

"You could have made it the rest of the way in that thing. Got four-wheel drive, right?"

"I think so. Yes. It was in four-wheel."

"Looks like you just got hung up on a rock," Jeri said, pointing toward the underside of the Escalade. "If you want I could try give you a pull. Shouldn't take too much."

"We would appreciate that very much," Rafe said, smiling and nodding at the others.

"I'll pull from the back. That looks the easiest," Jeri said. She drove forward, then backed the F-350 toward the rear of the Escalade.

The two men in the front stepped out. Rafe held up his hands signaling Jeri to stop. She looked out the window. "That's close enough," Rafe shouted.

"You stay here," Jeri ordered Michael. She climbed into the truck bed and lifted a heavy towing chain from the toolbox.

Rafe approached. "Here. Let me take that. I can hook it up. We're in kind of a hurry. Nice truck," he said, admiring the F-350.

Maybe they didn't need to look for another vehicle. Taking the pickup would have been convenient, but it also would have been easier to spot. Rafe decided to wait, to play along with getting the Escalade unstuck.

Jeri intended to connect the chain herself, to make sure it was done right. She had seen tow chains under stress come loose, flying back toward the tow vehicle. "That's okay. I can hook it up."

Rafe said nothing and grabbed the chain from her arms. She almost resisted, holding back after sensing something about the man that challenged the mutual trust between strangers finding common ground in trying to help one another.

"Be sure to hook it on to the frame," Jeri said in a loud voice. Did such vehicles even have a true frame? "Give me a wave when you're ready to start."

Half way to the Escalade Rafe stopped, turning around part way as if he had forgotten something.

She climbed into the truck, now conscious of feeling uneasy. "You ever seen these guys around before?"

Michael stared at them out the rear window, then back toward Jeri, indicating recognition with only the intensity in his eyes, but unable to release the words clenched in his throat.

She leaned out the window trying to see Rafe hooking up the chain. "I hope he knows what he's doing," she said quietly, mostly to herself. She looked back again. He seemed to be trying to find somewhere on the Escalade to attach the chain. She stepped out of the truck to go and help.

Rafe looked up, an ominous expression now replacing his initial charm. "I said stay there! Don't come here! I will do this."

Jeri stopped. The anger in his voice echoed back into remote corners of her mind, reawakening memories that she had been trying to hard to erase, or at least imprison. She stepped backwards to the truck, not taking her eyes off him. Now she wanted to run, to jump back into the truck and escape a situation that had mutated from helping someone in need into something evil and dangerous.

It was too late. Rafe had crawled under the SUV and managed to hook the chain to some part of the frame or suspension. He stepped aside and motioned Jeri to start pulling.

She shifted the truck into low gear and slowly depressed the accelerator. Michael looked intently out the rear window, enthralled by the action, his senses recording every detail. Jeri eased the F-350 forward, taking up the slack in the chain. She slowly accelerated. The huge tires slipped briefly on the grassy turf, gripping enough to move forward.

They heard a grinding, scraping noise coming from beneath the Escalade. It teetered and slid backwards off the rock. Looking back and seeing it resting free on all four wheels, Jeri eased off the accelerator, releasing some tension on the chain, but not all.

Michael poked her shoulder and pointed frontward.

FLASHING LIGHT BARS DANCED along the crest of the ridge ahead of them. A parade of law enforcement vehicles roared down the narrow, gravel road, two four-by-four pickups leading the way. The four-by-fours continued on where the road ended.

Leaving a contingent to investigate the old farmhouse and Randy Tollefson's abandoned patrol car, the main force pursued up the ridge, becoming clearly visible a quarter mile away.

Rafe saw too. He flew under the SUV and worked frantically to unhook the chain.

Jeri sat transfixed, her right foot still pressing the brake pedal keeping tension on the chain. In the rear view mirror she saw Rafe running toward them, and caught a glimpse of two others leaping from the Escalade, their hands gripping assault rifles.

She stomped on the accelerator. The F-350 powered ahead dragging the Escalade behind.

Rafe closed in and leaped toward the pick-up end gate. He pulled himself up hooking his arms over the top, struggling to climb in, shouting and cursing.

Tears of fear and anger burned down Jeri's face. She pushed hard on the accelerator and gripped the wheel in fury, fighting to keep the bouncing truck under control, and herself. Her eyes darted between the front windshield toward the approaching officers and the rear view mirror. Rafe still hung on, trying to climb in the truck bed. The Escalade bounced along at the end of the chain behind the roaring, churning heavy-duty pickup.

Jeri flinched at the sound of three loud, sharp explosions piercing the din coming from the engine and drive-train.

Michael leaned back in the window gripping a handgun. Jeri hadn't noticed him take it from the glove compartment. She looked in the rear view mirror and could not see Rafe. She kept the big truck churning forward.

Rafe lost his grip when the nine millimeter slug slammed into his right shoulder. Michael looked out the back window and could no longer see him until he came back into view, but not for long. He saw Rafe's surprise and panic a fraction of a second before the Escalade rode backwards over his flailing limbs.

A series of sharp cracks penetrated the V-8 engine's roar, followed instantly by metal smashing into metal and glass.

"Get down! They're shooting at us!" Jeri shouted. "Get down on the floor!"

She hunched down behind the steering wheel, barely able to see over the dash. Michael leaned forward, still holding the handgun.

"Get down!" Jeri commanded. "Where did you get that?"

Michael did not respond.

Jeri took a quick look out the rear window and kept driving forward dragging the Escalade, which blocked her view of Rafe's crumpled body. Turning frontward she saw the approaching emergency vehicles stopped. She kept the big pickup and trailing SUV moving forward.

Two Ames County sheriff's department four-by-fours started moving again and approached within a hundred yards, bouncing over the uneven terrain. She did not stop until they closed in, one on each side of the F-350.

Rapid-fire of bullets smashed into the sheriff's trucks. The doors flew open and officers dove out on the ground, some scrambling behind the vehicles or rolling over to rock outcrops.

Using the F-350 for cover one crawled to the front and looked above the hood.

"Are you okay?" he shouted.

"We're okay," Jeri tried to shout, but her voice felt weak and trembling, nausea rising in her throat.

"Just stay there and stay down."

The sharp, staccato fire from assault rifles sent swarms of lead ripping into the vehicles, tearing into the ground and ricocheting off rocks. Armed with handguns and two shotguns, officers returned fire toward the flashes coming from the rocks less than a hundred yards up the ridge.

Sheriff Schwartz' voice broke in on the radios.

"Give me a report."

He sat in the mobile command post in the driveway of the abandoned farm where they found Deputy Tollefson's patrol car.

Randy and Tom Otto had been found lying on the ground about fifty feet apart, arms and legs tightly bound and duct tape covering their mouths, but otherwise unharmed except for some bruises and contusions. The relief from that good news quickly ended upon hearing rapid gunfire echoing from the rocks farther up on the ridge.

"We're pinned down!" The sergeant's tense, controlled voice came over on the radio. "They've got some heavy shit."

"Anybody hurt?"

"Not among the good guys."

"Hold your ground. We're calling for assistance. The state patrol will send a chopper."

"We need more firepower, now. Forget the chopper."

"You want the K-9s?"

"Negative. We know where they are. They won't get far."

"We've got Lakota County coming in from the other side," the sheriff said.

"They better bring everything they've got. These guys have assault rifles."

"Remind me to mention this at the next county budget review. What's the situation with the vehicles?" Schwartz asked.

"We've got Jeri Otto and the Weaver kid in the pickup. They're still inside down on the floor but okay. They were towing an SUV, a white Escalade. We don't see anyone inside."

The deputy flinched and crouched lower in front of the F-350. Another barrage of gunfire came from the rocks farther to the left. Officers heard bullets slamming into metal, but it wasn't their own vehicles. The sound came from a short distance ahead, as if the Escalade had been the target.

"Everybody still okay?" the sheriff said over the radio.

"We're okay. I'm not sure. I think they're hitting the SUV."

"They know about Weed. I don't know what's going on there. That could be it."

"Who's Weed?" the deputy asked.

"Leuten had somebody on the inside, but he didn't exactly follow the game plan. Randy thinks he's tied up in the back of the SUV. See if you can keep them from moving too much. Keep them away from the SUV. When Lakota County gets on the other side we should be able to keep them inside a perimeter."

A JUMBLE OF ROCKS anchored in the soil lying at the foot of a rock outcrop became a small, natural fortress for two desperate men, each armed with a large handgun and an assault rifle. They could see Rafe's body; still and lifeless.

Within an hour they had been surrounded by sixty-two law enforcement officers and four K-9s. Every available officer from two neighboring counties, state patrol, and conservation officers joined Ames and Lakota County officers in the standoff.

"This is Ames County Sheriff Schwartz." His voice echoed loudly from a battery-powered megaphone. "The only way you will leave here alive is to lay down your weapons and come out peacefully."

Hearing Randy's descriptions of the men, the sheriff believed the odds did not strongly favor a peaceful resolution.

Schwartz waited five minutes.

Three hours remained until nightfall. He did not look forward to a night-long standoff with the slim chance they might escape in the darkness. It was inevitable that they eventually would be captured. He worried more that trying to escape would cause confusion among the surrounding force, with the possibility of injury or worse from friendly fire.

"Listen to me," Schwartz shouted into the megaphone. "We're not going anywhere. You're not going anywhere. You can end this now. The longer you wait the worse it gets for you. This isn't Mexico. You'll get your due process. You'll get an attorney. You can make it a lot easier on yourself by coming out now. Just toss out your weapons. Hands in the air."

Schwartz paused. "You think they can hear us?" he asked officers nearby.

They said they thought so. The words really didn't matter anyway.

Ten more minutes passed, seeming like ten hours, especially for Michael, who began to worry that he was going to pee in his pants. The officer stationed in front using the truck as cover had ordered them to remain in the truck crouching down on the floor. The stress of the situation was bad enough; the posture made it even worse. It felt as if his bladder would explode, but he would die before yielding to the indignity of letting it go.

"What's going on? What's he doing?" Schwartz shouted into the radio. They saw the truck's passenger door fly open and a small figure running.

"The kid took off." The sound of the officer's voice over the radio from in front of the truck wavered under the stress and in the wind.

"I can see that."

"You want us to pursue?"

"No. Stay there. You're too exposed. We're circling around the flanks. We'll get him."

About two hundred feet to the right of the truck Michael found a clump of squat cedars that somehow found enough soil and moisture among the rocks to survive the hot summers and bitter cold winters.

"Michael! Get back here!" Jeri shouted, keeping low and leaning toward the open door.

"Stay there!" the officer shouted. "Michael, stay there!" He addressed Jeri: "There's other officers over there. They'll get him."

"They'd never shoot at him, the bad guys," Jeri replied. "Would they?"

"I don't think so. Let's hope not. Why'd he do that?"

"I don't know. I think I saw him going to the bathroom."

Looking toward the cedars the officer saw someone grabbing the boy by the arm, but it wasn't one of the other officers.

"Oh shit. They've got him." He spoke into the radio microphone. "Sheriff, they've got the kid. They're about seventy-five yards out at ten o'clock from the red truck."

The bad news halted the sheriff's plan to deploy two officers with sniper rifles.

"Anybody got ahold of Leuten yet? He's got to get his ass out here," Schwartz fumed. "It wasn't supposed to happen like this. Somebody wasn't following the game plan."

Weed, the informant, had been feeding information to the state BCI about drug traffickers bringing meth into the state from labs in Mexico. Most of the action occurred in the larger cities, although how it was getting distributed remained to be discovered. Schwartz did not believe allegations about any involvement by Tom Otto, even after Leuten claimed to have found the plastic egg in the delivery truck. Perhaps cases of similar eggs, but not just one. Leuten's arrogance and apparently willingness to push circumstantial evidence, while annoying enough, raised questions that so far no one had voiced.

After learning Weed's real identity and previous record, the Ames County investigators understood the motive for the drug gang's visit to the Weaver farm Tuesday, something that Leuten and the Drug Enforcement Agency agents had not seen coming.

They always return to the crime scene, in this case, the remote farmhouse used ten years ago by a small group of drug users and dealers. Although he knew about Weed, Schwartz never had met him. After hearing the descriptions provided by Deputy Tollefson and Tom Otto, he realized Weed's identity and past as the leader of the gang operating out of the old Wegman farm. After the bust, the investigation and clean-up found no hidden cache of money other than what they found in the house, but the rumors persisted.

The Lakota County sheriff came on the radio. "Lakota County is in position."

"What's your twenty?" Sheriff Schwartz asked.

"We're probably two hundred yards out from the vehicles. We see one suspect down about fifty feet or so from the white SUV. We saw someone running from the red pickup."

"That's the kid. We think they have the kid. Do not approach. Even if you take fire, do not return fire. Maintain your positions and keep them surrounded. We are starting negotiations. BCI is on the way."

Sheriff Schwartz lowered the microphone. He rubbed his eyes and sent up a silent prayer: *God, please don't let the worst happen. These guys don't negotiate. For the kid's sake, help us end this without anybody getting hurt.*

"Sheriff, look." The detective pointed toward smoke rising from behind the rocks and brush ahead, streaming at an angle toward the two vehicles still attached by a tow chain. A fifteen-mile-per-hour northwest wind pushed a spreading arc of flames through dry, old-growth grass and brush overpowering the new growth.

The sheriff called all area fire departments to roll their tankers and grass rigs. He radioed the officers stationed by the Otto's pickup. "Get Jeri and pull back. Did you see anything how it started?"

A minute passed.

The officer called back. "She won't go without the truck. It looks like the fire line might come this way."

"Let her drive it out then."

"It's still hooked to the SUV."

"We want that, too. Can't lose any evidence."

With the wind pushing the spreading grass fire, tongues of flame now leaped ten feet high. Dark gray smoke billowed in clouds.

The officers in front of the F-350 ran back to their vehicles and motioned Jeri to drive forward dragging the Escalade. The fire emergency pushed aside her panic about Michael's safety. She started the engine and accelerated, providing cover for the officers. They glanced back and saw the fire line advancing toward the body of the man in the dark green polo shirt, not knowing whether he was just unconscious or dead.

"You little son-of-a-bitch! What you think you're doing?"

One of the men smacked an open palm across the side of Michael's head. Both men started stomping on the burning grass. They could not keep up as flames and smoke spread. The wind blew like a steady blacksmith's bellows pouring oxygen into the bright orange and yellow combustion spreading through dry thatch, consuming it in an instant and moving on to the next. Flames swept up into the green grass creating clouds of smoke.

Michael took off running in the opposite direction.

The men had been holding Michael in their hiding place among the rocks, arguing over the odds of getting any benefit from a hostage situation. Michael sat on the ground with his knees pulled up to his chin and arms wrapped around them. He saw the pack of cigarettes fall from a pocket of one the men and the book of matches stuck in the wrapper.

Slowly, he reached for the pack. Unnoticed, he lit a match, quickly extinguished by the wind. He lit another, touched it to the whole book of matches and tossed it into a clump of dry grass. It took a moment for the men to react, but was too late.

"Ames County, we see the kid. He's running this way," the Lakota County sheriff radioed.

"Let him come to you," Sheriff Schwartz replied. "If he sees you approaching he might run again. What's the fire situation on your side?"

"It's moving away from us."

"Give us a report when you have the kid."

"Ten-four."

The grass fire advanced along the ridge toward a cluster of towering wind generators.

22

"Give me a report from the house," Sheriff Schwartz ordered, not looking at anyone in particular. His eyes remained fixed on the approaching vehicles ahead and the slow growing grass fire.

The sudden arrival of two DEA agents surprised the sheriff. They intended to make certain the drug suspects were apprehended. They ordered caution in the advance on the abandoned farm house. They had been doing a lot of ordering since Tuesday, even before they arrived in Buffalo Ridge. They briefed the sheriff on a need-to-know basis.

"We're in position. We're moving in." The deputy's voice on the radio sounded choppy, the words clipped in competition with gasping breaths.

With so many law enforcement vehicles streaming by the old farmhouse, and the mobile command post stationed at the end of the driveway, the question of using stealth tactics approaching the farmhouse was moot. Schwartz ordered it anyway, mostly because the department had just completed stealth training. It could be justified by the present situation, and served to reinforce the training. And it was much more fun to suit up in camo and sneak through the woods.

"Find out when Leuten will get here," one of the DEA agents asked the sheriff. "Where the hell is he?"

"I think he's out on a boat ride. Back in St. Paul."

"Does he have a paddle?"

"What?"

"Never mind."

The DEA agents had showed up Wednesday. They briefed the sheriff and a detective on the informant working inside the drug ring. Schwartz thought they seemed irritated about having to do so. They apparently had not expected to be diverted to a small prairie town.

Monday evening, when the tracking device on the white Escalade showed it moving out of St. Paul, far out into the countryside, they decided against following immediately. They alerted the sheriff and FBI to look for the Escalade. If spotted, the locals were to contact the DEA agents, but not to approach the vehicle. Sitting in their office later Tuesday morning, they watched and wondered as the point on the GPS monitor that showed the vehicle stopped several miles south of Buffalo Ridge.

"He should be here any minute," Hank said. "He's flying out in a state patrol chopper. So who's in command here?"

"For the record, you are," the agent replied.

"I feel better already."

They stood outside the command post, a small trailer crammed with work tables and communications gear, watching the distant action around the red pickup. Trucks from the Buffalo Ridge Fire Department and the Department of Natural Resources regional office turned off the main county highway onto the gravel road speeding toward the grass fire.

"So why didn't you move in sooner on these guys?" Hank asked.

"You're not going to blame us for what happened Tuesday," the agent said flatly, a statement, not a question, that left Hank feeling irritated.

"If you knew they were in the area, we could have grabbed them," Hank said. "Now we've got one homicide and possibly two."

"This is way out of your league. These guys would cut you up before you even knew what happened. We were closing in on their distribution network. This little excursion out here in the boondocks didn't exactly fit their routine. We don't know why it happened," the agent admitted.

"Well it did, and now we have to clean up the mess."

Officers escorted Tom and Randy into the command post trailer. EMTs checked them over and dressed their minor injuries. A county detective and one of the DEA agents entered, asked Randy to leave, and began the questioning. The other agent remained with the sheriff.

Tom's explanation that he just happened to be in the area by coincidence and went to the old farmsite mostly out of curiosity, met with visible skepticism and more persistent questions from all angles.

"It just doesn't sound like you," the detective said.

"How do you know what I sound like," Tom retorted.

The detective stared back. Tom tried to suppress an agitated feeling. "You listening in on cell phones now?" Even as the words slipped out he wished he could take them back. The detective's face showed no reaction.

"You know what I mean. I mean when you're on the route you don't mess around. You always have a long day. You work hard. It just doesn't seem like something you would normally do."

"I swear it was just a coincidence."

"You just stopped the truck and decided to sneak up on this old farmhouse?" the DEA agent asked. He accompanied the county detective interviewing Tom while his partner stayed with the sheriff.

"Well, I did see the SUV. It was an Escalade, right?"

"That's right."

"I was about, I don't know, maybe a mile away. I saw it turn into the gravel road. Something just told me to follow it."

Tom explained again how he crept through the grove, hid in the old chicken coop, saw Randy captured. How he sneaked over to the patrol car and tried to call nine-one-one until his capture.

"When did you take the meth?"

"What?"

"When did you use meth?"

"What are you talking about?"

"Have you ever taken meth?" The agent spoke calmly, studying the young man's expressions and movements more intently than any words he expected to hear. He knew all the scripts. Only in rare cases did the body language fail to reveal the truth.

"Hey, are you nuts? I don't use that stuff."

"Have you ever tried it?"

"C'mon. We got a freakin' emergency going on here. My wife is out there. And the kid, Michael. Why are you guys still going after me? That plastic egg that BCI dude said he found in my truck, that's bullshit," Tom said, feeling a surge of anger.

"There's just a lot of questions, that's all," the detective said. "We have to ask them. So, have you ever used meth?"

"No, I don't use that stuff." The lie felt like a cold block of ice in his gut.

The detective sat back on the small stool, folded his arms and gazed silently. They had heard Tom's voice on the radio. Something in it triggered the thought that if they had heard it in person, they would have been better able to ascertain the possibility of impairment caused by meth, or alcohol, or perhaps some other controlled substance.

"We're just curious," the detective said. "I see all these big trucks on the road. Hour after hour behind the wheel. Hell, I get tired just driving to the cities, especially in the afternoons. I can't imagine what it would be like behind the wheel of an eighteen-wheeler trying to stay awake."

"What's that supposed to mean? You saying I'm using meth to stay awake on my route?"

"I'm saying that it makes me wonder in general. A lot of times the truth is right there in front of your nose, but nobody talks about it, nobody sees it or wants to."

"I said I don't use it. I use caffeine. That's it."

"That's good to hear," the detective said. He paused, "I hope you're telling us everything."

"I am. I swear."

They heard a radio call asking the sheriff to come back to the farmhouse immediately. The DEA agent thanked Tom and left the trailer.

"Sorry, Tom. We just have to play their game here. It's nothing personal. We should be glad these guys are here. They've had a lot more experience in the big leagues," the detective said nodding toward the departing agent now out of hearing range.

He sat up to look out a window of the command trailer. A convoy of sheriff's four-by-fours and the big red pickup approached.

"Okay. Let's go see how Jeri is. We'll be talking about this some more. Thanks." He forced a smile and gave Tom a friendly pat on his shoulder. Tom flinched, rose quickly and stepped out of the trailer.

Dwayne Gleason decided to take the big truck. He hung up the phone and looked up at the poster-size Ames County map.

When the deputy described vehicle and location, using the tandem-axle tow truck seemed justified, and would bring in a larger fee.

He caught only the tail-end of the scanner traffic. It sounded like a big deal. Something was going down with possible suspects in the murder case that had been dominating conversation around town. It sounded like an army had converged somewhere up on the ridge. An Escalade was large enough, and the possibility of going off-road up on the ridge to retrieve it were reasons enough to use the big tow truck normally reserved for semis and other large trucks.

Turning off the county highway on to the narrow, gravel township road leading past the vacant farm it seemed to take up the entire width. It barely squeezed by the mobile command trailer.

"Holy smokes, what'd he take that thing for?" Randy interjected, relaxing for a few seconds from his turn facing the detective's questions. "You see that? Dwayne took his big honkin' truck. He must be having a slow week."

The detective smiled, waiting several seconds before resuming.

"What do you think Tom was doing here?"

"I already said I don't know for sure. I know you guys are looking for something on him."

"Not really. We just want to know what happened. You ought to know that."

"I think Leuten was trying to set him up. That's what I think," Randy said. "And I think the feds are on to him. To Leuten. He gives me the creeps anyway."

"I'll pretend I didn't hear that."

"That plastic egg that Harmon claims he found in Tom's truck? Hell, I was there. He didn't say anything about it when we were in the truck. Then outside he just pulls it out of his pocket. You think he would have said something. He would have showed it to me right away."

"Maybe, maybe not. You ever think Tom has used meth?"

"God, I hope not. I don't think so. He's talked about it. He told me once down at one of the warehouses in the cities, somebody tried to sell him some. I just don't see it. You'd know if he was."

"That's true. But still, you don't sound a hundred percent sure that he doesn't, or hasn't."

"Can we talk about this later? I don't want to sit around in here with all the action going on. Just lay off for awhile. We're on the same team, aren't we? Yeah, Tom's my friend but I want to do my job. I want find out the truth as much as you do."

The detective smiled. "We both know sometimes the truth is tough to take. Sometimes we resolve a situation without really getting at the truth, or wanting to."

"Maybe it's like that with you guys higher up the food chain. Not me. You want the truth you go to the foot soldier. That's all I am and right now that's all I want to do."

"That's why I'm asking you all the questions," the detective smiled again.

THE SMUDGES OF DARK FACE PAINT FAILED to camouflage expressions of shock on several of the officers. They stepped out on the back porch after searching the farmhouse. They stood for a moment as if not knowing what to do.

"Sheriff, you better come in to the house," an officer radioed.

Schwartz wanted to stay with action, the red pickup approaching, the grass fire getting knocked down, any report from Lakota County about the suspects and the kid.

The dearth of information in the radio call from the farm house only increased the dread of seeing what they had found. Reluctantly Hank got into a patrol car with a deputy at the wheel and rode back to the farmhouse.

Sometime in the 1940s a bathroom had been carved out of a part of the kitchen and a pantry. It held barely enough room for a sink, toilet, and a full-size cast iron bathtub. An officer taking photos backed out and stepped aside for Sheriff Schwartz. He entered and looked down at the tub.

"Jesus," he said softly.

For a moment the only sound came from feet shifting on the creaky kitchen floor. Hank's eyes scanned across the tub cradling a still, human form, identifiable as such by its torso, limbs, and head, but not much more than that. Still clothed, blood covered almost everything. Streaks of blood on the floor leading into the bathroom indicated that the vicious beating occurred in the kitchen, and the body dumped into the bathtub. The stage of coagulation said the violent assault on human life and dignity happened within the last hour or two.

The search for Stan Weaver was over.

THE STATE PATROL CHOPPER ARRIVED a few minutes after 6:00 p.m. It approached high to stay clear of the surrounding wind towers and set down in a grassy area between the house and chicken coop. The huge rotor pounded the air driving it down, pressing the grass flat, scouring loose bits of soil and thatch sending them swirling away into the air.

BCI agent Harmon Leuten hopped out, instinctively raising a hand to cover his head. He hurried away from the rotor wash toward the farm house.

From a distance the sheriff didn't recognize him at first. He wore khaki shorts and a golf shirt instead of the usual suit and tie, creating a noticeable difference in the measure of authority that clothing conveyed.

Approaching the officers standing on the back porch, the expression on his face seemed unfamiliar. Instead of his usual demeanor of looking past the other person and talking in a command voice, this time his eyes scanned the others, their acknowledgement of the two DEA agents barely perceptible.

"How was the fishing?" Harold asked when Leuten stepped up onto the porch.

"I wasn't fishing. Who said I was fishing?"

"In a boat out on the river. I just assumed you were fishing."

"We weren't fishing. So what do we got? Where's the kid?"

"He's okay. He's already on his way back to town."

Harold stepped aside extending his arm, inviting Leuten to enter the house ahead of him. "Let's go inside. I guess we can remove one more name from the suspect list."

Leuten gave a slight nod to the DEA agents. He went into the house following an officer toward the small bathroom. He stood in the doorway. Focused on Stan's body, his eyes showed no reaction. It seemed as if he didn't know what to do. He went back outside to the group standing on the porch.

"Where's Weed? Have you interviewed him yet?" Leuten asked.

"He hasn't said much," Hank replied. "He seems to be in some state of shock. He's okay otherwise. A few bumps and bruises."

"Did he say why they came out here? To the Weaver farm?"

"Not that I know of. You can ask him yourself."

Leuten turned to the DEA agents. "You guys know anything? Why they were here?"

"All we know is what the sheriff told us," one agent replied. "The legend about the money hidden somewhere on the Weaver farm. Sounds like that could be the motive. We can't think of any other reasons why these guys would have come out here. Maybe Weed had something to do with it."

"Who is he working for, anyway?" Leuten asked.

A fleeting glance passed between the DEA agents. "As far as we know he's working for you," one finally said. "We just found out this week. What are you getting at?"

"Nothing." Leuten's breath carried the pungent, sour scent of alcohol.

JERI EMERGED FROM THE COMMAND POST trailer, clutching the handrail as she stepped down to steady the weakness she felt in her legs. Tom stood waiting, uncertain about what to expect. She walked over slowly and embraced him. She buried her face in his shoulder; tears squeezed from her clenched eyelids.

"I want to go home. I just want to go home," she sobbed.

"Don't cry now baby. Everything's going to be okay. We can go now." Tom held her close and struggled to make his voice sound calm, squeezing through the tightness in his throat.

"They were asking me all kinds of questions," Jeri said.

"I know. They grilled me, too."

"I mean, questions about you, too. What are they trying to do? When is all this going to be over?"

"I don't know. I think it's Leuten. He's still after me."

"Why? Why doesn't he just back off? I can't believe it. But what were you doing here?"

"I was just driving back towards town. I just got done with the north part of the route. I saw this big SUV turn onto the dirt road here. I remembered the old farm house back here. I just got curious and turned in. What were you doing out here with Michael?"

"We were going back into town. After Newton Case brought him over, I just took the long way."

"Some long way, half way around the county."

"I just had to be with him for a little bit. It wasn't hurting anything." Jeri fought back tears.

"Okay, okay. Sorry."

"How did you get caught? You and Randy?"

Tom tried to explain again everything that happened. Again he pressed Jeri on how she and Michael ended up where they did, and the details of their encounter with Rafe and the gang.

"It was stupid, but it turned out to be a good thing leaving your gun like that in the truck," Jeri said. "I still don't think the sheriff believes me about that. It happened so fast. Michael just grabbed it and leaned out the window and 'pop-pop-pop' just like that. And then he doesn't talk. It's like he's in some kind of trance or something."

"You know it doesn't really surprise me, though. When we'd see him at the Weavers and all the stuff he knew how to do. Sort of takes after somebody else we all know and love," Tom said with a little grin. Jeri smiled and it felt good, as though something good might arise later from the pain and tragedy inflicted by Satan and his evil on good people, or trying to be.

"I feel so bad about Stan," she said. "Why couldn't they just have let him go? He was so nice. I just don't get it."

"They were bad people, Jeri. They would do anything to anybody. I thought they were going to kill me and Randy. And that other guy, whatever his name was, Weed or something. I know they were going to kill him."

"But he was one of them."

"I don't get it, either. Randy said something about him being an under cover guy, somebody working for the cops. He said he might have been one of those guys there before, before Stan and Tulie took over the place."

Jeri pulled back. She held his shoulders and stared into his face. "Are you serious?"

"That's what he said."

"What did he look like?"

"Why?"

"Oh lord." Her voice trailed off. "What did he look like?"

"I don't know. I never got a good look. Why? Was he one of those guys?"

"I hope not. Can't you remember at all what he looked like?"

"I don't know. He was probably a little taller than me. Kind of skinny. Dark, greasy long hair. I didn't really see his face too good. Maybe a big nose. His skin looked shitty."

"I don't know. I'm not really sure, I guess," Jeri said. She hoped that this time her intuition was wrong.

SHERIFF SCHWARTZ WALKED OVER, asked if they were doing okay, and said they could go. He asked if they would stop into the office on Monday to go over things again. Tom said he would shorten his route and try to make it in around four; Jeri said she would see if she could use a couple hours of vacation and go into work late. Hank hailed a nearby deputy and told him to escort the Ottos to their home.

Dwayne Gleason's big truck rumbled past towing the Escalade, followed by an ambulance transporting the body of Rafe, born thirty six years ago in Tiajuana and christened with the name of Rafael Gonzales, which in recent years had become one of several that he used, depending on the situation.

Another ambulance remained at the scene while an emergency medical technician treated Weed for multiple contusions and lacerations, mostly to the head. Two officers stood guard. The sheriff would have preferred more, but couldn't until the two remaining suspects were captured.

A deputy in a patrol car escorted Tom and Jeri back to town and home, leading Jeri in the pickup followed by Tom in the delivery truck. Lynn had already fed

Jade and Trace, who were outside playing on the swing set when the vehicles entered the driveway.

They sat around the picnic table in the front yard, suddenly noticing hunger, which had been deferred by the events on the ridge. Returning to the Ottos with Jade and Trace, Lynn had picked up a bucket of KFC and potato salad. At first, Jeri's stomach still felt queasy. Tom chomped on a juicy, extra crispy chicken leg; the spicy, greasy aroma soon triggered Jeri's appetite.

Lynn rested her chin on her hands, her gaze switching between the kids on the swing set and Tom and Jeri eating, savoring the interlude of contentment inspired by a soft, sweet scent of leaves and grass washed in warm, subtle breeze.

"It's a good thing you found Michael," she said, quietly, thoughtfully.

"Yeah, Newton Case found him," Jeri said.

"I wonder why he did that? I don't know too much about him."

"He's not crazy like some people say." Jeri didn't think her mother knew about how she and Michael got to the hospital that January morning eight years ago. No one remembered much of anything from that time, or at least didn't acknowledge anything.

"That's too bad about Stan," Lynn said. "Did you find out anything about what happened to him?"

"I asked Randy and he wouldn't tell me anything," Tom said. "He just said he'd been pretty messed up."

"It just makes me sick," Lynn said. "They were so nice, such good people."

"Why does God let stuff like this happen?" Tom asked.

"You can't blame God."

"Why not? If God's all powerful, can't he just stop it from happening?"

"It's not that simple. Satan is powerful, too. It's in the Bible. Somewhere it says Satan is the god of evil in the world. Bad things happen because of it. But in the end God will win."

"Let's hope so."

"Well, he will if we help."

"What's that supposed to mean?"

"God uses us to do good things and fight evil."

"Apparently, not everybody got the memo."

"Oh, I think most people got the memo," Lynn said. "It's called the Bible. But not everyone does what it says."

23

Weed finished his breakfast and lay back on the bunk. He gazed up at the narrow, horizontal window high on the wall of his cell in the newly-built Ames County jail, thinking about his previous incarceration in the old jail eight years ago, since demolished and replaced by a new, larger facility.

Some people thought the brick walls of the old jail seemed to have more warmth and character than the barren concrete block walls of the new jail, although Weed was not one of them. Awareness of such attributes no longer registered among most of the occupants. However, he was conscious of the new surroundings. They compared well with the state prison of recent vintage where he spent five of the last eight years, but he could no longer relate to such sentiments. He could not explain why, nor would he even try to. Survival and revenge now defined his life even more than before.

Farther back than he could remember, Quentin Oakes had learned to avoid any introspection that attempted to examine his beliefs and behavior. He got the nickname, Weed, back in high school where he was known for selling and using copious amounts of marijuana. As the years passed the ability to look inward and accept responsibility for his actions gradually dissipated, evicted by a growing hatred of others, of the world, but mostly of himself and his existence.

But he could not erase completely the memory of the young girl who ran around with their loose association of meth cookers and assorted crackheads. They moved around, mostly to older, remote farmsteads. He once asked her to leave with him, and she almost did until one of the dogs attacked her little boy. The emergency and her response to it eventually led law enforcement to the old farmhouse, ending their existence of meth cooking and using, soaring and crashing, burning through a time of life God intended for building careers, families, homes, and communities.

He almost felt relieved that the recent charade had ended, although angry that it had not happened in the way he had intended.

Now he gravely regretted causing the diversion that brought Rafe and the others out to the old farm south of Buffalo Ridge. He had been sensing a growing suspicion about his true allegiances other than himself, at least in Rafe if not the others. He would have known if they had been talking among themselves.

He thought they might see the trip out to the countryside in search of about fifty thousand cash hidden on an old farm as an entertaining lark, that would distract them from further investigation of his bargain with agents of the U.S. Drug

Enforcement Agency, and later, Harmon Leuten of the state Bureau of Criminal Investigation.

Leuten had tried to get him alone Friday evening, but the DEA agents would not leave. Weed refused to answer questions anyway without legal representation present, and the only two public defenders in Buffalo Ridge had left town for the weekend.

The agents pummeled him verbally until almost two a.m. Weed knew the system and held out, mentally and physically, until they gave up. The DEA agents didn't talk much, leaving most of the questioning to Leuten. He must have asked fifty times why they went to the farm, and what happened with Stan and Tulie.

Weed's story, what he would tell of it, did not change: They intended no harm. They just wanted look around under the pretext of shopping for fresh, organic chicken, hand-crafted wood furniture, and home-made wine. When Tulie spooked and came at them with a shotgun, Rafe tried to take it from her in self defense. During the struggle the gun discharged striking Tulie's midriff. Leaving the farm, they passed by Stan cutting alfalfa with the horses. He was making a turn close to the road, close enough to wave and get a good look at the vehicle and its occupants. Rafe stopped; Stan walked out of the field and up to the road to see what they wanted. Rafe stuck a forty-five automatic in his face; the other two bound his hands and feet and stuffed him in the back of the Escalade. Weed insisted that he did not know what happened when they took Stan into the old house on the abandoned farm site on the ridge.

He acknowledged that Rafe confronted him about his allegiances, accusing him of being an informant. He swore that he had not admitted to anything, had not revealed any details about the arrangement. Finding him with injuries from a beating and tied up in the back of the Escalade, the agents believed most of his story, what he told of it.

The other two drug gang members were being held in the Lakota County jail and were to be transported to Ames County in the morning. They surrendered after K-9 units tracked them down on the broad plateau of the ridge, and then were flushed out staggering and gasping in a cloud of stinging, blinding tear gas.

DURING THE INTERROGATION ORDEAL late Friday and into early Saturday Weed had been tempted to play his trump card. He had sensed that the DEA agents did not want him to reveal any clues about it, his multiple allegiances although he was unsure to whose advantage that would become.

Now he was glad that he hadn't.

The DEA agents entered his cell at 9:00 a.m., one hour before his arraignment Saturday before a district court judge, finally getting him alone without raising suspicion among the other state and county investigators.

"Nice place here," one said looking around the cell. "You couldn't wait to get back."

Weed lay on the bunk staring at the ceiling.

"What the hell were you thinking? Obviously you weren't thinking," the agent said. "Why in hell did you come out here?"

"I told you. They were on to me. Rafe. He was getting suspicious."

"So what did this little escapade have to do with that?"

"I thought it would distract them, give me some cred."

"Like that's ever going to happen. You should have said something. You should have told us."

"I didn't think it would hurt. We would just zip out here, look around, and head back. Rafe went for it."

"You said it again."

"Said what?"

"Think. You talk but you don't think. Your brains if you have any left have been so messed up it's a miracle you've made it this far. You better start thinking now because you're so deep in shit we can't help you."

"I told you what happened. It was Rafe."

"Well I guess we won't be hearing his story now, will we? He wouldn't have been here anyway if it wasn't for you."

"What about Leuten?"

"What about him?"

"He could have had something to do with it. It could give him the chance to slither away from everything. You still need me."

"He has nothing to do with this. That is still on track. But the train might come in to the station a little sooner, that's all."

"Not without my help."

"We don't need your help anymore. You're on your own now, pal. You've already had your share of luck. If that young lady hadn't come along when she did?

They would've messed you up so bad, and you would have been conscious to savor every bit of it."

The agents left Weed's cell.

His thoughts wandered among the events of the past twenty-four hours, the past week. He began to calculate his chances.

The DEA agent was right. Instead of suffering a slow, excruciating death, Weed lay on a bunk in a small, clean room, digesting breakfast, his fate resting in the criminal justice system, not on the vicious whims of a mid-level *especulador* in a Mexican drug ring.

He recalled the glimpse of the young woman and the boy. He didn't see her face, but everything else about her fit into the outline of a memory. During the past eight years he had almost forgotten about her, the cute, young local high school girl whom they met at the race track.

When she continued to play along with their flirting, they asked if she wanted to go to a party out in the country, which she did. Two weeks later she ran away from home to move in with them at the old farm house. In return for the chance to party all night and sleep all day, she provided recreation and soon proved very capable and industrious at cooking meth.

After the bust she got off easy because of the kid.

Not until recently, after the DEA recruited him in prison to become an informant, did he try to remember anything about the old days on the old farm meth lab, and whose kid it was.

For a moment, lying there on the bunk, he even became slightly intrigued. When they first learned that she was knocked up, they made a game of arguing whose it was. After the baby arrived and their instincts eroded by drugs and alcohol, gradually they grew irritated at the intrusion.

He figured there was a one-third chance that the kid was his.

24

"Tom, c'mon in now and help get the kids to bed," Jeri shouted from the kitchen door. In the early Saturday evening Tom stood in the yard watching the sky.

The excitement that nature could provide helped him shake off the sour mood remaining from mid-afternoon when he had called Randy to see if he wanted to take the four-wheelers out for a spin at the abandoned gravel pit. If he couldn't take the truck out, he at least could ride the four-wheeler for awhile.

Randy said he had too much to do at home. He seemed distant, uncomfortable in even talking with Tom.

"I'm just looking at the storm. Just give me a minute, will ya?" Like the brewing storm his resentment approached the boiling point.

"C'mon! I've still got dishes to do. You shouldn't be out there anyway."

Jeri stepped back inside and slammed the door. The hot, muggy afternoon had exacerbated the tension building all week, waiting to strike. She switched the television channel to a news and weather station. Ames County was included in the tornado watch area scrolling across the bottom of the screen.

"I want to go outside with daddy," Jade whined. "Me too. I want daddy," Trace begged, becoming angry.

"We can't go outside. There's going to be a storm. Daddy's coming back in. It's time for bed anyway."

"I don't want to go to bed," Jade cried.

Jeri looked out the window and saw the pickup backing out of the shop. She commanded Jade to stay with her brother and ran out the door.

The hot, south wind that had been blowing all day had stopped as if the weather maker had simply switched off a hair dryer, leaving the air quiet and calm. Leaves hung limp and parched, suddenly resting quietly after hours of hanging on for life. To the southwest, through gaps among the tree branches of the grove surround the old farmstead, she saw the dark almost black wall cloud. She ran toward the pickup waving her arms, and reaching it tried to open the door. Tom pressed the unlock switch and she jerked it open.

"Where do think you're going?"

"I'm just going out to look at the storm. There might be a tornado," he said.

"Like heck you are. You get back in there and help me with the kids. They're bawling their heads off."

"I'll just be a few minutes."

"If you leave I'm taking the kids and go running down the road after you."

"C'mon. Don't be like that. It's no big deal. I'll be right back."

Jeri looked toward the southwest. The dark wall cloud appeared much closer.

"Tom! Look at that thing! What's the matter with you!" she started crying. "The TV said we're in a tornado watch! It's coming right at us!"

"Then let's go! Get the kids and let's out of here!" he shouted.

"You're not supposed to do that! They say you're supposed to stay inside. We should all get back inside, in the bathroom someplace."

The dark, roiling clouds approaching overhead shook loose a downpour of enormous raindrops, the first waves landing in large, wet plops thumping the hood of the truck. Hail soon followed, some as large as nickels. A wall of wind blasted into the grove ripping at the leaves and bending branches. Tom felt momentarily paralyzed in dilemma: drive the truck back into the shop to protect it from hail and ride out the storm hiding in the house, or load everyone into the truck and make a run for it.

"Let's get out of here!" he shouted over the growing roar of the wind. "Get in. I'll drive up to the house and get the kids."

"No! Let's stay here! I'm not going!"

"We're better off in the truck! If it's a tornado we don't have a chance in that tin can we live in! I'd rather take my chances making a run for it."

Jeri climbed in. "You're not supposed to do that," she said, angry yet resigned to his stubborn decision, only because she knew that if a tornado did strike the old mobile home would be flattened or tossed around like a cardboard box.

Tom drove across the yard up to the kitchen door. Jeri rushed into the house, ducking under pummeling rain and hail. Carrying Trace and holding Jade's hand, she hurried back and they all climbed into the truck, rain-soaked and crying.

The big wheels spun muddy trenches in the grass by the front door. The truck narrowly missed the picnic table as Tom drove out to the road.

"We're going to be okay." Jeri tried to sound calm addressing the kids, now more distracted than frightened by the excitement of going for a ride in the truck in a storm. Tom turned left out of the driveway. "Let's go north."

"That looks worse," Jeri said.

"I know, but we know what's there. If there's a tornado it will be behind us. You're supposed to go at right angles."

The hail let up but not the rain. The westward sky lightened as the swirling storm cell moved eastward, the path passing just south of Buffalo Ridge.

"You see that?" Tom said, looking back over his left shoulder. Jeri tried to see out the rear window. "What?"

"Does that look like a tornado to you?"

"I can't see anything. I've never seen one."

"Look at that spiral cloud. It's kind of starting to snake down. That's a funnel cloud!" Tom's eyes shot back and forth between the road, what he could see of it, and the corn field west of the grove of trees sheltering their home. Now less than a thousand yards away, the demonic vortex of wind spinning in a one-hundred-and-fifty-mile-per-hour spiral about two hundred yards across, churned a weaving scar into the earth, sucking up soil and young corn stalks, and sending out a deep, rumbling, roar.

"Oh God, please let's get out of here," Jeri cried, making the kids even more terrified.

Tom gripped the wheel. He glanced back and saw the funnel closing in on the grove, relieved that they were out of its path, yet unable to comprehend what might happen to their home. Their only major possession with sufficient insurance coverage was the pickup.

They drove north to the main highway and turned left. Tom parked the truck on the shoulder. They all looked back toward the southeast at the receding funnel cloud, appearing grayish white, slowly undulating like a sinuous serpent rising from the earth into the clouds. Light moving in from west behind the storm cell reflected off what looked like bare bones of trees amid the grove that once sheltered their home.

They looked back in silence. In the rear view mirror Tom saw the flashing lights of emergency vehicles approaching from the direction of town.

"Mommy, what's going on? I want to go home," Jade whimpered.

Tom and Jeri locked eyes, knowing that something dreadful had just occurred, fearing what they would find, searching for hope and strength.

"It's okay baby, we will," Jeri's voice trembled. "It's over now."

"You can say that again," Tom said grimly. "You thinking what I'm thinking?"

"It's probably okay," Jeri said, trying sound confident. "We'll just fix what we have to. What else can we do?"

"Not if it hit the house."

A sheriff's patrol car rolled to a stop behind the pickup. This time the flashing light bar was a welcome sight. The Ottos assured the deputy that everyone was okay. Tom made a U-turn and followed the patrol car back to their home site.

Jeri sat on the picnic table, which for some unexplained reason still sat in the front yard, apparently untouched by the funnel cloud that tore through their home site. Staring vacantly toward the shredded, twisted remains of the shop, she opened the cell phone and called her mother.

Trying to make herself sound calm and composed, she told Lynn they were all okay, all except for the house and the shop, the newest structure of greater value than even the older mobile home. An old granary remaining from the days when a succession of families made their living off the surrounding one hundred sixty acres, stood mostly intact.

Jeri's composure crumbled at the sound of her mother's voice.

"Can we stay with you?" Jeri pleaded. "I don't know what we're going to do."

"Of course you can stay with me," Lynn said. "We're just thankful everyone is okay. That old trailer wasn't worth much anyway."

"Don't say that," irritation momentarily replacing Jeri's sorrow. "That's all we have. And all our stuff and furniture? We can't afford to replace everything. Why did this have to happen to us, and of all times why now?"

Tom sat next to Jeri with Trace on his lap and holding Jade close. Usually the first in a crisis to respond with action, he did not know what to do, as if he were waiting for the nightmare to end. He reached his other arm around Jeri's shoulders, looking blankly across the debris-littered yard at the deputy twisting closed the valve on the propane tank, even though mostly empty after toppling from its stand, rupturing the copper tubing gas line.

"Sometimes we just don't know why these things happen," Lynn said. "We pray to God that we'll be spared, and if we're not spared, then for the strength to see it through. I know it's hard to understand now, but I know it will all work out."

"That's easy for you to say. You should see this place." Jeri began sobbing again.

"Just hold on. I'm coming out."

Tom carried the kids to the pickup. Jade sat quietly, trying to comprehend the change in her surroundings, the overwhelming assault on the security of all that she knew up to this point. Trace acted irritable, from sleepiness disrupted by events beyond his full understanding.

A caravan of emergency vehicles assembled in the yard, maneuvering around tree branches, chunks of what had been walls and the roof, furniture and other belongings strewn about. A two-by-four from the frame of the shop stuck like a spear into a basswood tree by the driveway.

A piece of the roof from the shop rested on the dash of the delivery truck, encircled by jagged edges of the smashed windshield; otherwise, the truck showed little damage.

Holding Trace on his shoulder, Tom climbed into the pickup. He pulled Jade close to his side and stared at the destruction. On the horizon of his mind he saw sneaking and slinking through the aftermath thoughts of why it all happened, and what would become of them.

Randy Tollefson picked his way through the debris toward the pickup.

"Hey, man, gosh." He looked around with a pained expression, then to Tom and the kids. "Everybody okay?"

Tom nodded. "Looks like we won't be hitting the trails tomorrow," he said sardonically. "Ain't this the shits?"

"Hey don't worry. You'll get through this. This is just stuff. As long as you guys are all okay, that's what counts."

"It's a good thing we left when we did," Tom said. "Look at that trailer. That's where we would have been otherwise."

Randy looked toward the flattened and shredded remains, quickly subduing the thought that it really was no big loss. "You got a place to stay? You can stay at our place."

"Thanks. We're going to Jeri's mom's, for now anyway."

Sheriff Schwartz approached and said he would try to find someone to watch the place overnight.

The tornado chewed a weaving path through the countryside south of town, in some fields shredding a promising corn crop, damaging three other houses, some outbuildings, and two poultry barns. Already people were calling to offer cleanup assistance.

On the road a stream of vehicles passed by with people drawn to the aftermath of disaster. Vehicles slowed, some stopping for a few seconds, all occupants struggling to see the destruction, driven by the energy from a brew of curiosity, awe, concern, and relief. The parade tapered off after deputies were stationed at both intersections to control traffic.

25

BECAUSE HE RAN FROM THE BROCK'S FRIDAY AFTERNOON after the incident on the ridge, against Jeri Otto's vehement protest, officers transported Michael to the youth detention facility in Lakota County. When she complained about this to Sheriff Schwartz, he also reminded her that the young boy, while in her unofficial custody, allegedly had taken a handgun and fired three shots at another human being, scoring with two, not to mention the grass fire that he allegedly started.

The explanation helped to ease the conflict in the sheriff's initial thoughts: he wanted to say 'yes, take the boy with you'. He wanted to believe the boy would be safe and secure in her custody, that he did not deserve what he might encounter at the youth detention facility.

At first officers believed her when she said she shot Rafe. No one else saw it happen. No one could conceive of another explanation, until one of the officers among the first to arrive began to question how someone could be driving a large pickup truck over rough terrain towing another vehicle, and at the same time fire a weapon from an awkward position actually hitting the target. From a distance they saw the trucks moving continuously. To do such a feat would almost certainly require stopping.

As Jeri told her story officers listened with unspoken respect, approaching admiration, for using force to the extent most of them had never done, to fire their weapons at another human being.

After investigators took fingerprints from Tom's handgun, which definitely did not match Jeri's, their respect grew into awe toward the ten-year-old boy. Michael remained mute throughout. He sat stoically in the back of a patrol car, his eyes cast downward, never responding to gentle, probing questions from a high school counselor who worked summers for the county family social services department.

Confronted with the fingerprint evidence, Jeri admitted her attempt to take the blame in defense of her son. For Sheriff Schwartz, it removed the doubt about where the boy would be staying Friday evening, the only question being how long.

The question haunted Jeri all day Saturday, until the tornado struck and its aftermath, resurfacing Sunday morning, fueled by a dream that awakened her just after 5:00 a.m. to find her and Tom in the old double bed in Lynn's spare bedroom.

THE SOFT, PRE-DAWN LIGHT filtering through beige curtains at Lynn Meyers' apartment early Sunday morning barely illuminated the faces of Jade and Trace lying on the guest bedroom floor, in slumber the faces of sweet cherubs.

Jeri raised her head off the pillow gazing at them, relishing for a few seconds the peace, love, and fulfillment they unknowingly created. The mood quickly crumbled, confronted with a counterattack from the pending contentions of the day. She lay back on the pillow under the weight of what awaited, dealing with the destruction of their home, the welfare of Michael, the suspicion toward Tom in the Weaver case, and all the usual strains of trying to make a living and raise a family.

"You awake?" She whispered. She drew close trying to discern a response, or create one.

Tom stirred, gradually losing his grasp on the nocturnal unconsciousness that had provided temporary refuge, slowly awakening to thoughts better suited for a nightmare. Foreboding thoughts that he must face as the new day emerged.

Tom turned on his back, stretching and yawning. He cradled her head with his arm. "What time is it?"

"Just after five. I couldn't sleep anymore."

"That makes two of us."

"What are we going to do?"

"Wish I knew."

"How's the delivery truck?"

"I think it's just the smashed windshield."

"How much does that cost?"

"I don't know. Three, four hundred bucks. It might take a few days to get it replaced."

"You think we'll find much stuff left?"

"Most of it's trash. We used to be trailer trash. Now we're just trash."

"Don't talk like that," Jeri scolded.

Tom remained silent, regretting that this particular day started way too early, even though he was accustomed to rising early on Sunday mornings, mostly because of habit from his weekday schedule.

"I wonder how Michael's doing," Jeri said.

"I'm sure he's fine. I still can't believe that. I remembered leaving the gun there. I just forgot to get it out of there."

"Why did you do that anyway? What if one of the kids found it?"

"Sorry. It was just a mistake. Maybe it was a good thing. What if he hadn't done that?"

"I don't think it would have made any difference. The cops would have been there in a minute."

"Maybe. Maybe not. If that guy had gotten to you guys, you never know. After what Randy told me what they did to Stan, they were some nasty dudes."

"It's all my fault," Jeri said.

"What's your fault?"

"This whole thing. The meth, everything. Michael. It's going to haunt me the rest of my life. That's why they were here, you know."

"I know. I know," Tom consoled. "It's not your fault, this part. You just got caught up in it back then. That has nothing to do with this. That's all in the past."

"Except for Michael."

"I thought we'd left that in the past, too."

"I did. Or thought I did."

"We've got our kids. That's enough. We should be worrying about where we're going to live. Michael'll be okay."

"I know, but it's been gnawing at me all week. Now that Stan's gone, too, they're orphans, except Michael."

"Just let it drop, will you?"

"I can't."

"What are you going to do about it?"

"I don't know yet."

"Well we certainly ain't going to get anywhere if we don't have a place to live," Tom said. "Just forget about it for now. Let's go out there now. It's getting light enough. I can't sleep anymore anyway. At least for a little bit. We can come back soon."

TOM STARTED BACK TOWARD the scrap pile that had been the shop, casting a tentative glance over his shoulder to see if Newt followed.

The unfamiliar presence of the old man momentarily frightened off thoughts, ghostly shadows slinking around perimeter of Tom's mind. As he sifted through the wreckage of the shop his thoughts kept returning to something Pastor Gabe said in the sermon.

They had followed Lynn's suggestion to interrupt the clean-up and attend the ten-thirty service at the Gospel Tabernacle, where their church community enveloped them in a warm flood of genuine compassion. For Tom the effect lasted until Pastor Gabe during the service acknowledged the Ottos and the destruction of their home.

Pastor Gabe said the text for the sermon, Romans chapter eight, verses twenty one and twenty two, was more than a coincidence. He said the Spirit was trying to help them understand why bad things happen to good people. All Creation suffers waiting for God's return in the body of Jesus. In the meantime, Satan and the forces of evil are working mightily to turn us away from God. They have the power to inflict such things as tornadoes, floods, hurricanes, disease, accidents, Pastor Gabe preached.

Hearing the word 'tornado' turned Tom's attention away from a whirl of worries about their future. He listened to Gabe's words and they almost absolved him of his secret, the meth that he took Friday afternoon, and of the thought that struck him awakening in the early dawn Sunday morning, that the tornado was God's punishment for yielding to temptation, which at the time he rationalized the action as being necessary to prevent falling asleep at the wheel.

Newt took several long strides catching up to Tom walking toward the shop location.

"Sorry about all this," Newt tried to sympathize.

"What are you being sorry for?" Tom felt a sharp edge rising in his voice, belying his conscious effort to seem conversational, when such interaction with the crazy old man did not seem normal at all.

The response bounced off Newt, failing to dislodge what he had to say. "The main thing is, everybody's okay. Nobody got hurt. All this stuff is just stuff."

Tom looked at Newt, trying to figure out why the old man all of a sudden was being so friendly, why he was even there. He began to see a real person behind the image of an old eccentric, thinning gray hair, bib overalls over a T-shirt more than several days in use, salt-and-pepper whiskers well into a second week of growth.

"And look at the Weavers, their kids especially," Newt said. "That must have been tough, finding Tulie like that. What they did to Stan was horrible. What I'm saying is, you'll pull through this."

"Thanks." Tom nodded. The furrowed appearance of his face softened, involuntarily letting go a slight smile. He turned away suddenly embarrassed, and toward the work of sifting through the wreckage. Newt followed, asking questions occasionally about whether or not to keep something, revealing a wide difference in perception of value. He deferred to Tom's wishes, saving his energy for the attempt to pass along information that he had acquired over the past week, but not too much so as to reveal his sources.

They worked in silence until Tom asked Newt to help him lift a section of wall that had landed on the four-wheeler. Tom scanned the Polaris noting dents, a bent handle bar, and a shard of window glass impaled in the seat. Newt stood by appearing similarly concerned, seeing an opening.

"That Leuten, the state guy, what'd you think about him?" Newt asked.

"Huh?" Tom turned his attention back to Newt. "I don't know. An asshole I guess, after how he ripped into Jeri on Friday. Him and Clymer. Why?"

"Well that's what I mean. Ain't something about those guys seem fishy to you?"

Tom paused, trying to imagine anything. "Clymer's always been an asshole. That just goes with the territory. Leuten's just doing his job I suppose. He was kind of spooky I'll admit. I never knew him or saw him around here before all this. Did you know he tried to frame me? Tuesday at the Weaver's?"

"How so?"

"When they were searching my truck—I said 'sure, go ahead'—he came out with this little plastic egg. Said there was meth in it. Randy Tollefson, you know Randy, one of the deputies? He told me later that was bullshit. Leuten was up to something."

"Why do you think he'd do something like that?"

"I had eggs in there. I sell a lot of them. In the city, too. I don't know why he'd do that. It's like he knew something, like there's something going on that I don't know about. Why? You know something I don't know?"

"On your route, your travels around the countryside, into the city, you ever see stuff that looks suspicious? People doing things, places that look like meth labs, things like that?"

"Not really. Most of those little meth operations are getting cleaned up." Tom held back from saying more. For a moment he felt that he could trust the old man, tell him about the offer of meth that he received from another delivery driver at the warehouse in the city, but not that he actually tried for the first time on Friday.

"You ever think how stuff like that gets around, gets delivered?"

"They asked me about that," Tom said. "What makes you so interested?" Tom said with rising irritation.

"I know how they operate. You were just a kid back when they put me through the legal wringer. I don't want to see it happen again, to someone who don't deserve it."

"I ain't done anything wrong."

"But somebody else has, except they're trying to make damn sure somebody else takes the rap."

"What the hell are you talking about?"

"I tried to warn you earlier. I probably should have been more direct."

"I don't remember any warning." Tom climbed on the four-wheeler to see if it would start. He wished Newt would leave him alone. He glanced at Newt, who seemed to be trying to say something without words, only a steady gaze. "Was that you?" He looked directly at Newt, a faint connection emerging in his thoughts.

"Was that me what?"

"Those phone calls, late at night?"

"You got me," Newt smiled slightly.

"Really? Was that you?"

Newt nodded.

"You sure as hell didn't say much."

"I ain't going to say much now, neither."

"Just maybe you don't have much to say."

"I'll say this. This ain't first time Lyon Clymer and that Leuten have met. If they make things hot for you and Jeri, then I'll step up."

"Step up and do what? How do you know this stuff? Why should I believe you?"

"I got my ways. Let's just leave it at that."

Tom pressed the starter button on the four-wheeler. He revved the engine, looking at Newt, his belief growing that the old man was a kook. He shut down the engine and climbed off. "Well happy Father's Day to you, too," he said, and started walking away.

"Same to you," Newt said.

Tom left Newt at the shop and headed for the house. Eloise Baumgarten intercepted him, carrying a large plastic box. "Tom, what do you want me to do with this?"

"What is it?"

"A box of baby clothes. That's what the label said anyway. Want to know where I found it?"

"Where?"

"It was across the road in the field. I saw it when we were driving here. We stopped and picked it up. It had to be from here. What should I do with it?"

"Baby clothes? We don't need baby clothes any more. At least I hope not."

"I took a peek. It was all intact. Isn't that weird? They looked brand-new. Most of them looked like they were for an older child, older than a baby."

"I've never seen it. Maybe give it to Goodwill. I don't know. Ask Jeri."

Eloise nodded and walked off to find Jeri.

26

With a few small exceptions, the investigation into the Weaver homicides disappeared from the pages of the Buffalo Ridge Banner, replaced by the usual news and events—the Buffalo Days summer festival, Fourth of July, government business, and assorted small crimes and accidents.

The Weaver case remained the top priority for Sheriff Hank Schwartz, and clouded the otherwise warm sunny days for the members of Harvest Our Prairie Ethically organic food producers. They took turns doing chores at the Weaver farm until the chickens and other stock could be sold. One member expanded her chicken production to fill the void left by the Weavers.

The Ottos moved into a vacant house north of town, half-way up the southwest-facing slope of the ridge.

Once a small farm on poor soil, the land and buildings went to an accountant in a nearby town who had handled the financial matters of the former owner's estate, a widow in her nineties, whose descendants had no interest in the property other than the money, which the accountant provided although at a bargain price, which proved more so each passing year as demand grew for marginal farmland used for private hunting preserves. Acquainted with the accountant and aware of the transactions, Jon Brock made sure that some of the financial benefit passed along to the Ottos enabling them to rent the house for only one-hundred fifty dollars per month.

Jeri threw all her energy and passion at cleaning, painting, and wallpapering, for which the landlord waived the first month's rent. The work helped her vent anger at the injustice of her dismissal from Prairie Pride.

Lynn complained about the distance from town—eleven miles—and resented their decline of her offer that they could stay with her as long as they liked, rent-free.

Except for wear and weathering, the house had changed little since it was built during the 1920s. Smaller than most prairie farm houses of that era, a living room and kitchen comprised the entire first floor. A steep, narrow stair in the kitchen led to a wide, second-floor hallway flanked by two small bedrooms. The outer edges of their ceilings sloped downward with the angle of the roof. The plaster-and-lathe interior walls appeared mostly intact, showing only a few cracks and small holes. The putty holding the glass into the casement windows, one in each room on the gable end wall, would need replacing. Until then, opening the windows would require a gentle force, if they would open at all.

Someone from the rural electric power cooperative checked the line leading to the house and installed new main fuses, leaving the responsibility for the smaller, individual circuit fuses to the new tenants. Inspecting the oil-burning parlor stove could wait, the need for space heating being unlikely in the middle of June. The well worked, surprisingly, since it looked like a home-made conglomeration of the necessary ingredients—electric motor, belts, pulleys, transmission for converting a rotating force to the reciprocating movement of the shaft descending into the well pit, where a pump sucked water from a perched aquifer about fifty feet beneath the small, once-white shed between the barn and house.

The man from the power company said they were lucky. Finding suitable ground water that far up the ridge had proved challenging. Along with the poor, rocky soil, the scarcity of water contributed to the number of similar abandoned farms in the area. A county public health nurse visited one morning and suggested having the water tested. If it showed a high level of nitrate, unsuitable for the children, she recommended using bottled water for drinking.

Donations of furniture, appliances, assorted household goods, and clothing sufficiently filled the house, closets, and drawers.

Tom's delivery business resumed, even gaining some new customers from the attention brought by the tornado and its aftermath.

Jeri went to several job interviews while still refurbishing the old house. Michael rejoined his siblings staying at the Brock's after Jeri and the director of the county family services department insisted that he should not be held at the youth detention center.

SHERIFF SCHWARTZ DROVE ALONE to the new Otto residence, without calling first, hoping to find Jeri home.

Two weeks had passed without any significant new leads in the Weaver case. The county attorney, anxious for some progress, had been insinuating the presence of sufficient evidence connecting with Tom Otto, which Hank knew to be absurd. The attorney seemed to be rationalizing based on several indiscretions arising from Tom's past exuberance with loud pickup trucks and beer in his early twenties, which might be enough to sway public sentiment toward accepting him as a suitable if not certain perpetrator upon whom the blame could be placed. Hank was certain that Harmon Leuten had been pressuring the county attorney to order Tom's arrest, not for the murder of the Weavers, but for drug trafficking in a scheme that somehow was connected with the murders. To his credit, Hank thought, the county attorney had been resisting the pressure, although calling for a grand jury seemed extreme, at least at this point.

"Hi sheriff. Come on in." Jeri opened the screen door, smiling, inviting him in. Startled at first by the sound of a vehicle approaching the house, she relaxed seeing who it was, someone she knew and trusted for the most part, not a stranger, which never used to bother her until now.

He nodded a silent hello and entered the house.

She studied the concerned expression on his face passing by, telling her that the reason for his visit caused him discomfort, and soon would do so for her.

"How you folks doing?" Hank pulled a heavy wooden bench away from the seven-foot-long trestle table that dominated the kitchen. He sat down and ran his hand over the silky smooth finish on the maple the color of caramel. "Nice table."

"It was one of Stan's," Jeri said. Remnants of embarrassment from receiving charity still lingered even though the Hamiltons and other HOPE members insisted on making the donation after the tornado. "We're fine. Used a lot of elbow grease fixing this place up. It's a little farther from town than we'd like. That's not a big deal for Tom, but my mom don't like it. So what brings you out here?"

Hank scratched his chin, using the pause to choose the right words.

"You want some coffee?" Jeri asked.

"No. No thanks." He looked up at her where she leaned against the oil-burning parlor stove. "When you were with Michael, did he ever talk to you?"

"Michael? Hardly. Mostly he just nodded yes or no if I asked him a question. Sometimes not even that. Why?"

"We've been trying to get through to him, you know, because he's a key witness. We've got some psychologists working on it, but we're not making much progress. It's really holding up the investigation."

"So why won't he talk? I don't get it. He always did before. He talked when he was two-years-old for crying out loud." The spoken reference to the past pulled back the wall that had shielded her from the heart-rending scene when a social worker carried away her two-year-old son, from the startled look on his face, from his last word 'mommy' as they passed through the door, never to see him again as her son.

"I know this is tough on you," Hank said. "But I don't know what else to do. I should tell you that they're going to convene a grand jury. If we could just get him to talk, it would really help the case. A grand jury is secret, you know. He wouldn't have to face a full court room."

"Oh come on. You're not going to make him do that? What he's been through? What they've all been through? He's just a kid!"

"But a grand jury is just to determine the evidence in a case. To see if charges should be filed. You know as well as I do that they've been looking at Tom, too."

"What? What are you saying?" Jeri's eyes flared.

"Just hold on. Not about the Weavers, although he was the one who found them. I shouldn't tell you this, but they've been investigating drug trafficking, mostly meth, some cocaine."

"I've heard that. That's BS."

"There is circumstantial evidence, slim, but in some people's mind's it's there."

"What people? It's Leuten, isn't it? I didn't like him the first time I saw him. Pure slime if you ask me. The way he treated Michael, it's no wonder he won't talk to anybody."

"But a grand jury would get all that stuff out in the open, as far as the investigation is concerned," the sheriff pleaded. "If we could get Michael to testify it could really clear things up."

Jeri leaned against the stove, her right hand under her chin, "you know who he did talk to, at least a little bit?"

"Who?"

"Newt. Newton Case. When he brought Michael to our place that Friday, after he ran from the Brock's. I know they'd talked. Newt even said so."

"You think he would talk to him now?"

"I don't know. Maybe. It's more likely that Newt won't cooperate."

"We can make him. Contempt of court if we have to."

"Good luck. They tried all that stuff on him twenty years ago. Listen, I'll talk to Newt. He probably knows more about all what's going on than anybody."

"How so?"

"He's not as dumb as people think."

"Oh, I know that."

"I'll talk to him. You let me know when and where to meet. I'll let you know if he'll do it. Just make sure the location is some neutral territory, not the law enforcement center or courthouse."

Sheriff Schwartz agreed. He shook Jeri's hand on the way out the door. She waved watching the patrol car depart down the driveway.

27

"How's he doing?"

"Fine. Outwardly at least. Come on in." Jon Brock stepped back holding open the door.

Sheriff Hank Schwartz and a detective entered the front hall of the Brock residence. "Where's Newt?"

"He called. He'll be here any minute." Jon led the way into the living room. "Where's Duane?" Hank said the county attorney drove separately and should arrive soon.

"You want to see the set-up?" Jon asked. Hank nodded. Jon led him into the den. Two small digital video cameras sat on the fireplace mantle, one at each end, each hidden behind a family photo in a free-standing frame, and aimed at chairs opposite one another in front of the fireplace.

"How are the other kids doing, Anna and Jonathan?" Hank asked.

"Amber and Ashley took them to the park."

"You really think this is going to work?"

"I hope so. Jeri seems to think so."

"I mean entering this as testimony."

"That should be no problem. If the declarant, that's the actual witness, is unavailable for some reason, but authorizes someone to convey the testimony, that can be argued as an exception to the rules of evidence. At least I hope the judge agrees."

"What if he doesn't?"

"Let's take one thing at a time," Jon advised. "Let's see how this interview turns out. Maybe we won't get anything."

"I still wish we could do this at the office."

"That would be an advantage in arguing this," Jon conceded. "But I agree with Amber and Jeri, Michael would totally clam up there. We'll just have to take our chances here."

The doorbell rang. "That must be Duane." Jon went to the front door to welcome county attorney Duane Harstad, who still had been showing signs of the disagreement over conducting the interview at the Brock's. He stepped in and set down his briefcase. "Nice place. You don't see woodwork like this anymore," Duane said. Jon accepted Duane's attempted cordiality. "Thanks. That's one reason why we bought it. Downside is that it takes a lot of upkeep."

"Sorry I'm a little late."

"No problem. Newton Case isn't here yet. Come on in and see the set-up."

"If he even shows," Duane said.

Jon understood, recalling past disputes between the eccentric, tax-protesting old farmer and the county attorney.

"He will."

Jon didn't have to repeat the argument of that was why the interview should be at his home, where the kids were staying, and not at the courthouse or sheriff's office, where Newt feared to go.

As Jon closed the front door, he saw a late 1990s Pontiac roll to a stop behind Duane's car. Who could that be? A young man emerged. His short, reddish hair still held a slight curl. He wore dark slacks, a striped dress shirt, and dark tie. The shirt told Jon he wasn't a Mormon or Jehovah's Witness missionary, but who was he?

"Duane. Come here. Who is that?"

Duane looked out a small window in the front hall. "I thought you knew. It's some young punk law clerk. From Sioux Falls. The judge said he wanted a neutral third party present to observe the interview."

"Doesn't he trust us?"

Duane hesitated before refraining to say what first came to mind, relating to his scorn for the hot-shot attorney from the big city. "He just wants to do this right. It's a little unorthodox. He doesn't want any unnecessary openings for appeals."

"I doubt there will be any appeals. I doubt it will even get that far. So what do we know about this kid?"

"I don't know any more than you do. He's just an observer."

Jon decided against pressing the point, spared in part by another arrival. "Here's Newton Case."

Newt got out of his pickup and held the door open. Harvey jumped out, grunting on the landing. The old beagle followed Newt up the sidewalk with a stride almost like a waddle resembling Newt's stride with a sideways rocking motion from stiff hips, even after a short ride.

"What's up with the dog?" Duane asked.

"That was Jeri Otto's idea. She says the dog will help put the boy at ease."

"That's not what I recall. You weren't around eight years ago. The kid was pretty messed up by a dog, a pit bull, out at that crack shack. It makes you sick, what they do to the kids."

"Well then he's come a long way thanks to the Weavers," Jon said. "What happened to them is much worse, losing two wonderful people like that to drug crimes. It's a shame that stuff was so rampant around here in the first place."

Duane felt a little sting from what he took as Jon's sarcasm, in part from the condescension he perceived emanating from Jon's big city background. "You saying we haven't been doing our job?"

"Not at all." Jon immediately sensed the sentiment behind Duane's response, arising from a usually well-concealed insecurity. "This is nothing compared with Chicago." Seeing the accusing look in Duane's eyes, Jon knew he did it again, making comparisons. "Having the dog here makes sense to me. He tracked the boy down and found him by the creek. The boy-and-his-dog bond worked. And it's not the first time they met, at least that's what Jeri Otto says. Newt and Harvey, that's the dog's name, found them on the road eight years ago."

Duane looked away, indicating boredom. "I know all that. I'm the one who handled the case."

Jon rolled his eyes, enough to notice but just below the threshold of obvious annoyance. "We're temporarily suspending our 'no dogs in the house rule'. I just hope he's had a bath and doesn't shed."

Duane offered a slight, conciliatory smile. "Who? The dog, or Newt?"

"Both."

MICHAEL WEAVER FOLLOWED JON from the family room to the den. He wore new blue jeans and a Hard Rock Café T-shirt from Paris. Jon invited him to sit in front of the fireplace on the folding chair opposite Newt. Harvey's tail wagged in greeting. He rose from where he lay at Newt's feet and waddled over to sniff Michael's hand, his eyes peeking from under drooping upper lids and almost popping out from sagging lower lids revealing their moist, rose-colored dermis. He looked up with a glint of recognition. Michael responded with a barely noticeable, flat smile, holding it back from turning up at the corners. He petted Harvey's head and scratched behind his ears.

"Michael, we invited Mr. Case here because he wanted to see how you were doing. He's thankful that he and Harvey found you by the creek. He just wanted to stop by and visit. Is that okay with you?"

Michael looked up at Jon and nodded.

"Good. Do you want anything? Pop or something?" Michael shook his head 'no'. "How about you, Newt? Coffee or tea?" Newt said no thanks. "Okay. I'll just leave you two here. If you need anything just holler. I'll be in the family room." Jon smiled, patted Michael's shoulder and left the room. He went to the kitchen where the others stood looking and listening before a laptop screen. "I hope this works. Newt said there'd be no guarantees."

Harvey lay down next to Michael's feet. He looked at Newt, then at Michael, waiting for some cue. Hearing or seeing none, he laid his head on his outstretched front paws.

"He likes you," Newt said. "I remember when I was your age, we had a dog that wouldn't listen to grown-ups. Us kids could tell him to do anything. When our dad said something he'd just sit there. We thought it was kind of funny."

Michael seemed to listen with apparent interest, once reaching down to run his hand over Harvey's back.

"Why are you here?" The firm, clear sound of Michael's voice surprised Newt. The boy's eyes looked straight at him.

Newt tried to remember the coaching from the psychologist. Stay relaxed. Listen. Advance gently with questions for clarification, like a climber on the face of a vertical rock wall.

"Michael, we need your help. We need you to tell us what you know, what you saw."

"They caught the bad guys. Why don't they just put them in jail?"

"They have to be convicted in court. They have to be found guilty. To do that they need evidence, more evidence."

"I lit the fire."

"What fire?"

"In the grass. After they grabbed me."

Newt recalled hearing the radio communications that Friday evening nearly three weeks ago. "How'd you manage to do that?"

Michael described how he acquired the book of matches, ignited all at once and tossed it into the grass.

"Are they going to put me in jail again?"

"You're not going to jail."

"They did right after that happened."

"I don't think it was because of the fire. Do you remember anything else? Before the fire?"

Almost visibly, Michael pulled back, behind the wall. Newt shifted in his chair, mostly to try ease the soreness spreading across his back, and possibly to find a new position that might re-establish the wisp of rapport. Harvey's head popped up when Newt hoisted himself up from the creaking chair. "You mind waiting for a minute? I got to go to the bathroom. You stay there, Harv." Newt tottered toward the door to his right.

"Bathroom's the other way," Michael said.

Newt stopped. "I was going to get some coffee, too. Mr. Brock said they had coffee. You want anything?"

Michael shook his head 'no'.

Newt entered the kitchen, hoping for some guidance from the five men standing around the laptop. The screen showed Michael still in his chair, reaching down to pet Harvey.

"This ain't going too well," Newt said.

"You're doing fine," Jon replied. "Give it some time."

"I don't think he's going to talk about anything else. If he saw anything at the crime scene I think he's just stuffed it so far down it'll never come out. Hell, even if he talked normal it'd be tough to get out. I ain't no shrink you know."

"You're all we have right now," Duane said.

Newt savored the taste of retribution. A former nemesis now depended on him. If he hadn't known about Michael's past and his connection to Jeri Otto, he wouldn't even be here.

Jon handed Newt a mug of coffee. "I'll go back in there. But I ain't promising anything."

Newt returned to the den and sat down, setting the mug on a low table by the couch. He asked Michael to try to remember anything about that Tuesday morning when the bad guys came to their farm. Michael closed his eyes. In a few seconds they opened seeming focused on the edge of the carpet between them, as if he saw some invisible portal to a secret hiding place for memories best buried from daily life. In a quiet, steady, even voice he began to describe what he heard, what he saw not long after breakfast that Tuesday morning at the Weaver farm, and also early Friday evening up on the ridge.

THIS TIME NEWTON CASE WORE a western-style shirt and a new pair of blue jeans. No one told him to dress up for the occasion. This time, instead of obstinance, he wanted to cooperate with the court system. He took the stand at the preliminary hearing to testify a confirmation of the recording of his interview of Michael.

County attorney Harstad tapped a key on the laptop, launching the recording projected on a screen in the corner of the courtroom. The judge motioned to the bailiff to close the curtains. Duane paused the recording.

"Do you want me to go back to the beginning?" Duane asked the judge.

"No, that's okay. Go ahead." The playback of the DVD recording so far only showed Michael entering the room and sitting down opposite Newton Case.

Duane tried to increase the volume when Michael began to describe what he heard, what he saw that Tuesday morning. They were having breakfast when a full-size, light-colored SUV drove up to the house. Everyone was excited, visitors are always a welcome sight. "Mom went to look out the window. She came back from the window and told all us kids to go down the basement. I had to almost carry Jonathan. He was bawling and didn't want to go. Then Anna started crying too. Mom got real mad and kind of pushed us all toward the secret door, the one in the closet that goes down into the basement. We all went down there and I had to almost cover Jonathan's mouth to keep him from crying. We stayed down there. We heard mom talking with these guys, kind of like she was mad. We were scared. Then we heard the shotgun go off. I wanted to run up there but Anna was hanging on to me so hard I couldn't go up the stairs. Then the shotgun went off again. I pushed Anna back and went up the stairs anyway. I sneaked up and peeked out the door from the closet. Then I saw…"

Michael's voice faltered. Harvey looked up at him.

"What did you see?" Newt asked quietly.

Tears spilled from Michael's eyes. He buried his face in his hands. Newt told him something he had never told anyone. "It's okay. I've cried before. It's okay to let it out. Sometimes we all have to. It don't mean we're weak or sissies. If you can tell us anything it'll help us get the bad guys for sure.

Michael continued. "I couldn't see real good. Mom was on the floor. I saw this guy. He had a knife…"

Grief that had been stuffed for three weeks made a rush to get out all at once, jamming up in his throat.

"What happened? With the knife?" Newt tried hard to speak softly, battling his own tension of the moment.

"This one guy made this other guy stab mom."

"Can you describe them?"

"It was the guy with the long hair and crappy face. It was the other one that I shot."

"You mean the long-haired guy had the knife?"

"Yes."

"Then what happened?"

"The bad guys took off. I went to help mom." Michael became silent.

"That's okay. It's hard to talk about."

Michael seemed to recover his composure. "I tried to call dad on the cell phone. He didn't have it. Then I heard Anna coming up the stairs. I went and made her go back down. She was bawling. Jonathan was bawling, too." He looked again as if we would start crying.

"When did Tom Otto come?"

"It wasn't too long after. We were all back down in the basement. Anna and Jonathan were trying to go upstairs. I wouldn't let them. Then we heard someone in the house hollering." Michael described how Tom Otto entered the basement from the outside door and found them.

He continued, describing how he took off from the Brock's and took the kayak down the creek. Newt said he didn't have to talk about when Newt and Harvey found him and took him to the Otto's, and he didn't have to talk about going in the pickup with Jeri Otto if he didn't want to. Michael said he didn't remember taking the gun from the glove compartment. He did remember using it to shoot at the guy coming after them, Rafael Gonzales.

"That's pretty much it," Duane said to the judge.

Newt had left the recording, followed by Harvey. Jon Brock came into view and knelt by Michael and said something too quiet for the microphones. Michael rose from his chair and followed Jon out of the room, but not before he leaned toward the fireplace mantle trying to see what sat behind the picture, a tiny, round eye with a wire leading from it.

28

BCI AGENT HARMON LEUTEN'S INCESSANT BADGERING continued half-way into July, yet he failed to convince Ames County Attorney Duane Harstad to file charges against Tom Otto in connection with the double homicide of Stan and Tulie Weaver and drug trafficking. After interviewing Tom three times, Sheriff Schwartz believed he was telling the truth about what he knew of the incident that Tuesday morning in June, and the circumstances surrounding it.

Leuten claimed he had sufficient evidence for an aiding and abetting charge. He guaranteed one piece of evidence that clearly linked Tom with the drug dealers, although he would not reveal it until charges were filed. Duane scoffed; how could he file charges without knowing all the evidence?

He was skeptical about the plastic egg containing crystal meth that Leuten claimed to have found in Tom's truck during the search the day after Tulie's body was found. Allegations that Tom knew about the legend of money hidden on the Weaver farm, and somehow was linked to the drug dealers' visit there in search of it, could be a possibility.

Like many families in and around Buffalo Ridge, the Ottos could have used a little extra money. Prairie West Bank, where the Otto's held checking and savings accounts barely above and sometimes below the minimum balance, and owed nearly $15,000 on a personal note to finance Tom's delivery business, provided evidence supporting a financial motive for involvement in drug trafficking.

AND THE CHILDREN.

Jade and Trace always appeared well-cared for, well-dressed, and entertained by an array of toys and playthings that would blend in well with any affluent, big-city suburb.

Jeri worked at the chicken plant, which everyone knew paid hardly more than $20,000 a year. Those in whom she confided had doubts about the profitability of "Tom's Fresh Meats and Produce—Naturally" food delivery service.

Their farmsite was worth something more than the mortgage, in part because of the new shop, but the trailer house that they lived in could be a liability.

If argued forcibly enough, which Leuten relished doing, one could be convinced that the Otto's, or at least Tom, were somehow tapped into the other economy, where drugs, extortion, prostitution, theft, and murder comprised the primary engines of commerce, challenging law enforcement and the courts on a daily basis, visible only in the shallow, generally inaccurate crime reports in newspapers, and dominating superficial, sensational television reports that claimed to provide all the news you need to know.

Leuten's insistence of the possibility began to tell Duane another story, one that could raise questions about Leuten's motives, but the county attorney's focus on charges against Quentin "Weed" Alt and the two other drug dealer-murder suspects, kept those questions at bay, for the time being.

WAITING FOR THE JUDGE to enter the courtroom, Tom Otto appeared calm and relaxed, as much as he could be, sitting inside the courtroom on a warm August morning instead of at the wheel of the delivery truck. He saw flashes of memory from the last time he sat there awaiting his turn before the judge on charges of underage consumption and driving under the influence.

He felt confined mostly by the buttoned collar of a scratchy, new, light-blue dress shirt. In the men's clothing section of the J.C. Penney store in the mall at Sioux Falls he first felt embarrassment, then disdain, for not remembering how to knot a tie, so he chose a clip-on. In the high-ceilinged courtroom where floor vents sent a tepid air flow from the under-sized air conditioning system retrofitted some years ago in the century-old building, having one less thing around his neck became an advantage.

It did little to compensate for missing another day's work, especially a Monday and the first in August, by which time some of the fresh garden produce from the organic growers of HOPE that he delivered to the city warehouse was ascending toward the peak season.

Jeri sat close on his right, her left hand clasping his right, her right hand reaching across and resting on his forearm. She wore khaki, pleated slacks, also newly-purchased from the Wal-Mart where she worked, and a rose-colored knit short-sleeved top that she often wore to church Sundays.

She leaned closer and whispered. "I remember the last time I was in here."

"So do I."

She leaned away to look in his face. "You weren't there. I didn't even know you then. I knew who you were."

"I meant I remember being here, too."

"Oh, that. I didn't know you then. I mean, I know who you were, but I was toasted by then. Well here we are again."

Tom sucked in a deep breath and stared straight ahead. Jeri took the cue and left the past where it belonged.

Jon Brock entered the courtroom and sat in the row behind, greeting them with a handclasp on Tom's shoulder and a confident smile. Tom and Jeri turned their heads with tentative smiles of acknowledgement from a measure of confidence they gained from Jon's briefing about what would happen and how to act when Tom was called forward as a witness.

In order to accompany him, Jeri had to switch shifts with a co-worker at the Wal-Mart in Watertown, which posed some risk since she had only been working there just over a week, and her performance was still being assessed. She liked the work and the people. The worst part so far was the forty mile commute one way.

Her 11:00 a.m. to 8:00 p.m. shift meant that her mother had to watch the kids a few more hours longer each day, which she didn't seem to mind. And if she drove fast enough she could get home in time to see the kids at bedtime, and have a few hours with Tom before he went to bed around ten.

She spent mornings working on the old rented farm house on the ridge, cleaning and painting. Scraping off multiple layers of wallpaper in the kitchen took more effort and time than she had anticipated.

A small barn that once held eighteen dairy cows appeared only several years away from collapse. Tom removed enough junk to make room for the ATV, snowmobiles, mower, and all his tools. The car and trucks sat outside.

Pacing before a jury of seven women and five men, County Attorney Harstad presented the state's case against Quentin Alt-Weed—in connection with the murder of Stan and Tulie Weaver, kidnapping, and assorted drug and weapons charges.

After the preliminary hearing, based on the testimony of Michael Weaver mediated through Newton Case, the judge agreed with Harstad that Weed's case should be separated from the other two suspects.

Weed entered the courtroom escorted by two deputies.

"Man, they sure cleaned him up," Tom whispered.

"Did you see him much before?"

"When everything came down at that old place up on the ridge. I didn't get a really good look."

"That was stupid."

"What?"

"Doing that. Trying to sneak up on them like that."

Annoyance swept through Tom. And guilt. He thought it was over. He had tried to explain why he decided to sneak up on the abandoned farm. He still couldn't explain it thoroughly, even to himself, much less to Sheriff Schwartz. He sensed that others remained skeptical about his actions, and the judgment underlying them. The guilt arose from the meth he ingested that mid-June Friday afternoon. He rationalized, arguing in his thoughts that it prevented him from falling asleep behind the wheel, something he struggled with almost every day.

"And what if I hadn't? What if I hadn't called in on Randy's radio? Then what?"

Jeri let it go. She glanced back toward Jon. If he had been listening he didn't show it. She turned her view frontward toward Weed.

His shorn hair actually seemed stylish, full and soft, almost black, barely brushing the collar of his bright, orange jumpsuit. Now on a regular diet and absent the drugs and alcohol, he had gained weight, which softened the pock marks on his face. The deputy released the handcuff around Weed's left wrist; his ankles remained shackled.

Weed turned his head in the direction of the Ottos. He first seemed to be taking a measure of Tom, then rested his gaze on Jeri, showing a slight, knowing smile. It made her spine feel like burning ice.

Tom whispered out the side of his mouth. "Why's he looking at us?"

It was him.

The nose mostly, protruding above thin lips that revealed several gaps in rotting teeth. Jeri shivered as the recognition took hold, despite her attempt at a nonchalant dismissal of the mounting clues. She tried to look away, trying to resist some magnetic force pulling her awareness, if not the direction of her eyes, toward him.

Follow-up news stories in the Buffalo Ridge Banner about the showdown on the ridge, the investigation, and the start of court proceedings involving the suspects, included only limited information about them. One story mentioned a possible connection between one of the suspects and a previous raid on a suspected meth lab at the former Wegman farm, before the Weavers bought it. The Ottos did not subscribe to the newspaper, looking through it only on occasion at the café or at Jeri's mother's. When Lynn told Jeri about the suspect's connection with the past, outwardly she shrugged it off. Curiosity drove her to the Ames County Public Library, where she found the back issue of the paper and read the story.

So what? She wrestled her thoughts back into a mold that held only her family and the future. She did not respond to Tom's observation.

"All rise." The bailiff, about sixty and with a graying comb-over, stood at attention to the right of the bench, a vacant look in his eyes, his wiry frame not quite filling out the gray uniform of a sheriff's deputy.

Judge Charlene Hawes entered brusquely from a tall, narrow door in the right corner behind the bench, her black robe fluttering almost audibly. At forty-eight, she was the youngest judge and only woman on the bench in Ames County District Court. Unsure which of the three judges would benefit the prosecution, County Attorney Harstad declined to lobby, instead leaving the assignment to their regular rotation. Judge Hawes rapped the gavel, announcing court to be in session.

QUENTIN "WEED" ALT KEPT LOOKING at Jeri, even as he leaned to the side toward his attorney, who was whispering something.

Jon Brock had been studying the attorney, trying to find a name, a place in his memory. He should have known better than to assume that the defendants would be represented by one of the local public defenders. The defendants had money. They had outside connections.

The attorney, a stocky man appearing to be in his fifties with a meticulous, full head of graying hair, wearing a finely-tailored dark suit, was giving Weed some last-minute instructions. Weed nodded, turning his view toward the jury, all showing attentive expressions.

The last murder trial Duane Harstad prosecuted occurred three years ago. Actually, a murder-attempted suicide. The defendant won the jury's sympathy and walked out with a manslaughter conviction based on weak evidence of self defense.

Duane and Weed's attorney took turns cross-examining law enforcement officers. They watched the video recording of Newton Case's interview with

Michael Weaver, which the judge had allowed despite the motion after the preliminary hearing by Weed's attorney arguing that it should be inadmissible.

After the viewing he objected again, unsuccessfully, and tried once more to convince the judge that a recorded interview, conducted by a citizen not directly connected with the case and not by a law enforcement officer, should be stricken from the record. He argued that he did not have an opportunity to cross-examine the witness. He claimed the boy's age and the usual discrepancies arising from selective observation and faulty memory seriously compromised the integrity of the process. Judge Hawes quickly overruled the objection.

Although Duane had been briefed beforehand, he felt some curiosity and surprise when the defense attorney called Weed to the witness stand. Not long into his cross-examination, Duane began to understand that the defendant seemed to relish the process, with a plausible answer for every conceivable question.

Weed parried every assault on his version of what happened that Tuesday morning at the Weaver farm. They had only stopped to look at Stan's furniture. Tulip Weaver confronted them with a shotgun. Rafael Gonzales wrested the gun away from her; it discharged, mortally wounding her. He denied the part about the knife. They saw no one else, no children. He alluded to the boy's age and its propensity for youthful imagination. He implied that it played into the possibility of coaching by investigators to elicit the answers they were seeking, evoking a sharp rebuke from the judge.

What happened to Stan Weaver was another matter. Weed said he protested against Rafe's decision to kidnap Stan. Later, he said he tried to intervene when the others began to viciously beat him.

The drug charges brought the strongest evidence. Harmon Leuten took his turn on the witness stand. Under questioning by Harstad, he described the surveillance of the drug dealers. He revealed the Bureau of Criminal Investigation's arrangement with Quentin Alt to serve as an informant inside the drug dealer ring. He waited until the cross-examination by Weed's attorney to drop hints about how meth and other drugs might be transported, directing several brief glances toward Tom Otto, and drawing two objections from Harstad, which surprised everyone, and which the judge sustained.

Harstad attempted to question Weed about his past affiliation with the meth lab at the old Wegman farm eight years ago, quickly drawing an objection from Weed's attorney, sustained by the judge. Duane tried to argue that it was part of the reason for their return. Judge Hawes would not yield.

"No further questions, your honor," Duane said, and Weed stepped down.

Duane called Tom Otto to the witness stand. Tom described again, what seemed like the hundredth time, what he found and did the morning he drove onto the Weaver farm. The story did not vary. Tom denied again knowing anything about the meth inside the plastic egg that Harmon Leuten produced after the search of his truck.

The county attorney concluded his questioning, turning the witness over to the defense attorney. He stood slowly, brushing and tugging straight the bottom of his suit jacket. He clasped his hand behind his back and walked slowly toward the witness stand, looking down as if deep in thought. Approaching the stand, he lifted his head and drilled his gaze into Tom's eyes.

"Mr. Otto, how often do you go into the food warehouse in the city?"

The question came unexpectedly. "Uh, well, almost every day, week days." Tom felt hollow, almost disembodied from the sound of his own voice.

"Would you describe to the court your business, what you do?"

Duane jumped up. "Objection. Your Honor, What the witness does for a living is irrelevant."

The judge looked up at Duane, then at Weed's attorney. "And what is your rationale for such a divergence?"

"Your Honor, it's common knowledge that circumstances and even some evidence surrounding this witness raise questions, questions relating to drug trafficking."

"Counselor, he is not on trial. He has not been charged with anything."

"Your Honor, the circumstances could have a bearing on his testimony. Of course, this trial is about my client and events that occurred back in June. But I contend that in order to get at the truth, we must consider all the facts in a wider context that still relate to this particular case. My client was risking his life to work for the citizens of this state by infiltrating a drug trafficking ring. Circumstances beyond his control placed him at the scene of the incident. We have not seen clear evidence that he committed any crime related to the homicides, except perhaps to be present when a case of self-defense turned deadly."

"You claim he was an informant, that's all."

"If law enforcement would tell the truth, I would prove it, your Honor. May I proceed?"

"I'm curious, but be warned, the witness is not on trial." The judge looked over at Duane. "Objection overruled."

The court listened to Tom's description of his daily routine. Weed's attorney asked him about the Bibles that he had started selling on the side. It brought another objection from Duane, which again was overruled when it was mentioned that only a few counties away, a drug task force uncovered a scheme of transporting meth hidden inside Bibles with the middle of the pages cut and removed.

"My client has been accused of drug-trafficking and murder. He has been accused of invading a peaceful farm in search of hidden money, the legacy of a past life. He has since paid his debt to society, he has enlisted his aid to eradicate the meth scourge, and yet the illicit trade continues. How? Why?"

"That's enough!" The judge's voice rose above decorum. Tension prickled throughout the courtroom.

The defense attorney's voice echoed loudly in return, "Thomas Otto, have you ever received meth? Have you ever taken meth?"

"Counselor! You are this close to contempt of court!" Judge Hawes held up her right hand, thumb and forefinger almost touching. "Your testimony is over!" She nodded toward Tom. "You may step down,"

Get up! Get up! What are you waiting for? Jon Brock sat up on the edge of the seat as if Tom could hear his thoughts, his right hand grasping Jeri's shoulder. Jeri glanced back at him, startled out of the numbness that had set in as the questioning progressed.

Tom lowered his head. His shoulders dipped forward, then lifted back, pushed by a deep breath filling his lungs, releasing a weight that had not seemed all that heavy, until now. He had almost forgotten. It would flash across his consciousness on occasion. He had prayed for forgiveness. He tried to avoid thoughts about Jeri's reaction if she ever found out. His throat burned, his stomach churned, his eyes grew moist. A few seconds of silence that seemed like hours pounded in his ears. He looked up at Judge Hawes.

"Once."

Weed's attorney smiled and gave a satisfied look back at his client. Whispers riffled through the audience, about thirty people. Jon Brock slumped back in his seat. Jeri stared at Tom, stunned.

Judge Hawes rapped the gavel. "Strike that from the record," she addressed the court reporter. "Mr. Otto, you have not been charged, you are not on trial today. Please step down."

29

THE BEST THING ABOUT THE OTTOS MOVING to the old place up on the ridge turned out to be the ridge itself. In the past, Tom and Randy Tollefson, and sometimes their spouses, usually took the four-by-fours off road down by the river.

After Weed's trial and acquittal on second degree murder charges, but conviction on drug charges, even though he had been an informant, and the absence of any formal charges against Tom, Randy could justify resuming their friendship.

Long shadows hid behind rocks protruding from the Buffalo Ridge landscape in the early morning sun in late August. Randy, Marlene, and their three kids arrived in their big Jimmy four-by-four at the Otto place feeling excitement, anticipating companionship, good food, and conquering the off-road terrain above the farmstead.

Jeri poured a cup of coffee for Marlene. They sat on the back porch watching the kids assault the climbing and swing set, a recent purchase using money donated by members of the Ames County sheriff's department and the Jaycees. Like a miniature, medieval battlement, the wood structure stood six feet tall and four feet square, covered by a yellow-and-green striped canopy, and surrounded by ropes, ladders and two swings.

They watched Tom and Randy depart in the trucks toward the rocky hills beyond the old barn.

"That was really nice of you guys," Jeri said, looking toward the kids on the play set, feeling their excitement.

"Thanks. It really wasn't all that much."

"Those things are expensive!"

"Yeah, but after what you guys went through, and it's not over yet."

"What do you mean?"

"Well, you can't live here forever. And the Weaver's kids, and Michael. I hope things work out."

"I hope so, too." Jeri looked back toward the swing set. "Jade! Watch your brother now! Watch him when he's on the rope!" she shouted.

"They'll be okay," Marlene said. "It looks like Tom's put enough sand around it."

"Yeah. I just remember last year though when Trace broke his elbow falling off the old swing set. It still really pisses me off, they way they grilled us when we took him to the hospital. It was like they thought we were doing child abuse or something."

"That happens more than you think. They're just doing their job," Marlene advised.

"It just makes me sick to think about that. And to think I was like that once."

Marlene glanced at Jeri, wondering how she should respond. "It wasn't you. It's the meth."

"I tried to take care of him, as much as I could."

"You dug yourself into a pretty deep hole, that's for sure, but you got out of it."

"Yeah, but Tom's little surprise during the trial sure stirred things up for awhile. All this time I really trusted him. I think he's telling the truth. I hope he's telling the truth. I don't know anybody who took that stuff just once."

"I think you have now," Marlene said.

"I hope so." Jeri paused, sipping her coffee and looking absently toward distant prairie below the ridge. "If Newton Case hadn't come along when he did, we, me and Michael, wouldn't be here today." Her voice trembled. "They would have found us froze to death. God saved us. He sent Newt. I can never wear open-toed shoes or sandals, you know."

Jeri leaned forward and removed her left shoe of the pair of slip-ons she often wore without socks.

Marlene watched curiously. "Oh my God!"

Instead of toenails, the three middle toes ended about half-way in fleshy stubs. "I just lost one on the other foot." Jeri replaced the shoe and slumped back into the deck chair. "I never showed that to anyone before, other than mom and Tom." She didn't want to say anymore, even regretting the mention. Marlene knew better than to press, a patience she'd learned whenever Randy returned home after a tough shift. All she did was to listen. Now she felt the need to say something, despite how weak and trite it seemed: "I won't tell a soul."

Jeri shrugged and tried to smile. "Don't worry about it. Like I said, it could have been a lot worse. You want any more coffee?" Marlene declined. Jeri went into the kitchen, returning with juice boxes for the kids.

TOM'S CONFESSION ON THE WITNESS STAND during Weed's trial that he took some meth the day the gang was captured had been stricken from the record by Judge Hawes. Weed's attorney challenged her ruling; he challenged everything throughout the entire proceeding. Judge Hawes said Tom's testimony ended the second she instructed him to step down from the stand. Whatever he might have said after that was off the record.

Instead of returning to his seat next to Jeri, Tom felt the urge to run out of the courtroom. He sat close to the edge of the bench, repelled by her stare of incredulity, disbelief, yet relieved of the weight of deception, which he feared would be replaced by anger and conflict. Sitting behind them, Jon Brock clasped Tom's shoulder in a silent offer of understanding and support.

The unexpected silence that enveloped Jeri since Tom's courtroom revelation persisted out of the courthouse, through the parking lot, and into the pickup truck.

"Let's just drive around for awhile." Softly, quietly Jeri said she didn't want to get the kids yet. They could stay at Lynn's for a while longer.

Tom searched for words that would explain his actions, profess his remorse, and seek understanding and forgiveness.

"Where should we go?"

"I don't care." Jeri stared straight ahead.

"Listen, I don't know what else to say. I did a bad thing. I'm sorry. I'll never do it again."

"You promised me when we got married," Jeri finally looked at him. "It's like you just forgot about everything, like it didn't matter."

"That's not true. I never used the stuff. It would have been so easy, but I didn't do it. The one time I did it could have saved my life."

"What? Saved your life? It almost got you killed!"

"I mean before that. I was falling asleep at the wheel. That whole week I hardly got any sleep. I was dying."

"Then you should just pull over and rest."

"It's not that easy to do. Whenever I've tried it, it doesn't do any good. I'd rather keep going."

"Where'd you get it?"

"At the warehouse, from one of the other drivers. He just gave it to me."

"That's how it starts, to get you hooked."

"I know that. That's why I didn't use it."

"Why'd you keep it? You could have just thrown it away."

"It's like I tried to forget about it. It was in a little salt-shaker thing, in my lunchbox."

"You brought it into the house, in your lunchbox?"

"No. I threw it in the glove compartment."

"So if you did that everyday how could you forget about it?"

"Then I just threw it under seat and left it there."

"I don't know which is worse," Jeri sighed. "Why'd you take it? You didn't have to take it."

"I don't know why. I just did. I told you I was really tired. I didn't really want to."

"It was stupid."

"I know. I'm sorry."

"What if somebody knows you had it? What if it's a set-up?"

"Nobody knows. And talking about set-ups, what that BCI agent tried was really stupid. I can't believe we haven't heard anything more about that."

"He was such a creep, treating Michael like that."

Tom saw the opening, a chance to change the subject. "Let's go get the kids."

"Okay. But promise me you'll never, ever do anything like that again."

"I promise."

NEWTON CASE INSISTED ON DRIVING himself to St. Paul. Tom offered to give him a ride. After receiving summons to appear before a federal grand jury, they had briefly conversed several times, even though they had been ordered to refrain from talking with anyone connected to the murders of Stan and Tulie Weaver, and investigation of the meth gang. Both felt nervous about what they faced.

Not long after the convictions of Weed and the other two gang members, the announcement of a federal grand jury surprised everyone.

Alone in his old Dodge pickup, Newt could have used the freeway escort. Puttering along at fifty miles per hour, several times he barely escaped rear-end crashes before taking the exit to downtown St. Paul. He cut across two lanes without signaling, forcing a semi-truck driver to hit the brakes and nearly sliding into a jack-knife.

Tom and Jeri took the F-350 pickup. Even though she would not be allowed in the courtroom, Jeri insisted on going along. They declined a ride offer from Duane Harstad, who brought the disk with Newt's interview with Michael.

Ever since the federal DEA agents showed up, Duane knew that something more was going on. He had done his part, winning convictions of the other two defendants in the Weaver case, at least on the drug charges. The grand jury would answer questions that had been growing from the day BCI agent Harmon Leuten took over the investigation.

If the Ames County courtroom seemed imposing, its counterpart in the St. Paul federal building created a feeling of awe beyond description. How anyone could tell anything other than the truth seemed impossible. Not knowing the truth, terrifying.

Creamy, marble columns fifteen feet tall flanked the door to the courtroom. A statue of Justice stood ten feet tall in the middle of a barn-size atrium, opening to two broad hallways in opposite directions. A curious, musty odor spiked with the scent of floor cleaner told of a place where laws, rules, decorum, and tradition controlled the thoughts and whims of mere humans.

A U.S. marshal escorted Newt out of the courtroom. The marshal nodded to Tom. "Your turn."

"Good luck," Jeri whispered and squeezed his hand. Newt signaled a 'thumbs up'.

Twenty-four men and women of the grand jury, young to old, black and white, watched the young man approach the witness stand. Tom stood as a marshal administered the oath. A federal prosecutor rose from a table, which held several stacks of documents.

On another smaller table sat a familiar-looking, large, white bag. It caught Tom's attention even before he took the stand. It was a bag of flour, the kind he delivered occasionally to the Home Bakery in Kasota Creek.

What he knew to be the truth had not changed. His testimony had been honest and consistent. Why a bag of flour sat on a table in a federal courtroom, he could not comprehend.

The U.S. attorney approached the witness stand. "Mr. Otto, thank you for your timely attendance here today. I hope you didn't have too much trouble getting here in the freeway traffic?"

Tom relaxed slightly. "No big deal. I drive a truck here almost every day."

"Right. I must have still been thinking about Mr. Case," the attorney said apologetically.

"Newt? Yeah, we offered to give him a ride."

"How well do you know Mr. Case?"

"Until all this happened I didn't know too much about him," Tom replied, curious about the opening questions, which he had not expected. "He's a little strange, but he's an okay guy I guess."

"You've had several occasions to meet him related to the events of our concern, is that correct?"

"Well, yeah, I guess he was at our place a couple of times. He found the kid, Michael Weaver, and took him to our place. He helped clean up after the tornado."

"What tornado was that?"

"It was that Saturday, after the thing at the Weavers. Before Father's Day. Our place got trashed, totally."

"I'm sorry to hear that. I trust you're making a recovery?"

"We're doing okay."

"Good." The attorney paused, returning to his legal role. "Mr. Otto, we have the transcripts of your testimony in the district court trials. We believe your testimony so far to be truthful to the best of your ability. But that's not why we've called you here today."

He gestured toward the bag of flour. "Would you describe to the court everything about your role in transporting those bags of flour?"

Tom looked over at the bag. His mouth suddenly felt dry as if the question sucked away moisture like a desiccating desert wind. "Them?" He struggled to think of some reason for its presence. "I just deliver some once in a while. There's a little bakery in Kasota Creek that gets them."

"Where do you get the bags?"

"From the warehouse, the same one that I get my other stuff."

"Who orders them?"

"The bakery, I suppose. I just haul them. They show up on the shipping manifest. I bring the fresh stuff in from our growers, then I pick up stuff in the city and haul it back."

"Do you know what is in the bags?"

Tom studied the attorney, trying to understand the logic of such a stupid question. He held back a smirk from his response. "Flour? It's just flour, isn't it? I thought it was just flour, going to the bakery."

The attorney asked a few more questions, thanked Tom, and released him from the witness stand. He stepped down and strode quickly up the aisle, feeling relieved and mystified. A marshal opened the door. Entering the atrium Tom turned left toward for Jeri. She gave a little wave, which ended with a slight gesture pointing to Tom's right. He turned to look, just in time to see Harmon Leuten entering the courtroom escorted by a marshal. On a bench farther down the hall sat Lyon Clymer with two marshals. He looked sharply in question back toward Jeri.

"How'd it go? I thought you'd be in there longer than that," she said.

"Me too. Let's get out of here." Tom's head rocked back slightly, gesturing toward Leuten. "What gives with him? And Clymer?"

"Can you believe that?" Jeri said. "I about fell off the chair when they came in. Then when Newt was leaving he slipped me a little note. Here, look at it. He wants us to meet him at a restaurant near here. I think he knows something." Tom read the note held out in Jeri's hand. "I know where that is. Let's go."

About an hour before the peak lunch crowd at the neighborhood café, Newt found a parking spot on the busy street. He spied a corner booth and hurried toward it. Sitting on the far side he could see the front door.

Tom spied Newt sitting in the back corner booth.

"Hey Newt. How'd you know about this place?" Tom asked as they neared.

"I been by here a couple times, but I never stopped."

"I used to come here back in the seventies," Newt said. "I worked at the fabricating plant down the street for awhile. We took over the farm in seventy-eight, from her folks. Great timing, huh?" He let go a grim smile. "Right before the farm depression."

An understanding of that time lay outside the scope of those who then were children, and not directly involved. Lacking an immediate, meaningful response, Tom and Jeri let the comment wither and recede back into Newt's memory.

"So how'd it go?" Jeri leaned forward, showing the intense gaze that demanded innermost truths, and sometimes evoked them. "What did you tell them?"

"Why were you even there?" Tom asked.

"Why was Clymer there? And Leuten?" Jeri added.

"Well you know we ain't supposed to talk about it. You gotta understand that anything we say here never happened," Newt said matter-of-factly.

The Ottos exchanged glances. Tom shrugged. "Sure. Why not? You can trust us."

Newt felt certain he could trust Jeri. Tom less so, but having become better acquainted with the younger man he felt trust growing.

A WAITRESS APPROACHED, took their lunch orders and quickly departed.

"I suppose you saw that bag of flour on the table?" Newt began.

"Hard to miss. What was that all about?" Tom asked. "They asked me what I knew about it. I just said I sometimes delivered them to the bakery, in Kasota Falls."

Newt's eyes narrowed, accompanied by a slight, knowing smile as he formulated just the right amount of information that he could divulge.

"Know what was in there?"

"Flour, I suppose. That's all I know," Tom replied.

"It's good that they must believe you," Newt said. "And what's flour like? A white, powdery substance, right?"

"Oh Jesus," Jeri muttered. "Newt, what are you saying?"

"I think you know what I'm saying. Mixed in with the flour. Meth."

"What? What the hell for?" Tom blurted, too many decibels above normal conversation and bringing an elbow from Jeri.

"You know those pastries they provided free at the chicken plant? I think you can figure it out."

"You mean there was meth in the flour in those rolls?" Jeri asked, disbelief contorting her face. "Why would anyone do that?" She sat back, beginning to absorb the growing revelation.

"How'd you know all this?" Tom asked, again drawing an elbow and 'shush' from Jeri.

"Let's just say I came across some information, heard some stuff."

"How was he getting it?" Tom asked.

"How was who getting it?"

"Clymer."

"I didn't say who it was."

"Well how was it getting into the bags? That's gotta take some planning. You just don't go into the flour factory and say, 'here, dump this white stuff into them bags, will ya?'"

"Will you be quiet?" Jeri said through pursed lips. "Let him talk!"

After imploring them again to never say a word to anyone, Newt told them some of what he knew about the conspiracy between BCI agent Harmon Leuten and Lyon Clymer, and the role of Quentin "Weed" Alt working as a double informant. For Leuten, Weed was the window into the drug ring bringing in meth from large meth factories in Mexico. For the DEA agents, he provided evidence for the investigation of the rogue BCI agent, who had been supplementing his paycheck with proceeds from providing access to meth for Clymer and a few other customers around the state.

The scheme emerged while he was driving back to the city over a year ago. Harmon assembled in his thoughts the pieces of a plan that might be worth something to the new manager at the chicken processing plant in Buffalo Ridge. He had been instrumental in Lyon Clymer getting the job at Prairie Pride in the first place. He anticipated the extra cash that he would be receiving in return, with very little real effort. A small voice tried to warn him about the risk, but, it could not stand up to the excitement, the money, and the power, which drew him to the profession in the first place.

THE METH GANG'S SUDDEN EXCURSION into the countryside in search of money hidden on the Weaver farm did not show up in anyone's game plan, the singular foray launched in desperation by Weed in an attempt to allay suspicions about his multiple roles, which he felt were taking root in the thoughts of Rafe Gonzales.

"If I told you everything, what is it they say, 'I'd have to kill you,'" Newt chuckled. He paused, "I guess that's not funny, is it? Anyway, I don't know why they, the meth gang, came out to the Weaver's. It just didn't have to happen. If we'd moved in on them a little quicker, it wouldn't have."

"Who's we?" Tom asked.

"I mean the cops, the feds."

"How come you know so much?" Tom persisted.

"Leave him alone," Jeri scolded. "I can see Clymer doing something like that. I never did trust him."

"Did you ever eat any of the rolls?" Tom turned to look at Jeri, stopping short of sounding too much like a tease, although just enough to suggest it.

Jeri shot him a hard stare. "Oh shut up!"

"Did you?"

"A couple times. I didn't know. At first he seemed okay except we were really pissed about them firing Ted for no good reason. Then when Clymer stabbed me in the back on that knife design thing, that did it. I wouldn't have taken a million bucks from him."

"Why would he do something like that? Seems stupid to me," Tom said.

"Think about it. Probably thought it would make us work harder. Don't make sense to me. Like it would be hardly enough to do anything."

"They actually used it for that reason," Newt said. "I think I remember reading somewhere that the Japs invented it. I don't know what for. In World War Two they used it for pilots, to keep them alert for long hours in the air. Maybe some other things, too."

"I wish they'd never done that. Invented it," Jeri said, a wistful veil softening her face. She looked at Newt. "Thank you, again."

"For what?"

"For being there, when you did."

"Oh." Newt understood. He welcomed the gratitude, which went a long way toward giving his life some meaning, if what he had done eight years ago on that bitter cold January morning had prevented the untimely end of two lives, which now were proving their value to a family and the community, and perhaps beyond. "Well, me and Harvey, we just did what anyone would have done."

Jeri smiled. "I still remember seeing all that stuff in the back of your truck. A bunch of old computers in there, too. I don't know why. You know how something just sticks in your mind."

"It just became kind of a hobby, I guess," Newt said. "Anyway, I'm glad everything's worked out okay."

"So far," Tom said.

"So far," Newt agreed. He reached for his lunch receipt. "I suppose I should hit the road. It was real exciting driving down here on that freeway." His eyes twinkled. "I don't see how you can do that almost every day."

Tom snatched the receipt from Newt. "It ain't so hard in a truck, actually. You're a lot bigger than the cars. Let us get your lunch."

Newt didn't argue. He thanked the Ottos and hoisted himself from the booth. "Good luck. I hope things work out. I don't think you're going to have to worry about Clymer anymore. Leuten, too, for that matter."

Newt's bib overalls stood out, drawing some looks on his way toward the door. A man sitting on a stool at the counter called him over, someone he had worked with at the fabricating plant many years ago. They engaged in animated conversation, covering a lot of ground in a few minutes. Newt shook his hand warmly, turned toward the door, and looked back with a wave to the Ottos.

30

With the new school year starting after Labor Day, and the Monday holiday falling five days into September, it gave at least an additional week to work on the placement of Michael, Anna, and Jonathan Weaver.

Amber Brock privately had been hoping that a more permanent solution would be found before the end of summer. She worried about Michael, how he would adapt to public school. She and Jon had discussed the possibility of continuing their foster care. So far they had not admitted concerns about the impact on their family. Ashley and Hunter had been tolerant, so far.

The Ottos' application to become a foster family to Anna and Jonathan, and to formally adopt Michael, created a bureaucratic tempest swirling through the hallways and cubicles of the Ames County family services department.

Some believed in Jeri, that she had more than passed the tests of those troubled years, that she deserved to regain parental custody of Michael, that it would be rooted in a mother's love, not merely a role prescribed by society and all its laws, rules and customs. They believed this outweighed the concerns, which had been expressed in great detail by others who argued against the application. They noted that neither Tom nor Jeri had received post-high school education. Financially, they lived on the edge, paycheck-to-paycheck. Living temporarily in a remote, worn out farm house ranked even lower than the trailer house they once inhabited closer to town.

The word about Tom's unofficial confession on the witness stand that he ingested meth had circulated around town, growing more grotesque with every passing.

Initially, it all added up to weigh against the application. As interviews with references accumulated, the scales began to even out.

Representing the members of HOPE, Ron and Wendy Hamilton attested to the attributes of character evident in their encounters with the Ottos. Honest, reliable, hard-working, loving parents, successful marriage, even-tempered, mostly.

"It's the right thing to do," Ron said. "It may not fit neatly into all the rules and regulations, but it's the right thing to do."

They sat around the table on the deck on a mid-morning of the week before Labor Day, Ron and Wendy facing the county social worker. She listened politely, writing in a notebook. "Have you ever been to their place, where they lived before the tornado?"

Ron and Wendy said they hadn't.

The social worker asked a few more questions. She thanked the Hamiltons for their time and left for the next stop, the Ames County sheriff's office.

Every morning at breakfast Jon Brock flipped through the Buffalo Ridge Banner heading toward the back pages and the legal section.

"Amber! Did you see this?" He stood abruptly, gripping the rustling newsprint, eyes focusing on a page of the Classified section.

She looked over from the stove where she stood turning pancakes browning on the electric griddle. "What?"

Jon looked around to see if any of the kids were near.

"Holy smokes! I don't believe this!"

"What? What is it?"

"This auction! It's about the Weaver property! Stanley Weaver estate. Eighty acres prime crop land, completely renovated buildings, 'Right out of Norman Rockwell' it says!"

"I thought that was already taken care of. The farm. I thought someone was setting up the trust for the kids."

"I thought so, too. Some lawyer from Stan's former life. Some law firm in Omaha."

"Well maybe they decided to auction off the property and put the proceeds in the trust."

"I thought they were going to hang on to the farm for awhile and rent it out. Something's going on there." Jon left half his pancakes and gulped some coffee. "I'm outta here!" He grabbed his briefcase and gave Amber a peck on the cheek. "I'll call you when I know something."

"Bye. Good luck."

"Same to you. They're coming over today for the interview?"

"Right. I'm sure it will be fine. I've talked with the kids about it. I think Michael's okay with it. It's hard to tell sometimes."

Jon's secretary was already working on it when he hurried in. Surprises such as this, although rare, ramped up the levels of energy and tension in the normally easy-going office into a legal onslaught.

Despite thorough research, the reality of Stan Weaver's marital status had eluded them. Jon called the Omaha law firm demanding to know just what the hell was going on. His secretary had already picked up the documents from the clerk of court's office.

Apparently, Stan Weaver had never been legally divorced. Nor had he and Tulie been legally married. His wife in his former life, having been contacted not long after the murders, filed a claim on the estate property. And Tulie, who remained an enigma, left no records anywhere. No relatives could be found. The title to the farm had been recorded in Stan's name only.

Jon leaned back in his chair, rubbing his hands over his eyes, sighing. "I don't believe this. How could I have screwed up so bad?"

"You did everything right, everything you could. They weren't your clients," Angela consoled.

"But the kids. We've got the kids to think about. Man, we're screwed."

"Oh come on. Are you kidding? The court's got to go for the kids."

"Yeah, but the wife, the legal wife, she's got the law on her side."

"But we've got truth and justice."

"Yeah, right," Jon groaned.

If Stan Weaver left a will, no one knew about it. A probate notice appeared in the newspaper toward the end of July, the same week that the Brock's took all the kids on a camping trip up north at a state park near Ely. For three days Amber stayed with Anna and Jonathan while Jon, Ashley, Hunter and Michael explored several lakes by canoe in the Boundary Waters Canoe Area. Somehow, with all the distractions around the criminal proceedings, claim on Stan's property eluded Jon. Unless some miracle intervened, Stan's estranged wife would get the property to do with as she pleased.

THE AUCTION BILL FOR THE WEAVER PROPERTY predicted a crowd of the curious and collectors along with full-time production farmers, among them Archie Daniels, who had coveted the eighty acres of rich, loamy soil. The livestock had already been sold, except for Zelda and Ernie, the matched pair of Percheron draft horses. What remained consisted mostly of shop tools and farm implements dating from the nineteen fifties and earlier, all well-maintained and in working condition. Everything was on the list, the house, barn, outbuildings, and eighty acres. If it didn't rain and a large crowd of buyers showed up, the sale proceeds would approach a half million dollars.

Although he dreaded attending the spectacle, Newton Case could not resist. The thought that the proceeds would be enriching some stranger from Omaha, who had no authentic connection to the Weaver kids other than being their estranged and absent step-mother, ascended into anger, bordering on revenge as he recalled the trauma of losing his own farm, and eventually his family, two decades ago.

Back then the attempt by his anti-government, tax-protesting compatriots to control and emasculate the auction crumbled. Although not justified, Newt took the blame; had he been less distraught, he might have pulled it off.

He dropped the newspaper on the kitchen table and reached for the phone. Ron Hamilton, who had become the de facto president of HOPE in the absence of Tulie Weaver, answered.

"You see the paper today?" Newt rarely made phone calls, and when he did, wasted few words on greetings and small talk.

"Hello? Who is this?"

"Newton Case. You see the paper today?"

Ron paused to assemble his recollections of Newt, a considerable amount consisting of hearsay bordering on legend. "Haven't had a chance. What about it?" He tried to recall the last time he talked with Case, curiosity priming him for what this conversation might produce.

"The auction bill. For the Weaver place."

"What auction?"

"There's going to be an auction."

"Who's doing the auction? Is that what they decided to do? I thought they were going to place the farm in trust for the kids and rent it out."

"Did you know about Stan's wife? Not Tulie. His other wife?"

Silence hung on the line for a moment while Ron sifted through his memory of Stan's past, consisting mainly of what minimal and sometimes mysterious things Stan might have said over the years of their friendship.

"I knew he was married previously. Back in Omaha or someplace. No kids there that I know of. Why?"

Newt explained what he had learned. A Mrs. Stan Weaver of Omaha had filed for probate action on the estate, prevailed, and hired a local real estate agent to dispose of the property.

"How many folks you got in your group, the organic farmers?" Newt asked. "That always make me laugh. It's all organic, you know."

"It's different," Ron said. "We don't use pesticides, chemicals. A lot of folks prefer that."

"How many you got?"

"About thirty. Why?"

"They got balls?"

"What?"

"*Cojones*! They ain't some old hippies, wishy-washy liberals?"

"I think you know who they are. What does that have to do with it?" Ron said, taking some offense.

"You remember what they tried to do back in the thirties? At some farm auctions?"

"You mean the 'penny auctions'?"

"Yeah."

"Are you serious?" Ron wanted to say more, something about Newt's reputation.

"It worked, in a few cases. I done a lot of research. It's true."

"So you want us to help you stage a penny auction? What's in it for you?"

"Get the farm for the kids. It should be theirs."

"I agree, but it doesn't look like there's much we can do about it."

"Can we at least talk about it?"

Ron's spontaneous reluctance retreated, confronted by growing intrigue. It couldn't hurt to at least talk about it. He agreed to contact other members of HOPE. Several hours later Ron, Wendy and two other HOPE members met with Newt at the truck stop café.

EVEN THOUGH IT MEANT GETTING BEHIND on deliveries, Tom took the day off to attend the auction at the Weaver farm. Jeri managed to persuade her supervisor at Wal-Mart to grant the same.

Following their marriage they attended several auctions to acquire appliances, furniture and tools. After Jade was born their auction attendance dwindled.

When they learned who would be the benefactor of the Weaver auction proceeds, a bewildering disbelief hung on to diffuse and dilute anger at the injustice of it all. How could Stan Weaver have deceived everyone, allowing such a thing to happen?

They found a space to park the F-350 out on the township road, lined on both sides with pickups mostly, some towing flatbed trailers. They walked in silence into the long driveway, to the left of which a mowed pasture held at least fifty vehicles.

The mid-morning sun in late August poured energy into the tall corn and leafy soybeans on the surrounding farms. Stan's thirty acres of corn stood just as green although shorter than the neighbors'. The alfalfa needed mowing and baling again. Archie Daniels had already harvested the oats and barley.

The auctioneer's staccato chant echoed among the buildings and drifted down the driveway, punctuated at every signal from either of two assistants scanning the crowd for bids. They already had gone through the first of three hayracks laden with small household goods, tools, and boxes of books and artifacts of daily life.

Tom showed his driver's license to the auction clerk sitting in a small trailer, registering as a potential bidder.

"Don't go crazy now," Jeri warned.

"I won't."

"We should have a limit. Twenty bucks."

"Are you kidding? Okay. I'm looking at one of Stan's hutches. That's got to go for more than twenty bucks. I thought you'd like one of those."

"Where would we put it? Yeah, it'd be nice. Let's see what happens, what they go for."

The sale of small items on the hayracks, furniture, implements and vehicles went past noon. The crowd of bidders had dwindled, many busy paying for and loading their purchases. By mid-afternoon all that remained was to auction off the property.

Tom and Jeri hung around to watch the bidding. They sat on the porch eating hot dogs from the lunch wagon. Tom had tried for one of Stan's hand-made hutches, but dropped out when the bidding exceeded a hundred dollars.

"It's funny, I thought there'd be more people here for this," Tom said. "I know almost everybody here. It's all the people from HOPE. There's Archie Daniels."

"Here comes Newt. How come he wasn't here earlier?"

Newton Case saw the Ottos sitting on the porch and walked over.

"You kids in on the bidding, or just here for the show?"

"Us? Bid on this place? We didn't win the lottery, Newt," Jeri laughed.

Newt studied them, wondering how much they knew, wondering what to say. "This one you just might be able to," he finally said. "But there's some strings attached."

"Always is," Tom laughed.

LOUD VOICES NEAR THE CLERK'S TRAILER drew their attention.

Newt looked away in concern. "You kids sit tight." He hurried in that direction.

A man dressed in a sport coat and tie stood facing Ron Hamilton, both talking loudly and gesturing. Others crowded around. They began moving in unison, herding the man away from the trailer and toward the driveway.

The auctioneer quickly walked over and stood in front of the house, his back to the Ottos sitting on the porch. About a dozen mostly HOPE members followed him. He seemed slightly nervous. He spoke quietly and did not use the loudspeaker.

"What am I bid for the property here, eighty acres more or less and all the buildings?"

The small crowd of men and several women stood close, looking sober, determined.

"One dollar," a man finally said.

"Any other bids?" The auctioneer paused about ten seconds. "Any other bids? Going once. Going twice. Sold to the man, what is your number? Three-forty-eight. Sold for one dollar to bidder number three-forty-eight. Thank you ladies and gentlemen. That's all for today."

He escorted the winning bidder to the clerk's trailer and quickly concluded the transaction.

The buyer and three others left with the sale bill for the courthouse. At the register of deeds office he transferred the title to the trust that had been established for Michael, Anna and Jonathan Weaver. In return, the buyer at the auction received one dollar, which came from Michael's own money that he had earned from selling farm-fresh eggs.

Everywhere he went, the man in the sport coat got the same story. Not much, really. The auction was over. No one knew anything about a conspiracy.

He barged into Sheriff Schwartz' office demanding that the auctioneer be arrested and charged with fraud. He claimed to be representing Mrs. Stanley Weaver and the Omaha law firm. The sheriff said the auction followed all the necessary steps, and was final.

Jon Brock avoided any connection with the event, but followed his curiosity to investigate the result. He had Angela call her friend, also the auctioneer's clerk.

After the auctioneer's cut, Mrs. Weaver in Omaha received nearly $75,000 from the sale of the furnishings, tools and implements. Enough to pay for some cosmetic surgery and a couple of trips, he thought. He decided that he would step in if a legal challenge to the auction developed. Angela was right. In terms of justice the outcome was fair. The children got the property. The estranged Mrs. Stan Weaver received a substantial amount, a windfall, really. The law had been followed, although strained.

Jon felt confident that he would be able to at least make a defense for what had happened; he deeply hoped that it wouldn't be necessary. He had already agreed to represent the Ottos in their attempt to gain custody of the Weaver children, at least of Michael. If Anna and Jonathan remained in foster care, perhaps it would be for the better if it meant also receiving payment from the county.

It certainly meant confronting County Attorney Duane Harstad, who had been looking for a scapegoat in the failure of sticking Quentin "Weed" Alt with a second degree murder conviction. The primary challenge emerged in Weed's service to the state as an informant, and the unorthodox testimony of Michael Weaver mediated through Newton Case. There clearly was reasonable doubt whether or not Tulip Weaver was still alive when Weed, at gunpoint by Rafe Gonzales, allegedly thrust a kitchen knife into her heart.

Complicating matters further, Weed's informant role gained access to a major drug trafficking ring, resulting in numerous arrests. The exposure of Harmon Leuten's involvement surprised everyone, and the link to Lyon Clymer at the Prairie Pride processing plant even more. Surprised everyone except for Newton Case.

As much as he desired to attend the auction, Jon could not. He waited for Angela to return from the courthouse with confirmation that the sale had occurred. He flipped through a stack of mail that had just arrived, stopping abruptly, staring at the envelope, fine quality paper, somewhat soft and textured, the return address being that of Quentin Alt's attorney.

31

Jon Brock agreed to represent the Ottos, with the understanding that any payment for his services would be negotiated later, and according to their financial ability.

They had a lot to talk about.

Jon didn't think the demand from Quentin Alt's attorney for a DNA sample from Michael Weaver had any merit. No matter what the result, he believed that it would not on appeal have any influence on Weed's conviction. Nevertheless, he would advise the county family services department to refuse the request. It amounted to only a distraction, a delaying tactic.

Jon focused his efforts on the attempt by the Ottos to gain temporary custody of Michael, eventually leading to Jeri regaining parental rights and adoption by Tom, and their application to become foster parents to Anna and Jonathan. If that were successful, there was even talk in the county family services department of allowing the Ottos to live on the former Weaver farm. Its ownership would remain in Weaver children's trust.

Already Jon had been thinking of a strategy to make that happen: Doing some remodeling in the house to alter the location of Tulie's untimely death, and having the Ottos make regular payments into a college fund for Jade and Trace and individual retirement accounts for themselves, all in lieu of having to pay on a mortgage. And getting rid of the F-350 pickup. If Tom needed a pickup, a good used F-150 would be sufficient and make more sense.

He was eager to hear about the offer to the Ottos of a business venture with Prairie Pride.

Since she had to work the weekend at Wal-Mart, Jeri was able to meet on a weekday afternoon. Tom shortened his route enough to arrive just after 3 p.m.

Angela greeted them and led the way to a small conference room. "Jon will be here in a minute. I think he's in back getting some coffee." Jon entered carrying a tray with a coffee pot and cups. Both Tom and Jeri accepted the offer.

Tom took a sip. "Good coffee."

"Thanks. I get it from one of your HOPE members. They started roasting awhile back. It's great, isn't it?"

Tom felt embarrassed. "How come I didn't know that?" he said, looking at Jeri. She smiled. "You don't know everything."

She returned her attention to Jon. "How are the kids doing? Jade said she saw Anna at kindergarten. Is Michael getting any better?"

"I think they're doing okay. Michael's seeing a special needs teacher. You know Wendy Hamilton. She knows the teacher working with him."

"That's good. I wish Wendy could, too. He knows Wendy."

"Even after just a week there's been some progress. That's what she said to Amber the other day. They've been through a lot."

"Haven't we all," Tom said.

"Right," Jon said. "I know you guys have been through a lot. Heck of a way to spend a summer, the tornado and everything. Things will start looking up. So tell me more about this business deal, with Prairie Pride." Tom described his conversation with Ray Morris at the Hardee's in Belle Prairie. Prairie Pride was interested in purchasing Tom's natural foods delivery business. He could stay on and help it grow.

"Sounds interesting," Jon said. "What do you think about it?"

"It makes me nervous," Jeri said. "I think I trust Ray. But I can't believe Clymer's still there. I couldn't have anything to do with that place as long as that creep's there."

"I don't think he'll be there long," Jon said. "I think the company's getting a little nervous, about their reputation around town. Everybody knows the story. I think when his case goes to trial, as far as the plant's concerned he'll be going, too. If you want my opinion, I think you should pursue the offer. What have you got to lose?"

Tom and Jeri agreed to continue working with Jon on the business venture. Their application for getting the kids was working its way through the system.

"Have you received any calls about the F-350?" Jon asked. Tom said that he hadn't posted a 'for sale' ad yet, but would do so soon.

They thanked Jon for all his help and stood to leave.

Jon stood and shook hands. "You have any plans for the weekend?" he asked casually.

"We're thinking of going to the drive-in movie on Friday," Tom said.

"Really? I didn't know any of those were still around."

"It's just outside Fairfield. It opened a couple years ago. This is the last weekend before they close for the season."

"That sounds like fun, I guess."

"It's cheap. Yeah, it's fun."

The Ottos left Jon's office for home, thanking him for what he had done so far, and what they hoped he could do.

So what about this Weed guy, Quentin Elk or whatever?" Tom asked as they drove away.

"What about him? I don't want to talk about it."

"This DNA thing. What if it shows he's Michael's biological father?"

"I said I don't want to talk about it, okay?"

"Okay. Okay."

They drove toward Lynn's apartment to get Jade and Trace.

"I don't want to go there yet. Let's just drive around a bit. Go get some coffee," Jeri said, hoping it would drain off the tension they felt.

"I know where we could go," Tom said.

"Where?"

"If we sell the pickup, we still need another vehicle, right?"

"I suppose. You got something in mind?"

"I know this used car place in Burnett. They've got good stuff, and reasonable. I drive by there all the time. Let's go take a look."

"We got enough time? I don't want to leave the kids at mom's all day."

"If we go right now and not dick around. Let's go!"

"How much are you talking about?"

"I saw a nice van for about a thousand. We can handle that. We'll be losing the payments on the pickup. C'mon!"

"A van? Are you serious? This I got to see."

They talked a little, but mostly listened to the radio on the forty-five minute drive to Burnett. Missing lunch earlier, they decided stop at a café on main street. They ate quickly and went to the used car lot.

"That's the one," Tom said, pointing toward a 1991 Astro Van. "It's got about a hundred and thirty thousand on it, but it's in pretty good shape."

The pickup slowed to a stop. Jeri's eyes scrutinized the boxy, light-blue van. "You really want to look at this?" Jeri said, wincing. "You'd actually drive this? Ain't it kind of a wuss-mobile?"

"You'd drive it, too, with all the kids," Tom said.

"So I'm the only one to drive it? Forget that. You're driving it, too."

"I just thought it would help. Jon wants us to get rid of this thing. I'd drive it."

"That'd be the day."

"I would. You don't believe me?"

"But if we got rid of this you were still going to get another pickup."

"We can afford it. A used one. Both of them together ain't as much as this thing."

At the office they enquired with the salesman, who gave them the key for a test drive. Returning to negotiate, they agreed on a purchase price of $925.

Concerned about their longer-than-planned absence from Lynn and the kids, Jeri left the checkbook with Tom and departed for Buffalo Ridge in the F-350. The salesman had offered to buy it for an insulting amount, which could have threatened to sour the deal on the Astro Van. Tom remained to close the deal and call their insurance agent to relay the vehicle information, after which he would drive it back.

"I'm sure you'll like this one," the salesman said. "You got kids? This'll be just the thing. Got a lot of good miles left on it."

The reality of handing over a check and actually taking possession of a mini-van began to invade Tom's thoughts, growing into a dilemma. Life had changed immensely in the past five years. Becoming a father with all its joys and burdens, becoming self-employed with the delivery business. The red F-350 had stood as a source, a symbol, of strength, power, individuality. Replacing it with a smaller model would help, but it wouldn't be the same.

Through the large, plate-glass window of the sales office his eyes scanned one last time the long row of vehicles on the display lot. One stood out, literally. An older limo, pale yellow or cream-colored, probably a Lincoln.

"What's that down there on the end?" Tom asked, pointing out the window.

"Which one?"

"The limo. At the end."

"That? I think it's a seventy-eight or seventy-nine. Let me look." The salesman flipped through papers on a clipboard. "Nineteen-seventy-eight Lincoln Town Car limo, unknown miles, good condition, eleven hundred ninety-five dollars."

"Ain't that kind of cheap? What's the matter with it?"

"You'll see."

"Can I take it for a test drive?"

"Sure. What about the van? Isn't that what you wanted?"

"If you say so."

"It's not me doing the saying. What about the little lady?"

"What do you care?"

"I'm just asking. I want my customers satisfied, that's all."

"You'd probably want to unload that limo instead of the van anyway. Am I right?"

The salesman ignored the challenge and handed Tom the keys. "Here you go."

Tom walked out to the Town Car, acutely conscious of any clues about the vehicle's condition. A closer look saw what seemed like hundreds of tiny dents covering the sprawling hood and trunk lid. Hail damage.

Tom opened the driver door and climbed in. The view through the tiny side mirrors barely conveyed the limo's long, boxy enormity. It was clean and seemed to have been well-maintained. The roomy passenger cabin appeared to have been thoroughly shampooed, erasing or at least masking remnants of exuberant social activity over the past twenty-two years.

On the drive back to Buffalo Ridge, the limo rode well. It almost felt longer than the delivery truck. Tom's thoughts worked on his responses to the surprise it would create. He only paid seven hundred and fifty. It was big enough to haul everyone and more. And it was not an eleven-year-old, light blue minivan.

THE KIDS SEEMED TO GET ALONG WELL, especially Jade and Anna. Michael remained inscrutable, although he had become a little more verbal after the school year started. Trace followed him like a puppy; Jonathan toddled behind as best he could.

When Tom and Jeri asked them, Jon and Amber thought it would be a good thing if the Ottos took all the kids, including their own, to the drive-in movie at Fairfield. Ashley and Hunter could take care of themselves, and would be able to help keep the younger ones from any danger. The Brock's agreed that the excursion had rewards for their own children as much as anyone. On a mild Friday evening in early September they were missing a high school football game, but they would be learning and gaining experience much more valuable than trying to talk smart among a cluster of middle schoolers.

The movie they planned to see was a re-make of Jack and the Beanstalk.

Jeri slowed the limo to a stop in front of the Brock residence.

After the initial shock and driving it, she relented to Tom's impulsive action. It came perilously close to a breach of trust, which had been rigorously tested over the past summer. But the limo was fun to drive, although a beast to maneuver in a parking lot.

She smiled, watching the kids tumble out of the Brock's front door and stampede toward the limo. Amber followed, carrying a small cooler with sodas and a large plastic bag of fresh popcorn. Jade and Trace poked their heads through the open sun roof, waving vigorously.

The clamor of seven kids laughing and jostling excitedly spilled out of the passenger cabin into the mellow early September evening, an hour before sunset. Jeri took command, issuing orders to sit still and behave. On the half-hour trip to the drive-in theater, Ashley helped to keep infractions in check, with occasional back-up from Tom or Jeri sending admonishments through the open sliding window between front and back.

The limo drew stares entering the line of vehicles for the drive-in theater ticket booth.

"I should charge you double for that thing," said the girl selling tickets.

Tom smiled. "Ten bucks, right? For a carload?" He handed her a twenty and waited for change.

"Enjoy the show," she said, smiling and waving at the pile of kids in the back.

"We should probably park toward the back," Jeri said.

"I'm not parking in back. You can hardly see the screen anyway." Tom guided the twenty-six-foot-long beast into the parking area. He made a wide turn into the first row behind the projection and concession building. They had arrived ahead of the main rush. He headed for several open spots to the right of the building.

With another wide turn followed by two back-and-forth maneuvers, he positioned the limo with the front and back jutting equally into their lanes. That put the front wheels slightly past the slight rise intended to raise the view from the vehicle.

"This ain't going to work," Tom said.

"I knew we shouldn't have taken this thing," Jeri said.

"It's the only thing we could take to fit all the kids. Plus, they can sit on the top and look out the sunroof. You couldn't do that with a van."

Jeri looked back through the sliding window, her attention irresistibly drawn to seven kids jostling for position and digging into the bag of popcorn.

Tom checked the rear to make sure all the kids still were in the car, and that nothing was behind it. He started the engine and backed slightly so that the front tire rode up on the rise, improving their view. It left little space for vehicles to pass behind. They were forced to slow with barely enough room to squeeze past. A few drivers expressed their displeasure with a horn honk and sour-looking glares. Others smiled at the scene, an old limo full of kids. They responded with smiles and waves.

Jeri looked back to see Michael. Was he having a good time? Was he talking with the other kids? She flipped open her cell phone and punched "one," the speed-dial for Michael's cell phone.

"Who are you calling?"

"Michael." On several earlier occasions, when she tried calling him, he would actually talk, more so than in person. "He looks like he's having fun. I just wanted to say 'hi.'"

She saw him retrieve his phone from his jeans front pocket.

"Hi. You having a good time?"

"Uh-huh."

"Good. How do you like the limo? It's kind of fun, isn't it?"

"Uh-huh."

"You have fun. We'll talk to you later. Bye." She looked back at him and gave a little wave. He waved back and smiled. After eight years and four months, the images of her young face as she held him, images sequestered during the years of nurturing love and care given by Stan and Tulie Weaver, resurfaced in his consciousness, connecting with her gaze hitting him like a laser coming from the front seat of the old limo.

Michael closed his phone.

"Who was that?" Hunter asked.

Michael pointed toward the front.

"Who? Them?" Hunter asked, pointing frontward. "What'd they want? Which one called?"

Michael pointed at Jeri.

"Your mom? Jeri? That's your real mom, you know. Can I see your phone? Let me see it. I want one of these. Mom and dad won't let us. How'd you get one anyway? Do you take it to school? You're not supposed to have them in school. If you get caught they take it away."

Michael fished the phone from his pocket. Hunter grabbed it, flipped it open and began to explore the phone book, settings and other contents. He selected

'Camera', pointed the tiny lens toward Michael, and captured a digital image. Michael winced. His patience kept him from grabbing back the phone. Hunter selected the 'In Camera' option, searching for the image he just captured. The screen filled with a checkerboard of tiny images. He selected the first, showing Michael the photo he just took.

"It makes me look funny," Michael said, feeling embarrassment and slight annoyance at Hunter's intrusion. While never becoming close friends to the extent that pre-teens achieve, they had experienced a cordial relationship over the past three months. Michael had become accustomed to Hunter's impulsive displays of confidence.

"You don't look funny," Hunter said. "That's a nice picture." He kept the camera-phone and chose several more images to expand, each in turn filling the small cell phone screen.

"Holy crap! What's this one!" He held the screen in front of Michael's face. "What's that guy doing?"

Michael grabbed the phone. Hunter had found the image Michael snapped, hiding in the closet leading to the hidden stairway to the basement on that Tuesday morning back in June. It showed a man, who could be identified as Quentin "Weed" Alt, crouching next to Tulie lying on the floor, a large kitchen knife in his hand. Michael's face flushed, his heart sped away from the danger rekindled by Hunter's discovery.

Hunter grabbed the phone and again stared at the image. "Who's that lying on the floor? What's that guy doing? Did you take this?" He beckoned Ashley, who was wiping Jonathan's face, which had been buried in a double handful of buttered popcorn. "Ashley! Look at this picture, in Michael's phone camera!"

She squinted at the tiny screen, listened as Hunter described what he saw. "We should tell dad. I think this is about the Weavers. Is that what this is?" she addressed Michael.

Michael nodded.

"Have you shown this to anybody? Can we show this to our dad?"

Michael shrugged his shoulders. "I suppose. I already told them everything I saw. I told Mr. Case, and he told them. Sure."

32

They agreed to meet at the Hardee's in Belle Prairie, the largest town between Buffalo Ridge and Minneapolis. Prairie Pride plant CEO Ray Morris was traveling to a meeting in the city. For Tom, it would be breakfast before working down a long list of pickups and deliveries.

Ray's call just before the Labor Day weekend to arrange the meeting bordered on astonishing. Tom had seen him around town, but had never met him. He knew about Morris only from common knowledge, and occasional references from Jeri during tirades about conflicts and injustices at work, although few against Ray.

His reputation of competence and fairness diminished somewhat when the new owners took over the plant. Loyal and bound by the benefits and entitlements of his position, he followed orders making changes, some of which he thought unwise, and a few bitterly distasteful, such as the dismissal of Ted Durand as production manager, replacing him with their corporate storm trooper, Lyon Clymer.

When the Hardee's came into view, Morris brushed off an impulse to skip out of the meeting. If someone saw him talking with Tom Otto, and if word somehow got back to corporate, it could raise suspicions. It certainly would require an ordeal of explanation and justification.

At first the drug conspiracy charges against Clymer seemed solid. Out on bail, he still came to work every day. Ray's attempt to fire him crumbled under corporate's dictate that a person is innocent until proven guilty, a principle they seemed to use selectively in staff hiring and firing decisions.

Their work relationship became even more strained as Clymer's arrogance seemed to have increased, particularly after gaining the representation of a high-priced defense attorney. The trial date fell in October, and each day the momentum seemed to be fading from the initial outrage that Clymer's alleged actions caused in and around Buffalo Ridge. He still was providing free pastries for employee coffee breaks.

Ray parked his Chrysler 300 on a side street and walked a block to Hardee's. He didn't recall the last time he had been inside a fast-food restaurant. He used a McDonald's or Burger King drive-through on occasion, usually for only a coffee.

Before opening the door, he scanned what he could see of the customers, hoping to not recognize anyone. The blue-collar breakfast crowd had dwindled.

A few moms kept busy herding and helping kids, their exuberant noise and laughter venting enviable energy. Four old retirees claimed a table where they sipped senior-discount coffee, expounded on the state of the world, and re-told a repertoire of stories from their pasts, occasionally refreshed with new embellishments.

Ray was early and did not see Tom or his truck. He bought a coffee and sat in a corner booth. In a few minutes he saw Tom's truck roll to a stop on the side street. He chuckled at the irony of the "Tom's Fresh Meats and Produce, Naturally" delivery truck next to a fast-food restaurant.

Tom bought a large coffee and looked around for Ray. He saw him giving a slight wave from the corner booth. It had to be him, the only person in sight wearing a suit and tie. Tom walked over and introduced himself. Ray thanked him for agreeing to meet. He asked how the delivery business was going, how the family was doing, especially after the tornado.

Tom answered cautiously. Everything was fine. He waited for Ray to say what this was all about.

"What do you think your business is worth?" Morris asked.

"What? The delivery business?"

"Right. What's it worth?"

"I don't know."

"Well what's the annual gross? What do you net?"

Tom had never faced such questions, other than Jeri's occasional attempts to raise them, and particularly from someone on a different societal plane who did not even register on the scale of trust. "Why? What's this about?"

Ray smiled, understanding the young man's reticence. "If someone wants to buy something, you need to know the price." He paused, waiting for understanding to develop in Tom's thoughts. "For some time now our company has been looking at ways to enter the natural or organic food business. Not too long ago I realized we have it right in our backyard, right under our nose. We'd like to discuss purchasing your business."

Tom sipped his coffee, staring at the person from another world, distinguished-looking in his dark suit, tan, chiseled face, neatly combed-back hair graying at the temples.

"I'm sorry. I didn't mean to create such a surprise. I suppose I could have hinted what this was about," Ray said.

"I thought you wanted to talk about Jeri or something, or Clymer."

"Oh? Why is that?"

"With Clymer doing what he did and all that? We maybe were hoping she'd get her job back. Except I didn't know why you wanted to talk to me about it."

"Maybe she could get her job back, in a sense anyway. If we worked out a deal and both of you stayed on to run the venture."

"You mean if you bought my business we'd still do the work?"

"Of course. Plus, you'd have access to many more resources. Together we'd make it grow."

"Sounds good. For you."

"You still could have an ownership share," Ray said. "You wouldn't miss out on the growth. It's a great opportunity."

"I'll have to talk to Jeri."

"Certainly. There's no rush. Things like this take time, within reason, of course. Maybe you could come up with some numbers and let me know."

"Jeri does the taxes. I think it grossed about forty or fifty thousand last year. Most of the expenses were for the truck."

"Work with us and we'll add some zeros."

"Thanks for the offer. We'll think about it."

"You do that," Ray smiled. He reached across the table to exchange a handshake and left, wishing Tom a good day.

With Jeri Otto no longer employed at the Prairie Pride plant, the union organizing effort withered. The rep from the meat cutters' union suggested holding off, but a vote had already been scheduled, and Hector Vasquez thought was too late to back out. Lyon Clymer was already gone, and for some workers that's all that mattered.

In the Oct. 31 election, the union failed by 12 votes, 96 for and 108 against.

Clymer's conviction two weeks earlier on drug conspiracy charges left a vacancy for plant manager. Absent from the plant during the trial, he never returned, even to collect personal items. The trial had been moved to St. Paul, and he remained in jail awaiting sentencing.

Hector was thinking about his family when he accepted the offer of acting plant manager. They needed the money more than the need to defend the principle of collective bargaining. Although sometimes he felt like it, he did not want to blame Jeri. The Ottos had been through enough, and still faced more challenges.

And when he heard about Morris' offer to Tom, he felt even less guilty.

Tom and Jeri hadn't discussed it much, until Jon Brock found out. He urged them to go for it.

They drove the pick-up to the meeting at Jon's office. The dark blue, 1999 F-150 half-ton headed south toward town into the already dark early November evening. They had accepted Jon's advice to get rid of F-350 one-ton truck, one more detail in the effort to show that they deserved to become foster parents of Anna and Jonathan, and adoptive parents of Michael, which Jon had been working on pro bono. The old limo was gone, too, the proceeds going toward the used F-150.

"What do you think we should do?" Tom asked. The solemn weight of important decisions waited for their thoughts to emerge during the drive home, where Lynn looked after the kids. They hadn't discussed it much since the offer was made two months ago. It re-surfaced when Jon's persistent questions about their financial plans and goals demanded answers, and Tom felt compelled to say something about it.

"Well, we're going to have to get more money from somewhere. Wal-Mart ain't going to cut it, unless I get lucky and get into management." Jeri held back from saying anything about Tom's delivery business, which hadn't increased much, despite promises of growth from HOPE. "They're not going to keep the offer open forever."

"I know."

"Look at Hector. Could you believe that a couple months ago?"

"I hope he gets it permanent," Tom said.

"Me too. What would they call it? The business?"

"Don't know yet. Morris never said."

Jeri chuckled, mostly to herself.

Tom's eyes left the road ahead and sent her a sharp glance, saying "What? What are you laughing at?"

"What if they called it 'Tom's', like it is now?"

"So what? What's wrong with that?"

"Nothing."

"C'mon, what?"

"Toms are turkeys. They're a poultry business, except it's chickens and not turkeys."

Tom ignored the lameness of it and let it go, along with the stubborn reticence which had first met the company's offer. "Let's do it. What the heck."

"What about the HOPE guys?" Jeri asked. "What are they going to do for shipping?"

"I don't know. I guess we'll have to work something out."

Until Newt's interview with county family services, few knew in great detail what happened on that bitter cold January morning more than eight years ago. His description of finding Jeri, stumbling barefoot and carrying her injured son, evoked a bewildered awe in the case worker, whose notes added another piece to the evidence that Jon Brock had been accumulating in favor of the Ottos.

But they still didn't know why Newt was traveling that early Sunday morning along the remote, gravel road.

Scavenging old computers and rebuilding them, he had gradually accumulated skills matching those needed by federal law enforcement agencies in surveillance technology. They found him when he had attempted to hack into FBI servers connected to the Internet. Leveraging his past infractions during the 1980s farm economic crisis, they convinced him that this time the consequences would be much more severe. He yielded to their offer, and agreed to join their electronic surveillance network throughout the heartland.

At first, they resisted when Newt said he wanted to install the gear high up in the old silo. After they became convinced that the roof would be weather-proof, they saw the value of its camouflage and elevation for clear signals.

After months of following mundane activity, Newt landed on a big case: A certain state BCI agent was under surveillance on suspicion of conspiracy involving drugs, particularly, meth. Newt's testimony helped lead to the conviction of Harmon Leuten, who would be spending the next 15 years in federal prison.

Newt felt even greater surprise when one of the other players in the case turned out to be one of the meth cookers in the old farmhouse down the road, Quentin "Weed" Alt.

Since early September, with the approval of county authorities, the Ottos had been taking the Weaver children with them to Sunday school at the Gospel Tabernacle.

By mid-November the excursions had escalated to having Sunday dinner with the Ottos and spending most of the afternoon out at the old farm house up on the ridge. The tenure of Michael, Anna and Jonathan at the Brocks had exceeded the span of time that Amber had anticipated when they took them into their home back in June, and the she welcomed the break from the responsibility, even though their absence all afternoon exceeded the original agreement with the county.

A fine rain started just before noon. Driven in a sharp slant by a 20 mile-per-hour southeast wind driving the barely 40-degree air, it felt like a shower of needles when Tom stepped outside the church. He went back inside and told Jeri and the kids to wait while he fetched the car.

Jeri stretched her arm holding open the church door, and the kids scurried out. Anna and Jade led the charge, followed by the boys, all seeming to clamber in at once. Tom waited until they settled in and buckled seat belts.

"Whew! That's nasty!" Jeri inspected her make-up in the visor mirror, and tried to fluff the dampness from her hair.

Tom smiled and waved to someone as he drove the van away from the church. "So, what do you think we should do?" he asked, turning toward Jeri.

Their original plan for the afternoon was taking the kids to Thorson's Farm. It was the last weekend for the annual fall festival, with pumpkin carving, pony rides, hay wagon rides, children's games, crafts, and food—carameled apples, apple cider, kettle corn and hot dogs among choices. It would have been their Sunday dinner.

"I don't know. I don't want to go home and eat," Jeri said, sourly, wistfully.

"Me neither."

"How about the Runes?"

"Really? I get tired of that place sometimes," Tom said.

"That's 'cause you go there so much. The kids would like it."

"All right. I suppose."

"Hey kids! What do you think if we go to the truck stop for dinner?" Jeri turned toward them and gave a big smile.

Trace lit up, "Yay, me too!"

"Of course 'you too'," Jeri laughed.

"What about the farm?" Jade whimpered.

"Look at the weather," Tom said. "That'd be no fun in this stuff."

"I want to go to the farm," Jade insisted.

Jeri announced that it would be best to have dinner first, and maybe the weather would improve. That was not likely, but they could stall and try to think of something else.

"What did you guys learn in Sunday School today?" she asked.

Jade said they talked about the Christmas program, now less than two months off.

"Michael, what did you guys talk about?" Jeri asked, hoping for an answer. She looked back toward him, anticipating at least a few words. He had been talking a bit more lately.

"It was about the woman at the well."

"About the Samaritan woman? That's a good one. So what did you learn from that?"

"That Jesus is here for everybody," Michael said.

"You bet!" Jeri couldn't think of more to say, so she just smiled at him.

THE OWNER OF THE RUNES CAFÉ had been contemplating closing on Sundays later in fall. Business slowed compared with weekdays and Saturday, and it would be nice to have a day off. But for some reason, on this particular Sunday, the parking lot was nearly half full. Inside found almost thirty people seeking refuge from the dreary, spitting rainy weather.

The Otto entourage burst through the entrance and claimed two open tables, pushing them together. Their clamor in the process of ordering provided entertainment and some consternation among the surrounding patrons.

The waitress, a weekend fill-in whom Tom did not recognize, brought over at his suggestion the coloring books and crayons reserved for children. Except for Michael, they plunged in to the task. Now feeling more relaxed, Tom and Jeri sipped coffee and watched their progress.

The respite vanished when Pastor Gabe and Tami entered the café, immediately spotting the Ottos and all the kids. With sincere obligation they approached, greeting everyone personally. Gabe said they were going to have a quick bite to eat, because they were due at the county jail for a service at 1 p.m.

Jeri was reaching to wipe ketchup from Jonathan's face, and waved goodbye to the Evans as they left twenty-five minutes later.

"Wonder if it does any good," Tom said quietly, sideways toward Jeri.

"Does what good?"

"Preaching to those guys."

"I suppose you got to try."

"He's still there, you know."

"Who?"

"You know who."

"You mean Quentin?"

"Yeah."

"How do you know? So what?"

"Randy said he hasn't been transferred yet."

Jeri didn't question any further. Just talking about him threatened to sour the rest of the day. "Whatever," she paused, giving the conversation time to fade away. "We still have to find something to do. Got any ideas?"

"I do." It was Michael.

The sound of his voice, not to mention the firmness of his statement, at first startled them, then grew into hope for a solution to their dilemma.

"Great!" Tom said. "Let's hear it."

"Maybe we should go visit him."

"Visit who?" Jeri asked.

"Quentin."

Tom's and Jeri's eyes locked, each trying to read the other. Several seconds seemed to last an hour.

"What for?" Jeri said, squeezing the words through a tightening throat.

Not expecting such a response, Michael teetered atop his protective wall, which he quietly had been trying to breach. Only the encouragement that he felt when Pastor Gabe had announced his afternoon engagement at the jail, kept him from falling back behind it.

"That's what the Sunday School teacher said this morning, about helping people even if they've done bad things, or they're different than us," Michael said, almost as an apology. "Jesus would want us to."

Tom studied Jeri for a response. It seemed as though it was developing, but he couldn't tell what it would be. "I guess we can't argue with that," he said quietly.

"Can we really do that?" Jeri asked, as if hoping some rule or restriction might intervene.

"People do it all the time, you know that," Tom said.

They felt Michael's gaze boring through their initial shock.

"Do you really want to do that?" Jeri asked.

"Sure."

THE BROCKS WERE HOME when Tom called. They agreed to take the four younger children while Tom, Jeri and Michael went to the county jail, to visit Quentin "Weed" Alt.

"I can't believe it," Amber said, closing the phone.

"Does anything from Michael surprise you? I don't see any harm in it," Jon said. "For what it's worth, he'll be together with his biological parents, at least for a little while. And maybe Quentin might realize there's something worth living for."

The windshield wipers scraped noisily as the Crown Vic pulled away from curb in front of the Brocks', and Tom switched them off. The pelting rain had subsided when they left the restaurant. Shafts of sunlight now angled through patchy breaks in the clouds.

Jeri leaned back, looking at Michael. "Have any ideas what you want to say, to Quentin?" she asked quietly.

"I just want him to say he's sorry, and that he'll never do bad things again."

Tom glanced at Jeri, trying to interpret the impassive look on her face. "Works for me," he said, hoping it was the right thing to say.

She turned to look at Michael, then to Tom, smiling just a little as peace seemed to settle over them softly. "Me too."

It didn't last long. The good intention and the peace that it wrought, retreated at the thought, of actually going to jail and facing Weed. "Maybe Gabe and Tammy will still be there," Jeri said, hope rising in her voice. "How long's it been since they left the restaurant?"

"Great. Just what I need, another sermon," Tom groused.

"Oh come on! They should be done anyway by the time we get there." Jeri looked back at Michael. "You really want to do this?"

"Sure."

"I don't know. I don't know what to say," Jeri said, looking at Tom.

"Who says you have to say anything? I just hope this doesn't take too long. It's starting to get nice out."

About two dozen cars and trucks sat in the parking lot in front of the jail. The solid brick and concrete block exterior of the jail opened to the world through a row of narrow, horizontal windows. A tall chain-link fence topped with spirals of razor wire surrounded the grassy lawn on one side.

They entered and waited for the guard to buzz them through the heavy steel door into the visiting area.

Friends and family of prisoners in orange overalls occupied three of the four tables in the center. The conversation, a mixture of Spanish and English, seemed much more lively and jovial than the circumstances might suggest.

An uniformed guard approached. "Did you make an appointment? I don't think Quentin was expecting you," he said.

"No, we didn't," Jeri said. "Maybe he doesn't want to see us." She glanced at Michael, whose impassive appearance remained unchanged.

"He was at the church service," the guard said. "I'll tell him you're here. Who are you again?"

Tom repeated their names.

The guard gestured them to sit at the open table. In several minutes he returned from the day room, Quentin following.

He sat down, his cautious eyes roving from Tom, to Jeri, and resting on Michael. He motioned them to take a seat across the table.

"You wanted to see me?"

Jeri spoke first. "Michael said he wanted to visit. You know who he is."

"The Weaver kid, I know."

What she wanted to say in reply, she couldn't. She turned to Michael. "What did you want to say?"

"I'm sorry I shot your friend."

Weed gave Michael a quizzical look. He glanced at Tom and Jeri, then to Michael. "I don't know what you're talking about."

"That day all that stuff happened on the ridge. When the other guy tried to chase us. I shot him."

"That was you?"

"I'm sorry." Now Michael showed signs of feeling, a slight qivering of his lip.

"He wasn't my friend," Quentin said. "You did what you had to do. I was doing what I had to do. Things just don't work out all the time," he said, looking from Michael and over to Tom and Jeri.

Silence intervened, until Quentin spoke. "Is that it? Is that what you have come here for?"

"There's one other thing," Jeri said. She looked at Michael. "Go ahead tell him what you said in the car, what you really wanted to say to him?"

"I just wanted you to say you're sorry, and that you won't do bad things anymore," Michael said.

"Okay. I'm sorry about what happened. I'll try. Can't make any promises, but I'll try." He held out his hand. Michael extended his and they shook.

"Thanks," Michael said. He looked over at Tom and Jeri. "We can go now."